Read what the experts are saying about *THE GIRLS OF MISCHIEF BAY*
An Amazon Best Book of the Month

"Once again, Susan Mallery has created an inviting world that envelops her readers' senses and sensibilities. It's not just a tale of how true friendship can lift you up, but also how change is an integral part of life... Fans of Jodi Picoult, Debbie Macomber, and Elin Hilderbrand will assuredly fall for *The Girls of Mischief Bay*."

—*Bookreporter*

"Mallery skillfully depicts three very different women in different stages of their romantic relationships who enter into unbreakable friendships... Will appeal to fans of women's fiction, especially such friendship books as Karen Joy Fowler's *The Jane Austen Book Club*."

—*Booklist*

"Fresh and engaging...the writing is strong, the dialogue genuine and believable. There's a generational subtext that mirrors reality and the complexities of adult relationships... filled with promise of a new serial that's worth following."

—*Fort Worth Star-Telegram*

"Romance superstar Mallery begins a new women's fiction series with a novel that is both heart-wrenching and warmhearted... A discerning, affecting look at three women facing surprising change and the powerful and uplifting impact of friends."

—*Kirkus Reviews*

"You will become totally invested in each of these characters and their struggles and root for a happy ending. Can't wait for the next installment from Ms. Mallery and *The Girls of Mischief Bay*!"

—*Fresh Fiction*

"Mallery's series debut is an emotional lesson in triumphs and tragedies told in her iconic eloquent style... Her exceptional handling of the climactic hard knocks and joyful events, and her tiny canine co-star, rocked."

—*RT Book Reviews*

Also by Susan Mallery

From MIRA Books

Mischief Bay

The Girls of Mischief Bay

Blackberry Island

Evening Stars
Three Sisters
Barefoot Season

From HQN Books

Fool's Gold

Best of My Love
Marry Me at Christmas
Thrill Me
Kiss Me
Hold Me
Until We Touch
Before We Kiss
When We Met
Christmas on 4th Street
Three Little Words
Two of a Kind
Just One Kiss
A Fool's Gold Christmas
All Summer Long
Summer Nights
Summer Days
Only His
Only Yours
Only Mine
Finding Perfect
Almost Perfect
Chasing Perfect

For a complete list of titles by Susan Mallery,
please visit www.SusanMallery.com.

#1 *NEW YORK TIMES* BESTSELLING AUTHOR

SUSAN MALLERY

The Friends We Keep

MIRA®

ISBN-13: 978-0-7783-1872-9

The Friends We Keep

For questions and comments about the quality of this book, please contact us at CustomerService@Harlequin.com.

www.MIRABooks.com

Printed in U.S.A.

First printing: March 2016
10 9 8 7 6 5 4 3 2 1

To Marla—May we always be the friends we keep. xoxo

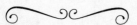

The Friends We Keep

Chapter One

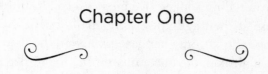

Was it wrong to want to pee alone? Gabriella Schaefer considered the question for maybe the four hundredth time in the past couple of months. In truth, she loved everything about her life. Her husband, her five-year-old twin daughters, her pets, her house. All of it was an amazing gift. She got that. She'd been blessed. But every now and then…okay, at least once a day, she desperately wanted to be able to go to the bathroom, like a normal person. To sit down and pee. Undisturbed.

Not with someone pushing open the door to complain that she was hungry or that Kenzie had taken her doll. Not with Andrew wandering in, a pair of socks in each hand, to ask her which one was the better choice. Not with a pink-toed cat paw stretching under the door or a basset hound moaning softly on the other side, begging to be let in. Alone. Oh, to be alone for those thirty or forty seconds. To actually be able to finish and flush and wash her hands *by herself.*

Gabby signaled as she got into the left lane, then slowed to wait for her turn. Fifty-seven days, she reminded herself. She had fifty-seven days until the twins started kindergarten and she went back to work. Sure, it was only going to be part-time, but still. It would be magical. And what she would never share with anyone was that she was most excited about being able to pee by herself.

"What's so funny?" Kenzie asked from the backseat. "Why are you smiling?"

"Are you telling a joke?" Kennedy asked. "Can I know?"

Because at their age, they were all about the questions, Gabby thought, keeping her gaze firmly on the road. When there was a break in the oncoming traffic, she turned into the parking lot and drove toward the end of the strip mall. There were still a couple of spots directly in front of Supper's in the Bag. She pulled into one and turned off her SUV's engine.

"I'm thinking funny thoughts," she told her girls. "I don't have any jokes."

Kennedy wrinkled her nose. "Okay."

Her voice was laced with disappointment. Both girls knew that what grown-ups thought was funny and what was *really* funny were usually two different things.

Gabby grabbed her handbag—a small cross-body with an extra-long strap—and got out of the car. She walked to the rear driver's-side door and opened it.

"Ready?" she asked.

Both girls nodded. They were already undoing the safety straps on their car seats.

Getting them out of their seats was never the problem. Getting them into them was another matter. Despite the fact that the seats were rated for kids up to sixty pounds, both girls wanted booster seats rather than their car seats. Car seats were for babies, she'd been informed several times already. The fact that car seats were safer didn't seem to be making an impact on the discussion.

She and Andrew were going to have to figure out a better strategy, she thought as she helped Kennedy jump to the ground. Kenzie followed. Gabby couldn't keep having the

same fight every day. Plus the arguments were taking longer
and she was having to build an extra five or ten minutes into
her routine just to get to appointments on time.

The problem was both girls took after their father, she
thought humorously. He was a highly skilled sales executive
with the gift of verbal charm. Even at five, the twins were
starting to try to talk themselves out of being in trouble.

"Is Tyler going to be here?" Kennedy asked.

Gabby brushed the girl's hair out of her eyes. Her blond
bangs needed trimming. Again. "He is."

The girls cheered. Tyler, her friend Nicole's son, was six
and soon to be in the first grade. In the eyes of two girls who
were excited and a little nervous about kindergarten, Tyler
was very much a man of the world. He knew things and they
both adored him.

Gabby reached past the troublemaking car seats for the
empty tote bags that came with her membership. The bright
green bags were covered with the Supper's in the Bag logo.
Every two weeks she joined a couple of her friends for a
three-hour session at Supper's in the Bag and when she left,
she would have six meals for her family. Meals that could be
thrown in the oven or grilled on the barbecue. They were
seasoned, portioned and ready to be prepared.

The premise of Supper's in the Bag was simple. Each session took about three hours. In the large, industrial kitchen-
like space were eight stations, each dedicated to a different
entrée. By following the clearly marked instructions, you
portioned meat, added spices and vegetables into recyclable
containers, basically doing whatever was needed to get the
meal ready for cooking.

At first Gabby had felt guilty about signing up for the
service. She was a stay-at-home mom. Surely she could get
her act together enough to cook for her family. *And yet*, she

thought, handing the empty bags to her daughters and then guiding them to the store. The days slipped away from her. Fortunately for her, the owner of Supper's in the Bag was the sister of a close friend. Telling herself that she was supporting a local business helped with the guilt.

Because Andrew was one of the good guys, he encouraged her to use the service. They went out to dinner at least once a week, so with the six meals she prepped here, that meant she only had to come up with six meals on her own.

The store was big and open, with the kitchen stations set up on the perimeter of the room. Industrial racks filled with pantry items stood in the center area. There was a cash register by the door and shelves for purses and the bags they all brought. The counters were stainless steel, as were the sinks.

To the left was a small seating area where clients could linger and talk, if they wanted. To the right was a small partitioned area that had been painted bright colors and set up with kid-sized tables and chairs. There were a few toys, lots of boxes of crayons and plenty of coloring books. Cecelia, the resident sitter, was already there. The petite, curly-haired college student grinned when she saw the twins.

"I was hoping you two would be by today," she said, waving at them. "We're going to have so much fun."

"Cece!"

The twins dropped their tote bags and ran to greet the teen. There were hugs all around.

"Is Tyler coming?" Kenzie asked anxiously.

"He is. I'm sure he and his mom are running late." Cecelia guided the girls toward a table. "Let's start on a picture, while your mom gets going on her meals," she said.

Gabby used the distraction to head for the aprons by the check-in area. She picked up her sheet, telling her which stations she would be using, and in what order.

Supper's in the Bag wasn't a unique idea. There were several businesses like it around the country. While Gabby had never been a fan of Morgan, the woman who owned the place, she had to give her kudos for wringing every dollar out of her clients.

Children were welcome for the price of five dollars per child per hour. For Gabby, that meant an extra thirty bucks, but it beat having to find a sitter herself. There were wine selections offered with each entrée, available for an extra charge. Gabby guessed the mark-up was a restaurant quality 100 percent. After-prep wine and appetizers were available, again for a cost.

Morgan's sister, Gabby's friend Hayley, came in early several days a week to prep the food. She did much of the dicing and slicing, the opening of spice bottles and tomato cans. Gabby happened to know that Hayley worked in exchange for meals.

While Hayley said she was getting the better end of the deal, Gabby had her doubts. No matter the situation, Morgan always seemed to come out ahead. Gabby doubted the arrangement with Hayley was any different.

Several more women walked into the store. Each session could handle thirty-two customers, although the daytime sessions generally had more like twenty-five. Supper's in the Bag was also open Thursday through Sunday evenings, from four until eight-thirty. She spotted Hayley, Nicole and Nicole's son Tyler. Nicole dropped her son off with Cecelia and they all met by the hand-washing sink.

"Hi," Gabby said as she hugged her friends.

Nicole was tall, blonde and enviably willowy. Gabby wasn't sure how much of her fit body was genetic and how much of it came from the fact that she taught exercise classes for a living. Gabby kept promising herself she was going to sign up for one. She was still carrying around an extra twenty-five pounds from her pregnancy, but given that the twins were starting kindergarten, she needed to either do something about the extra weight or stop blaming her daughters.

Hayley was also thin but in a way that made Gabby worry. As usual, her friend was pale with dark circles under her eyes, but for once she seemed filled with energy.

"I'm excited about the meals tonight," Hayley said. "The veggies were extra fresh and I think the new enchilada recipe is going to be a winner."

"You seem happy," Gabby said as she put on a green Supper's in the Bag apron. "What's going on?"

"Nothing much."

Gabby wondered if that was true. Hayley's life was a physical and emotional roller coaster as she tried desperately to carry a pregnancy to term. Her last miscarriage had only been a few months before and she was taking a break—on doctor's orders.

Nicole pulled her long hair back into a ponytail. "You sure?" she asked. "You're very bouncy."

Hayley laughed. "I don't think that's a flattering description."

The three friends stopped at their first station. Directions were written on laminated cards. The ingredients for layering the casserole were stored in bowls and bags. Spices were clearly labeled.

Each of them took a foil pan. "I can't believe it's already the middle of July," Nicole said as she layered corn tortillas on the bottom of the pan. "I was hoping to take Tyler away for a few days, but I don't see that happening. Between work and taking care of him, I'm constantly running."

"You own a business," Gabby said, ignoring yet another stab of guilt. She should own a business, she thought. Or be going back to work more than twenty hours a week. And cooking all her dinners from scratch. Honestly, she had no idea where her day went. The twins were in a summer program from eight until one every day. Makayla, her fifteen-year-old stepdaughter, was in a different camp that went from eight until four. Surely she could get her errands run, laundry finished, meals prepped and cooked, *and* do something to help the world. But it didn't seem to happen.

"There's always Disneyland," Hayley offered as she scooped chunks of chicken into her casserole. Rather than using a single nine-by-thirteen pan, Hayley used two eight-by-eights. Which doubled her number of meals. Of course it was just her and Rob.

"Tyler loves Disneyland," Nicole said. "It just seems like cheating."

"Be grateful it's close," Gabby told her.

The massive amusement park was only about thirty miles away from Mischief Bay. Less than an hour by car, if the traffic gods were on your side.

Gabby put her arm around Nicole. "It could be worse. There could be Brad the Dragon Land. Then you'd be totally screwed."

Nicole grinned. "I'd be tempted to set it on fire."

Hayley and Gabby laughed.

Brad the Dragon was a popular children's book series. Many young boys, Tyler included, loved B the D, as he was known by intimates. For reasons Gabby had never understood, Nicole disliked the character and had a serious loathing for the author. She claimed that she'd read an article once that said Jairus Sterenberg was only in it for the money, that he was evil and most likely responsible for any coming zombie apocalypse headed their way. Gabby was less sure about those claims. Of course there were plenty of parents who were desperately tired of all things *Frozen* or *Minion*.

"Was Hawaii amazing?" Nicole asked.

Gabby nodded as she remembered the ten days she, Andrew and the twins had spent in a condo on Maui last month. It had just been the four of them. Makayla had stayed with her mother.

"It was gorgeous! Beautiful weather and plenty to do. The girls had a fantastic time."

"How did Makayla do at her mom's while you were gone?" Hayley asked.

Gabby sighed. "Okay. Her mom doesn't love having her around more than a weekend at a time, so that makes things difficult. I don't get it. Makayla's fifteen. Sure, she can be a bit mouthy, but she's her kid. You're supposed to love your kid."

"She's back with you?" Nicole asked.

"Her mom dropped her off the first night we were home."

"Too bad you couldn't take her with you," Hayley said.

"Uh-huh," Gabby murmured neutrally, sprinkling cheese on her finished casserole before securing the plastic lid. Because while she probably *should* have wished Makayla could have gone with them, in truth she'd been grateful for the break from her stepdaughter.

Their first meal finished, they took their pans over to the wall of refrigerators and placed their entrées on their assigned shelves, then moved on to the next station. Hayley began pulling down spice bottles while Gabby and Nicole scanned the directions.

"Stew is interesting," Nicole said, her tone doubtful. "The Crock-Pot information is good."

"You don't sound convinced," Gabby murmured, her voice low.

"It's summer. I don't want to have to use the Crock-Pot in the summer." Nicole shook her head. "A classic first-world problem, right? But Tyler loves stew, which means a dinner that's easy and he'll eat. I'm in."

"Excellent attitude," Gabby told her, with a wink. "You get a gold star today."

"I live for gold stars."

Hayley pointed to the spice jars she'd lined up. "This is going to be delicious," she promised. "You'll love it. And the next station is all about grilling over fire."

"You *are* in a happy mood," Nicole said. "What's up? Your boss give you a raise?"

"No, and that's okay." Hayley opened one of the gallon plastic bags and began measuring the spices. "Gabby mentioned my mood, too. Am I usually crabby all the time?"

"Not at all," Gabby said quickly, not sure how to explain that for once, Hayley seemed happy and relaxed. If she hadn't known the other woman was on hiatus from trying to conceive, she would have wondered if her friend was expecting. Before she could figure out if she should ask anyway, Hayley picked up the bottle of red wine on the table, measured out a half cup and poured it into her bag.

Nope, Gabby told herself. Not pregnant. But there *was* something.

They worked through the rest of the stations, then loaded their meals into their totes. Gabby packed up the car before going back to get her girls.

"You ready?" she asked.

Kenzie and Kennedy looked at each other before nodding at her.

"They were great," Cecelia told her.

"We were very good," Kenzie added.

"I'm sure you were."

The twins were at that age where they were angelic with everyone but her. She'd read dozens of books on child rearing and from what the experts said, the need to be more independent battled with the need for Mom. So while everyone else got smiles and good behavior, she got push-back and tears.

She waited while her girls hugged Cecelia goodbye. They were growing fast, she thought with contentment. They were bright, inquisitive and loving. Given how right everything was in her life, she could deal with a little push-back now and then.

They left the child-care area and headed toward the front door. Today they'd chosen matching clothes. Blue shorts and blue-and-white T-shirts with little kittens on them. They'd lost that toddler chubbiness and were now looking like little girls.

They were fraternal twins, but so close in appearance that most people thought they were identical. They both had big hazel eyes and strawberry blond hair. They sounded alike and were both energetic.

But there were also differences. The shape of their chins. Kennedy had thicker, slightly curlier hair. Kenzie was a bit taller. School was going to be interesting, Gabby mused. Kennedy was more outgoing, but Kenzie had a level of patience her sister didn't. She wasn't sure which characteristics would mean success.

They reached her SUV and she opened the rear door on the driver's side.

"In you go."

The girls didn't budge.

"We want booster seats," Kennedy said firmly. "Car seats are for babies. Mommy, we're starting kindergarten."

"That means we're not babies anymore," Kenzie added.

Gabby didn't know which kid at their summer camp had said something about booster seats versus car seats, but she really wished he or she hadn't.

She thought about the bottles of wine waiting back inside Supper's in the Bag. She could give the girls back to Cecelia, have a couple of glasses and then phone Andrew to drive them all home. She could bang her head against the side of the SUV until that pain was bigger than the argument. Or she could suck it up, remind herself that she was blessed and lucky and every other good thing, and simply deal.

Despite the fact that the wine scenario was really appealing, she went with the latter.

"You are growing," she said, keeping her voice gentle. "And I love you very much. That's why I want to keep you safe. Please get in your seats so we can go home and get dinner ready for your dad."

The twins stayed stubbornly in place.

Gabby held in a sigh. Where was the win in this fight? She wasn't going to be blackmailed by five-year-olds. "Boomer and Jasmine are waiting for their dinners, too. I want to go home. Please get in your car seats now."

"We won't." Kennedy crossed her arms over her chest. Kenzie followed, because Kenzie always followed.

"For every minute we wait here, you will lose fifteen minutes of your television time," she told the girls. Kind of a big deal because TV was limited in the Schaefer household.

The twins glanced at each other, then back at her. Kenzie leaned over to her sister.

"Fifteen minutes is a *long* time."

Kennedy sighed heavily, then got in the SUV. Kenzie did the same. Gabby vowed that later she would talk to her husband and they would brainstorm a solution. Or at the very least have a glass of wine and remind themselves that in ten years, when the twins wanted to start dating, they would look back on the car-seat fights and tell themselves these were the good old days.

Chapter Two

"I heard the news," Cecelia said as she tidied the crayons scattered across the kid-sized table.

Nicole Lord held in a heavy sigh and faked a big smile. "Of course you did. Isn't it fantastic? We're all superexcited."

Cecelia stepped closer and lowered her voice. "It's okay. Tyler's over there."

Nicole glanced at her son who was across the room, playing with Hayley, then back at the nineteen-year-old babysitter. "Can you believe it? I can't. Of all the luck. Or lack of luck. Tyler's thrilled. He's counting the days. If his math was good enough, he'd be counting the minutes."

"And you?" Cecelia asked.

Nicole rolled her eyes. "I'm counting the minutes, too, but for different reasons."

"You're not going to attack him or anything, are you? I'd hate to read about you being arrested."

The question, meant to be funny, offered a visual that Nicole found tempting. Not being arrested. Despite the guilty pleasure of the show *Orange Is the New Black*, she was pretty sure she wouldn't do well in jail. Or prison. Either, really. But attacking Jairus Sterenberg was a different matter. She wouldn't mind smacking him really hard. Or maybe just giving him a piece of her mind. The angry, annoyed part.

"I will not attack him, I promise. Tyler loves his *Brad the Dragon* books and I would never hurt my son."

"What if he didn't find out?" Cecelia teased. She held up one hand. "I'll stop now. It's just, you really hate the guy."

"I don't *hate* him," Nicole said, hoping it was true. "How can I hate someone I've never met? It's just..." She shook her head. "That whole empire of his. The article I read on him a while back said he was a pretty awful person, making money off of kids. Which means he's little more than a weasel rat bastard who would merchandise air if he could figure out a way."

Brad the Dragon had started life in picture books and was now also in chapter books. And the merchandising! There were stuffed animals and clothes and sheets and games. The man was wallowing in money, she thought bitterly. All at the expense of kids and parents everywhere.

Worse, so much worse, she'd just discovered he lived in the area. And in what some people would mistakenly claim was a generous offer, he'd held a contest through the parks' summer programs. The same summer programs where Tyler spent his days.

Kids were invited to write a paper explaining why they loved B the D. The winning camper and his or her class got a personal visit from Jairus himself, along with an autographed book.

Tyler had been thrilled to find out about the contest and had spent two weeks perfecting his entry. Nicole would know—she'd helped him every step of the way. They'd come up with a B the D story line where Brad met Tyler. They had even included pictures.

"I know you don't think he's a bad guy," Nicole said. "But come on. Kids having to write a paper before they can meet the guy? Couldn't he just show up at the camp like a regular person? But *noooo*."

Cecelia laughed. "You have so much energy about that poor man."

"Trust me, he's far from poor."

"Still, what if he's not evil?"

"Then I'll feel really, really bad about trashing him."

"Think that's likely?" Cecelia asked.

Nicole grinned. "Not a chance."

She confirmed the upcoming week's schedule with Cecelia, then went to collect Tyler. She had to admit, if only to herself, that her loathing of B the D's creator was a recent thing. That in her heart of hearts, she understood that she just might be projecting her feelings onto a man she'd never met.

Nearly two years ago, her then-husband had quit his job to write a screenplay. Something he hadn't discussed with her or even mentioned until two days after the fact. There'd been no negotiation, no warning. Eric had simply up and quit, leaving her to support their household while he spent his days surfing to "clear his head" before he began writing.

It was right about that time when Nicole had started to find Brad the Dragon and all his merchandise the tiniest bit annoying. What was it about writers? Did they all have to be self-centered jerks? Or was it just the successful ones? Because Eric had gone on to sell his screenplay for the unbelievable amount of one million dollars. And then he'd left her.

"Ready to go?" she asked Tyler.

He stood with his thin arms wrapped around Hayley's waist as he leaned against her. Hayley hugged him back. The two of them had always been close. Hayley was a kid person down to her bones.

"See you next time," he told Hayley.

"I can't wait," the other woman said. "Have fun meeting Jairus."

Tyler grinned so broadly, Nicole knew his face had to hurt. "It's only five more days."

"Do you know how long that is in minutes?" Hayley asked, then slapped her hand over her mouth as Tyler turned to Nicole.

"Mommy?"

"I'm sorry," Hayley whispered. "I just made it worse, huh?"

"We'll survive."

Tyler rushed over and danced in front of her. "We can know how many minutes?"

"Sure. We can do the math when we get home. We'll need a calculator."

Hayley winced. "Now I'm making you do math."

Nicole hugged her friend. "I love you, even when you make me do math. But when I regrout my bathroom tile, you'll be the first person I call."

"It's a deal."

Nicole straightened. For a second she studied Hayley. As always, her skin was pale and there were dark circles under her eyes. She looked as if she were in the middle of fighting some awful illness. Nicole knew the truth was slightly less desperate, but still painful. Hayley was recovering from yet another miscarriage.

Nicole took Tyler's hand and led him out of the store. As she helped him into his booster seat, he chattered on about B the D and the upcoming visit by the prolific author.

Maybe it wasn't Jairus's fault, she told herself as she closed the rear passenger door. Maybe he was really a very nice man who loved children. She doubted it, but hoped she was wrong. Because she would hate for Tyler's heart to be broken by meeting a flawed hero.

On the bright side, she'd volunteered to be there for the visit. So if Jairus turned out to be a complete ass, she would do everything she could to protect Tyler and the other kids. At the very least, she could accidentally trip the man. And call him names. Possibly beat him with a stuffed B the D doll.

That image made her smile. Perspective, she reminded herself. So much of life was all about perspective.

"'And we're learning how to trust. And we're finally starting to live.'"

Hayley Batchelor tapped her fingers against her steering wheel as she sang along with the radio. The new Destiny Mills song had her swaying in her seat. When the light turned green, she drove through the intersection, and made a right.

At six-thirty on a Thursday night there was plenty of traffic—neighbors pulled into driveways, kids were out playing in front yards. The speed limit was only twenty-five, but no one went faster than that. It wasn't that kind of neighborhood.

Hayley saw that the house on the corner now had a second story. For months it had been in disarray. It had been interesting to watch the demolition followed by the reconstruction. Once finished, the house would be stunning. Most of the neighborhood was going through a similar process—updating, sprucing. Hayley knew there was a term for it—gentrification, maybe.

She turned at the next corner and drove down her street. Here there were more signs of the revitalization. She liked the fresh paint, the new front doors. But when she pulled into her driveway, she wrinkled her nose. Talk about shabby, she thought as she stared at the overgrown yard and peeling paint around the windows. The pale gray stucco was still in good shape, but the house looked like what it was—a place that had been neglected for a while.

She knew all the reasons why and they made sense, but things had changed. It was time for their house to reflect those changes.

She collected her Supper's in the Bag totes and made her way to the front door and went inside.

The house was small—just fifteen hundred square feet. When it was first built, the home had been only twelve hundred square feet, but the previous owners had added a master suite, complete with a small bathroom and walk-in closet. That brought them up to three bedrooms and two baths. The lot was a decent size and the location—just four blocks to the ocean—was prime.

The hardwood floors in the living room were original, as was the fireplace. Not that they ever used it much. Los Angeles wasn't known for cold winters. But it was pretty and every now and then the temperature dipped enough to warrant burning a log or two.

Hayley stepped into the kitchen and put away the dinners. Two went into the refrigerator while the rest were stacked in the freezer. When she was done, she turned on the oven and pulled out what she would need to make a salad. She folded the bags and stored them in the small laundry room, then turned back to look at the kitchen with what she hoped was a critical eye.

The layout was good. The counters—fifties tile done in two-tone green—weren't exactly contemporary, but they kind of suited the house. There was a lot of natural light and plenty of storage space. The cabinets were solid wood and beautiful, though they could use a good refinishing, along with updated hardware. She ran her hands across one and wondered what it would take to redo them. Was it something she and Rob could handle on their own?

The floor was a sad linoleum, but replacing it would be

too expensive. The sink was on the newer side and when their old stove had died, they'd replaced it with a nicer model.

If they left the tile and focused on the cabinets... That would make a difference. Some fresh paint would make a big impact, too.

She wandered down the short hallway that led to the main bath and two bedrooms. She and Rob argued about the bathroom a lot. It, too, was original to the house, with two-toned blue tile and a huge tub. He wanted to gut it and put in something modern. She liked the character of what they had.

The secondary bedrooms were easy. Paint would improve them a lot and maybe some inexpensive window treatments. The back bedroom, the smaller of the two, was a home office. The other one, well, she didn't go into that room. She knew what it looked like. Pale yellow walls and gleaming hardwood floors. A rocking chair sat in the corner. Otherwise the space was empty.

The master addition was on the other side of the house. Again, paint and maybe new bedding would make it look just fine. The house had good bones, was in a great neighborhood. They just needed to give it a little more TLC.

She heard the front door open and footsteps in the living room.

"I'm home," Rob called.

Hayley went out to greet him. "Hi. I just got in myself. We're having enchilada casserole for dinner."

Rob was about five-ten, with light brown hair and blue eyes. He wore glasses and had an easy smile. He was the kind of guy people instinctively trusted and Hayley had liked him from the first moment they'd met.

Now she stepped into his embrace and hugged him. He kissed her cheek.

"How was your day?" he asked.

"Good. Busy. I went to Supper's in the Bag."

"I figured. You know I love those enchiladas."

"I do."

His gaze settled on her face. "You feeling okay?"

"I feel great. Strong."

His expression was doubtful, but he smiled. "Good. It's a nice evening. We could eat outside."

Because while the rest of Los Angeles sweltered in the mid-July heat, Mischief Bay had the natural air-conditioning brought on by an onshore breeze.

"Great idea."

They walked into the kitchen together. While Rob washed his hands, she put the casserole in the oven before setting the small timer in the corner. He got two beers from the refrigerator and two tall glasses from one of the cupboards. He poured and handed her a glass. They went outside to the shade of their east-facing backyard. Chairs dotted the brick patio.

Hayley sat in her usual spot, her feet up on an ottoman. Rob sat across from her.

"How about you?" she asked. "Good day?"

He nodded. "Nothing blew up."

"There's a plus."

It was a comfortable joke, she thought. Six months ago Rob had taken the job of assistant manager of service at the local Mischief Bay BMW dealer. On his first day of work, there had been an explosion in one of the service bays. Something about compression and heat. No one had been hurt and no cars had been damaged but it had made for an exciting start.

The job had been a big step up for him—both career and money-wise. The hours were long, but he didn't have to travel and she liked having him around. He had good benefits, also a big plus. Eventually there would even be paid vacation but that was a few months away. Still, it would be good for when she had a baby. He had a second job, helping a friend restore old cars on the weekend. Easy work for a guy who loved cars.

"You're sure you're feeling okay?" he asked.

His tone was light, but she heard the worry behind the words. She also knew the reason. She could see herself in the mirror and knew that she looked like someone who had been through medical tough times. The price she had to pay, she thought grimly. That she would keep paying, no matter what. Because the dream was too important.

"I'm fine," she assured him. She lightly nudged his thigh with her foot. "You worry."

"I love you."

"I love you, too, and I've been thinking."

He paused with his beer halfway to his mouth. "Am I going to like what you've been thinking about?"

"You are. When I was driving home tonight, I was looking at the neighborhood. We have the ugliest house on the block and we shouldn't. This place is adorable. But with everything going on, we haven't had time to fix it up. I'd like us to talk about making changes."

Rob leaned toward her. "Yeah? That's great. I agree. We're an eyesore. I keep expecting the neighbors to start a petition. I have a lot of ideas."

Which didn't surprise her at all. She and Rob had always thought alike.

"The outside is an easy fix," she said. "It just needs time."

Rob looked doubtful. "Hayley, honey, you can't do anything strenuous. One of the guys at work has a brother in the landscaping businesses. We can get the yard cleaned up cheap in a couple of days, then you and I can get some new plants. That part we could do ourselves."

She hated the idea of wasting money on yard cleanup, but

he had a point. She was still pretty weak and he worked two jobs. "I don't want to spend too much," she began.

"I agree. I'll tell Ray to have his brother drive by and give us an estimate. We'll just do the front."

"Okay." Their backyard wasn't too bad. There was the patio and a few trees. The rest was lawn. If she started watering it more regularly, it would green up quickly.

"What did you think for the inside?" he asked. "We should remodel the kitchen."

She did her best not to flinch. "How about we start with paint," she said. "Maybe some new window coverings."

She thought he might push back, but he surprised her by nodding. "You're right. A kitchen redo is too much right now."

Guilt flashed through her. Rob was worried about her being overwhelmed. Because he always worried. They'd been through so much and he'd been beside her every step of the way. Their repeated attempts to get pregnant had left her body weak and their bank account depleted. They were emotionally exhausted by the roller-coaster ride they'd been on.

But her reasons for not wanting to do the kitchen were different than his. Some would say selfish. She would tell them they couldn't possibly understand what she was going through. What it was like to be denied the only thing she'd ever wanted.

She had a plan, she reminded herself. There was still hope. No way she was going to give up.

"The hardware store has the sale section in the back," she said. "After dinner let's go by and see if they have any paint we like. We only need a couple of gallons for the office and the master. I was thinking we'd do the kitchen, too."

Rob frowned. "You mean those leftover paint cans no one wanted?"

"They're not leftover, they're mistakes. When people try to color match or don't like what they bought. You can get a gallon of paint for like five dollars."

"I know it makes you happy to hear every penny squeak, but I'm pretty sure we can spring for a paint color we like, even if that means paying full price."

He was teasing. She could hear it in his voice, see it in his gentle smile. She forced herself to stay relaxed, to accept the comment in the spirit he meant it. To not shriek that they needed every possible dollar they could save. That babies cost money and in her case, getting pregnant costs even more.

But they'd fought enough about that. About everything. She was going to need Rob on her side to get through the next few months. They had to be a team. By this time next year, everything would be different. They would have a family. She was sure of it. Because this time, she knew there was going to be a miracle.

Chapter Three

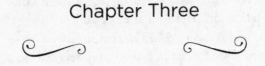

"Mommy, can Boomer and Jasmine get married?" Kennedy asked from her car seat on Friday afternoon.

"No, they can't."

"Because they don't like each other?" Kenzie asked.

"They like each other fine," Gabby said as she pulled up and joined the line of cars waiting to pick up teens from the twelve-to-fifteen-year-olds' summer camp. It was, of course, on the other side of the park, with the same start time as the one the twins attended. She sometimes wondered what the city planners were thinking when they decided schedules, start and finishing times, not to mention which streets went temporarily one way in the morning and evening. She wanted to believe they were doing what they thought was best to keep traffic flowing. That no one was secretly watching the mess everything became, giggling as mothers with kids in two different age groups scrambled to essentially be in two places at once.

"They can't get married because Boomer is a dog and Jasmine is a cat and we don't have pet marriages."

"But what if they love each other?" Kenzie's voice was dreamy as she asked the question. At five, "loving each other" was the ending to nearly every fairy tale. Well, and "they lived happily ever after," which was practically the same thing.

Gabby briefly thought that if she were a better mother she would find more self-actualized stories to read her daughters. Stories where women ran corporations or started businesses or became doctors rather than were princesses who got engaged because they were beautiful and vapid.

A problem for another day, she told herself, then groaned as she glanced at the clock on the dashboard of her SUV.

She was five minutes late because the twins had refused to buckle up when she'd collected them. Those stupid car seats, again. They loomed larger every day.

She inched forward, one in a long line of cars, and reminded herself that she only had to get through the next hour or so before she could relax. She would get the kids their dinner, then go upstairs into the master and take a long bath while Andrew—

"Sugar!"

It was as close to a swearword as she allowed herself these days. Because there was no bath in her near future. She'd forgotten she and Andrew had an event that night. Something work-related, maybe. Or maybe political. She couldn't remember. Double sugar. Were her black pants back from the dry cleaner?

The car behind her honked. Gabby realized she'd let precious space open up between her and the car in front. She eased forward, trying to figure out what she was going to wear, all the while listening to Kenzie and Kennedy discuss what Jasmine would wear if she and Boomer *could* get married. It wasn't the dress that stumped them so much as the wedding bouquet. How would a cat carry it down the aisle?

Gabby looked at the few kids still standing on the edge of the park and spotted Makayla. Her stepdaughter was tall with impossibly long legs. Her naturally blond hair hung halfway down her back. She wore a loose, flowy sleeveless shirt over shorts. She was pretty and still a little gangly, but in a couple of years she was going to have that easy beauty women everywhere envied.

Makayla looked a lot like her stunning mother. Around both of them, Gabby felt short and bottom-heavy, neither of which was Makayla's fault.

Gabby pulled up to the curb and watched the teen approach. Her stomach tensed as she tried to judge her mood. It was Friday on a visitation weekend, which meant things could go either way.

"Hi," Gabby said brightly as Makayla opened the passenger front door.

"Hi." Makayla slid onto the seat and fastened the belt before turning toward the twins. "Hey, munchkins."

"Makayla!" Both girls greeted her happily.

"We think Boomer and Jasmine should get married," Kennedy added. "In a white dress."

"Huh. I don't think Boomer would look good in a white dress, do you?"

The twins laughed. Gabby smiled, imagining their basset hound draped in white tulle.

"Not Boomer," Kenzie corrected. "Jasmine."

"Oh, that's different."

The knot in Gabby's stomach loosened. Makayla was okay. There wouldn't be shouting or door slamming this week. No sullen silences. She would get herself ready to visit her mother and then she would be gone for forty-eight hours. Odds were Sunday night would be awful—it usually was—but that was for then.

The highs and lows that came with being a fifteen-year-old were amplified by Makayla's relationship with her mother. It was erratic at best. Sometimes Candace wanted to be all in and other times she saw her daughter as little more than an inconvenience. Sadly, she didn't mind sharing that factoid with Makayla.

Gabby tried to understand that the resulting fits of rage and depression weren't about her. Makayla needed to blame someone and Gabby was a safe target. When things got tough, there was always chocolate, and the knowledge that whatever else was going on, Makayla loved her half sisters.

Gabby drove through Friday-afternoon traffic. The three blocks on Pacific Coast Highway took nearly fifteen minutes, but once they made it into their neighborhood, the number of cars lessened.

Gabby had grown up not five blocks from here. She and her siblings had gone to the same elementary school as Kenzie and Kennedy. She'd attended the same high school as Makayla. She knew where the kids liked to hang out, the exact amount of time it took to walk home and the quickest way to get from their house to the beach.

Sometimes she wondered what it would be like to have moved here from somewhere else. To discover Mischief Bay as an adult. For her there was only complete familiarity.

She pulled into their driveway. Makayla got out of the SUV, then opened the back door to help the twins. Gabby went to unlock the front door. She could already hear Boomer baying his greeting and scratching to get out. The only thing preventing him from going through the door was the metal plate Andrew had screwed into place.

As soon as she opened the door, Boomer raced past her to get to *his* girls. Because while Boomer loved his whole pack, Makayla and the twins were his girls. He followed them around, did his best to keep them in line and when they disobeyed his list of rules, he ratted on them.

Now he ran in circles, looping around all three kids, baying his pleasure at seeing them again, as if it had been weeks instead of a few hours. Gabby thought about pointing out that she'd been home much of the afternoon, but doubted that information would impress Boomer.

Makayla and the twins stopped to pet him before heading toward the house. Once they were moving, Boomer wiggled his way to the front and darted through the open door. The girls followed. Gabby made sure that Jasmine hadn't bolted for freedom, then stepped into the foyer and pushed the door closed behind her.

It was nearly four. By her calculations she had less than two hours to get the twins settled in for the evening, dinner started, the pets fed and herself turned from frumpy mom to glamorous, charming wife to successful Andrew Schaefer. It was going to be a push.

She went directly to the kitchen and dropped her handbag on the built-in desk that was her catchall for crap. Next she looked at the calendar posted on the wall, the one with all their activities color coded by person. Makayla's mom was picking her up at six, Gabby and Andrew were due to leave at six-fifteen and Cecelia, their go-to sitter, was due at five forty-five.

"Mommy, can I wear my purple hat to dinner tonight?" Kenzie asked as she ran into the kitchen. "Kennedy wants to wear her green one. I like my purple one better. It has feathers *and* lace."

"Did you pick up my dark-wash jeans from the dry cleaner?" Makayla asked as she, too, entered the kitchen. "I'm going to need them for this weekend. Mom's taking me to the movies and out to dinner and you know that means we'll be going somewhere nice."

"I did. They're in your room."

Which you would know if you'd bothered to go look. But she didn't say that. Nor did she mention she thought it was ri-

diculous that a fifteen-year-old was allowed to send her jeans
to the dry cleaner. Couldn't she wash them with the rest of
her clothes? But Makayla had deemed it critical and Andrew
had agreed. Gabby felt that if she was going to have to die on
some hill when it came to her stepdaughter, it wasn't going
to be the one about dry cleaning.

Makayla sat on one of the stools by the island. "Mom
said she's going to take me to her stylist and get my hair cut.
Maybe I'll get bangs. There's enough time to grow them out
before school starts. You know, if I don't like them."

As she spoke, she stretched her long arms out across the
granite countertop. Her hands were laced together as she
stretched. Kenzie watched closely and Gabby knew that in
the morning, she would see the same pose at breakfast. Because there was nothing the twins liked more than to imi-
tate their older sister.

"We might do some school shopping. She can get me in
to see all the fall clothes that aren't out yet. We went through
the look books already and I chose some things."

Candace was a buyer for an upscale department store and
had access to a lot of things, including styles and brands not
yet available for sale to the public. Gabby told herself it was
nice that Makayla got to feel special with her mom. That was
how it was supposed to be. Most of time she nearly believed
herself, as well.

Makayla raised one shoulder dramatically. "It's because I
have an eye for trends."

"You do."

Makayla eyed Gabby's baggy, knee-length shorts and over-
size T-shirt, the blue one with a stain on the front and a small
but growing hole near the hem.

"You want me to talk to Dad about giving you a makeover?"

"Thanks. Sweet, but no."

She told herself that she didn't have it so bad. Makayla was a pretty good kid. She had her moods, but most of those were either hormone or mother-induced. She loved her baby sisters and looked out for them.

What made things difficult was the nagging sense that Makayla wasn't treated like a member of the family. Her place was more revered guest, with everyone circling around her illustrious orbit. Like the dry cleaning. Seriously? For jeans? Or that Makayla *didn't mind* looking after the twins if Gabby needed her to. But only for an hour. Never for an afternoon or evening. And even the few minutes of watching was always a favor—never something Gabby could depend on. Giving Makayla orders wasn't allowed.

Second-wife syndrome, Gabby told herself firmly. Every now and then she got a twinge from having to deal with Andrew's past. The most he'd had to suffer through was an old boyfriend flirting with her at her ten-year high school reunion. And that was hardly the same thing.

"Mommy, I think Jasmine's gonna throw up."

Kennedy shouted the announcement from somewhere upstairs. Makayla and Kenzie took off running. Gabby paused long enough to grab a few paper towels. As she headed for the stairs she wondered if it was wrong to hope Boomer got there first and took care of things for her. The big guy could always been counted on to clean up messes.

By five o'clock, the household was in that delicate transition from chaos to calm. At least that was what Gabby told herself. Dinner was in the oven, Makayla was packing for her weekend and the twins were in their playroom, deciding on what to do that evening with Cecelia.

"Dress up," Kennedy said firmly, a small green hat perched on her head. "And Legos."

"Legos for sure," Kenzie agreed. Her hat was all feathers and lace. They were both adorable. Stubborn, but adorable.

Gabby found evenings with the sitter went easier if everyone went in with the right expectations. To that end she always provided a plate of snacks for both her kids and the sitter. She also made sure that toys, books and movies were chosen in advance.

The toys were picked out and put on the small, five-year-old-sized table. Next to it were three books Cecelia would read to them at bedtime, along with several DVD choices. Jasmine, recovered from her fur-ball attack, strolled in. She walked over to Gabby and gave her delicate girlie meow—the one that indicated all was right in her feline world. Boomer followed, his nose pressed into the carpet as he searched for fallen crumbs and who knew what else.

The twins pulled their pets close. Gabby used the distraction to escape to her room. She still had to shower—because she hadn't had time that morning—and do something with her hair.

For a while she'd been trying the blonde thing, but honestly, with three kids, it was too hard to get in for regular appointments. She was going to be starting back to work soon. If she didn't have time now, she sure wouldn't then. So she'd spent the past year or so easing the color toward her natural shade of sort-of-brown, sort-of-red. She was thinking of getting highlights to celebrate her return to the office, but only if her hairdresser promised her they wouldn't need touching up more than once every six months.

She managed to get in the shower without being called or having to deal with a crisis. By the time she was out, the twins, Boomer and Jasmine had moved into the master bath where the four of them lay on the floor, watching her as she reached for her towel.

Kenzie and Kennedy each had one of Boomer's ears in their tiny hands. They stroked his silky fur while leaning against him. Their dress-up hats were askew. Jasmine watched from the mat by the sink, as if in charge. Which was probably true. Jasmine did love to control situations.

"What are you going to wear, Mommy?" Kenzie asked. "You'll be pretty."

"Thank you. I'm not sure yet."

"A dress," Kennedy said firmly. "With high heels."

Because the twins loved to wear high heels when they played dress up.

"And lipstick," Kenzie added.

Gabby slipped on her underwear and bra, then walked into the big closet she shared with Andrew. While his side was organized according to the type of clothing, and then by color, hers was slightly more haphazard. A few things were piled on the floor, under the hanging racks. She wasn't sure if they were there by design or if Jasmine had pulled them off, and this wasn't the moment to find out.

Double racks and a built-in dresser should have helped with the organization but somehow that never happened. At least not for her. Andrew's drawers were meticulously arranged. Socks sorted by color, exercise T-shirts separate from the T-shirts he wore under dress shirts. Why was that? She put away the laundry. So she was the one who maintained his organized ways while doing nothing to move herself beyond controlled chaos.

The whys weren't important right now, she told herself as she dug through the single tall rack, searching for a reasonably clean, slightly dressy LBD. She found it in the back, next to a fuzzy pink robe she'd never liked.

The dress was long-sleeved, with a faux wrap bodice and knee-length skirt. She hadn't worn it in a while but it looked clean enough. Except for pink fuzz from her robe, which would come off easily enough with masking-tape strips. The bigger issue was would it fit?

She knew she had a killer Spanx slip hanging somewhere, but before she suffered through the indignity of that she wanted to see if the dress was even a possibility. She undid the side zipper, then pulled it over her head.

The arms felt tight and the fabric bunched right above her boobs. She pulled and tugged and shimmied until it settled over her body. Even before she reached for the side zipper, she knew there was going to be problem.

The dress looked awful. It accentuated her round middle and the roll above her waistline. The fabric gapped a good four inches at the zipper and no amount of prayer was going to make it close. Not even the killer Spanx would be enough.

How much did she weigh? She hadn't been on the scale in maybe a year. Sure, there were the extra few pounds since she'd had the girls, but this was unexpected. She hadn't actually put on *more* weight, had she?

Even as she thought about the extra cookie she had after breakfast most days and the secret stash of Hershey's Kisses in her nightstand, she told herself not to get off track. Andrew was due home any second. Cecelia would be arriving, Makayla was going to have a crisis before she headed to her mom's and the twins could only be counted on to be quiet and entertain themselves in twenty-minute increments. That time was rapidly drawing to a close.

She pulled off the dress and flung it on the floor, then reached for her go-to black pants. They were stretched out at the waist and in need of replacing, but none of that mattered now. They fit.

She pulled them on, then searched for a top that was on the dressy end of professional. She found a black blazer that always worked, only there was a stain on the front. She jerked the hangers across the racks, trying to remember what she owned that wasn't too small, too frayed or just plain ugly. Her throat tightened as panic set in. In her head she heard the frantic ticking of time going by too quickly melding with the horrifying realization that somewhere along the way, she'd gotten fat.

At the far end of the upper rack, she spotted a red sleeve. She pulled the shirt off the hanger and breathed a sigh of relief. Okay, the color wasn't good, but the loose, silky shirt would fit her. The fabric was a little see-through and had an unfortunate gold weave running through it. She had no idea what had possessed her to buy it. Still, she was grateful to have something to wear.

She pulled on a plain black camisole, grabbed the red shirt and hurried back into the bathroom. The twins lay across Boomer. Jasmine was nowhere to be seen. Not a surprise— the feline had excellent self-preservation instincts. She seemed to sense exactly when there was going to be a crisis of some kind and extricated herself before it could happen.

Makeup, Gabby thought frantically as she plugged in her hot rollers. Curl her hair, makeup, dinner prep, Makayla, Cecelia, feed the pets, talk to the twins and out the door. It was possible, she told herself. Unlikely, but possible.

She draped the red shirt over the side of the tub. Kennedy wrinkled her nose.

"Mommy, you said you were wearing a dress."

"No, you said that. I like pants."

"You're still pretty," Kenzie said loyally.

"Thank you, sweetie."

"Daddy likes you in a dress." Kennedy's expression turned stubborn. "And high heels."

"I'm going to wear high heels." High-ish, Gabby thought, already feeling her toes whimper in protest.

"Gabby, where are my white crop pants?" Makayla asked from the doorway to the bathroom. "I put them in the wash this morning."

Gabby reached for her comb. After sectioning her hair, she put in a hot roller. "I don't do whites on Fridays. I do them on Monday and Thursday."

"But you knew I need them for this weekend." Makayla's expression turned annoyed and the volume of her voice increased. *Danger.* "You didn't wash them on purpose."

The twins looked at each other. Identical mouths formed perfect O's as they waited to see what would happen next.

Every Friday Makayla was seeing her mother, Gabby thought grimly, there was a crisis, a fight, a something. And it was always her fault. *Sugar, sugar, sugar.*

Gabby faced her stepdaughter. Once again she was momentarily distracted by how pretty she was and how Makayla would spend much of her adulthood defined by her beauty. Oh, to be so cursed, Gabby thought ruefully.

"Makayla, you know I do laundry on a schedule. I've done it on a schedule since you came to live with us two years ago. I do the whites on Monday and Thursday. If you have a special request, I'm happy to try to help, but you didn't tell me about the pants. I had no way of knowing they were in the laundry."

Tears filled the teen's eyes. "You could have looked."

The unreasonable statement made her chest tighten. *Deep breath.* "And you could have told me. I can't read your mind. Is there something else you can take with you?"

"No, the weekend is *ruined*!"

"Why is that?"

The question came from the bedroom. Gabby felt the tight-

ness around her chest ease just a little. The twins scrambled
to their feet and raced toward the speaker, as did Boomer.

Shrieks of "Daddy! Daddy!" competed with barks and
Makayla complaining about her lack of white crop pants.

Gabby turned back to the mirror. The odds of her getting
close to Andrew in the next ten minutes were close to zero.
The girls and Makayla always claimed his attention when he
got home. Boomer needed his moment with the master of the
house. Even Jasmine would stroll in for a quick chin scratch.

Gabby finished rolling her hair, then quickly applied her
makeup. She had a five-minute routine that got her through
most situations. She wasn't sure who the fund-raiser was for
or the crowd they might face, so she took a little extra time
with her eye shadow and liner.

Ten minutes later she pulled out the rollers and finger-
combed her hair, then applied hair spray. Earrings followed.
She slipped on low pumps and hurried out of the bedroom.

She walked toward Makayla's room. The teen was folding pink pants.

"You doing okay?" she asked, careful to sound cheerful
rather than cautious.

Makayla nodded without looking at her.

"Okay, then. Come get me if you need anything."

Gabby hurried to the kitchen where she checked on dinner. She wasn't sure where the twins were, but she could
hear laughter and Andrew's low voice from somewhere in
the back of the house.

Boomer and Jasmine came into the kitchen. The calico
wound around her legs in what Gabby assumed was supposed
to be affection. Or at least a claim on her attention.

"I'm very clear on the time," she told her pets. "You're
next."

She put Boomer's food in a bowl and set it in the mudroom,

then got out Jasmine's dinner. Wet food with water mixed in, to keep Jasmine's urinary tract healthy. Gabby added a small bowl of kibble on the side and carried both to the laundry room, because there was no way dogs and cats could eat together. Not if the cat was going to get any food.

Jasmine jumped up on her table and meowed until Gabby set down the dishes.

The pets fed, Gabby returned to the kitchen and set the table for three, all the while glancing at the clock. She pulled out the plate of raw vegetables she'd cut up earlier. Because while the twins wouldn't touch a *cooked* vegetable, they would eat them raw.

Right on time, the doorbell rang. Boomer announced their visitor, in case he was the only one who heard the bell. The twins came running, yelling Cecelia's name. Gabby let in the teen and smiled gratefully.

"Hi," she said with a sigh. "I hope you like lasagna."

"Love it."

Cecelia had a backpack slung over one shoulder. Gabby knew that once she got the twins settled, she would study. In addition to her part-time job at Supper's in the Bag, Cecelia babysat and took classes in summer school. It was impressive.

Back in the kitchen for what felt like the forty-seventh time in the past ten minutes, Gabby explained about what had to be done for dinner. She went over the selected toys, books and movies for that evening and guessed as to when she and Andrew would be home.

"You have our cell numbers, right?" she asked.

"Programmed into my phone," Cecelia told her. "Don't worry. We'll have a great time."

"I know. I can't help it."

She glanced at the clock. "Candace is going to be here any second," she said. "I need to check on Makayla."

The twins, Boomer and Jasmine followed her down the hall to where Makayla stood with her suitcase. Her expression was tense, her body stiff. She looked more like she was heading to the dentist than to her mom's for the weekend.

For a second Gabby felt sympathy. Makayla didn't have it easy. Candace was an indifferent mother at best and she was often late. More than once, she'd phoned at the last minute to say she couldn't possibly take her daughter for the weekend. Sometimes it was a legitimate reason—like being out of town on business. But more often there was no explanation offered.

"Is she here?" Makayla asked anxiously.

"Not yet. I wanted to make sure you had everything you needed."

"Not the white crop pants."

Gabby knew she'd walked into that one and tried not to react. Kenzie slipped past her and stared up at Makayla.

"Do you have to go?"

The tension immediately eased as Makayla dropped to her knees and held out her arms. Kennedy came running and both girls hugged her tight.

"I'll be back before you know it," Makayla promised.

"You could take us with you." Kennedy poked her in the arm. "We'd be good. Promise."

"I don't think that's a great idea," Makayla said gently.

"Why not?" Kenzie asked.

"Because I would miss you too much!" Gabby said. "I'd be totally and completely sad without my girls here. It's bad enough that Makayla's gone. What would I do without my munchkins?"

The twins ran from their sister to her. She was pinned by thin arms hanging on so tight. She felt their love all the way to her heart. It filled it and made her world right.

In that moment she glanced at Makayla and saw fierce longing in the teen's blue eyes. The raw emotion startled her. Before she could figure out what to say, it was gone.

"Makayla, your mom's here."

Andrew's voice carried down the hall.

"Auntie Candace!" the twins screamed together as they turned and ran toward the living room. Makayla followed more slowly.

Gabby didn't want to go at all, but knew that would be rude. Not that Candace would notice. Their brief exchanges were always awkward and overly polite. Conversation between two people who were sure they couldn't possibly have anything in common. Ironic considering they had both fallen in love with the same man. Talk about sharing something intimate.

Gabby wasn't sure what Candace thought of her, but she knew exactly what she thought of the other woman. Candace was tall, thin and beautiful. Worse, she was successful. She was the head buyer for designer shoes and handbags for an upscale department store.

She had fashion sense, a wardrobe to die for and absolutely no cellulite. Gabby was sure of it. She might be shorter than Candace, but next to her she always felt as if she were taking up too much room.

She took a deep breath and walked into the living room. Andrew stood by the door, Jasmine in his arms. Boomer bounced around, his ears and jowls flapping as he tried to get Candace to notice him. The twins were talking and twirling, while Makayla stood beside her mother. And Candace, well, she was busy being tall and thin and beautiful. Not to mention perfectly dressed in a pair of narrow cream-colored slacks and a tailored shirt in the same shade.

White, Gabby thought in amazement, wondering how long it would take her to get a white shirt stained. Eight seconds? Nine? There was also her jewelry—fashionably layered necklaces and several rings. Even though she'd most likely put on her makeup nearly twelve hours before, it was still…perfect.

As Gabby made her way into the room, Candace looked her up and down, then smiled that mean girl smile of hers.

"Gabby. How delightful. Are you going out?"

"Yes."

"Your hair looks lovely. Well, you'll want to get changed, so I won't keep you. Makayla, darling, are you ready?"

"Mommy already changed," Kenzie said helpfully. "She's in her going-out shirt."

Candace's right eyebrow rose. At least as much as the Botox would let it. "Oh. Well. You look…very nice."

Heat burned on Gabby's cheeks, but she didn't let a little thing like embarrassment slow her down. She herded the twins back to the kitchen and helped Cecelia get them ready for dinner. When she heard the front door close, she exhaled slowly. One crisis down for the evening. Four hundred and thirty-seven to go.

She walked back to the living room and saw Andrew putting Jasmine on the sofa.

"At last," he said, turning toward her. "Hi. How are you?"

He kissed her before she could reply. While the kiss was light, the hug that accompanied it was not. Andrew gave good hugs, full-bodied embraces that lingered an extra second. When the world was spinning, he was her anchor.

"I'm okay."

He touched her cheek. "I know what you're thinking. How on earth did I marry such a bitch? I have no excuse. All I can say for myself is thank God I got it right the second time."

He was good with words, too, she thought gratefully. And life. Andrew understood life. He was successful—the vice president of sales for a large aerospace firm. He traveled a lot, but not more than he had to. He made sure he was home for significant events and he never once made Gabby feel that his work was more important than hers.

Now she resisted the need to cling to him, to complain about Makayla and the white pants, to ask that he go beat up his ex for being mean to her. No, those were her issues and she would deal with them.

"My day was fine," she told him. "What about yours?"

"Good. We hit our numbers for the quarter, so I'm golden." He flashed her a grin. "Until Monday, then it all starts again."

The familiar joke made her smile. Just looking at him made her smile, too. He was eight years older than her, but aging well. Dark hair and blue eyes. There was a touch of gray at his temples, which made him look even more appealing. It was the distinguished thing. Because Mother Nature clearly favored men.

"I don't remember the name of the fund-raiser," she whispered. "I'm sorry. I didn't put it on the calendar. Just the date and time."

He leaned in and kissed her again. "I didn't tell you the name." He pulled her close and lowered his head so he could whisper in her ear. "There is no fund-raiser, my sweet wife. I've rented a room at the Inn on the Pier. There's a bottle of champagne chilling. I was hoping we could have our way with each other for a couple of hours, then order room service before coming back home."

"I'd be willing to write a check to that cause," she told him.

Andrew leaned back his head and laughed, then put his arm around her.

Tears burned. Happy tears, she told herself as she willed them away. The tears of a woman who had won the husband lottery.

Chapter Four

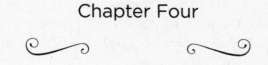

"Again!" Tyler said eagerly, not sounding the least bit tired, despite the fact that it was a good half hour past his bedtime and they'd had a full day. "Read it again."

Nicole leaned over and kissed the top of his head. "Are you thinking too much?" she asked her son.

He grinned at her. "I am. I'm excited, Mommy. It's better than Christmas."

If only that were true, Nicole thought, knowing there was no way to prepare a six-year-old for potential disappointment, yet aware she had to try.

They'd spent their Saturday together—something she was still getting used to. Divorce from Eric had been difficult on so many levels, but financial wasn't one of them. He might not see his kid very often, but he always paid his child support on time. The checks had allowed her to hire a couple of extra instructors at her exercise studio, Mischief in Motion, which allowed her to cut down on her evening classes and the luxury of not working on Saturdays. In a few short years Tyler was going to be too busy with school activities and friends to want to hang out with his mom, but until then, she wanted to take advantage of every second they had together.

She stroked his hair. "Meeting the author of *Brad the Dragon* is going to be great," she began.

"I know. He's going to be funny and nice and make everyone laugh."

Nicole wanted that to be true. But weren't authors authors for a reason? There was no way she could spend all day alone, staring at a keyboard, typing. She needed to be doing something and around people.

Of course, she probably had a ridiculous view of writers. Eric wrote screenplays, and while he did spend a fair amount of time alone at the computer, he was also out surfing most mornings. He took meetings, went to parties, did screenwriterly things, she wasn't sure what. Maybe Jairus was the same way—working fifteen minutes on a picture book, then using the rest of the day to count his money.

She sighed. She really needed to work on her attitude. She was going to be meeting the man in a few days. She didn't want to shriek at him in the first three seconds. Better for that to happen in the second hour.

The thought of yelling at the money-grubbing jerk made her smile. Tyler smiled back.

"You're excited, too," he said.

"I am." A white lie was allowed because she was a mom, she told herself.

"You won't forget?"

"Nope. I'm teaching at the senior center that morning but my afternoon is all Brad the Dragon, all the time. Just me and you-know-who."

As she spoke, she tickled Tyler's sides. He squirmed and laughed, then lay down. "One more time," he pleaded, pointing at the book. "I'll try not to think. I promise."

"Only for you," she murmured.

She picked up the book and turned to the first page. "Brad the Dragon had always been interested in flowers."

She read automatically, not having to pay attention to the dragonly antics. She knew the story by heart, along with each and every other one of them. The never-ending thrill of B the D was that he evolved. Thank God the series ended when Brad turned ten. There was no way she wanted to read about a teenage B the D getting his stupid driver's license.

Nicole finished the book, then kissed Tyler good-night. His eyes were closed and his voice slow as he whispered, "I love you, Mommy."

"I love you, big guy."

She walked out, careful to leave the door just a little open. So he wouldn't feel cut off from her. Or maybe she was the one who needed the connection.

Back in the kitchen, she finished cleaning up the dinner dishes. Normally she did them after they were done eating but Tyler had been so wired they'd gone for a long walk instead. As she rinsed pans and put them in the dishwasher, she thought about how much she was dreading the upcoming author event at the city park camp Tyler attended.

Maybe she was being unfair. There was the tiniest chance he wasn't totally awful. After all, she loved the *Fancy Nancy* books and they basically had the same trajectory as B the D. They started as picture books and moved to chapter books. She knew. She read them to Gabby's twins when she looked after the girls.

But Fancy Nancy was different, she thought, hearing the whine in her head. She was lovely and sweet and there was always a lesson to be learned. Not to mention vocabulary words. Brad the Dragon was just so…annoying.

She finished with the kitchen and started the dishwasher, then wandered into her living room. The house—a Spanish-style beauty she'd managed to buy for a rock-bottom price just before the mortgage bubble—was a testament to crafts-manship. There were arches and thick walls, lots of windows and a beautiful yard out back. She loved her house. Loved that Tyler was growing up here. If sometimes she got a little lonely for male companionship, well, that was okay. She'd been blessed in the rest of her life.

Her phone chirped, telling her she had a text. A quick glance at the clock told her it was after nine. She thought in-stantly of Hayley and her frail condition, then hurried to read the screen. Even as she told herself that if something bad had happened, she would get a call not a text, she couldn't catch her breath until she'd read—

"Damn him."

She read the message three times before tossing her phone on the sofa. "Lying, selfish bastard."

Nicole picked up her phone, ready to give Eric a piece of her mind. Then she read the words again.

Can't make tomorrow. Sorry. Next time for sure.

Sadness mingled with her fury. Because in the morning, she was going to have to tell her son that his father wouldn't be coming to see him. There would be no outing with Eric, no time for Tyler to see his dad.

The real killer was, Tyler wouldn't mind. He would shrug and go back to whatever it was he'd been doing. Because Eric canceled more often than not and Tyler cared less and less about seeing the man.

The disconnection had started long before the divorce, Nicole thought, somewhere around the time when Eric had begun writing his screenplay. He'd pulled back from his fam-ily—spending his time surfing, writing or going to classes and his critique group. Then after he sold the screenplay, he'd been busy with revisions and a new project. She and Tyler had become less and less important.

She'd thought she would have to fight him for custody, but Eric hadn't wanted more than one Sunday, every other week. That was it. And he blew off those days more and more.

She reached for her phone but instead of texting her ex, she sent a message to Hayley.

The bastard blew off his kid again. Is it wrong that I hate him?

Hayley's response came in seconds. No, but if it makes you feel better, I'll hate him for you. Doing okay?

I'll get through it. Thanks.

Nicole sank onto the sofa, drew her legs to her chest, and rested her head on her knees. If it wasn't for her friends, she wasn't sure how she would have survived the past year. It wasn't supposed to be like this. She and Eric were supposed to have been a family. That was what she'd always wanted, always hoped for. She hadn't known her own father. He'd left his family before she was born. With Eric, back when he was a software engineer, she thought she'd found someone good. Someone stable. Someone who would be there for their children.

She'd been wrong. About all of it. Some of that was on her, but some of it was purely him. He didn't care about his son. That was the bottom line.

She kept hoping he would change. That he would realize what he was missing. But so far there was no hint that he was having second thoughts about their custody arrangements. And Tyler no longer talked about missing his dad.

She had a sinking feeling that by the time Eric woke up to what he'd missed, it would be too late. That Tyler would be unreachable. But even worse was the very good chance that Eric would never care. Never ask for a second chance. That this was as good as it got.

She looked up at the Brad the Dragon stuffed animal sitting on a bookshelf by the TV. The creature was a happy shade of red, with big blue eyes. She glared at the dragon.

"This is all your fault," she whispered. And while she knew it wasn't, sometimes it felt really good to have someone to blame.

"Why does Boomer smell like corn chips?" Kennedy asked from her place on the floor next to the dog.

"I have no idea."

Gabby thought about pointing out that it was better than how most dogs smelled, but knew better than to encourage smell talk. It would lead to an entire discussion on farts, burps and other things that were hilarious, but often led to awkward moments around other people. She was still recovering from the classic, "That lady farted" event from three weeks ago at the grocery store. She'd been embarrassed, the older woman had been embarrassed and the twins had thought the situation was the funniest thing ever. They told nearly everyone they saw. Which was why she did her level best to not take them to the grocery store any more than necessary.

She held up a pink T-shirt. "One of my favorites," she said.

Kenzie, who was combing an incredibly patient Jasmine, nodded. "Me, too."

Kennedy didn't bother answering. While she was normally the twin in charge, when it came to clothes, Kenzie was the spokestwin. Gabby wasn't sure how they made up their rules but she mostly went along with them.

"And we are done," she said, staring at the five outfits, times two, chosen for the upcoming week.

In an effort to create order from chaos, when the girls had started preschool, she'd made it a point to choose their outfits in advance. Now it was something they did together every Sunday afternoon. It helped with the morning craziness and was a fun time for the three of them to have girl talk.

The twins abandoned their pets to put their outfits away in a special drawer in each of their dressers. When they were done, they looked at her expectantly.

"Daddy's next," Gabby said brightly.

Kenzie leaned over and picked up Jasmine. The cat submitted to being half carried, half dragged to the master closet. Boomer followed on his own, then flopped down in the doorway. Kennedy immediately draped across him, while Kenzie sat in the middle of the floor, prepared to offer fashion advice. Jasmine settled next to her and proceeded to lick her fur back into order.

Gabby picked up the sheet of paper Andrew always left for her on Friday evenings. It was his schedule for the upcoming week. His assistant emailed her his travel schedule every time a trip was added or changed, but Andrew took care of making sure she knew where he was all the time. It was something he'd started when they were first married. She remembered following him through the apartment they'd shared while they were waiting to close on the house.

"When will you be back?" she'd asked, knowing she sounded petulant. "It's hard when you're not here."

He'd turned to her, his blue eyes dark with concern. "Are you worried about being alone in the apartment? Do you want me to get an alarm installed?"

"No, silly. I just miss you."

He'd stared at her for a long time. She'd watched confusion change to understanding, relief and love. He'd hugged her so tightly, she hadn't been able to breathe. But that was okay. Andrew was more important than air.

The next morning she'd received her first email from his assistant. The following Friday, Andrew had brought home his schedule for the upcoming week. Because that was the kind of man Andrew was. He didn't want her to worry. He didn't want her to be concerned about anything.

From the night they'd met until their wedding had been nearly a year. He'd told her about his first marriage and what he thought had gone wrong. She would have sworn she knew everything about him. But until that night in their small apartment, she hadn't really understood what he'd been saying.

Candace hadn't cared. She hadn't bothered to keep track of his travel schedule or asked when he would be home. She'd rarely made time for Makayla. Her work was her one true passion. Gabby could understand loving a career, but not at the expense of people.

Now she looked at his schedule and saw the various meetings he had.

"Daddy's going to be home all week," she told the twins. "Yay!"

"Can we make him brownies?" Kenzie asked.

Gabby thought about her inability to fit into her dress the previous Friday. Since then she'd been thinking she had to do something. "Um, sure."

She could ignore the brownies, she told herself. Just because they were in the house didn't mean she had to eat them.

She sorted through Andrew's suits and shirts. Even with the pile of shirts to go to the dry cleaner's on Monday, there were still plenty to choose from. She held up a gray suit with a pale blue shirt.

"Which tie?"

Only Kenzie considered the question. "The one with the blue and pink stripes."

Gabby found it. She hung the suit, shirt and tie and moved on to the next selection.

While Andrew was perfectly capable of picking out his own clothes, she liked doing this for him. It was a connection, a way to quietly say she was thinking about him and that she cared. Like him leaving her his schedule.

When they were done, she led her posse back to the kitchen. She didn't need her wardrobe laid out and Makayla wasn't back yet from her mom's. Even if she had been home, she'd made it clear she didn't want or need the help. She was fifteen, after all.

Gabby briefly wondered if she'd been difficult at that age and figured she probably had been. It came with the territory. But knowing that didn't make her any more eager for Makayla's return. Sunday nights after Candace weekends were always difficult. The visits rarely went well and Makayla usually came home both hurt and angry. She needed someone to pay for what she'd been through and that person was usually Gabby.

She'd tried talking to Andrew about the temper, the snide comments, the door slamming. But Makayla was always careful to act out when her father wasn't around and if Andrew had a weakness it was his daughters. Not just Makayla but all three of them.

A trait she admired, Gabby reminded herself. So she would take the high ground. Or at least try. It was the only advice her own mother had given her when Gabby had been getting ready to marry Andrew.

"Being the second wife is hard. I've watched several of my friends go through it. Think before you speak and take the moral high ground whenever you can. It will make things easier."

Gabby had appreciated the advice and the love behind it, so she'd listened. She tried to keep her Makayla-based whining to a minimum and be as patient as possible. She wasn't perfect, but she did her best.

The dryer buzzed. She left the twins coloring at the kitchen table while she carried a load of clean clothes to the master. Although it wasn't her day for whites, she'd wanted to have the special crop pants done when Makayla returned. She wasn't sure if the gesture would be seen as caring or taunting, but she knew her motives were pure and told herself that would be enough.

Andrew strolled into the bedroom and crossed the carpet to help her. He picked up impossibly small socks and smiled at her.

"Remember when they were even smaller?" he asked.

"I know. They're growing so fast. I can't believe they're starting kindergarten."

"How many days?"

She smiled. He wasn't asking about the start of school. Instead he was inquiring about *her* start date.

"Fifty-four days."

"You excited?"

"Yes, and nervous. What if I don't remember how to hold down a job?"

"You will. You work hard and you're brilliant. They're lucky to have you."

She would be working for a nonprofit, part-time. The job wasn't anything spectacular, nor was the pay, but it was in her chosen legal field of immigration and she would be helping people who didn't have anywhere else to go. Plus there was the whole pee alone thing.

"I'm lucky they're willing to take a chance on me." She'd been out of the workforce for just over five years. That was a long time. Although she'd taken a few online classes to keep current on changes in immigration law, she'd been worried about anyone wanting to hire her.

"You'll be amazing," he assured her, setting down another pair of socks, then reaching into his jeans front pocket. "I have something for you."

He handed her a Nordstrom gift card.

She took it, then looked at him. "I don't understand."

"You'll need new clothes for work. Everything you have from before the twins is five years old. I want you to feel good on your first day back."

A sweet gesture, she thought, even as her mind replayed his words. Fear joined horror. Her work clothes *were* five years old. They were pre-twins, which meant there was no way any of them fit. The being out of style part was the least of it.

She turned the gift card over in her hands. "We have a charge card at the store."

"I know, but this is different. You can buy anything you like without me seeing the bill. You know I don't care what you spend, but you always want to justify every purchase. This is guilt-free shopping."

She stared into his blue eyes and felt a rush of love. "Andrew, you're very good to me."

"I want to be. I love you, Gabby." He took the card from her and slid it into her shorts back pocket, then rested his hands on her hips. "So, how much time do you think we have until we're invaded?" he asked, his mouth lowering to hers.

He kissed her deeply, sweeping his tongue against her bottom lip. She felt his passion, which ignited her own. Their evening together on Friday had been all about slow, sensual lovemaking, but Andrew was fairly spectacular at the "we have three minutes" quickie.

"It depends on when Makayla gets home," she said, already eyeing their bedroom door. "The girls are coloring. Five minutes, maybe ten."

He was already unbuttoning her shorts. "Think you can come in three?"

Andrew turning her on had never been a problem. Even before she felt the first brush of his fingers against her clit. The familiar combination of heat and ache had her wrapping her arms around his neck. He eased her toward the bed and leaned over her, rubbing his erection against her thigh.

"Mommy, Mommy, Makayla's home!"

Kennedy's high-pitched voice cut through the house more effectively than a fire alarm. Andrew swore softly before withdrawing his hand and helping her to her feet.

"Tonight," he promised.

She shivered in anticipation. "I can't wait."

He grinned. "Want me to stall the girls while you take care of things yourself?"

His suggestion made her blush. She swatted his arm. "You know I don't do that. I'd rather wait and make love with you."

"Not always."

Because sometimes she did touch herself, but only when he was there. Only when he was watching. She couldn't imagine doing that with anyone else. But Andrew always made her feel safe. Wanted.

They started for the living room. "I'm thinking of taking classes with Nicole," she said.

"Like knitting or something?"

Which was just like a man. "No. At her studio. An exercise class."

His look of genuine confusion made her want to hug him for about a thousand years.

"I've put on a little weight."

"Really? I don't think so, but if you want to take the class, have a good time."

There were implications. If she couldn't find a class when the twins were at camp, she would need to make sure Makayla could watch them. Or hire a sitter. The latter meant an added expense but Andrew was okay with that.

The twins were dancing around Makayla, competing with each other to tell her what she'd missed over the weekend. Boomer joined in, wanting to be petted by the returning member of the pack. Jasmine was nowhere to be seen but later she would settle herself on Makayla's bed and stay there for the night.

Gabby watched her stepdaughter, taking in the straight set of her mouth and the way she seemed to be forcing herself to interact with her sisters. Only time would tell how bad this week's reentry would be, Gabby thought. She called out a greeting to the teen, then walked back to the bedroom to finish folding clothes.

When she'd first met Andrew, he'd only had Makayla on weekends. Then, just before she and Andrew had married, Candace had asked for a change in the parenting plan—giving him equal custody. A few years after that, Candace had again asked for a change, this time giving Andrew full custody with Makayla visiting her mom every other weekend.

Gabby had known there wasn't a choice. That while Andrew asked her if it was okay, the truth was, she couldn't say no. Of course he wanted his daughter around more. The fact that he was at work and traveling, leaving her to deal with the teen, was immaterial. With Candace basically rejecting her only child, it was up to them to make the girl feel welcome. Gabby did her best, although sometimes it was hard.

She *wanted* to love her stepdaughter and was pretty sure she did. But *liking* her was more of a challenge. She wrestled with the expected emotions, like anger and resentment. But sometimes there was jealousy, too. Jealousy that Andrew had done the husband/father thing before. That no matter how she tried, she would never be first. There had always been another wife, another child before her and the twins.

She sorted the folded laundry by owner, then dropped it off in each bedroom. She paused in front of Makayla's open door, braced herself for the lingering effects of the weekend visit, then offered a cheerful, "Knock, knock."

Makayla was sitting on her bed, her unopened suitcase on the floor beside her. She looked up when Gabby entered.

"I know it's late for these," she said, placing the white crop pants on the dresser, "but I felt bad you didn't have them to take with you. If you tell me you need something, I'll try to get it washed."

Makayla's head was bent so her hair mostly covered her face. "Sure," she mumbled.

"I could teach you to do laundry yourself."

"No, thanks."

Gabby wanted to stomp her foot. The teen was plenty old enough to be washing her own clothes. All the books she'd read on teenagers said it was important that they be given clearly defined chores. But Andrew wasn't a fan of that. He wanted Makayla to, as he put it, "Have time to be a kid and not always have to deal with crap around the house." Then he told Gabby to hire a housekeeper so she wouldn't think the situation was unfair.

She already had a service every other week to take care of

the deep cleaning and even that made her feel guilty. But once she was back to work, they would be a necessity. At least that was what she told herself. And having a housekeeper wasn't the point. Makayla needed to be a contributing member of the household. Watching the twins when she was in the mood and setting the table wasn't enough.

Everyone had their flaws, she reminded herself. Andrew was a great husband and father and she could live with his unrealistic expectations of what it meant to be a teenager.

"Everything go okay with your mom?" she asked, then braced herself for the response. Because while Makayla didn't like to talk about her weekends, she complained when no one mentioned them.

"It was fine. I want to have friends over this week. After camp."

Andrew walked in and sat next to his daughter. He pulled her against him. "Friends? Do I know these friends? Are they in a rock band? Because you know how I feel about rock bands."

That earned him a slight chuckle. As Makayla leaned against her dad, her hair fell away from her face and Gabby could see she'd been crying.

Her low-grade annoyance at Makayla's easy life here gave way to anger directed at Candace. Why couldn't Makayla's mother care just a little? Would it kill her to be nice to her only kid?

"Just let me know what day," Gabby said. "I'll make sure the twins have plenty to do." Because there was nothing the five-year-olds liked more than hanging out with their big sister and her friends.

"Thanks. Maybe Wednesday. We have to decide."

"How many? I'll bake cookies." She'd learned that no

matter how surly the teenager, he or she could be bribed with cookies out of the oven.

"Three or four. Brittany, Jena and Boyd for sure."

Gabby's radar clicked on. "Boyd's been hanging out here a lot."

Boyd was an unassuming sixteen-year-old. Never in a million years would she think he was capable of anything. But she'd seen the movie *Juno* enough times to know looks could be deceiving.

Andrew looked up and chuckled. "Gabby, it's fine. Makayla's only fifteen. She's not into Boyd that way, are you, honey?"

Makayla rolled her eyes. "We're all friends, Gabby. It's not like that."

"Humor me on this," Gabby said lightly. "When Boyd is here, you all stay downstairs in the family room. I'll keep the twins in their playroom."

Andrew surprised her by nodding. "Good practice for when you bring home the football captain." He kissed the top of his daughter's head. "Jocks love pretty girls who are secretly smart. I should probably take up karate so I can take them on if they get out of hand."

He made a slashing motion with his arm. Makayla got up. "*Da-ad*, stop. You're not going to do karate on any of my boyfriends."

"There's an easy solution, kid. Never get a boyfriend. That way you won't break your old man's heart."

Andrew rose and followed Gabby out of the room. In the hallway, she turned to him.

"I'm worried about Boyd."

"Don't be." He put his arm around her. "I've seen the kid. He's probably gay. Plus he's too young."

"They're so not too young, but as long as they stay in the family room, we should be okay."

"You worry too much."

"I can't help it."

"I know and I love you for it."

Chapter Five

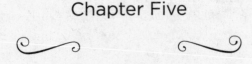

Nicole felt like the White Rabbit as she kept chanting, "I'm late, I'm late." She didn't add the "for a very important date" part, but she felt it. She could hear the *tick, tick, ticking* in her head as she circled the parking lot, looking for a spot.

The lot was packed. Had every family in Mischief Bay conspired to take advantage of the beautiful beach weather?

"Finally!"

She saw a spot at the very end and goosed the engine to claim it before someone else did. Then she jumped out of her SUV, grabbed her tote, slammed the door and hit the lock button on the key fob before dashing toward the park.

She wanted to say it wasn't her fault. Her class at the senior center had gone long because she'd been having a good time. There was something so sweet and life-affirming about watching a bunch of seniors dancing together. Especially the couples who had been married sixty and seventy years. Their bones might be frail, but their love was strong. She'd gotten caught up in the lesson and watching them and had totally forgotten that she had to be at the park to collect Jairus Sterenberg and bring him to Tyler's camp.

A psychologist would probably have a field day with her convenient memory lapse. He or she might point out that there was something very passive-aggressive about the whole situation and later, Nicole promised herself, she would have a good, long think about it. But until then, she was going to simply run as fast as she could, considering she was wearing three-inch heels and a purple tango dress with a very short skirt.

The irony of her *running* to meet the author of *Brad the Dragon* did not escape her. Nor was she unamused by the fact that she was the parent liaison. Yes, Tyler had begged, but she knew it was more than that. Life had a sense of humor. She was constantly reminded of that fact. Which meant she was frantically searching for a town car—God forbid the man actually *drive* himself—and the man who would step out of it.

She spotted the black vehicle pull up to the curb and hurried toward it. The back door opened and a guy got out. Nicole slowed to a walk, then came to a stop altogether.

She waited, knowing someone else had to get out of the car. The guy standing there couldn't possibly be the evil, nefarious money counter she knew he must be.

He was of average height—maybe five-ten or five-eleven—with dark hair and eyes, high cheekbones and sculpted jaw. His skin was a light café-au-lait color. He wasn't traditionally handsome, but she had to admit she liked the look of him. Adding to the appeal were broad shoulders and narrow hips.

She blinked, not sure which surprised her more. The sexy package or the lack of black cape and horns.

No, she told herself. This was the manager. He'd come to explain why jerk-off couldn't make it. He had to be.

She walked over. "Mr. Sterenberg? I'm Nicole and I'm—"

He looked at her, blinked twice, then held up his hands in the shape of a T. "Crap. No way. I can't believe it. They sent you? Here? Now?"

WTF? Nicole's warm, fuzzy, girlie feelings faded as quickly as they'd appeared. "Excuse me?"

"Look, this is really bad timing. I'm sure you're terrific and all." He glanced away, then returned his attention to her. He actually took a step back. "My friends are great. Assholes, but great. I can't figure out if this is a joke or what but I'll take it up with them later. But I have a thing I need to get to."

He pulled his wallet out of his back pocket. "I can pay you. You want the money, right? Or if they paid you already, I'll tip you, but you have to go away."

Words all spoken in English, yet they made absolutely no sense to her. Nada. What on earth was he—

"Oh my God, you think I'm a hooker?"

He stared at her, his eyes widening. Several twenties dangled from his fingers. "You're not?"

"No. I'm the mom sent to escort you to the event back at the camp."

His mouth moved, but no words came out. "Y-you can't be. Look at how you're dressed. This is not my fault. I saw a couple of my buddies over the weekend. I was bitching, ah, complaining about a long dry spell. They joked about fixing me up with someone. When I saw you—" He waved his hand up and down in front of her. "Look at how you're dressed. This is not my fault."

"You already said that." Nicole raised her chin and squared her shoulders. "I was substitute teaching dance at a senior center," she told him, using the haughtiest tone she could muster. "Helping a friend who's on vacation with her family. She likes to dress in a costume because it helps. Today was tango day."

His gaze dropped to the fairly spectacular amount of cleavage she was showing. No way she was going to tell him that it was mostly fake. Her somewhat meager assets were being pushed up by the wardrobe equivalent of chicken cutlets.

"Costume?" The word came out as a yelp.

"Costume," she repeated slowly. "Do you know how in-

sulting this is? I have a six-year-old son who worships you."
She dismissed him with a flick of her wrist. "Okay, not *you*
but Brad the Dragon. He wrote and rewrote his essay. He
didn't play, barely ate. Because of your books. Do you know
how many forms your stupid contest requires? I filled out
every one of them. I took time off work to be here. I left senior citizens to be here and you think I'm a hooker?"

"I'm so sorry."

"Like I believe that. I knew you'd be a jerk, but I never
expected…" She sucked in a breath. "Fine. Let me show you
where you're supposed to go." If only it were hell, she thought
grimly. She would love to show him that.

"And you'd better be nice to the kids. All of them. Especially mine."

"You're mad."

She started walking toward the camp area of the park.
"Wow. A rocket scientist. You're wasting yourself on kids'
books."

He kept up with her easily, but then he wasn't wearing
heels. "It was an honest mistake."

"Prostitution is illegal. I'm not even dressed that sexy. It
wasn't honest. It was sick. What kind of a man assumes a
woman is a hooker?" She swung around to face him. "It's
one o'clock in the afternoon. In a park. Did you think I was
just going to blow you in your car?"

He shifted uncomfortably. "I didn't think that part through.
And, no, I don't assume every woman is a hooker."

"Just me?"

He winced. "I'm sorry. Really sorry. But you have to
admit, you're dressed provocatively."

"No, I don't." She glared at him. "You're saying I look
like a slut?"

"I'm saying you're all that."

Under any other circumstances, she would have found him interesting. And maybe charming. But not like this. Not when he was that hideous author. She started walking again.

He slipped the money back in his wallet. "I'm sorry," he repeated.

"You should be."

"You really don't like me."

She barely glanced at him.

They went along the tree-lined path, toward the main camp building. Normally the kids were outside, but for this event, they were kept contained.

"Why did you assume I would be a jerk?" he asked.

"We are not having this conversation. I'm taking you where you need to go and nothing more. No. Wait. I'll be taking pictures of you with Tyler and you will pretend this is the best time of your life."

"Yes, ma'am."

"This is really important to him."

"I got that."

They reached the main camp building. She opened the side door before he could and stomped inside, then pointed. "Room five. Act happy. I've got mace in my bag."

Jairus nodded once and reached for the door handle. He turned back to her, but she only continued to glower and point. When he went inside, she crept close and watched through the window.

The kids screamed loud enough to shake the building. She spotted Tyler standing in front of everyone, his eyes wide, his whole body shaking with excitement. Jairus approached him and said something she couldn't hear. Tyler nodded. Jairus held out his hand. Tyler flung his arms around the man and Jairus hugged him back before glancing over his shoulder to where Nicole was watching.

"I got this," he mouthed.

She turned away and hurried to the bathroom. Once there, she checked out her reflection even as she was peeling off layers.

Okay, so the makeup was a little heavy for the middle of the day. And yes, the dress was kind of tacky-sexy. But she'd been teaching tango.

"A hooker," she muttered as she stepped out of her dress. She slipped on shorts and a T-shirt, then traded in heels for flip-flops. "Talk about a jerk. I knew it. I just knew it. That internet article about him was exactly right."

Too bad he was so appealing. That was just wasted. God should have given Jairus more ugly. The man deserved it.

She had makeup wipes tucked in a side pocket of her tote. She used them to remove her tango-centric eye and face makeup. It only took a second to brush out her hair and secure it in a simple ponytail.

Now she looked like what she was. A mom. She supposed it was her own fault for being late. If she'd gotten to the park ten minutes earlier, this never would have happened. Not that Jairus wasn't still going to have to pay.

She came out of the bathroom to find the party moving outside. The counselors had set up several tables with balloons and goody bags, along with a big cake. All part of the prize package. Not only were the kids being given a special afternoon with Jairus, they were taking home an advance copy of his next book. Oh, joy. She knew what she and Tyler would be reading before, during and after dinner. For weeks. Damn Jairus and his ridiculous creation.

Tyler ran up to her. "He's here!"

"I know. I met him."

"He's nice and funny and he told me secrets about Brad."

"No way."

Tyler nodded earnestly.

She dropped to her knees and took her son's hands in hers. "I'm so proud of you. You worked hard to make this happen. You and your friends are having a great day and it's because of you."

He hugged her. "This is the best day ever, Mommy. You helped, too."

"I know, but you're the one who believed. I love you, big guy."

"I love you, too."

Tyler ran back to where Jairus was sitting on the grass talking to the kids and answering their endless questions about Brad and why things had turned out the way they had in his various stories. He seemed to be genuinely enjoying the kids. When it was time for the cake to be cut, he did that himself and served it to all the kids and counselors.

Nicole wanted to say it was because she'd frightened him, but she had a feeling his actions had nothing to do with her. He was too easy with the children. Too comfortable. He must do these parties a lot, she thought, wondering if they were part of his deal with his publisher, or if he chose to interact with his littlest fans.

The afternoon wore on. She kept to the fringes of the event, watching but not getting involved. This was Tyler's moment. He reveled in the joy of being close to Jairus. The questions never let up, but the man took them in stride. Despite their disastrous meeting, Nicole had to admit Jairus was good at what he did.

Probably because he was so rested from counting all his money.

After about an hour, the goody bags were passed out. Jairus read the new book to everyone, then patiently signed every copy. Parents started arriving to pick up their kids. A few went over to meet him. He shook hands and posed for pictures.

One of the camp counselors walked over to join Nicole. "He's so hot," the twenty-year-old said with a sigh. "I tried to give him my number, but he wouldn't take it."

"You're probably too wholesome," Nicole muttered.

"What?"

"Nothing. Sorry. I was thinking of something else."

"He's been so great with the kids."

"He has."

She said the words reluctantly, but there was no denying the truth. Either Jairus truly liked children or he was the best actor on the planet. And as she refused to give him any credit for talent or ability, she was left with the uncomfortable fact that he seemed to really like children. And didn't that suck?

She wanted him to be pure evil. Or just slimy. Except for the hooker thing, he'd done well.

As the campers left to go home, the crowd around Jairus shrank. Tyler lingered and Nicole didn't hurry him, knowing this was important to him. They would leave when Jairus did. Tyler would want every second with his hero.

As she watched, Jairus said something to Tyler, then walked toward her.

"You look less hostile," he said as he approached.

"I didn't want to scare the kids."

"You're still mad."

"No. I appreciate you did a good job here." Man, that was hard to say.

"Thanks. I *am* sorry."

She looked at him without speaking.

He shoved his hands into his jeans front pockets. "This is the part where you say it was pretty funny and no big deal."

"That's not going to happen."

"Can I buy you a cup of coffee by way of an apology?"

His eyes were beautiful, she thought absently. He was obviously of mixed race—kind of a common thing in LA. She wondered about his heritage. A little something of everything, she would guess.

"Nicole?"

"What? No." That sounded rude. "Um, no, thank you."

"Can I get your number?"

She stared at him. "Why?"

He smiled. A sweet smile with just a hint of sexy. A smile that made her insides feel funny and her knees go just a little weak.

What? No! No way and no. She was not attracted to the evil, awful author of *Brad the Dragon*. She hated him. Hated. There was no way she was interested.

"To go out? I don't know you and you have friends who send you hookers."

"I only thought they did. There's a difference."

"Not much of one. The fact that you thought they did means they're capable of it. Those are not people I want hanging around my son. You did good here today. That's all I wanted. The rest of it doesn't matter."

"So that's a no?"

"That's a no."

"You're tempted, though. A little?"

"Don't you have to be somewhere?"

"Not really. And you do know me. Through my work."

She thought about the endless hours she'd spent reading his books aloud. "That doesn't recommend you."

He surprised her by chuckling. "Not a fan?"

"You have no idea."

He leaned close. For a second she caught a scent of something woodsy and clean. Nice. "I get that from a lot of parents, but the kids love me and I love them."

"Don't try to be nice now."

"I'm always nice."

And highly verbal, she thought. "You're a writer. I don't like writers. Look, you really have to go."

He studied her for a few seconds, then nodded. "It was nice to meet you, Nicole."

While she was happy this was over, a teeny, tiny part of her was sorry he was giving up so easily. Was it a writer thing? Because Eric had sure given up on them. Not that her marriage could be compared with her five minutes with Jairus, but still.

He walked back over to Tyler. They talked for a few minutes, then hugged. Jairus whispered something to the boy before leaving.

Tyler held his new book tight. "This was the best day ever."

Nicole brushed his hair out of his eyes. "I'm glad. He spent a lot of time with you."

"I know. He said he had fun."

"I'm sure he did. Want to get your stuff so we can go?"

Tyler nodded and ran back the room where he'd left his lunch bag. The camp counselor moved next to Nicole.

"He was asking about you."

"Tyler?"

"No, Jairus. You know… Were you single? Did you have a boyfriend? I think he was interested."

There was a distinct fluttering right below her rib cage. Nicole told herself it was because she'd missed lunch. She was hungry—nothing more.

"I hope you didn't tell him anything."

"Just where you worked."

Nicole groaned. "Why?"

"Did you see his butt? Plus, he's successful."

"Nothing will come of it."

"I don't know. He seemed pretty interested to me."

"You say that like it's a good thing."

"Are you kidding? He's so sexy."

"Not what I'm looking for."

"Uh-huh. Keeping telling yourself that and maybe it will be true."

Chapter Six

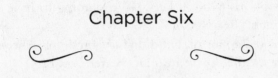

The waiting room was familiar. Hayley couldn't guess how much time she and Rob had spent here. Talking. Hoping. There were also the appointments she'd had on her own. While it would never be a second home—no one would want that—it was familiar. Sometimes the news was good and sometimes it wasn't. She'd cried here, hoped here.

She knew every painting on the walls. All landscapes. There were no pictures of families in this waiting room, no children. That would be too hard. The magazines were related to travel or cooking or sports. No smiling babies on parenting magazines.

Appointments tended to last a long time so it was rare to run into another couple. The process of having a baby when science had to get involved wasn't easy.

Rob sat next to her, his left ankle rested on his right knee. His foot bounced as he stared unseeingly at the magazine he'd opened. She might be the one going through the procedures, but he'd always disliked Dr. Pearce's office. Or maybe he disliked the reason they had to be here.

For the past four years, this place had defined their life. She'd been referred after her second miscarriage. There had been tests and discussions. It wasn't that she couldn't get pregnant, it was that she couldn't stay pregnant. Her body rejected the fetus and while there were many explanations, there didn't seem to be any solutions.

"It's okay," she told Rob. "You can relax."

"Not here."

She took his hand in hers. "We're going to have a good appointment. I can feel it."

He looked doubtful, but didn't say anything. Alice, one of the nurses, called them into Dr. Pearce's office.

"How are you feeling?" the nurse asked as they walked down the hall.

"Good. Taking my iron every day."

She had to. She'd lost so much blood with her last miscarriage. She was also bleeding on and off. If it were Halloween, she could easily do the vampire thing and be plenty pale without makeup. The thought made her smile, but she doubted Rob would appreciate the humor.

Dr. Pearce was already waiting for them. She was tall and in her early forties, with short red hair and a lot of freckles. She looked like what she was—a sensible, compassionate woman. Hayley had liked her from the start. She kept current on the latest infertility research and was willing to discuss unconventional therapies.

Dr. Pearce shook Rob's hand, then hugged Hayley.

"How are you feeling?" she asked.

"Good. Strong."

Dr. Pearce raised her eyebrows. "You don't look strong, Hayley."

"Okay, I'm better than I was. I'm eating right and taking my vitamins."

"Good. Your body has been through a lot. It needs time to recover."

Time was not Hayley's friend. She knew that fertility started a steep downhill slide and with no information on her family's medical history, she didn't know if she came from a long line of fertile women or those who had gone into peri-menopause at thirty-five.

She and Rob sat in the comfortable visitor chairs. Dr. Pearce slipped on reading glasses, then typed on her computer.

"We have your blood work from your last visit. It's better than it was."

Hayley pulled some papers out of her handbag. "Good, because I want to talk to you about this." She passed over the sheets. "They're doing great work in Switzerland. The clinic has had incredible success with women having trouble carrying to term. There's a new drug therapy and special monitoring. It's expensive, but we'll find a way. We always do."

She spoke quickly, careful to keep her attention on the doctor. Next to her, Rob stiffened. She knew why—this was the first he'd heard of the clinic in Switzerland. She hadn't mentioned it because she didn't want to hear all the reasons why it wasn't a good idea. Rob didn't get it. He thought they'd done enough. Been through enough. He wanted to give it a rest. Or adopt. No matter how much she explained neither option was possible, he didn't want to listen.

Dr. Pearce ignored the material and took off her glasses. She looked between Hayley and Rob, then drew in a breath.

"No," she said quietly. "I can't recommend you, Hayley. The reason I wanted to meet with you today is because you've reached your limit. Your body simply can't handle this anymore. The last bleeding episode was the worst, by far. I'm concerned about your health."

"No. I'm fine. I feel great." An exaggeration, but she did feel better.

"All the drugs and treatments have taken a toll," Dr. Pearce continued. "I'm sorry. I know how badly you want to have

a baby. There are other options that don't include carrying
a child to term."

Hayley went cold. She couldn't be hearing this right. "I
have to," she whispered. "We can't use a surrogate."

They'd tried, but her ovaries didn't respond to the drugs.
The attempt to harvest had failed.

"Hayley, listen to her," Rob said, reaching for her hand.
"That bleeding last time was scary. You can't risk your health,
your life. I don't want you to die."

She pulled her hand free and stared at the doctor. "I want
to go to Switzerland. They'll make it work. You'll see."

"That's not an option. Not for you. Hayley, this is so hard
to say and I know it's going to be hard to hear. You need a
hysterectomy. You're at risk of bleeding. I'm afraid the next
time it starts, we won't be able to stop it."

"No." Hayley wanted to cover her ears. She wouldn't hear
this. Couldn't. She wasn't giving up. She was never giving
up. There was an answer. There had to be. "No. You don't
understand. I have to have a baby. I have to."

"Sweetie, don't." Rob reached for her again. He touched
her arm. "It's okay. We'll get through this—"

She pushed him away and stood up. "A hysterectomy?
No. I won't." That would be the end. She could never have
a child of her own. Never have a family of her own. Something that was her. She needed that. Needed the connection,
the belonging. Why couldn't they understand? Why were
they ganging up on her?

She turned to Rob. "Did you know about this? Did you
talk to her?" She spun to the doctor. "Did you go behind
my back?"

"No," Dr. Pearce said quickly. "Of course not. Hayley,
I know this is awful for you. I wish I could help you, but I
can't. Let me be clear. If you get pregnant again, you will

bleed out and die. I strongly recommend you go to the hospital today for surgery, but I understand you have to think about this. Process it."

"I want to go to Switzerland." She had to focus on what was possible. Otherwise she couldn't get through it.

Rob stood and faced her. "You're not going anywhere," he yelled. "You're not getting pregnant. Let it go. Dammit, Hayley." Tears filled his eyes. He shook his head, then walked out of the office.

Hayley stared after him, but didn't follow. She sank back into her seat. "There has to be something," she whispered. She was cold. Desperately cold. Her stomach churned.

Dr. Pearce came around the desk and took Rob's seat. She reached for Hayley's hand.

"This sucks," she said bluntly. "You have done everything medically possible to carry a baby to term. I know how important this is to you. I wish you could know how I hate telling you this. I'm sorry, Hayley. If it's this painful for me, I can't imagine how awful it is for you. But you have to get through this. The surgery is necessary to save your life."

She reached for a card on her desk. "I'd like you to see another specialist. She's at UCLA. Talk to her. Get a second opinion and a third. But please, don't wait too long."

Because time was never on her side, she thought, the cold deepening until she couldn't feel anything else.

Hayley nodded. "Okay. Thanks. I get it."

She stood and collected the material she'd brought with her. She could feel herself moving, but something wasn't right. It was as if she were underwater, or fighting through being slightly out of space and time. The cold was the only constant.

"I'm sorry," Dr. Pearce repeated. "Hayley, you have my cell number. Call me anytime. I mean that."

"Sure. I will."

She walked out of the office and back to the waiting room. Rob stood there.

"Are you going to listen to Dr. Pearce?" he asked. "Did you hear what she was saying? I don't want you to die. We have to stop. You have to schedule the surgery."

As cold as she felt, she was surprised her teeth weren't chattering. She couldn't feel her hands or her feet. Her heartbeat sounded loud in her ears, making it difficult to hear what her husband was saying.

Maybe this was shock, she told herself. Maybe it was a bad dream.

"We should go," she said. "We're done here."

He looked at her for a long time. "I wish I could believe that."

Gabby had met Nicole over a year ago through Shannon, Gabby's sister-in-law. Casual conversation had turned to going to Supper's in the Bag together which had morphed into friendship. Gabby knew in her head that Nicole ran an exercise studio that specialized in Pilates. She'd seen her friend in various outfits and knew the other woman was in great shape. But all that intellectual knowledge had not prepared her for a class at Mischief in Motion.

Mat Pilates had sounded easy enough. The mat part implied lying down. At least she wouldn't be running and jumping. But halfway through her first class, she realized that the mat was just there to taunt her. There might not be running and jumping but there was more pain than she'd ever thought possible. Nicole wanted her to do things that the human body just wasn't meant to do. At least hers wasn't.

"Five more seconds," Nicole said, sounding more like a drill sergeant than a friend. "And hold. Three, two, one and relax."

Gabby fell onto her back. She was sweating and quivering. The sweating was gross but expected. What she objected to the most was the quivering. Even though the exercise was over, her stomach muscles continued to tremble. That couldn't be good.

Nicole, all skinny and fit in black exercise leggings and a black and hot-pink racer-back tank, knelt by her mat.

"You doing okay?" she asked.

"No. I can't move."

"Just do what you can. This is a pretty advanced class. When we're done here, let's go over the schedule and find something you'll enjoy more."

"You mean a class with fat, out-of-shape people with emotional eating problems?" Gabby was trying to be funny but had a bad feeling she only sounded pathetic.

"I was thinking that a class geared to someone who's been busy with her family might be better, but you call it what you want." Nicole rose. "Okay, everyone. We'll finish with the plank."

Everyone rolled over and shifted into the plank position. Well, everyone except Gabby. She tried to sit up only to find that her body failed her. Pain joined the quivering. She rolled onto her side and managed to push herself up so she was at least sitting.

She watched the other women in the class hold their pose as Nicole counted the time. Three of the women dropped out at a minute, which left Shannon and Pam still going. At two minutes, Gabby felt her mouth drop open. Shannon was in fantastic shape, damn her, but Pam was over fifty. She looked great and obviously worked out a lot. Gabby figured she could either be inspired or feel bitter. Right now, bitter was winning.

"Three minutes," Nicole said out loud.

"Ready to call it?" Pam asked, sounding out of breath.

"Yes. One, two, three."

On three they both collapsed. Everyone applauded. Gabby told herself she would remember this moment and when she was faced with cookies or brownies, she would think of Pam. She might also eat a cookie, but it would be with Pam in mind.

Shannon stood and walked over. "How are you holding up?" she asked.

"I have no idea," Gabby admitted.

The other woman held out her hand, to help Gabby to her feet. Gabby took it and forced herself to stand. Her legs were shaking and she felt a little sick to her stomach.

"I hate exercise," she admitted to herself as the rest of the students collected their things and left.

Nicole brought her a bottle of water. "Drink. Then come look at the schedule."

"You did great," Pam told her. "This is a tough class. Nicole works us extra hard, so the fact that you got through it shows grit. When I first started, I had the endurance of a noodle."

"I've always liked pasta," Gabby admitted.

The other women laughed.

Pam walked over to her tote bag. A head popped out. Gabby looked at the delicate Chinese crested and compared her to Boomer. They were barely the same species.

Lulu seemed more alien than dog, with a bare body that was sort of gray with white splotches. On her tail, head and feet, she had pure white fluffy fur. Today she had on a blue T-shirt with little hearts on it.

The dog might be weird-looking, but she was very well behaved. Boomer could learn a thing or two from her. Not that his lack of manners was his fault, Gabby admitted. She hadn't taken enough time to train him. Pam reached for Lulu and the little dog jumped into her arms.

Pam returned to the group and everyone sat down on the mats. Gabby joined them. She didn't have to be anywhere for a while.

"When's your next trip?" Shannon asked Pam.

"September." Pam turned to Gabby. "I have some friends I cruise with. We're doing a quick cruise around Spain and Portugal."

"They're wild women," Nicole added. "I keep expecting to hear you've mooned some island."

"I don't think my butt is big enough that I could moon an entire island," Pam said as she stroked Lulu. "Maybe a beach. Hmm, I'll get back to you on that."

Shannon patted her lap and the little dog jumped gracefully over. "You're going to stay with me, sweet girl. Aren't you?"

"Char and Oliver must love that," Gabby said. "The twins adore her." Lulu had quite the wardrobe and was happy to play dress up.

"How long will you be gone?" Gabby asked Pam.

"Nearly two weeks. The cruise is a week, then I'm staying with friends."

"Has anyone talked to Hayley?" Nicole asked. "I left her a message a couple of days ago and haven't heard back from her."

"I haven't, either," Gabby said. "I'll text her when I get home."

There was a moment of awkward silence. The women looked at each other. Gabby would guess they were each trying to figure out what to say.

"If something had happened, we would have heard," Gabby said. "Rob would call one of us."

"Even if he didn't, Steven would know," Pam added. "He

would have said something. He knows better than to keep something like that from me."

Despite being part of the Los Angeles metropolitan area, Mischief Bay was, at heart, a small town. Hayley worked for Steven Eiland who owned a plumbing company. Steven was Pam's son.

"Poor Hayley," Nicole murmured. "I worry about her."

"Me, too." Gabby knew her friend desperately wanted to have a baby, but she'd been through so much.

"Everybody has their own path." Pam stretched her legs out in front of her.

"You got that right. The baby thing is complicated." Shannon hugged Lulu. "Maybe I should get a dog."

"You work too many hours," Pam pointed out.

Gabby watched Shannon and wondered if her sister-in-law ever felt regrets. Shannon had an amazing career. She was CFO for a successful software company. But she was forty-one and hadn't married until the previous year. She and Adam, Gabby's older brother, didn't have any kids of their own. Adam had two from a previous marriage. He and Shannon had just finished up the paperwork and approval process to be foster parents. Talk about changing their lives. They were going to make a difference, but Gabby wasn't sure that was enough for a woman who really wanted kids. While she envied her sister-in-law her career, she wouldn't have given up the twins for anything. She'd always wanted both.

But that decision left her wondering if having it all meant doing a lot of it badly.

Chapter Seven

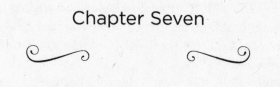

Nicole enjoyed the company of her friends. This was when her job didn't feel like work. To be honest, except for the paperwork and payroll, which she hated, none of it did. She'd been blessed, she told herself. Owning Mischief in Motion was a dream.

She shifted so she and Pam sat facing each other, legs outstretched, feet touching. They reached out and grabbed hands, then Pam pulled Nicole toward her into a forward bend. The hamstring stretch was perfect, Nicole thought, letting her body relax. She sat up and pulled her friend forward. Pam leaned into the motion.

"You're exhausting me," Gabby grumbled. "Can't you two let it be? Class is over. I still have to crawl to my car."

Nicole grinned at her. "You should stretch or you're going to hurt tomorrow."

"I'll hurt tomorrow anyway."

Pam released Nicole and patted Gabby's thigh. "Don't join the beginner's class. Stay with us. We're more fun."

"This class will kill me."

"You say that now," Nicole told her. "But trust me. In a few weeks, you'll be able to keep up."

Gabby groaned. "You're so lying."

The other women laughed.

Nicole knew she was telling the truth. Gabby was out of shape and needed to lose a few pounds—Nicole guessed close to thirty to be in fighting shape. But not everyone wanted to work out. That made no sense to her. She'd been active her whole life. But then when Hayley had tricked her into signing up for a knitting class, Nicole had hated everything about it. She'd quit rather than risk doing someone in with a knitting needle.

"It's whatever you want," she told her friend. "You are welcome at any of my classes. This one is more advanced, but you know everyone. My beginner's class is definitely easier, but less social."

"You can try the other one," Shannon suggested. "Then figure out what you want to do."

"Always with the reason," Pam said as she stood. "You continue to impress me, missy." She stretched up her arms, then shook out her shoulders. "I have to go. Lulu and I have a busy afternoon planned. See you all on Friday."

Pam collected her tote, picked up Lulu. Gabby limped after her.

"Take a hot shower," Nicole told her. "And an anti-inflammatory."

Gabby groaned, waved and walked out of the studio. Shannon went to get her things and Nicole headed for her office. She had a couple of hours until her next class. As she passed by the front door of the studio, she saw someone approaching. A man. A familiar man with dark hair and beautiful brown eyes.

She came to a stop, not sure what to do. There was nowhere to run. Nowhere to hide. Okay, she could hole up in the bathroom, but for how long?

She pressed a hand to her suddenly fluttering stomach. Well, crap.

"Nicole, are you okay?" Shannon asked.

Nicole twisted her fingers together and motioned to the door. Before she could speak, Jairus walked inside.

"Hey," he said. "You *do* work here. I wasn't sure the counselor at Tyler's camp was giving me right information."

Shannon walked briskly toward him. Despite wearing capri-length leggings and a tank top, she radiated control and power.

"Hello," she said, holding out her hand. "I'm Shannon. Who are you?"

"Jairus Sterenberg."

Shannon's eyes widened. "The *Brad the Dragon* guy. That was this week? Huh. I thought you'd have horns." She looked at Nicole. "Do we like him?"

"Horns?" Jairus repeated.

Nicole shrugged. "I don't know. I don't think so. He's not evil."

"You know I'm standing here, right?"

Shannon ignored him. "Was he good with the kids?"

"Yes, but it could have been an act."

Jairus frowned. "It wasn't an act. I like kids. That's why I write kids' books. And I'm still right here."

Shannon sighed as she looked at him. "We obviously don't care about that." She turned back to Nicole. "I'm going to make a phone call. I'll be by my car." She pointed. "Right there. Where I can see everything."

Nicole nodded, grateful for the not very subtle message that she wasn't going to be alone with Jairus. Because being alone with him was confusing. Or uncomfortable. Tingle-worthy but weird.

Nicole forced herself to face Jairus. "You're here," she said unnecessarily. Still, the obvious observation seemed to be the safest.

"I am." He smiled. "Hi."

He had a good smile. Easy. Friendly. Appealing. She found

herself wanting to step toward him. To smile back. To give in to whatever he was asking.

No, no and no. She took a step back and folded her arms across her chest. "Hello."

He didn't seem deterred by her body language. "I wanted to see you again."

"Why?"

The smile broadened. "You can't still be mad at me. I apologized sincerely."

"How do I know it was sincere?"

"You know. I was mortified."

She couldn't remember the last time a man had used the word *mortified* in a conversation. Huh. "You're right. You did apologize. So why are you here?"

"I thought we could get coffee."

"I'm at work."

He glanced around the empty studio. "You don't have a class."

"I will."

"Then dinner."

He was asking her out? This was the first time a guy had asked her out since she'd met Eric nearly eight years ago. She hadn't dated since the divorce, hadn't been interested. And she wasn't now, no matter how good Jairus looked or how easy his smile.

"No, thank you."

"Why not? I'm a nice guy, Nicole. I have a steady job, I like kids. Your son thinks I'm amazing."

"Tyler thinks Brad the Dragon is amazing. You're just the delivery system."

"Ouch." The smile faded. He pressed a hand to his chest. "Is it that you're mad about before or you just don't like me?"

"I don't know you well enough to like or dislike you, and I'm not mad. I'm just not interested."

He took a step toward her. The movement wasn't threatening, so she didn't move back. Instead it seemed as if he were trying to figure something out.

"Okay," he said slowly. "Goodbye."

He left. Just like that. No backward glance, nothing. Nicole stared after him, not sure what she felt. She'd thought he would make another run at asking her out. Apparently she'd been very clear in dismissing him.

Shannon walked back into the studio. "Well?"

"He's gone. He asked me out, I said no and he left."

Her friend glanced over her shoulder to where Jairus was driving away. His car was a black sedan. A BMW, but not overly flashy—at least for LA.

"Did you like him?" Shannon asked. "I know you hate all things Brad the Dragon, but I'm talking about the man. Was he nice? Were you tempted?"

"I don't know. Why?"

Shannon touched her arm. "You're my friend and I love you. I also worry about you. It's been over a year since you and Eric split. The divorce has been final for months and months, but to the best of my knowledge, you haven't gone out with anyone. Aren't you lonely? Don't you want a romantic relationship in your life?"

"I don't know," Nicole admitted, telling the absolute truth. "I don't let myself think about it."

Shannon's gaze turned sympathetic. "That's what I thought. Maybe this is a good time to find out why."

When Gabby was a kid, Legos had been a toy only boys played with. At least in her circle of friends. Sometime in the past twenty years, they'd developed a line of Legos for girls.

As she carefully applied the sticker to what would be a scale in a pink-and-purple vet's office, she thought this was actually kind of fun. Building things with her girls.

The directions were simple and visual. The twins took turns putting the pieces together. They had already named both the cat and the dog, and had big plans for adding this business to their Lego village.

She finished with the sticker and handed the little piece to Kenzie, who carefully snapped it into place. Her hands were so small, Gabby thought. With tiny fingers. Sometimes it was hard to imagine the girls would grow into adults in just a few years. While part of her looked forward to watching the evolution, she had to admit, having them stay her girls forever would be kind of nice.

"Anybody home?"

The question came from downstairs. The three of them looked at each other before the twins shrieked in unison and headed for the stairs. Gabby followed, wondering what brought Andrew home at three o'clock on a Wednesday.

"Daddy! Daddy!"

Gabby walked into the kitchen to find Andrew holding a twin in each arm. He smiled at her.

"My afternoon meeting got canceled, so I headed home."

She walked over and kissed him, then took Kennedy from him and set her on the floor. "It's a very nice surprise."

"I like surprises," Kennedy said.

"Me, too," her twin agreed.

Andrew winked. "Some surprises are very nice." He loosened his tie. "I thought I'd take the girls with me. We'll go pick up Makayla and grab dinner. Does that work for you?"

He was offering her an evening alone, to do whatever she wanted. A gift as rare as a natural blue diamond.

"That would be amazing," she admitted. What to do first?

A nap? Read? A bath? If she took a bath, she could also read *and* have a glass of wine. Talk about heaven.

"Thank you."

"Anything for you." Andrew lowered Kenzie to the floor, then picked up his briefcase from the counter. "Oh, I almost forgot. This weekend the new wheelbarrows are being unveiled." He frowned. "Revealed. Whatever it's called. We should go see them."

The twins clapped their hands together, then danced around him.

"Can we?" Kennedy asked.

"We want to go," her twin added.

The wheelbarrows were an interesting tradition in Mischief Bay. When the town had first been founded, criminals—mostly drunks—had been transported to jail in wheelbarrows. In the past ten years, they'd become a tradition in town. They were a fun charity moneymaker. People bid on the chance to decorate a wheelbarrow for a year. Gabby had first met Andrew at a fund-raiser for the wheelbarrows.

She'd been young—only a few months out of law school. She'd spotted him right away. He'd been talking with a group of people, engaged in their conversation, but also watching her.

She'd had boyfriends, of course, some of them serious. But no one like Andrew. No one that funny and sweet and together. He'd walked up to her and smiled and she'd been lost. The more she'd gotten to know him, the more she'd liked him. Their relationship had been a natural progression. Dating, falling in love, getting married. There hadn't been any drama, no questions.

She remembered the first time she'd spent the night at his apartment. They'd been dating about two months and while she'd wanted him, she'd been nervous. Her lovers had been guys her own age, most of whom weren't exactly experts. What if she'd been doing it wrong? Andrew was so sophisticated and out of her league.

When they were done—both out of breath, with her still trembling—he'd pulled her close. "You are so incredibly perfect," he'd whispered. "How did I ever get so lucky as to find you?"

She thought of that now, of how he always looked out for her. His caring wasn't always done in big gestures, like the Nordstrom card. There were little things, like taking the girls.

"I would love to see the wheelbarrows this weekend," she told him.

The girls cheered.

"Let me run upstairs and change," he told her. "Then we'll head off and you can start your evening."

"Perfect."

She took the twins to the bathroom they shared and put sunscreen on them. No doubt they would be outside at some point. There was a brief discussion about what to wear before Kenzie decided their shorts and T-shirts would be just fine.

Andrew joined them. He'd replaced his suit and tie with jeans and a deep blue golf shirt that matched his eyes.

He was still so attractive. He ran a couple of mornings a week and when he traveled, he always worked out at the hotel gym. She thought of her disastrous performance at Nicole's studio and knew that her unexpected free time would probably be better spent going for a walk or doing sit-ups, but there was no way that was going to happen. *Wine, bath and book, here I come.*

The four of them headed downstairs. "You'll pick up Makayla on your way," she reminded him.

"Promise."

She kissed each of the girls, then him. "What are you going to do?"

"I'll take them shopping before dinner."

"For what?" Kennedy asked.

"Something fun?" Kenzie added. "We need more Legos."

"You do not," Gabby said with a laugh. "If you get any more, we'll be forced to move and none of us want that."

The girls laughed. Andrew grinned. "I figured we'd go get booster seats."

The girls started dancing and shrieking.

Gabby felt her good mood fade. "What? Why? We decided they were going to stay in their car seats a few more months."

Andrew raised one shoulder. "We also talked about replacing them with booster seats. Come on, Gabby, they hassle you daily. Can you really deal with that for a few more months?"

Yes. Of course. They couldn't let five-year-olds dictate decisions like this. Nor did she want the twins learning that if they complained enough, their parents gave in. Talk about the wrong message.

Both girls stared at her. Gabby knew that if she told him no, he would back down. But then she would be the villain. The one who took away the new, shiny thing. That her life would be hell every time she tried to get them into their car seats. "But Daddy said" would be a constant refrain.

She battled against anger. This was so wrong, she thought. Making the decision without her. Telling the girls so that she couldn't really say no. She hated being put in this position.

"Is it really so bad?" he asked. "The car is safe and they ride in the back."

"You're not helping," she told him.

"Mommy, please," Kennedy pleaded.

"Yes, Mommy. Please, please, please."

Everything about this was wrong, she thought grimly.

From Andrew ambushing her to her giving in. Because it all came down to, as her husband often said, her willingness to die on this hill.

"All right," she said.

The girls flung themselves at her. Andrew leaned in and kissed her.

"Was that so hard?" he asked. "Go have fun. We'll be home around eight. I promise the girls will be tired and ready for their bath."

She nodded and watched them leave. She knew she'd been outplayed. Worse, she'd been weak. What she didn't understand was why it always seemed to come down to surrender or being the bad guy. When was there any middle ground?

Saturday morning Hayley woke before the alarm. She hadn't been sleeping well, which wasn't a surprise. Every second of every day she felt the weight of sadness and loss pressing down on her. She tried to forget, tried to tell herself that Dr. Pearce was wrong, but she couldn't escape the cold reality of the words.

Another specialist wouldn't matter. Not here anyway. Unless there was a miracle, she wasn't going to be able to carry a baby to term. And she was terrified she wasn't going to find her miracle.

Which left only Switzerland, she thought, as she stepped out of the shower. As she reached for her towel, she was careful to hang on to the counter with her other hand. She got dizzy so easily. It was the blood loss from her last miscarriage. And the one before. The toll the drugs had taken on her system.

She dried off and dressed, careful not to look at herself in the mirror. She knew what she would see. Too many bones sticking out. Unnaturally pale flesh. Shadows under her eyes.

A few weeks ago a lady had stopped her at the grocery store. The older woman had squeezed her hand and said she would say a prayer for her recovery. It took her a minute to realize the other woman thought she had cancer.

Nothing that drastic, she thought as she left the bathroom and walked to the kitchen and started the coffeemaker. Except for her body's stubborn refusal to carry a fetus to term and her stubborn refusal to accept that, she was golden. Cancer would have been a whole lot easier.

While the coffee brewed, she put the blender on the counter and began her morning ritual. Rich coconut milk went in first, followed by a double dose of high-grade protein powder. She added flaxseeds, avocado, blueberries and a few other powders designed to help her body heal, then flipped the switch and waited while the concoction melded into something not the least bit like food.

She glanced at her phone and saw she had a text from Gabby. The other woman was checking in to say hi. Hayley answered her, then put her phone back on the counter.

Rob walked into the kitchen.

"Morning," he said as he walked to the coffeemaker. "You sleep okay?"

"Uh-huh. You?"

"Like a log." He poured himself a mug, then took a sip. "You're going in to work today?"

"Just for a few hours. I'm not staying for any sessions."

She had a second job helping her sister with Supper's in the Bag. She went in early and did all the chopping and arranging. Mostly she was paid in dinners, but that was okay. It meant money they didn't have to spend on groceries. For the past four years, every dollar not necessary for survival had gone into their baby fund. Defying God was neither cheap nor easy.

"You okay?" Rob asked.

She wanted to scream at him. To cry out that no, she wasn't okay. She was destroyed. She'd trusted Dr. Pearce, had expected her to help. Now the doctor had betrayed her, as had her body. She was alone, desperate, scared. There was only one hope left and it was thousands of miles, not to mention a continent, away.

But she didn't say any of that. Because she knew that a happy marriage was good for a baby's well-being. She and Rob had to stay strong. Had to be a family unit.

"I'm all right. It's hard."

"I know, babe." Rob crossed to her and drew her against him.

He was warm and solid, she thought, leaning in to the embrace. Most days she was neither. She seemed to live a half life, waiting for what was really important. Waiting to have her baby.

He'd always supported her, she reminded herself. Even when he hadn't understood, he'd been there. He hadn't judged. He'd gotten a second job to help pay for the treatments, he'd gotten her ice chips when the hormone shots had made her so sick she couldn't eat or drink for days, he'd cleaned up gushes of blood from her miscarriages.

The fact that he didn't *want* a biological child the way she did wasn't his fault. He didn't get it. No matter how many times she tried to explain, he couldn't possibly know that adoptive parents simply didn't love their adopted children the same. But she knew. She knew what it was like to be the other. The one who didn't fit in, physically or emotionally. She knew what it was like to be the decision that was later regretted.

"I'm sorry," he told her. "For all of it. Do you want to talk to someone?"

"Like a psychologist?"

"Uh-huh."

She looked up at him. Was he insane? That was expensive. Even with their insurance, there would be co-pays. "I'm fine."

"I worry about you."

"Don't. Physically, I feel great. Stronger every day."

She waited for him to call her on her lies, but he didn't. Instead he reached for his coffee again.

"I'm telling Russ I'm quitting."

She poured her protein drink into the tall glass she used. It gave her something to do so she didn't turn on him and scream.

"Okay," she said slowly, when what she really meant was *How could you?*

"I'd like us to spend some time together, Hayley. I never see you. We're both working so much."

The translation was, they didn't need the extra money anymore. If there weren't fertility drugs and IVF and every other thing they'd tried, then they were fine, financially. Not rich, but comfortable. They could get by with them each working just one job.

She thought about the clinic information she'd hidden at the back of the closet. About how she checked flights to Switzerland nearly every day, hoping for a seat sale. That she'd already found a hotel where they were going to stay while she was at the clinic. It was close and cheap—both good because while Rob would only be there for a few days, she would have to stay at least two months.

"I'm working on a car with Russ now," he continued. "When it's done, I'm quitting."

She wanted to tell him he couldn't, but didn't. When she had their Switzerland trip arranged, he would understand that he couldn't give up the extra income. He would support her. But for now, all she said was, "Whatever you think is best."

"I wish I could believe you mean that."

She sipped her drink, then looked at him. "You can."

"I'm not convinced." He leaned against the counter. "Can we at least talk about adoption?"

"No."

"A child—"

"I want a baby. Our baby."

"Hayley, honey, your parents loved you. I saw them with you and they adored you. The problem wasn't them, it was Morgan."

"You don't know what it was like, Rob. We've been over this and over this. My parents were great people. They couldn't help loving their biological daughter more than their adopted one. I get that. I accept it, but I can't forget it. I want a baby of my own. A baby that is truly us. Only us. Then everything will be fine."

His expression turned pained. "Hayley," he began.

"I know. You want me to accept it's never going to happen." She glanced at the clock. "I have to go. I'll see you later."

He didn't try to stop her from leaving the room. Fifteen minutes later, she was driving to her sister's business. Rob's claims about her sister and her parents weren't new. Sometimes, she could almost believe him. The problem was, her parents weren't around to ask anymore. They'd been killed in a car accident nearly five years ago.

All she could go on now was how it had felt growing up—when everything was about Morgan and she was always thought of second. There were a thousand examples—like when she'd won the essay contest for the entire fourth grade. While her parents had said they were proud of her, the celebration dinner had consisted of Morgan's favorite foods, not hers. Or if they were each given a doll and Morgan broke or damaged hers, Morgan was then given Hayley's. Because Hayley would understand.

Sometimes she had but sometimes she'd held back tears until she could be alone and cry. Because it had never been fair.

She arrived at Supper's in the Bag a little before eight. The first customers today were scheduled at ten. Most of the food was delivered relatively prepped. It was amazing what a food-based business could buy these days. Her job was to get everything ready. Put out the day's menus and the instruction sheets. Chop up the fresh produce that was more delicate, like the tomatoes. Distribute the ingredients to each station and have it all done in two hours.

She unlocked the front door, then locked it behind her. After flipping on lights, she put on an apron and studied the menus for the day.

By nine-thirty, she had six of the eight stations set up. Everything was diced and in place. She heard keys unlocking the door and knew that Morgan had arrived.

"Oh my God, you simply won't believe it," Morgan said by way of greeting. "I swear, that husband of mine is a complete idiot. He knows I work every Saturday morning and week after week, he claims he forgets he's responsible for the kids until I can get home. I just want him put to sleep."

Hayley kept working. She checked the spice bottles she'd brought out of the industrial-sized pantry. The company bought in bulk, then she poured smaller amounts into restaurant-sized bottles for each station. The same with olive oil, soy sauce and other pantry staples.

"Did Brent think you'd use Cecelia to sit for them?" Hayley asked.

"I don't know. I didn't stay to listen. I just left. How's it going?"

"Good."

Morgan walked over to the unfinished station. "You're going to get to this, right?"

"I am."

Because Morgan didn't believe in doing work herself.

When their parents died, she'd used her half of their small inheritance to buy the franchise. She'd said she wanted something of her own. But when it came to running the business, she hadn't wanted to do anything with it. She'd hired a manager, but that had been a disaster. The company had lost money steadily until Brent had gone through the books and figured out the woman was stealing from them. He'd told Morgan to either run it herself or sell it. Morgan still complained about that ultimatum.

"The kids are making me crazy, too," Morgan continued, snatching up a cherry tomato and biting into it. "Amy has reached the whiny stage. Everything is about her. It's exhausting."

Hayley and Morgan couldn't be more physically different. While Hayley was small-boned, blonde and of average height, Morgan was tall, curvy and dark-haired. She had a vibrancy about her. When she walked into a room, she commanded attention. Usually it was just to complain, but still. People knew she was there.

Hayley was eleven months older. All through school, she'd heard the same thing. "Hayley was such a smart girl. So quiet. I had no idea Morgan would be so different." That was usually followed by a knowing chuckle. Sure, Morgan didn't get the grades, but she was a pistol. Stubborn, difficult, yet compelling. Morgan had a way of getting everything she wanted. It was a lesson Hayley wished she'd also learned—maybe then she would have a couple of kids of her own. As it was, she had a failing reproductive system and a niece and two nephews.

"Sometimes I wish they'd all just go away," Morgan admitted. "And leave me in peace."

"You don't mean that," Hayley said, as she put out the spices for the chicken cacciatore station. "You love your family."

"I do, it's just something… I don't know. I guess we all want what we don't have." She walked toward the office. "I need to do some paperwork before the idiots arrive. You'll have the stations set up?"

"I will."

"Good. It's nice to know there's someone I can depend on."

Chapter Eight

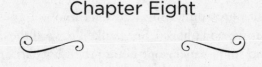

The giggling from upstairs was loud. Amazing, considering there were several layers of wood, drywall and even full rooms between them, Gabby thought. But here she was, in the kitchen, still able to hear the teenagers giggling.

She and her siblings were close enough in age that her mother had had as many as three teenagers at a time in the house. How had she stood it?

"Mom, you're even more amazing than I'd realized," she said, as she pulled the cookie sheet out of the oven.

The twins were watching a movie in the family room. Both girls had played hard at camp that morning and were exhausted. A happy state of affairs, Gabby thought. Jasmine and Boomer were both enjoying the Disney retrospective going on, as well. Makayla was up in her room with a couple of girlfriends. Gabby was caught up with laundry, she'd gone for a walk that morning and had yet to eat a cookie. All in all, it had been a spectacular day.

Now she put two peanut butter cookies onto a plate and took it in to the twins.

The girls thanked her, as did Boomer. He thumped his tail enthusiastically.

"Please don't give him too much," she told the girls.

She filled another plate and headed up the stairs. As a rule, teenage hunger seemed to grow in direct proportion to the fun they were having. Based on what she'd been hearing, Makayla and her friends had to be starving.

But as she approached the closed door, she realized there wasn't any sound at all. It was as if everyone had left. But wouldn't she have heard them go? They usually called out that they were leaving, plus just a few minutes ago, she'd heard the laughing.

"You girls must be starving," she said as she opened the door.

Only there weren't the three girls she'd let into the house two hours ago. There was only Makayla and Boyd. Sitting on her bed. Kissing.

They immediately jumped apart. Boyd stood and took several steps back. Makayla rose and got between Gabby and the boy.

"What are you doing here? Why didn't you knock?"

This wasn't happening, Gabby told herself. It couldn't be.

"When did you get here?" she asked Boyd, trying to appear calm. "I didn't see you come in."

Nor had she heard the other girls leave, she thought again. Had they snuck him in and then disappeared?

"What's going on?" she demanded.

"Nothing." Makayla's voice was defiant. She glared at Gabby. "This is my room."

"Yeah, I know that. And you know the rules. No boys in your room. Boyd, you need to go home now."

He nodded and walked past Makayla without saying anything.

"You ruin everything," Makayla yelled at her. *"Everything."*

"Then my day is complete. No boys in your room. Are we clear?"

Makayla nodded sullenly.

Gabby thought about adding she would be talking to Andrew later, but wasn't sure that was much of a threat. Still, she had to say something.

"No friends over for the rest of the week."

Makayla rolled her eyes. "Whatever. I'll just go there."

To which Gabby couldn't say anything because she wasn't allowed to ground Makayla on her own. Andrew had made that very clear. Because Makayla was *his* daughter, not theirs. Not that she was allowed to say that, either. Talk about a one-way road to disaster.

So no grounding, but she could withhold cookies, she told herself. A small, petty act, but it was all she had. She carried the plate back out and headed down the stairs.

A boy in her room. That was bad. Makayla was a beautiful fifteen-year-old girl. Maybe hormones weren't ruling life yet, but they were making a run at it.

Once back in her kitchen, she told herself she was overreacting. That everything was fine. The trick was making herself believe it.

"Are you sure?" Andrew asked a few hours later, when Gabby told him what she'd seen. "They couldn't have been kissing. Boyd isn't that kind of guy."

"I know what I saw. He's sixteen and they're all that kind. Don't you remember?"

"Yeah, but that was different. Boyd's kind of geeky."

"I'm sure he has a working penis."

They were in their bedroom. She'd waited until everyone had gone to bed to fill him in on what had happened.

"They were kissing, Andrew. This is serious. Not only did she break the rules, for which she should be punished, but we need to talk to her. Candace isn't going to. Makayla has no idea what she's getting into."

Andrew finished brushing his teeth. He rinsed out his mouth, then straightened. "Gabby, you're a doll to worry, but trust me. Nothing is going on. Kids these days don't date. They travel in packs."

"They still have sex."

He shook his head. "I'll talk to her." She started to speak, but he held up his hand. "And I'll make sure she's punished for having a boy in her room. What seems fair? The weekend without her phone?"

Gabby nodded. "That seems okay."

He moved toward her. "They're just kids," he said as he reached for her. "They have no idea what they're doing. I, on the other hand, know exactly what you like."

She leaned into him. Even as she kissed him back, a whiny little voice in her head said this was a bigger deal than he was acknowledging and while she was easy to distract, that didn't mean the problem was going away.

The Pacific Ocean Park—otherwise known as the POP—had started life in Santa Monica. The pier, little shops and restaurants had eventually lost favor with residents and tourists. Years ago, the POP had been torn down and discarded. Several citizens in Mischief Bay had gotten together to pick up the pieces and move the whole thing a few miles south. Now it was a bustling tourist attraction and a place for locals to hang out. The very heart of the POP was a beautifully restored carousel.

Nicole stood with Gabby by the wooden horses, watching her son and Gabby's girls go round and round.

"I think it's a big deal," Gabby said, her gaze on her daughters.

"Of course it is." Nicole grimaced. "Back in high school I knew a girl who got pregnant in the tenth grade. In her senior picture, she was holding a toddler. Talk about a nightmare."

"There's a scary thought." Gabby pressed her lips together. "I really don't like this. The worry, the lack of control. Makayla needs more structure in her life. More rules. Andrew is still acting like he only has her on weekends, but that's not the case. We're full-time parents to her and we need to act like it. Plus, what about the twins? They look up to her and want to be just like her. I do not want them learning to get pregnant while they're still in high school."

Nicole heard the worry and frustration in her friend's voice. She couldn't imagine what it would be like to have to raise someone else's kid, yet not be given any authority. Or very little. Talk about having to do it with both hands tied behind your back. Gabby was in an impossible situation.

"Can you talk to her?" she asked.

"Not really. Makayla and I aren't enemies, but we're not friends, either. She resents me. Or something. I honestly have no idea what she thinks of me. We rarely talk. I've tried, but she shuts me out."

"You think it's about her mom?"

"Maybe. If she likes me, she's being disloyal. She's good with the twins, which I appreciate. Maybe that's enough."

"Not if she's having sex," Nicole pointed out.

"Tell me about it." Gabby shook her head. "I don't want to talk about this anymore. It's too depressing. But I appreciate you listening."

"Think about going back to work instead," Nicole said with a smile. "That will make you happy."

"It does. To be back in the professional world. I can't wait." She looked at Nicole. "Was it hard for you to go back to work?"

"A little. Tyler was younger than the twins and in day care for part of the time. I didn't like that. But it was still good to get out. Of course I had a job waiting for me, so I didn't have to deal with the transition you're having."

Nicole had gone back to work because she and Eric had needed the money. Gabby was working because she wanted to. Nicole had no idea how much Andrew made in a year, but based on their nice cars and the big house, it was plenty.

She couldn't begin to imagine what it would have been like to grow up with financial security. She'd been the only child of a single mom who'd wanted nothing more than for her to be famous. There had been dance lessons and voice lessons and auditions. Money had been tight and schooling had come second to her dancing and acting.

The irony of her current financial situation didn't escape her.

"What?" Gabby asked. "You have the strangest expression."

"I'm just thinking."

The carousel stopped but all three kids stayed on. Gabby and Nicole had bought them each three rides and they would be lucky if they only wanted to stay on that long. Lately, every time they came to the POP, Tyler said he was getting too old to ride the horses, yet he continued to do it happily. Nicole knew the day would come when he would actually mean it. While it would be yet another sign he was growing up, she knew she would miss the little boy things they'd done together.

Things Eric missed every day.

She drew in a breath. "Eric bailed on Tyler again. I don't think they've had a day together in six months. It makes me crazy."

"I'm sorry. What does Tyler think?"

Nicole looked at her friend. "That's the worst of it. I don't think he cares anymore. Dad is just a concept, not a person. He doesn't miss him because there's nothing to miss. I keep thinking that Eric is going to wake up to the fact that he's losing the one thing that can't be recovered. Time. I worry that he genuinely doesn't care. Then I wonder if it's my fault."

"How could it be your fault? Eric's his father."

"I know. It's just that Tyler and I are so close and maybe Eric feels shut out."

"No. Tyler is his son. He's responsible for his own relationship with him."

"I guess." Nicole bit her lower lip. "Sometimes I worry that I feel guilty about the divorce."

"Guilty in what way?"

"That I didn't suffer enough. Eric left and that was bad, but financially things are better. I have the house and Tyler. Our lives are great."

"Isn't that a good thing?"

"So many women have a hard time after a divorce."

Gabby drew her brows together. "You think you should be in more emotional and financial pain and because you're not, you're a bad person?"

"Okay, when you put it like that, I sound like an idiot."

"You kind of are," Gabby said gently. "Nicole, divorce is hard, no matter what. You and Tyler have made a great adjustment. Be grateful, don't beat yourself up. Not that you'll listen. You do have an interesting set of rules about things. Remember buying your new car?"

Nicole winced. When her car had coughed its last breath, she'd been forced to buy a new one. She'd agonized for weeks, driving everyone crazy. It wasn't that she didn't have the money, it was that she felt she didn't deserve a new car. Her friends had finally insisted on an intervention. Armed with statistics and safety reports, they narrowed her choices down to three, then Rob and Andrew had taken her car shopping.

"Okay, I might have some issues," she admitted, then confessed, "Shannon says I'm stuck."

"Shannon is right. You are. You aren't pining for Eric, but you're not moving forward, either."

"She told you about Jairus?"

Gabby stared at her. "What about Jairus? OMG, something happened, didn't it?"

"OMG?"

"I live with a fifteen-year-old and don't change the subject. You said it was no big deal. You said he was surprisingly nice and good with the kids. There's more, isn't there?"

"Maybe. Yes. I don't know."

Gabby laughed. "You liked him. I can't believe it. You who hate all things B the D liked the guy who created him."

"I didn't *like* him."

"You're acting like you're sixteen and pretending not to notice the football quarterback standing right beside you. Tell me what happened. Everything. Start from the very beginning. You said hi and he said hi and…"

Nicole groaned. "He thought I was a hooker."

"What?"

Nicole told her about the first meeting with Jairus and how he'd asked her out.

"One of the counselors told him where I worked and he showed up after the class you came to. Shannon was there. She went outside so we could talk, but she didn't leave until he did."

"That's just like Shannon. So where does the stuck part come in?"

"He asked me out again and I said no. Shannon thinks I'm avoiding relationships."

"She's right. You've been separated for well over a year and divorced for months and months. Don't you want to stick your toe in the water, so to speak? Don't you miss having a man in your life? Not just for sex, although that can be great, but to have someone who cares about you. Someone who is more than a friend?"

Nicole laughed. "Why don't you tell me what you really think?"

Gabby's expression turned stricken. "Was that too much? Was I too blunt?"

"No. You were exactly right. I appreciate the honesty." It stung a little, but she knew Gabby had her best interest at heart. Just as important, she was telling the truth. There were things Nicole *did* miss about being in a relationship, but whenever she thought about dating, she had a million reasons not to try.

"I'm scared," she admitted. "I had no idea things were so bad with Eric. I mean I knew there were problems, but not that we were headed for a divorce. After he left, I had a lot of time to think about all the things I'd done wrong. I don't want to mess up again."

"So it's better not to try?"

"It's safer."

"But the best things in life aren't safe. What moves us, what we want the most, always means taking a risk. Isn't that what makes things worthwhile?"

"You're so logical."

Gabby smiled. "I wish. What I do know is that you have to make decisions from a position of strength. And that means understanding your motives. If you're not dating because you're perfectly happy on your own and can't see what value a man would bring to the mix, then great. But if you're hiding, then you need think about that. You're a positive person who takes charge. Hiding isn't like you."

It hadn't been her lately, Nicole thought. She might not want to face the truth, but that didn't change it. She'd made sure all of Tyler's needs were met, she'd seen to her business and her house, but when it came to herself, she'd been on autopilot. Gabby was right. If she wanted to be alone, then that was her decision. But hiding—that wasn't her at all.

"Hey, Mom," Gabby called as she opened the back door of her mother's house and walked into the kitchen, the twins right on her heels. As soon as they stepped into the big kitchen, they started yelling.

"Grandma, Grandma!"

Marie Lewis walked into the room. Her arms were open, her expression happy. "My best girls," she said as she crouched down to hug the twins. "What a fantastic surprise."

Gabby watched her mother fuss over the girls before ushering them to the giant island and getting them settled. Next would be snacks and plenty of conversation. Marie was the perfect grandmother. She was warm, caring and just stern enough to keep everyone behaving.

Once the twins were in their seats, Marie hugged Gabby.

"How are you doing?" she asked.

"Great."

Her mother patted her cheek, then turned her attention back to her granddaughters. Lemonade was poured into plastic glasses and cookies produced.

If Shannon was Gabby's career ideal, then Marie was Gabby's maternal role model. Despite five children, an assortment of pets and plenty of potential for chaos, the house had always run smoothly. Sure it had been loud, but there hadn't been a constant scramble for things to get done. With two kids of her own and a teenage stepdaughter in the house, Gabby felt she lived three steps behind. She honestly didn't know how her mother had done it.

She joined her daughters at the island. The kitchen was large, with white cabinets and blue-and-green tile accents. Not what she would have chosen, but nice.

Gabby watched her mom. Marie was sixty-one and still a size eight. Talk about incredibly depressing. She colored her hair but otherwise didn't do anything to defy her age and she could pass for someone in her late forties. Gabby hoped she'd inherited the same genes.

"How's camp?" Marie asked the girls. "Having fun?"

"Every day," Kennedy told her. "We have art project and playtime."

"Sometimes we work on our letters," Kenzie added. "We know them all and we can read some words."

"Can you? Way to go. I knew you were smart girls the first time I saw you."

They both laughed.

When the cookies and lemonade were finished, the four of them moved out to the backyard. A new swing set had been installed when the first grandchild had been born. By the time the twins came along, it was well-worn and comfortable. Now the twins ran to it and settled on the seats.

"Are you still looking forward to be going back to work?" her mother asked, watching her grandchildren.

"You have no idea."

"I don't understand why you want to. You could stay home and have more babies."

A familiar discussion, Gabby thought. "We have Makayla full-time now. Three is plenty."

"Makayla will be gone before you know it and the twins

are already heading off to kindergarten. More children would be a happy thing."

"Not for me, Mom. I'm ready to get back to my career."

Marie pressed her hand to her chest in mock distress. "All my friends compliment me for raising two sensible, career-oriented daughters. Little do they know how I wish you were both more like me."

Gabby laughed because it was expected, but in her heart, she thought maybe her mother was telling the truth rather than joking. She *would* have preferred either of them to be a stay-at-home mom. But Gabby's older sister was a veterinarian and Gabby was ready to get back to her law practice.

"I guess it's up to one of the boys," she said.

Marie laughed. "I don't see that happening, either."

For a second, Gabby thought about telling her mom about Makayla and Boyd and the kiss. Her gut told her she wasn't making too big a deal of it, but Andrew insisted all was well and Makayla had accepted her punishment without a whimper. Maybe she should just keep quiet and be grateful she hadn't discovered them doing anything worse.

Chapter Nine

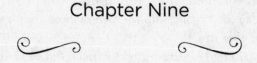

Tuesdays and Thursdays, Nicole taught the late-afternoon class. Cecelia picked up Tyler from his summer camp, took him home and got dinner started. By the time Nicole had wrapped things up and driven across Mischief Bay, it was usually close to six when she walked in the door. But still a much better arrangement than when she'd been teaching until seven or eight at night.

In the early days of her separation from Eric, she'd had a nanny—at Eric's insistence. Nicole had kept her until she'd been able to cut back her own work hours. Not only wasn't she the nanny type, she preferred to take care of Tyler herself.

Her cell phone chirped and she glanced down to see she had a text from Gabby.

Checking in to say hi, her friend typed.

I'm good. Anymore kissing?

Not that I've seen. What about you? Any kissing at all?

Nicole chuckled. Very funny. No and no. Did I mention no?

LOL. TTYS

She put down her phone and checked to make sure the right play mix was in place. She'd changed it out for her own workout earlier. She had a feeling that her clients wouldn't really appreciate her strange combination of country and rap. It was confusing at best.

Several clients strolled in. She greeted them. Her Tuesday-Thursdays four-o'clock session was a mat class, done with minimal equipment. Some people thought that made it easier and maybe in some places it was. But not at Mischief in Motion. She prided herself on a killer workout. People were taking time out of their lives and paying money for their workout. She made sure they limped away knowing they'd gotten the best bargain possible.

"Hey, Judie," she called as a pretty blonde with brown eyes walked in. "How's it going?"

"Great. I'm ready for you to kick my butt."

Nicole grinned. "You'll be kicking your own butt."

"I really hope you mean that as a figure of speech and not literally."

"You'll have to wait to find out."

A couple more clients walked in, followed by the one person Nicole had never, ever expected to see in her studio again. Jairus wore loose jersey shorts over fitted bike shorts, and a T-shirt. He had on sandals, but carried a pair of Pilates socks in his hand.

"I called earlier," he said. "I was told I could be a walk-in if the class wasn't full."

Nicole opened her mouth, then closed it. No. This wasn't happening. He couldn't be here. He couldn't take a class.

She wanted to say she was full. That he had to go away, only the mats were laid out on the floor and it was obvious that two were empty. As it was 3:59, the odds of anyone showing up in the next eight seconds seemed slim.

She wanted to say the class would be a hundred and fifty dollars. Or five hundred. Or whatever number it was that would make him go away. Behind her she heard low rumbling. No doubt the women were upset that there was going to be a guy in class. A man always changed the dynamics, and generally not in a happy way. She didn't know what to say, what to think and she really, really hated how deep down in her chest there was the smallest little *ping* of interest.

"Have you been to a Pilates class before?" she asked.

"Never. I run and lift weights."

"Interesting but not useful. You're going to be sore tomorrow."

"I'll risk it."

His dark, curly hair was too long and he hadn't shaved that day. He should have looked scruffy, only he didn't. He looked…good.

She pointed to the empty mat on the end. "We need to get started."

He nodded and walked across the studio. He kicked off his sandals, then faced the six women already sitting on their mats.

"Ladies, I'm sorry to invade your class like this. I promise, it won't be a regular thing."

Judie raised her eyebrows. "So we should pretend you're not here?"

"That would be great."

Nicole stood in front of her class. If she turned just a little to her left, she barely had to see Jairus. She told herself he was just another student. She would do what she always did.

"We'll start with the hundred," she said.

Jairus had put on his Pilates socks. He glanced at the other women and assumed the same position—balanced on his butt, his arms straight, legs straight and raised.

"Tummies in and up," Nicole said. "Begin."

She counted to one hundred, patting her hand against her thigh between each number, stretching out the length of time, as she usually did. Jairus hung in to about forty-seven, then he started flagging. By eighty, he was flat on his back.

The class continued. He did his best to keep up. Leg circles were easy for him, although he didn't have much control. The open leg rocker was more difficult and toward the end, he went over on his side.

Several of the women giggled. A couple called out advice. Nicole had to give him points. He tried hard and he didn't complain.

He also had a pretty decent body. He hadn't been lying about working out. She could see he had muscles and endurance. Just not the right kind for what they were doing here.

About twenty minutes into the class, the students seemed to forget he was there. Conversation flowed—it was the usual discussion of husbands, kids and bosses. Jairus didn't join in, which surprised her. She was sure he would want to offer advice.

"Teaser," she said toward the end of the class. She glanced at him. "You should sit this one out."

He looked at the other women. They all lay on their backs, their arms extended up over their heads. As she gave the count, they rose gracefully into a V, toes pointed, arms straight.

"Good idea," he muttered as he collapsed onto the mat.

She held in a smile. Class wrapped up quickly with a few stretches. Everyone applauded when it was over and got to their feet.

Jairus moved a little more slowly. A couple of the women spoke to him before leaving. When he was the only one left, he stood and hobbled over to her small desk.

He was sweating just a little. She would like to think he was nervous, but knew it was a lot more about the workout.

"You teach a great class," he said.

"Thank you."

"It's hard."

"It's supposed to be."

He ran his fingers through his damp hair. "Look, this is my last shot. If you say no, I'm done. I'm not interested in being some weird-ass stalker guy. I like you. I'd like to get to know you better. You're interesting and that's important to me."

"Plus you haven't been getting any lately."

He winced. "Did you have to bring that up?"

"Yes."

"You're not easy."

"That's true." She studied him. "I like that you don't go to prostitutes."

"I hope you like more than that because otherwise, you need to work on your standards."

That made her laugh.

She thought about what Shannon and Gabby had said to her about hiding. She thought about how long it had been since she and Eric had split up. She thought about how Jairus had been a trouper in her class. He'd made a real effort. That had to be worth something.

"Dinner?" he asked.

"Dinner."

Hayley pulled a dress off the rack and studied it. Spending money on something as ridiculous as clothes bugged her, but she needed a few things for herself. Her clothes were all so threadbare. It didn't take much for a seam to rip. In the past week, she'd had two skirts and a shirt fall apart in the wash. She'd been careful to throw them out before Rob saw. He didn't understand why she wouldn't just go to a department store, like everyone else. Even a discount one. He believed if they needed something, they should get it. For him, it was only money. For her, wasteful spending might mean the difference between having a baby and not.

"Great selection this time," Nicole said from the other side of the rack. "Did you see this one?"

She held up a simple blue wrap dress. The knit material would wear like iron and the subtle pattern meant stains would be less noticeable.

"Love," Hayley said, walking around the end of the long rack.

It was lunchtime and she and Nicole were spending their precious hour at the local thrift store. The Goodwill was bigger, with a better selection, but too far to go to on a lunch break.

She'd dressed for their outing in a tank top and shorts, so it was easy to pull on the dress and wait for Nicole to react.

"Looks great," her friend said. "Nice color. And hey, five bucks. You can't beat that."

Hayley went over to the large mirror on the wall and studied herself. She was too thin and pale. She still looked sick. She hadn't had a period since her last miscarriage, so she wasn't ovulating. Dr. Pearce had warned her that all the hormones would mess things up and she'd been right.

It was going to get better, Hayley promised herself. Once she got the hundred thousand dollars she needed for the treatment in Switzerland, she would get pregnant and stay pregnant. Then she would have a baby. Everything would be worth it after that.

Nicole walked over with another dress. A simple, sleeveless, red sheath made of a quality woven cotton.

"With a black sweater, it could be perfect," she said. "Seven dollars. Still a steal."

Hayley didn't want to spend more than twenty dollars. Which meant she could get both dresses plus a couple of tops.

Nicole found a few shirts and shorts for Tyler while Hayley looked through the women's shirts. There was a nice green blouse that looked as if it had never been worn. As she slipped it off the hanger, it drifted to the floor. She bent over to pick it up only to realize a half second too late that she'd stood up too fast. The room spun, folding at the corners before she could grab on to the rack.

Nicole was immediately at her side. "Are you okay?"

"Just dizzy." Hayley straightened and forced herself to breathe slowly. The room steadied. She smiled. "I have low blood pressure. It's not hard for me to get light-headed. Don't worry."

"I do worry." Nicole's gaze was sympathetic. "You're still recovering, aren't you?"

Hayley nodded. "It takes longer each time."

Her friend squeezed her hand. "That was your third miscarriage?"

"My fifth."

"That many? Is that okay for your body?" Nicole shook her head. "Sorry. That was the wrong question to ask. Do you need to get something to eat? Would that help?"

"I have a sandwich back at the office. I'll be fine." Hayley never knew how much people wanted to hear. She also didn't know how much she wanted to listen to. Tell someone you'd miscarried and chances were they had advice. Especially women who'd had successful pregnancies, like Nicole.

Was it worth it? Did she have the right doctor? What about adoption? Sometimes Hayley wanted to grab the speaker and shake them. Really? Was it possible she and Rob hadn't already had that conversation fifty-seven times?

"I have a protein bar with me," her friend said. "You're welcome to it."

"Thanks." She held up the blouse that had fallen. "I think it's pretty."

"Me, too. With white or khaki now and with black in the winter." Nicole smiled. "It's not like we have to worry about it getting too cold in January. A light sweater over that top would be great."

Hayley relaxed. "Thank you for not lecturing me."

"Not my business."

"That doesn't seem to matter to most people."

"The heart wants what it wants. Having a baby by carrying it to term is important to you."

The right words, Hayley thought. "But you don't get it."

"I don't have to. I'm not dealing with what you are."

No one was. At least Nicole understood that. But she was only one of a few. Nearly everyone else wanted Hayley to get over it. To accept reality and adopt.

Nicole unbuttoned the blouse and held it out. "Let's see how you rock this. Then we'll buy what we found and head back to work. On the way, we'll splurge with a latte at Latte-Da."

"They'll cost more than this blouse."

Nicole grinned. "Which is what makes it a splurge."

Gabby, we know you can hear us. Gabby, we love you. Come back to the kitchen and eat us.

Gabby wasn't sure which was more psychotic—hearing the cookies downstairs calling to her, or wanting to answer.

It was her own fault, she reminded herself. Her family was perfectly happy with store-bought cookies. But did she buy those? Of course not. Instead she made them from scratch so the smell of chocolate and peanut butter wafted through the entire house.

It was day six of her diet. Day six of being hungry and annoyed and had she mentioned hungry? She missed sugar and bread. She missed not caring about what she was going to eat next. She missed the feeling of being so full that she never wanted to eat again. Even if that only lasted for a few hours. These days she was either starving or ravenous, there wasn't much in between.

She reminded herself that she'd already lost two pounds and that she didn't give a rat if it was only water weight. The scale was going down. She would be strong. She *was* strong. Hear her roar. Or maybe that was just her stomach.

She sorted the load of laundry by owner, then started folding. In theory she could take Makayla's clothes back to her and the teen would fold them, but sometimes that wasn't worth the argument. Which made her just as guilty as Andrew on the mixed-message front. Of course, it was tough to be strong when she was weak from hunger.

"I can do that."

She turned as her stepdaughter walked into the master.

"Those are mine," Makayla said. "I'll fold them."

"Thanks," Gabby said, even as she glanced out the window to see if day was now night and it was raining some strange animal. As the weather seemed completely normal, she pushed the pile of whites to the other side of the bed.

In her shorts and a loose tank top, her hair pulled back in a braid, Makayla seemed younger than usual. More approachable. Jasmine lay tucked between the decorative pillows on the bed and stuck out a paw to catch stray socks.

"School's going to start soon," Gabby said, not sure if she

was supposed to make conversation or wait for Makayla to talk. "Your sophomore year is a big one."

"Uh-huh. Cami's getting her learner's permit."

Cami was one of Makayla's friends and a little older than the other girls. As Makayla had just turned fifteen at the beginning of summer, Gabby and Andrew had a few more months until they would be faced with that. Fortunately California had graduated license requirements. Teens had to earn their way into a driver's license, which meant even if Cami got her permit, there would be no driving her friends around anytime soon.

Makayla finished folding her clothes and pairing her socks. She sat on the bed and picked at the duvet cover. "I'll be taking geometry for math. Everyone says it's hard."

"Geometry is weird," Gabby said. "From what I could tell, either you get it or you don't. If you get it, it's super easy. If you don't, it's very challenging. But you've always done well in math."

"Yeah."

Gabby finished with the twins' clothes. Even though the next logical step was to pick up the items and take them to where they belonged, her gut said to stay where she was. Until she found out what Makayla wanted.

She had no idea where the conversation was going. Was this about body piercing? A tattoo? Going on a trip with one of her friends and her family? Painting her room purple? There was really no way to tell. She didn't think she had to worry about Makayla being bullied. She was popular with her friends and didn't seem to have that many who were mean.

For a second she thought about mentioning Boyd and the kissing. To try to find out how far things had gone. She held back, wanting Makayla to get to whatever was bothering her first.

"When did you know you were in love with my dad?"

Of all the questions, that was not even close to being on the list of those expected.

"About two months after we started dating," she said. "He was a really great guy. Kind and funny and smart." She smiled. "He cared about you a lot and that was important to me."

Makayla finally looked at her. "Why? I thought second wives hated the kids from the first family."

"Not at all. I liked how your dad was with you. I knew he was the sort of man who would put family first." The answer was automatic, while Gabby processed the *I thought second wives hated the kids from the first family.* Was that the problem? Did Makayla really think Gabby hated her?

Sure they didn't always get along, but hate was so strong. Gabby felt herself flushing as she wondered if she'd been more bitchy than she realized. Had she made the teen feel unwelcome?

"Some of my friends have stepmoms who are really mean," the girl said, turning her attention back to the duvet cover.

"I'm sure it happens." Did she fall in the mean category?

"You were planning on having the twins, right? They weren't an accident."

"I was trying to get pregnant," Gabby said. "I didn't think there would be twins."

"That would be hard." Makayla looked at her, then away. "Um, a friend of mine thinks she's pregnant and doesn't know how to be sure. I, ah, said I'd ask you."

Gabby was incredibly grateful she was sitting down because if she were standing, she would have collapsed. Now all she had to worry about was screaming. Or swearing. Something she hadn't done out loud since the twins were born. This time "sugar" was not going to cut it.

Pregnant? *Pregnant?* She flashed back on the kiss. They

hadn't seemed like they were that intimate, she thought frantically. If anything, she would have said they were awkward together. Maybe there really was a friend.

"How far along is she?" Gabby asked.

"A few months. Maybe two or three."

Makayla's voice shrank with each word until there was barely any sound. By the end of the sentence, the world shattered and Gabby knew there was no friend. Makayla was pregnant. Now what? What were they supposed to do? Was being pregnant better or worse than being on drugs? Better or worse than stealing or being a bad person or...

Gabby stood. "Can you please stay with the twins? I have to go to the drugstore."

"Um, sure."

Gabby started for the door, then turned back. "Start drinking water. Lots and lots of water."

Chapter Ten

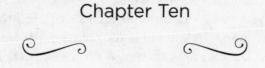

The pregnancy test sticks were lined up on a paper towel in the master bath. Each one of them showed the same result. Whether it was a plus or lines or the word *yes*, the answer was clear. Makayla was pregnant.

They stood as far apart from each other as the small room allowed. Gabby was by the counter, the teen was by the tub. Silence filled the space, pressing in on them.

"I'm sorry," the teen whispered. "I'm sorry."

Me, too. Not that Gabby could say that. She couldn't say much of anything. Right this second, it was hard to catch her breath. Her chest was tight, her legs shaking. Makayla was pregnant. That changed everything. What were they going to do? Worse, she was faced with the dilemma of when to tell Andrew. The how would come later. Unless...

"Do you want to tell your dad or should I?"

"Could you?"

No! I couldn't. Only she was the adult. She was the one who had to stay calm and sensible and understanding. She had to be the rock when on the inside she simply wanted to scream. Take the high ground, as her mother had once advised her. Only Marie would never have imagined this moment. No one could.

"After the twins are in bed," she whispered, trying to figure out what she was going to say. "I'll tell him and then we'll come talk to you."

Makayla's eyes were huge and filled with tears. Her lips trembled. "I didn't mean for this to happen."

"I know."

Gabby wanted to grab her girls and run. She wanted not to have to worry about this. Not deal with it. Not have their lives forever altered. But if she was this scared of the future, what must her stepdaughter be feeling? She was only fifteen.

"We'll figure it out," she said with false cheer. "You'll see."

"You think?"

"Of course." Gabby walked over to her and hugged her. "It's going to be okay."

Makayla surprised her by hanging on tight. By hugging back as if she would never let go. The girl started to cry. Harsh, choking sobs that shook her body and left her gasping. Gabby stayed close and prayed that she wasn't lying. That everything really was going to be all right. But in her heart, she knew it wasn't.

"We have to talk."

Andrew looked more amused than worried as he stretched out on their bed. "I got that from the way you pulled me into the bedroom." He patted the space next to him. "Come on. You can tell me what's going on while I feel you up."

"This is serious."

His smile faded and he sat up. "You have my attention, Gabby. What is it? The girls seemed fine at dinner. Makayla was a little quiet. Did you two have a fight?"

She twisted her hands together. Sitting wasn't an option. She had to stand or better yet, pace. Only, she wanted to be looking at him as she told him. She wanted to know what he was thinking. If he blamed her. Because she was worried about that. Being blamed.

"Gabby?"

"Makayla's pregnant. We did three different pregnancy tests. They were all positive."

Andrew went completely still. For a second, she wasn't sure if he was even breathing. Then he swore—angry words directed at no one but upsetting all the same.

He rose until he was standing in front of her.

"You're sure?"

She nodded.

"Boyd?"

"I don't know. Honestly, there hasn't been time. I went and got the tests and she took them. By then the twins were done with their movie and I had to start dinner."

She was shaking. Everything hurt. Nothing felt right. She was braced for him to start yelling at her, to tell her what she'd done wrong. Even though Andrew never did that.

Was it her own guilt? If she'd tried harder with the teen. If they were closer.

Andrew charged out of the room. Gabby hurried after him. He opened Makayla's door without knocking. She sat on her bed, her back against the pillows, her knees drawn up to her chest. She'd been crying and wiped her face when they entered.

"Is it Boyd?" Andrew asked.

Makayla nodded.

He turned around and walked out.

Gabby stared after him. What?

"Daddy, no!"

But Andrew didn't listen to his daughter's plea. He disappeared and a few seconds later, Gabby heard the slam of his office door, which was a whole lot better than the garage door opening. At least he wasn't going to confront the teenage father-to-be right now.

She stood in the center of the room, not sure what to do. Makayla began to cry again. Gabby sucked in a breath, then went over to the bed and sat down. Makayla threw herself at Gabby, wrapping her arms around her waist and burying her head in her lap.

"It's going to be okay," Gabby said automatically, stroking the girl's back. Like this, broken and hurt, Makayla seemed younger. Smaller.

"It's not. He hates me."

"He's known for fifteen seconds. Maybe he gets some time to figure out how to deal with the information."

"You didn't reject me when you found out."

"Your father hasn't rejected you, but he does need to process all this. He loves you and we'll get through this as a family." Was she saying the right thing? Was there a right thing?

She sat there while the girl cried. After a few minutes, the tears quieted and the teen sat up.

Gabby touched her cheek. "You're a mess. Still way too beautiful, but a mess."

Makayla didn't smile. "What am I going to do?"

"Wash your face, brush your teeth and get into bed. The rest of it can wait. You're not having the baby tomorrow. I'll talk to your dad tonight and we'll come up with a plan."

Makayla nodded and climbed off the bed. She walked to the bathroom, then turned back to Gabby.

"Can you stay until I fall asleep?"

An unexpected request. "Of course."

"Do you hate me?"

"No."

"You're sure?"

"I'm not happy, if that's what you're asking. But I'm going

to guess you're not happy, either. We'll deal. Nobody hates you."

Makayla nodded. For a second Gabby was afraid she was going to ask the next logical question. *Do you love me?* Of course she would say yes, but she wasn't sure it was the truth. Loving Makayla wasn't easy. The teen pushed her buttons. And right now, well, it wasn't anything she wanted to talk about. But Makayla didn't ask, so there was no need to lie.

Less than ten minutes later, Makayla was in bed. Gabby pulled up the chair from her desk and sat close. The only light came from the half-open door and the hallway beyond.

She'd thought Andrew might return to say something, but he hadn't. While Makayla had been in the bathroom, Gabby had crept into the twins' room and pulled out a couple of books. Now she opened the first one.

"You're not going to read to me," her stepdaughter said. "I'm too old."

"It will help you fall asleep."

Gabby opened the first book. It was a chapter book by Jane O'Connor in the Fancy Nancy series. "Nancy Clancy, Super Sleuth," she began. "Chapter One."

It took a while, but eventually Makayla fell asleep. Gabby put the chair back, then walked out into the hall. She left the door open a little and the overhead light on. In case the teen woke up. Then she made her way downstairs.

She was tired. No, bone-weary. In a few short hours, everything had changed. She didn't know how this was going to end, but it wasn't going to be good. She could feel it.

She walked into Andrew's office. He sat behind his desk, staring at the wall. When he saw her, he rose and crossed to her. After taking her hands in his, he looked into her eyes.

"I'm sorry. I was wrong. About Boyd and the kissing. I should have listened to you."

She nearly melted with relief. "I had no idea they were so involved. This is a mess. It's been awful, trying to act normal, waiting to tell you."

"You had to. We couldn't discuss this with the twins around." He pulled her close. "I hate that sniveling little shit for doing this to her, but that's beside the point. We have to figure this out. Talk about a giant fuckup."

Despite everything, she giggled. "That's one way to put it."

He looked at her. A smile tugged at the corner of his mouth. "No pun intended."

"Too bad."

He put his arm around her and led her to the sofa under the window. "What do you think we should do?"

"Talk to her and find out when this all happened. Talk to his parents. Present a united front."

He nodded. "That makes sense. I also have to make things right with Makayla in the morning. I need to remember I'm upset with the situation, but she's still my daughter." He squeezed her hand. "I'm so lucky to have you, Gabby. We'll figure this out and go forward together."

Exactly what she wanted to hear, she thought, as she smiled at him. As long as they were united, they would get through this.

"I know why they didn't want that one," Rob said as he stared at the murky purplish-brownish color on the side of the paint can. "It had to have been a mistake."

"I hope so." Hayley pointed to another can on the shelf in the back of the hardware store. "What about these?"

"Yellow? Not my favorite. You know, we *could* just buy the color we want. It's paint. We can probably afford it."

Hayley shook her head. "Come on. Think of this as a chal-

lenge. Or a scavenger hunt. We'll use the money for something else."

She had a feeling he was thinking window coverings or
carpeting while she was thinking Switzerland, but they were
having such a good time this morning. There was no reason
to mention that.

"If we don't find anything we like, we're picking a color."

"Agreed."

They continued to study the shelves of discounted paint
cans.

"Hey, look at this one." He held up a can with a brush of
sage green on the side. "It's kind of nice."

She walked over and studied the color. It was just the right
shade of green. Not too yellow and not too dark.

"I like it a lot. How many cans are there?"

"Three. Which should be enough. We'll need to do a coat
of primer because the walls haven't been painted in so long
but we can get that tinted." He glanced at her. "They tint
for free, so don't freak."

"I don't freak."

"About money? Yeah, you do. So we're sold on the sage?"

"We are." She smiled at him. "You're so handy."

"Just one of my many charms. Come on. Let's go get the
primer."

When the paint had been loaded into their cart, they made
their way to the garden section. The morning was warm and
sunny, even with the awning overhead. Plants were laid out
in rows—some on tables with the larger ones on the ground,
grouped by type—shade, flowering, annuals, perennials. Now
that their front yard had been cleaned up, it was in obvious
need of fresh plants. But there were too many choices.

Hayley looked around at all the offerings, then back at Rob.
"I don't know anything about plants. You?"

"Same."

"We could ask someone."

"You're assuming we know the questions."

"Oh, right." She pointed to the roses. "I know what they are. I think they're a lot of work."

"Then not for us."

She sighed. "I'm clueless."

"But pretty and that counts, right?"

She pretended to slug him in the arm. "Very funny. So maybe we should go home with what we have and walk the yard. Figure out what's dead, what just needs watering and come up with a plan. Then we can go online and learn a few basics before coming back."

"An excellent idea." He kissed her lightly. "Not so clueless after all."

They made their way through the Saturday afternoon crowd and got in line to pay for their purchases. After loading everything in the car, they drove home and carried the cans and paint supplies into the house.

They'd already emptied the master of everything but their bed and the dresser. They would take the curtains down in the morning, just before they started painting. Hayley picked up a roll of blue tape.

"I'll start with the baseboards if you want to do the windows," she said.

Rob took the tape from her and dropped it onto the floor. "Or we could do something else," he whispered right before he kissed her.

The feel of his mouth on hers was nice, but surprising. When his arms came around her, she knew exactly what he wanted.

"I don't know if I'm ovulating," she admitted. She hadn't taken her temperature in weeks. There hadn't been any point.

Between her body recovering from the miscarriage and the way the last batch of hormones had messed her up, she had no idea where she was in her cycle.

"That's okay," he said, kissing along her jaw before moving to her neck.

But what about Switzerland? A question she thought but didn't vocalize. Because nothing could happen before then. She had to let her body recover before the treatments began.

"But I…"

Understanding dawned just as Rob straightened. His brows drew together in annoyance.

"Not everything has to be about getting pregnant," he told her. "We're married. We used to do this just for fun."

Guilt burned hot and bright in her belly. Not only because she wasn't telling him her plans but because he was right. There had been a time when they'd wanted to make love all the time for no reason other than it felt good to be with each other. Their first year of marriage, they'd made love every day, sometimes more. They'd laughed and touched, smug in the knowledge that they would be in love forever.

He stepped away.

"Rob, wait."

He looked at her for a long time. "Is it ever not about getting pregnant?"

"Of course." The words were automatic. "It's just…"

"That's what I thought. I'll be in the garage."

She let him go. She could have called him back, could have gone to him and kissed him. Could have held him. Changing his mind wouldn't be that difficult. Instead she sank onto the floor and sat cross-legged on the carpet.

She hurt all over. Not just the usual cramping, but everywhere. Her arms and legs were too heavy. She wasn't sleeping well. Wanting a baby wasn't a crime, she told herself as she rested her head in her hands. She wasn't a bad person. Rob had to understand that.

The problem was, she was pretty sure he did understand. But the journey had gone on too long, and understanding wasn't going to be enough anymore.

Boyd's parents lived on the Torrance side of Mischief Bay. It was a pretty two-story house on a small lot. Gabby would guess there had once been a cute little bungalow that had been torn down to make room for the larger home. It was happening all over.

The yard was manicured, the front door freshly painted and the living room pristine. Gabby thought of the endless stream of books, stuffed animals, dog and cat toys, books and dolls she was constantly picking up in her own family room. Given three days' notice, she couldn't get close to her house being as well-ordered as this one.

The living room had been decorated in a palette of white, ice blue and pale gray. Two large sofas faced each other. She and Andrew sat in one while Boyd's parents sat in the other. The teenagers were perched on two chairs. They weren't physically together, but they still seemed oddly united.

Boyd was a tall, skinny sixteen-year-old with too-long dark hair and hunched posture. Looking at him, Gabby would guess he was more into computer games than sports. Surprising. She would have guessed Makayla was more the jock type. But what did she know? This time last week she would have laughed off the notion of her fifteen-year-old stepdaughter being pregnant.

His parents—Thomas, not Tom, and Lisa—had identical looks of disapproval and judgment, with a bit of pinchy face thrown in. Gabby had the brief thought that she should have downed a shot of something before the drive over. Maybe being tipsy would take the edge off. An inappropriate giggle wouldn't make things any worse.

At least Candace wasn't here to add her two cents to the uncomfortable mix. Andrew had put a call in to her, not saying what was wrong, but asking to speak to her. She'd texted back saying she was traveling in Europe and couldn't possibly be bothered until she was home.

Gabby looked around at the tall vases, the view of the pool, the draperies that were probably silk. The differences in their lifestyles weren't about money. They were about having five-year-olds and pets. Gabby resisted the urge to glance down at her shirt to make sure there weren't any stains.

She became aware of the silence filling the room. Since the slightly awkward introductions, there hadn't been any conversation. She reached for Andrew's hand. He gave hers a slight squeeze, then took a breath.

"It seems we have a problem," he began.

"We do." Lisa, a tall, slender brunette with small eyes, turned her attention to Gabby. "A problem your daughter created."

Gabby stiffened. "Excuse me?"

"If you'd known what was going on in your own house, none of this would have happened. Don't you have rules?"

Of course they had rules, Gabby thought, not sure what to say. Rules that had been broken.

"We didn't do it there," Makayla said quickly. "It was here. Both times."

"Back at you," Gabby told Lisa, even as she wanted to scream at the heavens. Twice? They'd done it twice and Makayla had ended up pregnant? She knew the biology, so of course it was possible, but hardly fair.

The other woman flushed. "I'm not sure the where is what matters."

Right. Because it had mattered three seconds ago.

"I agree." Andrew leaned forward. "We have to come up with a plan that makes the most sense."

"They're children." Thomas glared at his son. "Irresponsible children. I don't understand. We talked about this, Boyd. You were supposed to wear a condom."

"How about not sleeping with a fifteen-year-old?" Gabby snapped, not sure where the words came from.

Andrew squeezed her hand. "Gabby," he murmured.

She nodded, knowing she wasn't helping.

Lisa rolled her eyes. "It's not Boyd. Don't expect me to believe this was Makayla's first time. I'm sure she seduced him."

"What?" The word exploded from Gabby's lips.

"It was," Boyd said quickly. "I swear. There was blood and she cried. Mom, you're not helping."

Gabby felt bile rising in her throat. She was going to be sick—right there on the pale gray rug. Talk about a bitch. The situation was difficult enough, but Lisa was making it worse. She risked a glance at Makayla, who was staring at her lap, her fingers twisting together. Gabby wanted to run over and hold her until all this went away. But that wasn't an option.

Andrew cleared his throat. Gabby recognized the sound. It was him trying to keep control.

"If we're done trying to assign blame," he said, his voice low, "perhaps we could work on a solution."

"We have one." Boyd reached for Makayla's hand. "We're in love."

"Dear God, you're sixteen." Thomas glared at his son. "You're too young to know what love is. Or good judgment, apparently."

"We want to be together," Boyd said stubbornly.

"And have our baby," Makayla added.

Not a surprise, Gabby thought, but a kick in the gut all the same. How on earth were they going to keep a baby? Raise it? There were other options. While she supported a woman's right to choose, she wasn't sure how far along Makayla was in her pregnancy. If the teen was talking about being in love and raising her child, then abortion was off the table. Which left adoption. Weren't infants supposed to be sought-after?

"You're not getting married," Lisa said flatly. "You're too young."

"We can wait." Boyd raised his chin. "Makayla and I are going to stay together."

Gabby had to give the kid kudos for standing up to his parents. She wondered if that happened very often and had to guess that it didn't. Would he be able to stay strong or would they work on him until he caved?

Her gaze shifted to Makayla. The teen stared at Boyd with hope and love. They were both so young. They had no idea what they were facing.

"We need some time," Andrew said. "We know what these two want. Gabby and I need to talk about where we are in all this. I assume, Thomas, that you and Lisa want to do the same. Let's agree to talk in a couple of weeks."

For the first time since they'd walked into the house, Lisa smiled. "That's an excellent idea, Andrew. We just found out and we all need time to process the information. Why don't you and I stay in touch?"

Because she and Thomas were lessor mortals in the *My kid is pregnant* club?

Gabby shook off her annoyance. She was going to have to deal with Lisa for the next few months. Possibly longer if, God forbid, there was any reality to the plan of Makayla and Boyd staying together and raising their baby.

Chapter Eleven

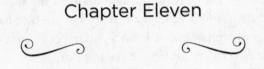

Pescadores was a popular Mischief Bay seafood restaurant. Nicole knew there was some complicated history between this place and The Original Seafood Company down the street. People often assumed that any part of metropolitan Los Angeles was faceless and nameless due to size and population, but they would be wrong. There were small town-like enclaves everywhere and Mischief Bay was one of them. Feuds flared up, people took sides, words were spoken, shopping decisions made. Then time passed and no one could remember why they never went to a particular deli, but the rules stayed in place.

All of which was terribly interesting and not the least bit relevant, Nicole thought as she got out of her car but kept hold of the door handle. It was nerves. Fluttering, twisting, nausea-inducing nerves. She'd never been one to self-medicate beyond the occasional glass of wine, but this seemed like a really good time to start. Did she know anyone who might have a prescription for Valium or Xanax? She didn't want a whole pill. Just half. Something to take the edge off.

It was Saturday night. A traditional date night. She knew that. She used to date, back in the day. But that had been about eight years and a whole marriage ago. Now she was a divorced, single mom who didn't know what on earth she'd been thinking when she'd said yes to Jairus's invitation.

She felt stupid. And out of place. Not to mention confused. Everything was wrong. Her dress, her hair, her being here in the first place. Two days ago, she'd realized she had nothing to wear. She'd borrowed a dress from her friend Shannon, a pretty floral print number with a square neckline, scooped back, fitted to the waist before flaring out.

Nicole hadn't recognized the name on the label, but she was pretty sure it was a designer dress that had cost more than a couple of months' mortgage. But Shannon had been generous and hadn't mentioned how much it had cost. Nor had she pushed to know the event it was needed for beyond Nicole's slightly untrue, "I've been invited to a client thing." Which sounded like a house party or benefit. Not a date.

This was *all* his fault, she told herself. If that stupid man hadn't asked her out, she would be home now with Tyler. Watching a movie, eating popcorn. She would be comfortable. Content. She would not be afraid she was going to throw up.

"Hi."

She jumped—a serious mistake in three-inch heels—and turned to find Jairus walking toward her. Her first thought was that he looked good in a dark blue shirt and black pants. His hair was still too long, but he'd shaved. He was smiling. A sexy, happy-to-see-you kind of smile that made her tummy even more unstable.

"Hi," she managed to answer, then told herself she had to let go of the door handle. At some point he would be expecting her to walk into the restaurant with him and wouldn't that be awkward with her dragging a car behind?

Jairus tilted his head. "You okay?"

"Fine." She should have stopped there. Instead, sadly, she

kept talking. "I'm nervous. About this. The date. That it's not going to go well. Or that you're annoyed about meeting here instead of picking me up at the house. It's just, I don't really know you, so why would I trust you? Plus Tyler. He loves B the D and you're, well, you know who you are. I don't want him thinking things. I don't know what they would be, but something."

She ordered herself to stop talking. If she didn't stop voluntarily, she was going to be forced to physically hold her lips together. Which meant she really, really had to let go of the door handle.

She did both—releasing the metal and shutting her mouth. She even managed a tight smile. She hoped it looked less scary than it felt.

"B the D?" he asked.

"It's short for—"

"Oh, I know what it's short for." The sexy smile returned. "It's kind of cute. B the D. Like his street name."

"I'm not sure a pudgy red dragon gets to have a street name."

The smile faded. "Pudgy?"

"Kind of."

"He's big-boned. And a dragon. They're not skinny on purpose. Brad's a good-looking dragon."

His defense of a fictitious creature eased some of her nerves. "Sorry. I wasn't trying to disrespect Brad."

"He's not fat."

"I got that. Just big-boned."

"And a dragon."

"Absolutely. A very fit, handsome dragon."

Jairus studied her. "You're mocking me."

"A little, but that's okay."

"From your perspective. Ready to go in?"

She was. Breathing was easier and her stomach had settled. They started for the restaurant.

"You look good," he said as he held open the door. "Very good."

"Thank you. Um, you, too."

Pescadores was decorated with a distinct nautical theme, but they hadn't gone over the top. There were a few anchors and seascapes on the wall and there was plenty of wood and rope between booths, but other than that, it was a simple and elegant restaurant. The tablecloths were white, the plates heavy and the servers quiet and knowledgeable.

Nicole and Jairus were shown to a table by the window with a view of the marina. As soon as she sat down, the nerves returned and with them, the need to bolt. Even thinking about Brad being "big-boned" didn't seem to help.

"You all right?" Jairus asked.

"Mostly. I don't, um, date that much. Since the divorce." She set her small handbag next to her and leaned forward. "I can't figure out if I'm being careful or shutting myself off. I know how my friends would vote on that one."

"Shutting yourself off?"

"Totally."

"I knew there had to be a reason you didn't jump at the chance to go out with me. Now I know what it is."

She laughed. "You're not all that."

"I am. Really. Ask anyone."

Humor twinkled in his eyes. Nicole relaxed a little. Their server came and told them about the specials, then took their drink orders. Nicole knew she would be driving at the end of the evening, so she got a glass of chardonnay. Something she could sip over several hours.

"You're divorced?" Jairus asked when the server had left.

"Yes. Eric..." What? Left? That sounded too dramatic,

even though it was the truth. "He wanted to be a screen-writer. So he quit his job to write a screenplay. The problem is we didn't discuss it first. He quit and told me two days later. It was terrifying."

Jairus leaned toward her. "Of course it was. What the hell. You're partners. You talk about stuff when you're married."

"According to Eric, he didn't say anything because he knew I wouldn't support his dream."

"Was he right?"

"I have no way of knowing. Seriously, I can argue both sides of it. So I supported him while he wrote and surfed."

Jairus groaned. "No. Do not tell me he's giving writers a bad name."

"He is. Kind of. But it turned out he was talented. He sold his screenplay for a lot of money. A couple of months after that, he moved out." She shrugged. "I was completely surprised and yet not at all, if that makes sense."

"It does."

"We'd grown apart. He wanted different things. I'm okay with that. People change. It's just, he has a son and he never sees him. Eric pays his child support on time but he won't show up. He has Tyler one Sunday every other week and he blows him off more than half the time. It's horrible."

"I'm sorry."

"Me, too. The worst of it, Tyler doesn't talk about him anymore. It's like he doesn't miss him. I guess you can't miss what you don't remember. I keep hoping that one day Eric is going to wake up and realize what he's lost, but what if he doesn't?"

She paused for breath, only to realize how much she'd been talking. And about what?

"Oh, no." She pressed the tips of her fingers to her nose,

then dropped her hands onto her lap. "So, if you weren't convinced before that I don't date much, you have clarity now."

"It's fine."

"It's a little scary. You should be checking out the closest exit."

"It's behind me and I'm fine."

Their server appeared with their drinks. Jairus asked that they have some time before ordering.

When they were alone again, he raised his glass. "To your dating life."

"It might be dangerous to toast that," she told him.

"I'm willing to risk it if you are."

He was nice, she thought. That was unexpected. "What about you?" she asked. "Tell me something incriminating or at the very least, personal. So we're even."

He'd ordered a vodka tonic. Now he moved the glass against the tablecloth. "I'm divorced, as well."

"I'm sorry."

"It happens." He glanced at her, then away. "I had an older sister, Alice. She had Down syndrome. She loved picture books and we would read them together. One day, when I was about eight, it was raining and my mom couldn't take us to the library to get more books. I forget why. So I started drawing. Those scratches eventually became Brad."

He smiled. "Alice loved Brad. She thought up some of the story lines. We had fun. I would write and draw and she would color him. She's the one who said he had to be red."

Nicole told herself it was rude to stare, even on a date, but she couldn't look away. Nothing he was telling her was what she'd thought. *He* wasn't what she'd thought. Wasn't what she'd read in that online article.

"I knew that when my parents were gone, I would be responsible for Alice. I wanted that. So when I was older and started dating, that was always in the back of my mind."

"Oh, no," she breathed.

"Yeah. You guessed right. By college, I was getting serious about Brad. I looked for a publisher and I was lucky. He sold and he sold well. Then I met Mindy, who was sweet and sexy and claimed to love Alice."

"But she didn't."

"No. My parents were killed while traveling and Alice moved in with us. Within a couple of months Mindy was talking about how Alice would be happier with her kind." His mouth twisted. "Those were her exact words. *Her kind.* Like she wasn't human. That was the day our marriage ended, at least for me. We fought more but in the end it came down to a choice. Mindy or my sister."

Nicole was torn between being impressed and so incredibly sad. Eric couldn't even suck it up enough to see his son for an afternoon. Jairus had stepped up without question.

"Mindy didn't get it," she said quietly.

"Not even close. A few months later, Alice got pneumonia and died."

Nicole stiffened. "Oh, no. I'm sorry. That's horrible."

"It was. She'd always had trouble with her lungs, but I'd hoped she would live a long, happy life. I was with her until the end."

"Of course you were."

"Mindy came back."

"What?" Her voice came out louder than she'd planned. She cleared her throat. "Sorry, but are you kidding? Like you'd take her back after what she did? You could never trust her. Alice was your sister. It wasn't the promise, it was that you loved her." She clamped her hand over her mouth. "Oh, no. You didn't take her back, did you? Because if you did…"

He raised his eyebrows. "You just stuck your foot in it?"

"Technically, yes, but you're an idiot, so I would say we're even."

He laughed then. A big, happy laugh that had her laughing with him.

"I didn't take her back."

"I'm glad."

"She was pissed."

Nicole rolled her eyes. "Oh, please. She was in it for the money."

The brows went up again.

She swore silently. Really? Was she that bad at the whole dating thing? "Um, what I meant was you're so amazing, I'm sure she was crushed."

"Better. And you're right. She was in it for the money."

"And you."

"Yeah. Sure." He took a sip of his drink. "So, you read some stuff about me online, didn't you? Bad stuff."

She did her best not to flush. "What? No. Never. Maybe. Yes."

He grinned. "I figured. Mindy got a friend who works for an online gossip site to write it. The article got picked up and circulated. For what it's worth, I don't spend my days counting my money or whatever it was they said."

"Good to know." They looked at each other. She reached her hand across the table. "I'm sorry about Alice."

"Me, too." He rested his fingers on hers. "Brad and I miss her."

Nicole carefully withdrew her hand. "You and Brad? You speak to Brad?"

"Sure. We're partners."

"That's, um, nice."

The grin returned. "Gotcha."

She groaned. "I hoped you were pretending, but he's a compelling guy, so it's hard to be sure."

They ordered, then had dinner. Conversation stayed on a slightly more informational-slash-superficial level. Jairus was from Mischief Bay and had gone to the California Institute of the Arts—a school found by Walt Disney. Nicole told him about her dance scholarship at Arizona State and her disastrous attempt to make it in New York. When she happened to glance at her watch, she was shocked to find over three hours had passed.

"I told Cecelia I wouldn't be late," she explained, as they got up to leave.

"I had a good time," Jairus told her as they walked outside. "I'd like to see you again."

They reached her car and she faced him. The sun had set. The parking lot was well lit, but the quality of light was different than daylight. Still, he looked good. Even better, he'd been easy to talk to. He was a decent guy. These days that was so much more important than handsome.

"I enjoyed this, as well. But I have to tell you something."

"I'm listening."

She sighed. "It's Brad."

"The dragon?"

"Yeah. He's, ah…" She pressed her lips together. "Sometimes he drives me crazy. All the merchandise, the stories. I know he's a good role model, but he is everywhere in my life. Did you know there are Brad chapter books?"

One corner of Jairus's mouth twitched. "Yes. I wrote them."

"Oh, right. Well, that means Brad and I are going to be together for a few more years. It's not that I hate him, but if you're expecting me to be wild about him, I'm not. And if your whole house is a shrine to Brad, then there's a problem, because I am not a groupie."

"You're saying you're not in this for my cartoon alter ego?"

"Exactly."

"Good."

He leaned forward and kissed her. Just a light brush of his mouth against hers. Simple. Easy. A little zing whipped through her, starting at her toes and working its way up. When Jairus straightened, she was the tiniest bit out of breath.

"I'm going to call you," he promised.

"Okay."

"You're going to answer."

She grinned. "I will."

"We'll do this again."

"I'd like that."

He waited until she got in her car, then waved and walked away. She drove out of the parking lot, then turned toward her house. As she pulled into her driveway, her phone buzzed. She parked, then looked at her phone.

I'm not calling. It's too soon to call, because that would make me look needy. I'm saying good night. Brad says good night, too, but you probably don't want to know that.

Nicole laughed, then tapped her phone. Tell Brad I'm sorry I judged him so harshly.

He understands. He's a forgiving sort of guy.

Nice to know. I had a good time.

Me, too. Night.

Nicole walked up to the front door. Dating wasn't so hard, she thought happily. At least not anymore.

Andrew poured two glasses of brandy and handed one to Gabby. She settled at one end of the big leather sofa in his office. The kids were in bed, the office door closed for privacy. Boomer lay on the ottoman and Jasmine was stretched along the back of the sofa. Andrew took his seat and closed his eyes.

"Hell of a Saturday," he said.

"I know." Gabby inhaled the scent of the brandy before taking a sip. Dieting meant trying to avoid liquor, but she thought maybe an exception could be made considering what they'd been through.

"Thomas seems reasonable," she murmured. "But Lisa's just awful."

"She runs the family and she's going to be difficult." Andrew took a drink, then leaned back and scratched Jasmine under the ears. "Boyd's not staying."

"What do you mean?"

He shifted his gaze to her. "They're not going to be together long."

"No way. They're in love. He defended her to his mother and from what we've seen of Lisa, that can't be easy."

Andrew raised one shoulder. "Did you see his eyes? He wouldn't look at her. Or any of us. Sure, what he did has screwed up everything, but he's a sixteen-year-old kid who got a girl pregnant. He's a stud."

Despite everything, Gabby smiled. "I don't think anyone says stud anymore."

"Then whatever the word is. He's the man. I know he said all the right stuff, but he's not long for the relationship. Makayla's going to be crushed."

Gabby knew there would be pain, but she had to admit

that in the scheme of things, losing the boyfriend would be the least of it. At the end of the day, there would still be a baby to deal with.

"We'll know more in a couple of weeks—at least when it comes to Boyd," Andrew said. "But in the meantime…"

Gabby nodded. "A thousand things to deal with."

"I'm going to have to tell Candace when she gets back from her trip."

"Assuming she will make time for the call." She sipped her brandy. "Was that too bitchy?"

"Not at all."

"Good, because she's going to blame me."

"You don't know that."

"Really?"

"Okay, she's going to blame you. I'll be sure she knows it didn't happen here."

Gabby settled more deeply into the sofa. "Twice. Did you hear that? They did it twice and Makayla is pregnant. Poor Hayley can't carry a baby to term and she's desperate for a child. It doesn't seem fair."

For a second she thought about mentioning they could give Hayley the baby, thereby solving several problems at once. But it was too soon, not to mention awkward. Once Makayla decided to give up the baby, there would be issues to deal with—both legal and emotional. Having the child living a mile away might mean never getting over what she'd been through.

She sipped her brandy. "I'll do some research," she said. "If you're right about Boyd and he's going to bail, then we need to be prepared. I'm assuming you're not excited about the two of them staying together forever and raising the child together?"

"God, no. They're too young."

She felt herself relax a little. Good. At least they were on the same page when it came to Makayla giving up the baby.

"Candace isn't going to take this well. Even if she doesn't blame me, she's going to freak." Gabby thought about the other people who would have to know. "I want to wait to tell my parents. And the twins. They don't need to know yet."

Andrew sighed. "I know it's wrong and selfish, but I keep thinking how this is going to affect us. What people are going to say. That we're to blame."

"We are the parents. Makayla lives with us."

"Think we can get a sign that says *Don't blame us. She didn't do it in our house*?"

"Technically, we can, but I don't think it's very helpful." Besides, Andrew would have it easy. He would head off to work and she would be the one taking Makayla to the doctor's appointments and…

"Crap. She needs to see a doctor." Gabby put down her drink and pulled her cell phone out of her jeans pocket. "I'll send myself a note so we can get in as quickly as possible. We don't even know how pregnant she is."

"She didn't say?"

"Not really. She says two or three months, but I'm not sure I believe her. She's young and skinny. She could be four months along. You know there are all those news stories about teenagers hiding their pregnancy with baggy shirts."

She typed the note and emailed it to herself. "You're right. Everyone is going to judge us." Her mostly. She was the mother figure and therefore the one to blame.

He slid his glass onto the coffee table, then leaned forward and gathered her into his arms. "I couldn't do this without you, Gabby. You know that, don't you? You're my everything."

She hung on to him. "You're mine. We'll figure it out. Step by step."

"I'm sorry I didn't listen when you told me about them kissing. I still can't believe it. She's a kid."

While it was too late to change anything, hearing the apology was kind of nice. She let herself relax against him. Tomorrow was plenty of time to panic. Right now they had the beginnings of a plan and each other. Until morning, that was enough.

Chapter Twelve

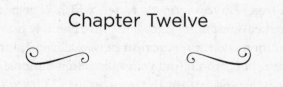

"The location is perfect," Lindsey Woods, an attractive fifty-something blonde, said as she walked through the living room.

"We're going to be painting," Hayley told her, hoping she sounded calmer than she felt. "In the kitchen I thought we could replace the hardware."

"Inexpensive bang for the buck."

Lindsey moved into that room and looked out the back window. "Nice layout. It hasn't been renovated, but I think there are buyers who would rather do that themselves. To be honest, you're better off letting the price reflect the lack of updating than to do a cheap job on the sly. Most buyers today aren't fooled."

Hayley smiled and nodded, anxious about how long the appointment was taking. She only had an hour before she had to be back at work. But Lindsey had promised to be quick as she viewed the house. Once she assessed the property, she would get some comps from other homes in the area, then write up a full report. It would include a marketing plan, a suggested price, along with easy, inexpensive fixes to get the house ready to be listed.

Armed with that information, Hayley would then have the job of convincing Rob this was the right thing to do.

Lindsey checked out the bedrooms, then did a quick tour of the backyard. When she walked back into the kitchen, she nodded.

"It's lovely, just as you said. The age of the house isn't really an issue. Buyers want character, which your home has. The market is booming right now. Mischief Bay is a sought-after location and the school district is excellent. I think with very little TLC, you'll find yourself fielding multiple offers."

Hayley leaned against the door frame. "That would be great." A bidding war would be better. They needed to get at least a hundred thousand dollars from the sale but more would be better. More would mean having money to put down on another house.

They probably wouldn't be able to purchase in Mischief Bay at that point, but maybe somewhere close so Rob didn't have to commute. She didn't love the idea of moving into an apartment, but that couldn't be helped. She'd thought and thought, and short of winning the lottery, there was simply no other way to raise that kind of money for her treatment in Switzerland.

"It will take me a couple of days to get everything together," Lindsey told her. "Let's say by end of business Wednesday? I'll email the material to you."

"Thank you."

As Hayley started toward the front door, she heard a car pull into the driveway. She pressed a hand to her chest. No! Why was Rob home now? He was supposed to be at work. She'd deliberately scheduled the appointment with Lindsey in the middle of the day.

The front door opened and Rob walked in. "Hayley? I saw your car. Are you okay?"

Lindsey walked toward him, her hand outstretched. "This is nice. I didn't think we were going to get the chance for introductions today. I'm Lindsey Woods, Rob. Nice to meet you."

Rob shook her hand, then pushed up his glasses. "Hayley, what's going on?"

Lindsey's smile faded. "I'm the real-estate agent your wife called. I'm here to look over the house. For when you list it?"

Rob looked between them. "I see."

Hayley had no idea what to say. Rob wasn't an idiot. He would figure out that she'd done all this behind his back. He would know why, too. Because he didn't want to sell the house. He didn't want her to keep trying to have a baby. He wanted her to give up.

Lindsey hesitated a second, as if sensing tension and not sure if she should say anything. Then she smiled again. "All right. I'll see myself out. Hayley, I'll be touch."

The door closed behind her.

The house was quiet. Hayley heard the refrigerator kick on. She waited for Rob to say something. When he didn't, she wondered if he was expecting her to speak first. Maybe to apologize.

She knew that it was wrong to go behind his back, but it wasn't as if she was going to sell the house without his permission. She just wanted to get all her facts together. They needed the money. He had to see that.

"I forgot my lunch," he said, at last looking at her. "I came home to get it."

"Oh."

Rob walked past her to the kitchen. He collected his lunch from the refrigerator, then walked back to the front door and opened it.

"I can't believe you'd do something like this," he said, staring out at their yard. "I knew having a baby was important to you, but I didn't think..." He swallowed. "The doctor was really clear, Hayley. You can't get pregnant again. You need surgery."

"I'm not going to have it. I don't care what she said. I want to try the treatment in Switzerland." Her voice was pleading. "Rob, you have to understand that I need to do this. Having a baby is the most important thing to me. It always has been. We need this."

He looked at her for a long time. "Whatever happened when you were growing up has nothing to do with us now. We don't need a baby, Hayley. Not to be happy. We need each other. We need our marriage to work."

"I need the baby."

"More than anything. Yeah. I got that." He shook his head. "I'll see you tonight."

Hayley waited until he'd driven away before leaving herself. She felt unsettled inside, and a little scared. Rob wasn't the type to scream, but he'd been too calm and quiet. He had to be mad.

As she drove home after work that afternoon, she tried to figure out what she was going to say. Maybe if she admitted she'd been wrong to talk to the agent without him, he would understand. If not, she was back to where she always was, trying to explain the emptiness inside her. The need to connect on a biological level. She knew nothing about her birth family. The adoption had been closed and she'd been unable to find out anything. She was a single entity in a sea of connected families. She wanted what most everyone else took for granted.

Just one baby. Was that asking too much? A baby of her own. Of their own.

She pulled onto their street and was surprised to find Rob's car already in the driveway.

The fact that he was early could be both good and bad. He

probably wanted to talk, but maybe he'd realized why they had to do this. Maybe he finally understood just how much she needed to have a child of her own. To not adopt or foster. To give birth.

The living room was empty. She heard noises coming from the bedroom and went down the small hallway.

A suitcase lay open on the bed, shirts and slacks lying next to it. Socks and underwear filled part of it. Rob walked in from the bathroom, jeans and T-shirts draped over his arm.

"You're home," he said. "Good. I didn't want to have to leave a note."

Her heart raced. She felt each breath as if it were a unique sensation. There wasn't pain, but there was something. Something that left a bitter, metallic taste—like blood—on her tongue.

"You're leaving." Not a question. Of course he was leaving—the man had a suitcase. You didn't pack a suitcase if you weren't leaving.

He started folding clothes. "I'll get the rest of my stuff over the weekend."

"Rob, you can't just go."

"I have to."

"But we're married." *You love me.* She nearly said the words, then thought perhaps that wasn't the best argument right now.

He put down the half-folded shirt and faced her. His mouth was straight, his jaw determined. He wasn't angry. Maybe resigned? "I love you, Hayley. You're right. We're married and I thought we were a team. But what you did today… I can't forgive that."

"I wasn't going to sell the house without talking to you. I wanted information so we could make a decision together. I was just getting information."

"You think that matters? You lied to me. You didn't want

to fix up this place for us. You planned to sell it all along. I thought we were making a start. A fresh start. We talked about the yard and the bathrooms. It was all a crock. You betrayed more than me. You betrayed us."

"No." Tears burned, but she blinked them back. "Rob, don't. Stay. We can talk about this."

"Are you still determined to get pregnant and have a baby?"

"Of course."

He turned back to his packing. "That's what I thought."

"You're going to leave me because I want a child? That's horrible."

He spun toward her, his eyes wide and dark. "No. I'm leaving because I won't watch you kill yourself. Did you hear what the doctor said? You are going to die. You need a hysterectomy, Hayley. If you don't get one, you're at risk of bleeding out. Every single day I wonder if this is it. If I'm going to get a call saying you're gone. That it's too late. Every day."

She sank onto the straight-back chair in the corner. "You never said anything."

"I don't talk about it. I figure you're under enough stress. You want a baby. I get that. I know you've always felt your parents loved Morgan more than you. That's not true, but me saying it doesn't help. So we've tried. We've tried everything." His voice softened. "Hayley, you have to stop. You have to accept there are simply some things your body can't do. We have each other, and we can get a child another way."

"No. I need my own baby. I need to be part of something. I need the connection."

"You're part of us."

She looked at him. He stared at her for a second before turning back to the suitcase.

"Yeah," he said slowly. "It's not enough. I know. That's why I'm leaving. I want children, but I want you more. You can't say that and because of your obsession, you're going to die. I can't do this anymore. I can't watch it happen."

Tears spilled onto her cheeks. "Rob, no. I need you."

He didn't bother looking at her. "No you don't. You can get sperm anywhere." He put in the last shirt, then zipped up the suitcase. "Look at the bright side. If we split up, we'll sell the house. Maybe your half will be enough to pay for what you want."

"That's mean."

"Maybe, but it's the truth." He looked around the room, then back at her. "If you change your mind, give me a call. If you don't, good luck. I hope I'm wrong. I hope you continue to heal and everything is fine. But I don't think so. I do love you. So very much. But I can't be a part of you killing yourself. Not anymore."

He picked up the suitcase and walked out. Hayley heard the front door close, then the sound of his car engine. Silence followed. Silence broken only by the sharpness of her desperate sobs.

Whoever said it took twenty-one days to form a habit, hadn't been dealing with the complication of a pregnant fifteen-year-old, Gabby thought as she settled into the corner of the sofa in Andrew's office. She'd been on her diet well over three weeks and still wanted to eat the entire house. Preferably doused in chocolate and whipped cream. The stress wasn't helping at all.

On the bright side, there was something comforting about knowing that her day was going to end here—with her husband. The two of them discussing what was going on. Which so far had been nothing. Still, connecting seemed to be helping them both.

He held up the bottle of brandy. She shook her head.

"I'm still going to class at Nicole's studio. I'm not sure I see the sense of working that hard, then drinking the calories later."

"I'm impressed," he told her.

"Thanks. I think the class makes me feel as if I'm in control of something."

He sat next to her and laced his fingers with hers. "What a mess."

"It is, but we're getting through it." It was day three of having learned about Makayla's pregnancy, so they still had a long way to go, but still. A start. "I appreciate that you canceled your business trip to stay home this week. It helps."

"It's the least I can do. Anything to report?"

Gabby thought about her day. "I made an appointment for Makayla with my doctor's office. The practice is all women, so that will help, but it's not going to be easy." There was peeking and probing when one was pregnant. When the mother-to-be was excited about having a baby, the visits were a small price to pay.

"Thanks for doing that," Andrew said. "Candace texted and asked if she could trade this coming weekend for the next one. I agreed, mostly because it means putting off telling her, at least for a couple of weeks."

"I would have done the same," Gabby told him.

She shifted so she could lean against him. He put his arm around her.

"Candace is going to tell her to have an abortion."

"We don't know how far along she is."

"I'm sure she'll offer to find a doctor who will do it anyway."

Gabby sighed. "Makayla is fifteen. This is traumatic enough without throwing that into the mix. She says she wants to have the baby. I don't think we need to push her into any other decision right now." There would be plenty of time to get the adoption process going once they had more information.

"We are talking about Candace," he pointed out. "This is the same woman who didn't understand why she had to give up three weeks of work after having a baby. I swear, if it had been up to her, she would have gone back to the office the next day."

Gabby believed it. Candace had been the one to change the parenting plan to spend less time with her daughter, not more. Whatever her thoughts on Makayla getting pregnant, the conversation wasn't going to go well.

"This is going to be my first grandchild," Andrew said with a sigh. "Not how I imagined it."

Gabby sat up and faced him. "That means I'm…" She couldn't say it.

He smiled. "No. She's your stepdaughter. It's different."

"Not really. I'm thirty-three. I can't be a grandmother." She was the mother of five-year-olds. That was more age-appropriate. "We are not having this conversation."

"Yes, ma'am."

He pulled her close again and she relaxed against him. A grandmother. Impossible. Well, she just wouldn't think about it. At least not for tonight.

Gary's Café had been around forever. The original Gary had been dead at least twenty years and when his widow had sold the place, there'd been concern about changes. But the new owners had respected the idea of great food in an old-fashioned setting and had kept everything exactly the same. So despite three spruces and one complete remodel, Gary's

Café still had red vinyl booths, the specials written on a chalk-board and the best burgers in town.

Hayley stared at the familiar sign over the low, one-story restaurant and told herself that she was getting out. Having lunch with friends. That was good. A distraction, which was something she desperately needed in her life. Because if she stopped moving, stopped doing things, she would start think-ing, and thinking meant having to feel something. She didn't want to feel anything.

Rob still wasn't back. It had been nearly a week. He'd gone by while she was working—just as he'd said he would—and collected the rest of his things. He hadn't phoned, hadn't been in touch in any way. He was just gone.

She couldn't believe it. They were married. A couple. She thought he loved her. Yet he'd walked away without look-ing back.

She knew she was still in shock—and that was probably for the best. She didn't want to have to deal with all the messiness and pain when the truth set in. Disbelief and a little righteous indignation were far easier to manage.

As she collected her purse and got out of her car, she thought about how much she missed him. Their small house echoed without him. The bed was too big, the nighttime hours too long.

She wasn't sleeping and it was difficult to eat. In the hours between four in the morning and dawn, she allowed herself to admit the truth. That Rob had every right to be furious with her. Not for wanting to try to have a baby—that was her decision. But about the house. Going behind his back like that had been wrong and she knew it.

She crossed to the entrance to the diner and saw that Ni-cole was already there.

"How's it going?" her friend asked, giving her a quick hug. Nicole paused. "Are you okay?"

"I'm fine. A little tired." Hayley forced a smile and hoped it looked natural. She still hadn't decided if she was going to tell anyone about Rob leaving. "How about with you?"

"I'm doing well. Busy with work. The usual." Nicole glanced away, as if she had something else to say, but before Hayley could press her, Gabby joined them.

There were more hugs before they were seated at a booth, with Hayley seated on one side and the other two on the other. Their server took their drink orders right away, before leaving to let them look over the menu. Hayley told herself having lunch with her friends would make her feel better. If nothing else, the love and support would help and she certainly needed the meal.

Gabby studied Nicole. "What?" she demanded. "There's something."

"Seriously? You can tell?"

That got Hayley's attention. "What happened?"

"I had a date with Jairus," Nicole blurted.

Hayley had no idea who that was. Even more startling was her friend going out. Nicole hadn't been on a date since the divorce was final. "Did I know you were interested in someone?"

"Who's Jairus?" Gabby asked at the same time.

Nicole groaned. "You're going to make me say it?"

"Apparently," Gabby murmured. "Why does that name sound familiar?"

Nicole raised her eyebrows and waited.

"Jairus… Jairus… OMG, you went out with Brad the Dragon."

"The author of *Brad*," Nicole corrected. "I've been out of

the single world for a long time, but not so long that I have to resort to dating fictional characters."

"You went on a date!" Gabby hugged her. "Good for you. How was it? Not that it matters. You did it. The second time won't be so scary. So how was it?"

Nicole wrinkled her nose. "Better than I thought," she admitted. "He was nice and we had a good time. He made me laugh and that was unexpected."

"That's great," Hayley said, happy for her friend.

"It's unexpected," Nicole admitted. "I'm confused about the whole thing."

"Are you going to see him again?" Hayley asked.

The server arrived with their iced teas. Everyone ordered the burger special—the house burger topped with guacamole and bacon.

Nicole waited until she'd left to say, "I am. Even if nothing comes of it, I could sure use the practice. But it feels very strange, I have to tell you."

"What does Tyler think of all this?" Gabby asked.

"I'm not telling him. It's too soon. Plus with the whole B the D connection, he's going to get super excited. I don't want him thinking Jairus is sticking around. I mean, it was one date."

Nicole had always been sensible, Hayley thought. She ran her own business, managed her divorce with grace and strength. Nicole would never spend five years and tens of thousands of dollars chasing an impossible dream. She would figure out that she wasn't meant to have children and move on.

While Hayley admired that about her friend, she couldn't emulate it. Of course, Nicole didn't have her past.

She debated telling them about Rob but honestly didn't know what to say. She didn't want the sympathy or the comfort they would offer. Either would break through her carefully constructed shield. Then she would crumble. What if she fell apart in so many pieces there was no putting her back together?

"Okay," Gabby said, drawing in a breath. "I have something to say." She looked at Hayley. "I just don't know how."

Gabby had figured out Rob was gone, Hayley thought frantically. She didn't want to start crying. If she did, she might never stop. But how to distract her friend?

"It's about Makayla."

"What? Is she okay?"

"Yes. No. I just…" Gabby pressed her lips together. Her brown eyes were dark with emotion. "Hayley, I'm sorry. Really, really sorry. You're going to find out and I'd rather it was from me. But it's making me sick to say this."

Hayley pressed a hand to her chest. "You're scaring me."

"I don't mean to. Well, sugar. Makayla's pregnant."

Hayley waited for the "and she's dying" but Gabby didn't say anything else.

She lowered her arm to her side. Relief chased out apprehension, leaving her a little light-headed, but otherwise okay. The news was shocking, but not the worst thing ever. Why would—

And then she got it.

"Oh, Gabby." Hayley reached across the table and squeezed her friend's hand. "You're sweet to worry about me, but Makayla getting pregnant doesn't have anything to do with me beyond how it affects you. Are you okay?"

Tears filled Gabby's eyes. "No, but that's not the point. It's so unfair. I know you and Rob are trying everything and you can't stay pregnant while my fifteen-year-old stepdaughter does it twice and gets knocked up. That totally sucks."

"It does, but it's not your fault."

Nicole bumped Gabby's shoulder with her own. "She's right. This has nothing to do with any of us, but we're here for you."

"Thanks." Gabby sighed. "I appreciate your attitude. I'll admit, I was worried. You're my friend. I don't want to hurt you."

"You didn't."

"Are you sure you're okay? You seem way more calm than I thought you'd be."

"I'm a little bitter, but I can deal." Funny how two weeks ago the news would have shattered her. Although it wasn't fun to hear, it couldn't touch her. Not with Rob gone.

"How are you managing all this?" Nicole asked. "Talk about a game changer."

"I know. It's a nightmare. We were stunned when we found out. The father is only a year older. They say they're in love and they're going to stay together, no matter what, but we have our doubts. His mother is awful—that doesn't help." Gabby folded her arms across her chest. "Makayla's a kid herself. There's no good outcome. Whatever happens, her life is changed forever."

"Is she giving up the baby for adoption?" Nicole asked, darting a glance at Hayley.

"We haven't talked about it, but I'm assuming so. She can't keep it. She needs to finish high school and go to college."

"Exactly."

For a second Hayley wondered if Gabby was going to offer her the baby. On the surface, it would solve so many problems. But Hayley didn't want someone else's child and Gabby knew that.

"I'm sorry," Hayley told her. "About all of it. Poor you."

"Thanks. We're getting through it. Andrew's been great. We haven't told anyone yet. The twins don't know. We figured they could wait for a while. I'm taking Makayla to the doctor and then we'll know how far along she is. I'm guessing she's close to four months."

Hayley had gotten to four months with her first pregnancy. But after that, she'd never made twelve weeks. Not that she needed to be thinking about her miscarriages.

"You'll get through this," Hayley told her. "So will Makayla. Hopefully she'll learn from what happened."

"That would be wonderful, but I'm not holding my breath. Anyway, I wanted to tell you."

"I'm glad you did. I'm okay."

Gabby smiled at her. "I hope you are, but if you're lying to protect me, I want you to know I really, really appreciate it."

Hayley managed a laugh. "I'm not. I swear." Hearing the news wasn't fun, but compared to having lost Rob, it didn't matter at all.

Chapter Thirteen

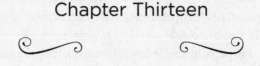

Nicole's case of nerves for her second date with Jairus was different from the one before her first date. Then she'd been worried about *dating*. It had been too long. The rules had changed. She was out of practice. She wasn't ready. Whatever. There had been a thousand reasons, but none of them had been about the man.

This time was different. This time the fluttering, slightly anxious woozy sensation was specifically about Jairus. She didn't like that. She didn't like it at all.

She hadn't wanted to like him. The man was responsible for the hell that was Brad the Dragon. But having gotten to know him a little, how could she not? He was basically a very nice man, who was also funny and sexy, and when he smiled she felt quivers.

She was doomed. Worse, she had nothing to wear.

Nicole stared at the contents of her closet and groaned. There was nothing new, nothing cute and she hadn't wanted to borrow from Shannon a second time. Once was understandable. More than that would be tacky.

But nothing she owned seemed appropriate. She was meeting Jairus for dinner at McGrath's Pub. They were having a weekend barbecue, which sounded completely casual, but wasn't. It was a special once-a-year event that required tickets. For that, she needed something cute and a little bit sexy.

White crop pants, a stylish sleeveless top and some killer flat sandals. Or a swingy little dress. What she had instead was an entire wardrobe of workout wear, ratty shorts and tank tops, and a sundress that was not only stained but at least six years old. She honestly couldn't remember the last time she'd bought herself something new. Even from a super discount store.

"Is Gabby right?" she asked herself as she studied her clothes. "Am I punishing myself for the failure of my marriage?"

Really good question, but not helpful right now. Clothes first, she told herself. Self-analysis later.

She dug through her closet again and found a white denim skirt with the tags still on it. It was shorter than she usually liked, which explained why it was unworn. She tossed the skirt on the bed and went in for a second round of closet digging. She found a couple of tank tops, along with a sleeveless wrap shirt in red. Then she turned to study her options.

The wrap shirt was adorable, but cut practically to her navel. While she exercised regularly and didn't mind being seen in tight workout clothes, she wasn't going to flash her boobs to the world. But she did have a plain white tank top. If she tucked that into the skirt and wore the red top over it, she would be layered, not exposed.

Wardrobe crisis solved.

She dashed into the bathroom and did her makeup. The event was going to be on the boardwalk, which meant sun, wind and possibly ocean spray. She pulled her long blond hair into a high ponytail, fluffed her bangs, then applied two coats of hair spray. She got dressed, remembering at the last minute to snip the tag from the skirt. While her plain brown sandals weren't killer, they would have to do. Five minutes later, she and Tyler were on their way to Pam's condo.

Pam had moved the year before, turning her two-story house over to her daughter and moving into an oceanfront condo. She'd bought the condo from their friend Shannon, who had married Adam and moved in with him. It had been a fun time of musical houses.

Nicole pulled into the visitor parking. She and Tyler went up the stairs to Pam's door. He rang the bell and they immediately heard Lulu barking.

"Okay, little girl," Pam said, her voice muffled by the closed door.

Lulu went quiet. Nicole knew that meant she'd been picked up. Nicole had a feeling that if she owned a dog it wouldn't be anywhere near as well behaved as Lulu. The little Chinese crested seemed to speak English as well as most people.

"Hi, you two," Pam said as she let them in. "Tyler, what do you think? I thought you'd appreciate Lulu's outfit."

Due to her lack of hair, Lulu had to be protected from both sun and cold. She wore sunscreen and little shirts or sweaters, depending on the season. Today Lulu sported a doggie-style tank dress in camouflage.

Tyler laughed as he petted the dog. "She's a girl."

"Girls can be soldiers," Nicole said automatically. "Maybe not Lulu, but other girls."

"Not ones that small," he pointed out.

"There is that."

"I'll admit Lulu isn't military grade." Pam set the dog on the floor. Lulu immediately ran over to greet them. "But she has a big heart."

Tyler sat down in the entryway and held out his arms. Lulu scrambled onto his lap, planted her tiny front paws on his chest and proceeded to kiss his entire face. Tyler laughed and hugged her.

Nicole let her date worry fade for a second as she appreciated the fact that Tyler was gentle and kind. Hormones and peer pressure would eventually toughen him up, she thought wistfully. But she really hoped those qualities survived the growing-up process.

"Thanks for looking after him tonight," Nicole said.

"I love having him over and you know it. It's good practice for when my grandson gets a little older, assuming Jennifer will ever relax enough to let me babysit him without her hovering all the time." Pam studied her for a second. "I have the perfect necklace for that outfit. Come with me."

Nicole followed Pam into the condo's spacious bedroom. Sliding glass doors led to a balcony that faced the beautiful Pacific Ocean. Views didn't get much better than this, she thought.

Pam crossed to a free-standing mirror and pulled on the small knob. The front of the mirror swung open to reveal a hidden jewelry cabinet. Necklaces hung from hooks and there were little shelves that held bracelets and earrings, along with spaces for rings. It was beautifully organized—no surprise, considering the jewelry's owner. Pam eyed Nicole's outfit again, then reached for a chunky silver necklace with red stones set in the shape of a daisy.

"Red coral," Pam said, as she held out the necklace. "I have matching earrings, but I think that would be too much. Your silver hoops are simple and pretty."

"Thank you." Nicole took the necklace and put it around her neck, then fastened the clasp. "I'll guard it with my life."

"No need to get crazy. Just bring it back when you come get Tyler." Pam smiled and lowered her voice. "So, you and Jairus have sex yet?"

Nicole felt herself flush. She glanced toward the half-open door, then shook her head. "It's only our second date. It takes longer than that."

"I don't know," Pam teased. "You young people today. I haven't had a first date in over thirty years. So is sex the third date? Or the fourth?"

"You make me insane." Nicole grinned. "I don't know and it won't be anytime soon, I promise."

"Which is very different than saying never. You like him."

The nerves returned, bringing with them that icky, unsettled feeling in her tummy. "I don't want to talk about it."

"That means yes."

Nicole touched the necklace. "Thank you for letting me borrow this and for looking after Tyler."

"I'm very excited about our evening together. We're having dinner at Gary's Café, then coming back here for some Lulu time and movies. Just so you know, I'm letting him stay up as late as he wants."

Nicole laughed. "You know he'll be zonked on the sofa by nine."

"I do, but we'll still have fun. As will you, I'm guessing. Even without doing you-know-what."

Nicole covered her ears. "Stop, I beg you." She hugged her friend, then went back into the living room. Tyler was sitting on the floor by the couch, Lulu next to him as he read from one of the books Pam always had around.

"Bye, sweetie," she called.

"Bye, Mom. I'll see you later."

"Yes, you will."

She waved and let herself out. Tyler was growing up so fast. He wasn't going to be her little boy much longer. She would miss that, but also looked forward to seeing what kind of man he grew into.

She took the stairs to the ground floor, then headed out onto the boardwalk. From Pam's it was an easy walk to Mc-Grath's. She was going to leave her car in Pam's visitor space rather than drive the short distance and fight for parking closer to the restaurant.

Fifteen minutes later, she spotted Jairus sitting on the short wall by the lifeguard station near the restaurant. He was looking in the opposite direction, which gave her a second to catch her breath.

He looked good. Tall and fit, with an ease about him. He was a man comfortable in his own skin. He wore jeans and a long-sleeved shirt with the sleeves rolled up to his elbows. Boat shoes with no socks and sunglasses.

He was an appealing man, she thought, not sure what to do with the information. She was pretty sure she liked him. Which left her confused. Pam's teasing question about sex hadn't helped her emotional equilibrium. What was he expecting from her? What did she want to offer?

He turned in her direction. She knew he'd spotted her because he went still for a second. Because of the sunglasses, she had no way of knowing what he was thinking.

He stood as she approached, then removed the glasses. His brown eyes were warm, his smile welcoming.

"Right on time," he said, then bent down and kissed her cheek. "You look beautiful."

"Thank you. We're not having sex tonight."

She hadn't meant to say that, exactly, but there was no way to call back the words.

Jairus looked at her for a couple of seconds, then smiled. "I can't wait to meet your friends."

"What?"

"Your friends. I look forward to meeting them. I'll bet they're a lot of fun."

"I don't understand."

He put his arm around her. "Someone said something about how long you're supposed to wait, right? Which got you thinking about dating rules and how long it had been since you had to worry about that. You freaked out, because you're not sure about any of this."

She pulled away. "How do you know that? Guys aren't supposed to be insightful. Stop it right now."

He laughed. "Sorry. I'm a writer. I observe people. I think about things. It can't be helped." The humor faded. He stepped closer to her and touched her cheek.

"Nicole, I get it. You're nervous. Hell, I'm nervous, too. You're really hot and if you were offering, I'd be there in a heartbeat. But you're not and that's okay. I can wait."

"What if it's a long wait?" she asked, her voice a whisper. "We both know you're not into hookers."

He laughed again. "I'll live, okay? I want to get to know you. I want you to get to know me. The rest of it will happen in its own time. You don't have to worry. I'll never pressure you."

She wanted to believe him because it all sounded so amazing. And she wanted him to be lying because if he was telling the truth, then she was in way over her head. How was she supposed to stay safe if he was really that honest, decent and nice?

"You look concerned," he said.

"I am, but I'll live, too."

He pointed to the restaurant. "Ready to go get your summer barbecue on?"

"I am."

They turned toward McGrath's. Nicole sucked in a breath, then, as casually as she could, reached for Jairus's hand. He laced his fingers with hers and they walked inside.

While they waited to be seated, Jairus turned to her. "You know I have a new book coming out."

"Yes. It's very exciting."

"Liar. I'll be going on tour. That means I'll be traveling on and off over the next few weeks. There's going to be a local signing. I thought you and Tyler would like to come. I can get you VIP tickets."

That was a lot of information, she thought. "There are VIP tickets?"

"Of course. Brad's a VIP kind of guy." He squeezed her fingers. "He wouldn't have to know about us, Nicole. It would just be a signing."

There was an us? A them? As in… She didn't know as in what, but knew there was no way she could ask.

"That would be very nice," she told him. "Tyler would love that. Thank you."

"Anytime." He winked. "You've made it to Brad's inner circle. Hang on, babe. It's a hell of a ride."

She was still laughing when they were shown to their table.

Hayley started the cleanup as soon as the last of the clients finished with a station. It had been another busy evening at Supper's in the Bag, with lots of happy people taking home meals for their family. She stored away the leftover food and made a note of which pantry staples they were low on. Tomorrow they would do the same thing again.

She had no idea how much money her sister made on the business, but she would guess it did reasonably well. Especially considering that Morgan only had to work about thirty hours a week.

When the customers had left, Morgan pulled out a chair and sat down. "I'm exhausted. Being a small business owner is crap. I wish I'd married someone rich so I could stay home and not have responsibilities."

"Would be nice," Hayley said, joining her sister. Normally she was anxious to get home, but tonight there was no reason to hurry. "Being taken care of."

Morgan snorted. "Like you'd ever let that happen. You're always working."

Not because she wanted to, Hayley thought. To earn money to pay for her various treatments. No one enjoyed working sixty hours a week.

Morgan leaned forward and pulled another chair close, then put her feet up and sighed. "Brent is making me crazy. That man. He's just so into the kids. There are too many activities and he wants to be a part of them all. But on Saturday morning he never remembers I need him."

"Most women would be thrilled their husband was devoted to the children."

"That's a crock. What about me? What about my needs? Maybe I made a mistake picking him."

Hayley liked Brent a lot. He was a hardworking guy who wanted to do the right thing. He deserved someone who made him happy. Unfortunately for him, he had a wife whose first concern was herself.

Just another way she and her sister were different, Hayley thought. Morgan had always had a plan. Find a good guy and get married. She hadn't been interested in a career. She wanted what she saw as an easy life—being a wife and a mother.

Brent had been interested in a family, too, but first he'd wanted to finish college and maybe go to grad school for his MBA. He'd talked to Morgan about his ambitions and had encouraged her to develop her own. She'd assumed his graduation celebration would include a marriage proposal. Instead, he'd told her he'd been accepted at several grad schools, including a couple back East. Not only hadn't he proposed, but he'd started talking about them seeing other people while he was gone.

Morgan had gotten pregnant within a few weeks. Brent had done the right thing. He'd bought a ring and gotten down on one knee. Morgan had pretended to be shocked, then she'd accepted. They were married two months later and his dream of getting an MBA was never discussed again.

"Brent's a sweetie and he loves you," Hayley pointed out. "Be grateful for what you have."

"Why? You got the good husband. I should have made a play for Rob instead."

Hayley felt her mouth drop open at her sister's ugly statement. Did Morgan really think that Rob would have preferred her to Hayley, if only he'd had the chance?

Hayley reminded herself that Rob had never much liked her sister. That Morgan was just being Morgan. That when Rob came back, she would tell him about the conversation and he would laugh. He would hold her and tell her he loved her and—

Her eyes began to burn. Too late she realized she'd crossed that mental line that allowed her to stay in control. Longing and hurt and fear swelled inside her. She was so tired and she hurt everywhere, as if she'd fallen down stairs over and over again.

"What's wrong with you?" her sister demanded. "Your face is weird."

"Nothing. I'm fine."

"You don't look fine. Are you sick? You're not going to start bleeding, are you?"

"No. It's not that." Hayley swallowed. "Rob left me. He moved out a few days ago."

She knew that in the name of self-preservation, telling Morgan was an absolute mistake. At the same time, she wondered if she was doing this to herself deliberately. Making the wound deeper. Because she knew she'd been wrong and deserved it?

Her sister sat up. "No way. He didn't. That man is crazy about you." Her eyes narrowed. "What did you do?"

Hayley told her. About the clinic in Switzerland, what the doctor had said, the real estate agent, everything. Morgan listened openmouthed.

"You are a complete moron. You know that, right? Dear God, let it go, Hayley. You can't have a baby. Boo-hoo. Get over it. Adopt."

The words stung. "You don't understand."

Morgan rolled her eyes. "Oh, please. You're so sad. Poor little adopted girl. Your life was hell. I was loved and you were hated."

"I wasn't hated. It was different for me." Their parents had loved her, they just hadn't loved her as much. Time and again they'd allowed Morgan to have whatever she wanted—usually at Hayley's expense. Morgan was their biological child and Hayley wasn't. That was reality.

Morgan waved her hand. "Quit being such a damned drama queen. You had it easy. You were chosen. They picked you. I'm the one they got stuck with. You think I don't know that?

"Grow up. Move on. The rest of us have. You're going to lose the best thing that ever happened to you if you don't. Talk about stupid."

Hayley stood and reached for her handbag. "I have to go."

"I'm right," Morgan yelled after her. "I'm right and you know it."

Chapter Fourteen

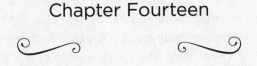

Gabby had been seeing the same gynecologist since she'd graduated college. Dr. Mansfield was part of a larger practice in the Mischief Bay area. But with a thriving practice came difficulty getting appointments, so it was nearly two weeks before she could get Makayla in to see the doctor.

Andrew had planned to talk to Candace first, to give her the option of taking her daughter to the doctor. But Candace had blown off her last two visits with Makayla and time had become more pressing. Which was why Gabby was now standing at the receptionist's desk.

"Gabby Schaefer. My stepdaughter and I have an appointment. Makayla is a new patient."

The fortysomething woman behind the computer nodded. "Did you fill out the paperwork already?"

Gabby handed over the sheets of paper, along with their insurance card.

"Thanks. I'll take a copy of this and get the co-pay." The receptionist glanced at the paperwork, then at Makayla.

"She's pregnant?"

Gabby told herself there was no judgment in the tone. Nothing critical. But she felt as if the other women waiting were all staring at her.

"Yes," she said as calmly as she could.

"All right." The receptionist nodded toward the door lead-ing to the examination rooms. "She'll need to give us a urine sample."

"No problem." Gabby turned to Makayla. "You're going to have to pee in a cup. Have you done that before?"

The teen looked blank and shook her head. "Why?"

"They'll confirm the pregnancy and test for other things in your urine," Gabby told her. "Sugars and I'm not sure what. The doctor can explain it. Let me take care of this and I'll walk you back. There's a whole process."

Gabby passed over her credit card, then signed the paper-work. It occurred to her that she wasn't sure of her legal stand-ing when it came to the underage teen. Would she count as a guardian, because she sure wasn't a parent.

A problem for another time, she told herself.

She and Makayla went to the restroom. Gabby walked the girl through the steps to secure the urine sample, then went back into the hallway to wait.

As she stood there, the receptionist walked up to her with her clipboard. "I want to confirm a couple of things. The date of her last period is unknown?"

Gabby nodded. "She doesn't keep track."

"But she does know the dates of intercourse?"

Gabby raised her chin. "I think so. Yes."

The other woman nodded. "And her date of birth is cor-rect?"

"May 2, 2001."

"That's what I needed."

All polite words, Gabby thought as she waited. But there was *tone*.

She almost couldn't blame the other woman. Gabby knew she would have been thinking fairly judgmental thoughts her-self, if she saw a pregnant fifteen-year-old. What she wanted to tell her was this wasn't her fault. That she'd been the one to insist on the no-boys-upstairs rule. That when she'd tried to express her concern about the kiss, she'd been dismissed. That she was the stepmother, with all of the pain but none of the power.

But no one was listening, she reminded herself. Everyone was busy living her own life. They didn't have time to do much more than judge and move on.

Makayla emerged from the bathroom. She had her sample cup in her hand.

"Over here." Gabby pointed to the collection tray. Makayla put it down, then returned to her side.

They went back to the waiting room.

"What will happen at the appointment?" Makayla asked when they'd sat down.

"The doctor will ask questions about your health and listen to your heart. Then she'll give you a pelvic exam."

"What's that?"

Oh, God. "Have you ever been to the gynecologist before?"

"No. Just my pediatrician." Her big, blue eyes were so trusting. "Is it different?"

Gabby held in a groan. "It is. She's going to have to examine you and feel where the baby is." Why hadn't she thought to ask before? They could have gone online together so Makayla would be more prepared.

Makayla drew back. "You mean she's going to touch me… *there*?"

"Dr. Mansfield is really nice. You'll like her. She was my doctor when I was pregnant with the twins."

"No way," Makayla said, coming to her feet. "I won't do that."

The other women in the waiting room glanced at them.

Gabby rose. "I know it's uncomfortable to think about, but it's for the sake of the baby. Don't you want to make sure he or she is okay?"

"I guess."

They both sat back down. Gabby wished they could be anywhere but here.

"You wear a weird hospital gown and there's a paper blanket for your lap," she said. "I can stay in the room, if you want, or wait outside. It's up to you." She glanced at the teen only to find her head bent. "Makayla?"

"You should stay," the girl whispered. Tears dripped onto her lap.

Gabby lightly touched her back. "I'm sorry. I know this is a lot. The exams get easier, I promise. But the first time, everyone is embarrassed. It's a strange thing to go through, but we all do it."

"Thanks. I know it will be worth it when Boyd and I have our baby." She sniffed and raised her head. "We'll be a family."

Not anything Gabby wanted to hear.

One crisis at a time, she told herself. Today she simply had to get Makayla through her first appointment. She would deal with the rest of it later.

Hayley arrived early at Latte-Da. She wanted to be able to pick a good table, one that would allow her to see Rob arrive. She didn't want to be surprised by having him walk up from behind.

She ordered a latte at the counter, then took her seat. She pulled out a book so she could pretend to read. As if she were a normal person, doing okay. Just out on a Saturday morning, enjoying herself with a latte and book.

The truth was very different. She was tired, so desperately

tired. How could she sleep when the bed was so empty? Plus she hadn't been eating very much and without the right nutrition, it was nearly impossible for her body to heal.

She was a complete and total mess. Without Rob, she had trouble getting through her day.

Somehow, with all the stress of trying to get pregnant and her miscarriages, she'd forgotten that without her husband, nothing mattered. She'd become so focused on where she was in her cycle, with her drugs, with her ovaries, that she'd lost track of the man she loved. She didn't know when everything had changed, but it had. She would guess it had happened slowly, over time, but the end result was the same. He was gone and she didn't know how to get him back.

She never would have thought it would come to this. When she and Rob had first met, she'd been in her second year of college. She'd been working close to full-time and only taking a couple of classes a semester. She'd planned on being a business major—maybe marketing. She'd gone to a party with a friend and had met Rob.

It had been one of those things. She'd taken one look at him and had known he was the one. Maybe it had been how he'd smiled at her, or that he was such a sweet guy. Whatever combination of chemistry and conversation, she'd fallen hard.

She'd been careful to play it as cool as she could. When he'd asked for her number, she'd given it to him without shrieking with excitement. When he'd asked her out, she'd pretended to check her calendar to see if she was free.

They'd gone out the next night and the next. By their fifth date they were lovers, by their eighth, they'd admitted to being in love. By the end of month two, they were engaged.

Hayley had dropped out of college. She couldn't work enough to support herself, go to college *and* be in love with Rob. There simply weren't enough hours in the day. So college had been sacrificed so she could work full-time. Six months after the wedding, she'd been promoted to John Eiland's personal assistant. With that responsibility had come a nice raise.

She and Rob had started saving for a house right away. They'd had a plan. Three years of marriage, then kids. She'd gotten pregnant the first month they'd tried. They'd both been thrilled and happy. Then she'd lost the baby.

"Here you go."

"Thank you." Hayley smiled at the teen who brought her the latte. She took a sip, then returned her attention to her book. But instead of words, she saw the empty room at their house. The one they'd been so sure would be a nursery.

They'd been so happy once, she thought wistfully. Back before they'd realized how hard it was going to be for them to have a child of their own. When they hadn't known there were problems, that she couldn't seem to carry a fetus to term. That her eggs weren't easily harvested—meaning a surrogate wasn't an option.

"Hayley."

She'd been so caught up in her thoughts, she hadn't noticed Rob approach. Now she looked up and saw him standing next to her small table.

"Hi. Are you getting a coffee?"

"I'm good."

He sat down across from her.

He looked the same as he always did. The same haircut, the same glasses. Maybe he looked a little tired—she thought there were shadows under his eyes, but maybe that was just the light in the shop. He didn't seem happy to see her, but he wasn't mad, either. At least not that she could tell.

"What are you reading?" he asked.

She raised the book so he could see the front cover, mostly because she had no idea what she'd thrown in her bag.

She hadn't seen him in nearly two weeks and now that he was here, she didn't know what to say. "I miss you" was the obvious choice, but was it the right one?

"How are you?" she asked instead.

"Busy at work. How about you?"

"The same." She picked up her latte, then put it down. "I thought we should talk."

"I agree."

He was still wearing his wedding ring. That was something. Because she'd been afraid he would take it off. That being married to her didn't mean anything to him anymore.

"Where are you staying?" she asked.

"I'm renting a room. A couple of college kids and me." He smiled briefly. "I think I cramp their style, but the check clears so they put up with it."

"You could come back," she whispered. "I miss you. Us. We could see a counselor or something. If that would help."

His gaze was steady as he listened to her. When she was done, he leaned toward her. "I love you, Hayley. More than you know. I miss you, too. I want to come home. It's where I belong."

Some of her tension eased. "That's wonderful. So come home."

"Have you talked to the doctor?"

"What do you mean?"

"Have you scheduled your surgery?"

"No. Of course not. I can't do that." She leaned toward him. "Rob, please understand. I *have* to do this. I have to try. A baby is everything to me. You've always known that."

"I have."

"Then you know how wonderful it will be when we have a family of our own. You want that, too."

"I want you more." His mouth turned down at the corners and sadness filled his eyes. "You're still planning on going to Switzerland for treatment."

He wasn't asking a question, but she answered anyway. "Yes. As soon as I can raise the money." She reached for his hand. "I want you to be a part of that. I want—"

He pulled free and rose. "Goodbye, Hayley."

With that, he turned and walked away. She was left with her cooling coffee and a book she knew she could never, ever read.

"You look beautiful, Mommy," Kenzie said.

Gabby turned back and forth, letting the full skirt flow around her. "I am a princess," she said dramatically. "You servant girls, do my bidding. You there." She pointed at Boomer. "Fetch my carriage."

The long-suffering dog, dressed in a ridiculous yellow-and-purple-striped jacket, wagged his tail. The twins collapsed onto the floor in a fit of giggles. Jasmine, sensing trouble, had fled long before the dress-up party had gotten started. Gabby would guess the feline had safely hidden under the king-size bed in the master, where she would stay until things quieted down.

It was late afternoon on Friday. Andrew was taking Makayla to her mother's for the weekend. Candace knew he had something to discuss but didn't know the topic. Gabby tried not to imagine how the conversation was going. Andrew would share all when he got home.

She secured the "tiara of power" more firmly on her head and pointed at Kennedy. "You will quack like a duck," she said imperiously.

Kennedy sat up and made the appropriate noise. Kenzie joined in and Boomer bayed. Her bidding completed, Gabby took off the tiara and passed it to Kennedy.

"I yield my princessness to you."

And so it went. Everyone got a turn being the princess and bossing the other two around. A little before five, Gabby ushered the girls out of the playroom and into their bathroom.

"Hands washed," she said briskly. "Hair brushed and then we're off."

A very brave Ellie Davidson from the summer camp was having four girls over for dinner. Gabby had no idea why. Lunch, sure. An afternoon birthday party, yes. But dinner? Late in the day meant tired kids. There was more potential for disaster. But she hadn't been consulted. When the invitation had come, the girls had been excited to get it.

Twenty minutes later they were walking the three blocks to their friend's house. Kenzie and Kennedy each had a small gift bag in their hands.

"It's nice to take something to the hostess," Gabby explained. "To thank her for the invitation. Adults bring flowers or wine. Sometimes a dessert. We could have chosen hair ribbons or a book."

"Mrs. Davidson will like the cookies," Kennedy said. "They were delicious."

Gabby only had their word to go on. Despite the ongoing Makayla crisis, she'd been faithful to her diet. According to her scale, she was down nearly eight pounds. A fantastic victory. She'd been attending classes at Nicole's studio twice a week and eating way more vegetables than a biped should. She was a little less crabby than she had been at the beginning, but just as hungry. Still, she was seeing results and that was what mattered.

She was waiting to go clothes shopping until the week before she started work. Hopefully she would be in a smaller size by then.

They arrived at their friend's house. Gabby had the girls ring the bell, then they waited to be invited in. She greeted Mrs. Davidson, confirmed the pickup time and that she had Gabby's cell number, then left the twins to play.

The late afternoon was still sunny and warm. She could smell food grilling, which made her stomach growl. She and Andrew had a couple of steaks ready for their own dinner and she'd prepared a big salad earlier. Since it was Friday, she was going to allow herself a glass of wine. Just one. And no dessert. Talk about grim.

But thoughts of hunger and dieting faded when she rounded the corner and saw Andrew's car in the driveway. She hurried the last few yards home.

"I'm back," she called.

"In the kitchen."

She found Andrew by the island, pouring himself a glass of scotch. He looked tired.

"How did it go?" she asked.

"Candace doesn't disappoint," he told her as he held up the bottle of red wine she'd left on the counter.

She nodded. "In a good way or a bad way?"

"It's Candace."

"So bad."

"She swore. She blamed us. She swore some more. She talked about how disappointed she was, how she didn't have time for this. Pretty much what we expected."

Andrew didn't look at her as he spoke. Gabby knew that his attention on opening the bottle of wine was a lot more about what he *didn't* want to say.

She knew Candace well enough to fill in the details. There had been no "we" in the conversation. Candace would have put the blame squarely on Gabby's shoulders. There would have been talk about irresponsible and inadequate supervision and how Makayla needed a better role model.

Candace hadn't liked her from the start and Gabby had never been sure as to why. She and Andrew hadn't met until after his divorce was final. Even if she had known him before, Candace had been the one to end the marriage, not him. While Gabby was a few years younger, Candace was by far more glamorous and beautiful. She had a fantastic career, lots of friends, plenty of travel. Yet Candace had always been condescending and difficult.

"I'm sorry she was a pain."

"Me, too." He handed her the glass of wine. They went out onto the patio. "What a week."

They sat next to each other on the love seat. Andrew toasted her, then sipped his drink.

"I don't know how much Makayla heard," he continued.

"Even if she didn't, she can guess all the things her mother would say. I wish Candace could be more supportive."

"You and me, both. I'm glad Makayla is living with us and not her. We'll make sure things go smoothly through the pregnancy and after."

Gabby nodded. The adoption was going to take a lot of planning. She'd done some online research and it seemed that they could pull it all together in a few months. With the teen still convinced she and Boyd were in love, this wasn't the time to bring up the various options, but they would have to have that conversation soon.

"Once the baby is born," she said, "life can return to relative normal."

"There will have to be some changes." Andrew looked at her. "More rules. I need to listen to you more."

She smiled. "Yes, you do. Makayla's a great kid, but she still needs to have boundaries. No more sex with boys."

He chuckled. "Is this where I say something about too little too late?"

"Maybe, but I still think it's a good rule." An unrealistic one, but for that moment it was nice to think they could actually have that much control.

There were going to be lots of discussions and decisions, she thought. Did they put Makayla on birth control? She wouldn't even be sixteen when the baby was born. What a nightmare. She wanted to ask how this had happened, but they all knew the answer to that.

"Have you heard from Boyd's parents?" she asked.

"No."

"Me, either. I can't help thinking that's not a good thing."

"Yeah." He leaned back against the cushions. "We should look into counseling. This is going to be stressful for all of us. I don't want to screw up and I don't want you getting too stressed out."

Which was one of the reasons she loved him so much, she thought. "Counseling is a very good idea. I'll ask around and get some recommendations."

He grinned at her. "Are you saying some of your friends are crazy?" He held up a hand. "That's humor, Gabby. I know going to counseling is a good thing."

"I accept the comment in the spirit in which it was delivered. As for being crazy, I think we all have a little bit of that in us."

Chapter Fifteen

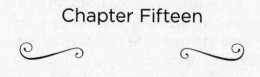

Hayley stood in the small, empty bedroom. The walls were painted a pale yellow, with white trim. They'd replaced the carpeting with hardwood because it was easier to keep clean without harsh chemicals. She'd been four months along when she'd miscarried the first time so they hadn't had time to get serious about buying furniture. There was only the empty room and the painted walls.

She crossed to the closet and opened the door. There weren't any baby clothes, no stacks of impossibly small linens. No miniature blankets or sheets. Just an old scrapbook—the one her mother had put together for her.

Now she got it down and walked to the patch of sunlight in the corner and sank to the floor. She sat cross-legged, the book resting on her legs.

She and Rob had talked endlessly about their baby those first few months. They'd debated names and talked about the merits of different types of cribs. They'd touched tiny bootees and had tried to imagine the glory of holding a child of their own.

All that had ended with the first unexpected cramps.

She'd been at work when the miscarriage had started. At first she'd thought she was having some kind of stomach flu.

But when she'd gone to the bathroom, there had been spotting. The spotting had turned into a flood of blood and by the time she'd gotten to her gynecologist's office, the baby was already gone.

She remembered the devastation. How Rob had held her and they'd cried together. It had taken weeks for the emptiness to go away. Her parents had still been alive then and her mom had come to stay with her. She'd miscarried before, so she understood how horrible it was. How people said foolish things like "Oh, it happens to everyone," or "It's nature's way of taking care of a problem."

Fuck that, Hayley had thought. She didn't want to think her baby had been a problem. It hadn't been. Her baby had *died*. And it *didn't* happen to everyone. It didn't happen to most women. She didn't want platitudes, she wanted revenge.

Her mom had promised it would get better and although Hayley and Rob hadn't believed her, over time, the wound had scabbed up. It had never gone away, but they'd been able to move forward. To try again. It was only after the second miscarriage that they'd started to realize something else was going on.

Now on that hard floor, with the sun warming her back, she opened the scrapbook and saw the announcement of her birth. Well, not her birth, exactly. The announcement of her going home with her parents. There was a picture of her dad holding her, then one of her mom doing the same. There were a few handwritten notes about what they'd each been feeling. And a letter from her mom.

My Dearest Hayley,
There are no words to describe my joy in bringing you home. It's been ten days and I still can't believe you're here and you're ours. Every night I wake up two and

three times to check on you. To stand in your room and listen to you breathing. You are so perfect. Everything about you is wonderful. Your father and I love you so much. We will always love you, dearest daughter. You are our miracle.

She traced her finger along the letters. She hadn't been their miracle for long, she thought. A few months later, her mother had found out she was pregnant. And this pregnancy had gone to term. Morgan had been born less than a year after they'd brought Hayley home. Morgan, who had been a crying, colicky baby. Morgan who had grown into a difficult toddler and a loud, pushy little girl.

Hayley turned the pages of the scrapbook and watched herself grow up. There were copies of her report cards, certificates and various awards and even a few cards from her parents. There were also photos, some posed, some candid. The last one had been taken at Christmas, a few months before their parents had been killed.

Hayley touched the smooth surface of the picture, wishing her mom were still with her. She would know what to say about the situation with Rob. She would have good, solid advice about everything. She would hug Hayley so tight that for those few seconds, she could believe everything was going to be okay.

But there had been so many times when her mom had been too busy dealing with Morgan to bother with Hayley. Silly things, really. Like when it was Hayley's birthday, Morgan got a present, too. Otherwise, she would make everyone miserable with her crying when she was young and later her complaining. But on Morgan's birthday, Hayley was expected to simply watch her sister be the center of attention.

Morgan was always seen to first, whether it had been shopping for school clothes or when they'd both come home sick from school. It was never Hayley and Morgan—it was always Morgan and Hayley.

She looked at the pictures and notes and cards and wondered how she was supposed to reconcile what had happened. Her sister told her to suck it up and get over it. Was that good advice, or just Morgan once again protesting at not being at the center of the universe?

When their parents had unexpectedly died in a car crash, Hayley had been devastated. She'd barely held it together. Rob had been upset as well, but he'd taken care of so many of the details. At the reading of the will, Morgan had thrown a fit when she'd found out that their parents had left them each half of their modest estate. Morgan had argued that she had three kids and Hayley didn't have any, therefore she should get the lion's share. But the attorney had been firm. The will was not to be contested. If it was, Morgan would get nothing.

In her head, Hayley could justify every action her parents had made when it came to their daughters. But in her heart, she was unable to reconcile the love they proclaimed with how she had often felt. Second best. Less than. Yes, she was an adult and she should get over it. But looking back, her eight-year-old self hadn't understood why Morgan got more presents every Christmas. Why Morgan's demands for a new dress were answered with a new dress while she was told to make do. Why Morgan got two bedtime stories and she was read only one. Why Morgan wasn't punished for some things when Hayley was. Whatever message they'd meant to send, the one that had been received had been clear—Morgan mattered more. And Hayley had only ever come up with one explanation.

Somewhere in all that, a need had been formed. The burning desire to have a baby of her own. One she would love as he or she should be loved. A child who would never lie awake and wonder why Morgan was cared about so much more.

Rob had tried to understand, but to him, adoption was an easy solution. They wanted children. There were thousands of children looking for families. Problem solved.

But she couldn't do it. She couldn't risk having anyone feel the way she had. It had hurt too much. What if her parents hadn't acted the way they had because Morgan was a difficult, demanding kid? What if it had been because, in the end, it was easier to love Morgan?

Hayley supposed that was at the heart of it. The fear that if she adopted she might find out that she really hadn't been loved simply by virtue of not truly being theirs. What if she, too, couldn't love a child she adopted? If she didn't know for sure, she could maintain the illusion, but if she found out that horrible truth, she risked losing everything.

She closed the scrapbook and placed it on the floor next to her, then curled up in the sun and closed her eyes. She hurt all over. She was so very tired, and she was alone. There was no possible way out of this, she thought sadly. No happy ending. Just long, lonely days and the looming possibility that she would never, ever have a child of her own.

Tyler practically danced from the car to the entrance of the hotel. "Can we get another copy of the book?" he asked. "Do you think Jairus will remember me? Can I have his autograph?"

Nicole held his hand as they went through the double glass doors. "Yes, yes and yes," she teased. "But first we have to find out where we're going."

One of the bellmen approached. "You're here for the signing?" he asked. "The ballroom is that way." He pointed.

Nicole pulled tickets out of her bag. "We're here for the pre-event," she said. "In the Blue Pacific Room."

"That way." He pointed to the left. "Follow the signs. You'll see a long line. You can ignore that and keep going."

"Thanks."

Nicole followed his instructions, then saw the arrows that pointed her in the right direction. At the next corner they saw the long line of families waiting to get into the signing.

There had to be a hundred people there, she thought, looking at all the kids holding *Brad the Dragon* books and dolls. There were tweens and toddlers and every age in between. It seemed that business in Brad's world was very, very good.

"Whoa." Tyler clutched his Brad stuffed animal more tightly. "That's a lot of people."

"It is. Come on, big guy. We have a party to get to."

As promised, Jairus had sent over VIP tickets. The start time for that event was an hour before the signing. Nicole was curious as to what would happen. Did he speak at both functions? Circulate? Well, not at the second one, she thought. Not with a hundred people already in line.

She and Tyler found the Blue Pacific Room. Two hotel employees stood at the entrance.

"Your tickets, please," a young woman said with a smile.

Nicole held them out.

The man winked at Tyler. "Excited to meet Jairus?"

"I've met him. He came to my summer camp and signed a book for me."

"You're a lucky guy."

"I know."

The woman handed Nicole back her tickets. "Have fun," she said, as she held open the door.

Nicole took Tyler's hand again. They stepped into a big, open room decorated in all things B the D. There were balloons, streamers, piles of books and every possible kind of merchandise. She would guess there were about forty people milling about. An equal number of adults and children. Some of the kids were in wheelchairs. There was a little girl on crutches.

A volunteer in an *I Love Brad* T-shirt came over with a big tote bag. He handed it to Tyler.

"You can take one of everything," the teen said with a grin. "There's a buffet over there, and a soda fountain on the back wall. Jairus will be out in about fifteen minutes."

"Thank you," Nicole murmured, blown away by the sheer proliferation of goodies for the kids.

She and Tyler went from table to table, collecting his gifts. One of the mothers came up and greeted her.

"You look shell-shocked," she said with a laugh. "Your first time?"

"Yes. We had no idea."

"I know. Jairus and his publisher throw a party like this every time he has a book out. It's pretty amazing. I'm Veronica."

"Nicole." She pointed to where Tyler was studying a *Brad the Dragon* DVD. "That's Tyler."

Veronica waved to the other side of the room. "My husband is with our son. Mason doesn't do well in crowds. He's autistic. But wow, does he love Brad. This is our third year."

"How did you find out about this?" Nicole asked.

"One of Mason's therapists contacted the publicity firm the publisher uses and nominated him. Jairus has always supported special-needs kids. His foundation is very generous financially, but he does this personally. I've heard rumors that he had a family member with special needs, but he doesn't talk about it much." Veronica looked at Tyler. "Your son wasn't nominated by his doctor?"

Nicole hadn't been expecting the question. "No. We, um, Tyler won a contest for his summer camp a few weeks ago. Jairus came to see him and the camp group. They all loved it."

All true, but not exactly how they'd gotten in. Still, she wasn't comfortable admitting to a personal relationship with Jairus. Not when it was so new and they hadn't discussed what exactly they were doing. Plus, finding out he kept the information about his sister to himself made her doubly cautious about oversharing.

"He knows how to put on a good show," Veronica said easily. "He's so good with the kids. Mason doesn't like to be close to strangers. Jairus seems to sense that and never pushes. He lets the kids come to him. He's not put off if they scream at the wrong time or are in a wheelchair. You gotta love that."

"You do."

Veronica excused herself. Nicole joined Tyler at the buffet. There were all kinds of kid-friendly foods. Everything from hot dogs to cupcakes decorated in B the D colors, of course.

But she couldn't seem to summon her general annoyance at the dragon's bright red universe. Not when it seemed that Jairus wasn't such a bad guy after all. She'd been enjoying getting to know him, but that was as the man. She still hadn't been sure what he was like as king of the B the D empire. From what she could tell, he wasn't half bad there, either. Which meant resisting his considerable charms might turn out to be more difficult than she'd imagined.

"Mommy, can I invite Jairus to a barbecue?" Tyler asked. "You always say that it's 'portant to invite back. He had us here, so we should have him at our house."

Talk about a big step, she thought, pressing her hand to her suddenly fluttering stomach. But maybe it was time to walk on the wild side. Or at least stroll very, very slowly.

"I think that would be nice. He's going to be on his book tour, so it might not be right away."

"I know he's busy. He's got a lot of kids to make happy." Tyler smiled up at her. "This is the best day ever."

She laughed. "You know what? It kind of is."

Hayley pulled the card out of the printer and handed it to her boss. Steven shook his head.

"How do you do that?"

She smiled. "It's not hard, but I refuse to show you. I consider my skill with your schedule my job security."

"You got that right." He glanced at his list of appointments for the day. "I have a teleconference in ten minutes."

"Yes, you do."

Hayley generally gave Steven his appointment card every workday evening, but he'd lost the one for today. The man did a great job running the company, but he couldn't keep track of his schedule if his life depended on it.

She touched her phone. "I have the phone number right here. I'll buzz you when you're connected."

"Thanks, Hayley." Steven leaned against the door frame of her office.

He was tall and nice-looking, a lot like his dad. Last year, when Steven had stepped in to take over the company, they'd all wondered how it was going to go. But John had trained his son well, as had Pam. Steven was a fair boss, honest and understanding without being a pushover. From her point of view, the pay was good, the hours completely reasonable and whenever she'd needed time off, he'd worked with her.

She thought about mentioning the trip to Switzerland, but honestly didn't have the energy. With Rob still gone, there wasn't much reason to think about getting pregnant.

She didn't want a child on her own—she wanted them to be a family.

But they hadn't spoken since their meeting at the coffee shop. She'd wanted to call, but didn't know what to say. She knew that until she was willing to tell him she'd let go of her dream, he wasn't coming back.

She returned her attention to her boss. "You'll need the notes on the contract," she told him. "Let me grab them."

She rose so she could cross to the file room just off her office. She knew she made it to upright, but wasn't completely sure she got past that before the room started spinning.

How strange, she thought, more confused and intrigued than scared. This wasn't like when she stood up too fast and got light-headed. It was completely different. Almost a kind of slow motion. As if everything were turning and turning, like the carousel at the park. She'd always liked the carousel. The white horses, especially, with pink ribbons and—

Something hot and wet dripped down her legs. The sensation surprised her. She glanced down and saw her jeans were stained. She touched her hand to her thigh and then looked at her fingers. Blood, she thought with surprise. That was strange. So very strange.

"Hayley!"

The frantic voice came from far away. Steven, she thought as she crumpled to the ground. He sounded worried. She needed to tell him she was going to be all—

Chapter Sixteen

Gabby carefully pulled up the zipper of the black Akris pants she'd bought. They were ridiculously expensive—even on sale—but so gorgeous, she'd been unable to resist. They were also a size smaller than she'd been this time last month which made buying them with her shiny gift card even more exciting.

"Yay, me," she whispered as she looked at her reflection in the mirror. She still had a ways to go, but considering everything going on in her life, she was doing great.

Andrew strolled into the walk-in closet. Normally he would have been long at work, but he had a flight out later that morning and had decided to not go into the office first.

With the kids off at camp already, they'd had a rare couple of hours to sip coffee and talk about their upcoming week. Now he looked at her as she turned in front of the mirror.

"Very sexy," he said.

She grinned. "They're black pants, honey. That means they can't be sexy."

"They are, on you."

"Sweet man." She studied her reflection again. "Only four more weeks. I can't believe it. Four weeks from tomorrow I'll be walking into my new office. It's going to be exciting."

She shimmied out of the pants and carefully hung them

back on the hanger, then pulled on her jeans. Andrew watched her. His dark eyes filled with something awfully close to sympathy. Or was it regret?

"What?" she asked.

"I'm sorry."

"About?"

He put his arms around her. "All you're giving up. I'm glad you're excited about work. You need to enjoy it as long as you can. You know if there was another way, we'd find it. Gabby, you can't know how much I appreciate this and how bad I feel."

She pulled out of his embrace. Their closet was spacious, with plenty of light and lots of storage space, but right this second, it felt small and stifling. Maybe it was the apprehension tightening her chest.

She moved into the bathroom and faced him. "I have no idea what you're talking about."

He tilted his head. "Your job."

"Yes. I start in four weeks."

"I'm saying I feel badly that you're so excited about going back to work when you'll only be there a few months. I appreciate everything you're giving up for the family and I'll do my best to make it up to you in any way I can."

Heat burned through her. She knew she was way too young for her first hot flash, but even as the thought formed, she was suddenly cold. Nothing made sense——certainly not Andrew.

"Why will I only be working a few months?"

His look of genuine confusion matched her own. "Because you'll be staying home with Makayla's baby, after it's born."

Gabby reached blindly for the counter behind her. Stay home? Stay *home*? "No, I won't. Why would you think that? I'm not staying home. Even if I didn't want to go back to work, which I do, by the way, Makayla is going to give up her baby for adoption."

Andrew shook his head. "She's not. She's keeping the baby. I don't understand. We've talked about this more than once. Even if she and Boyd don't stay together, she's going to keep the baby. She'll need our help."

"No." She couldn't breathe. Panic threatened. A to-the-bone fear that made her tremble. "No, that's not what we discussed. We talked about her and Boyd being too young. That they were both too young to deal with a baby. You said it and I said it."

"They *are* too young. That's why she needs our help. Gabby, this isn't hard to grasp. Why are you acting like this?"

"Me? This isn't about me. I never said I would stay home with her child."

"You have to. Honey, I don't get it. We talked about this. We both agreed that we wanted life to get back to normal."

"Right—*after* the adoption."

"No, with the baby. Makayla can't do it herself. I love my daughter, but we both knew she's nowhere near prepared to be a mother. She's only fifteen. She has to have the chance to be a kid. She needs to be going to school, preparing for college and her future."

"So she gets to have a life, but I'm supposed to give up mine? She gets to have the baby and walk away without any consequences, but I'm supposed to give up everything to take care of it?" Her voice tightened.

"I don't understand your reaction. We talked about this so many times before we had the twins. That a child needs a parent at home during the first five years of life."

"A parent. That would be Makayla or Boyd. Not me. I'm not the parent."

"But she can't do it. You have to see that."

No, she didn't, she thought, wondering how he could sound so calm. As if she were the irrational one. Nothing about this was right. Or fair. Or reasonable.

"So I'm the point of sacrifice," she said, trying to keep from sounding shrill. "I give up everything while she goes on as if none of this ever happened? How is that right?"

"Of course she'll have responsibilities," he said, his voice annoyingly soothing.

"Will she? Really? Because you don't even make her do her own laundry. She has virtually no chores in this house. None. She lives here full-time and we treat her like an honored guest. Now you're telling me that I'm expected to raise her baby? To give up my career, everything I've been waiting to get back to, so she can go off and have a good rest of her childhood?"

Her voice rose with each word until she was shrieking. Andrew's phone chirped.

They stared at each other. She was breathing as if she'd just run a mile and he still looked more confused than upset.

"Obviously we have to talk about this more," he said as he pulled his phone out of his shirt pocket. "My car is here. I have to go."

She nodded. Right. Because he had a business trip and life went on.

She wanted to throw something at him. Like a shoe. Or a building. What on earth had he been thinking? No way she was giving up her life for Makayla's baby. A baby that would be adopted soon enough.

He crossed to her. "I'll call you tonight," he said and kissed her cheek.

She nodded without speaking.

He walked toward the bedroom, then paused and turned back to her. "Are we all right?"

She nodded. They weren't, but what was the point in saying that now? He had to leave. Better that things be reasonably pleasant. They would talk again when he got home. There was time for her to get him to understand that there was absolutely no way on this planet she was giving up her career to take care of Makayla's baby. Not now, not ever.

Hayley was aware of movement around her long before she opened her eyes. There was an annoying steady beeping, along with low conversation and the occasional sensation of warmth. Drugs, she thought hazily. Someone was giving her drugs.

She surrendered to them as much as she could. A voice—no, that was too strong—a feeling told her not to wake up until she had to. That surfacing, having to face whatever had happened, would be bad. So she didn't stir, didn't open her eyes until finally she couldn't keep them closed anymore.

The room was unfamiliar, as was the bed. She closed her eyes, then opened them again as pain settled on her. The kind of pain that could only be dulled, not deadened.

She inhaled slowly. She was breathing on her own. That was good. She moved her arm, then winced as she realized there was an IV attached. The beeping was her heartbeat.

"How are you feeling?"

The voice was familiar, but not the one she wanted to hear. She turned and saw Dr. Pearce standing beside her bed, watching her with an awkward combination of relief and concern.

"Sore."

"You're on an IV for the pain. Can you push the button yourself or do you want me to?"

"I can do it."

Hayley found the button and pressed it. Relief was almost

instant. Drugs, she thought hazily. She'd never done them as a kid, but they were magical.

"Do you know where you are?"

"The hospital."

"Do you remember what happened?"

Hayley fought against the swirling sensation she recalled. The blood. There'd been so much blood.

"I made a mess at work on the floor."

Dr. Pearce smiled. "I think they'll be okay with that."

Hayley nodded slightly. "You're right. Steven's good that way."

The doctor's smile faded. "Hayley, you were hemorrhaging. I'm sorry. I wish there had been something else I could do to save you from—"

"Stop," Hayley whispered. "Don't say it."

Not that the words would make it any more or less real. She already knew the truth. Could feel it in the tightness in her insides, the pain from the incisions. She simply didn't want it spoken out loud.

"If there'd been another way..."

"I know." Hayley felt tears on her cheeks, although she wasn't aware of crying. It was done. There was no going back now. She was done. Totally and completely done. She closed her eyes.

"How close did I come to dying?"

"Close enough. You lost a lot of blood."

There hadn't been a decision to make. She understood that. At least in her head. Her heart was different. Her heart screamed out at the unfairness of it all. Her heart sobbed and cried and began building walls that would never be scaled.

"I'm going to let Rob know you're awake."

Hayley opened her eyes. "He's here?"

"Of course. He just went to get more coffee. Steven called

him after he called 911. Rob got here within a few minutes of the ambulance." Dr. Pearce squeezed her hand. "It's been nearly forty-eight hours. We were all starting to wonder when you'd wake up. Let me go get him." Dr. Pearce left the room.

Rob was here. Hayley hung on to the thought, then forced herself to fight the drugs and stay awake until she saw him walk into her room.

"You look awful," she told him, her voice scratchy.

There were dark circles under his eyes and two days' growth on his jaw. His clothes were wrinkled and his glasses dirty.

"Hayley."

He breathed her name, then lowered the railing on the side without the IV and slid onto the narrow bed until he was stretched out next to her. He touched her hair, her cheeks, then wiped away her tears.

"You nearly died," he told her. "You nearly bled out. They wouldn't let me see you. You nearly died."

She heard the fear in his voice. The accusation. Because she'd done this to herself. To them. From his point of view, she should have given up. Should have stopped fighting.

She was so happy to see him and at the same time, she knew it didn't matter. Irony. Now that she'd had the hysterectomy, he would come back. They would be together. But without a baby, she wasn't going to be whole ever again. She wasn't going to be who she was. He would love her and she would be gone.

She knew she wasn't making sense. It was the drugs and maybe what she'd been through. Regardless, she knew the truth. There was a hole inside her. An emptiness that would never be filled.

She pushed those thoughts away and focused on the man next to her.

"I'm sorry," he whispered. "I shouldn't have left. I didn't know what else to do. How else to get your attention."

"It's okay." There was no point in him suffering, too.

"Everyone's been by," he told her. "All your friends. Steven and Pam and half the people from work. They all gave blood." He raised his head. "You had a transfusion. Did Dr. Pearce tell you?"

She shook her head. "Is Steven mad about the carpet?"

"No. He's happy you're okay."

It hurt to talk. She was tired. So very tired. She felt her eyes closing.

Rob got off the bed and replaced the railing, then pulled up a chair. "Go to sleep, Hayley. I'll be right here. They want you to stay another night. I've already moved back home. I'll be there to take care of you."

She nodded because there was nothing left to say. He was back in her life. He loved her and he was back. Too bad it was all for nothing. It was too late. For both of them.

Let's Do Tea was quintessentially cute. The building had once been a private home, built in the 1920s. The architecture lent itself to charming retail and Let's Do Tea took advantage of that. The main floor held the grocery store side of the business, offering everything edible and British from ginger beer to scones. There was also a take-out counter. A restaurant filled the upstairs. The menu was on a spectrum from ploughman's lunches to high tea.

Nicole saw Gabby had already been seated and waved as she made her way to the table. Gabby rose and they briefly hugged.

"I'm a mess," Nicole admitted as she took a seat. "Which is really sad because none of this is happening to me."

"It was scary," Gabby told her. "Rob was terrified when he

called. I haven't heard all the details, but it sounds like they weren't sure Hayley was going to pull through."

"I know." Nicole shuddered. "Pam said that Steven couldn't believe how much blood there was. He thought she was going to die right there on the floor of the office. Poor guy. Apparently he's still in shock. But she pulled through. Did you give blood?"

Gabby nodded. "I'm O negative, so they love me. The universal donor. Rob said she'll be coming home today. I'm going to wait a bit before visiting."

"Me, too. I don't want to tire her. I just wish there was something concrete I could do. You know—babysit, pet sit, regrout her bathroom."

Gabby smiled. "Regrouting isn't a traditional get-well gift, but it should be."

Nicole picked up her menu, then put it down. While Gabby was saying all the right things, something was off. There was a tension in her voice, a strained set to her shoulders.

"Are you okay?"

Their server chose that moment to walk over to their table. "Good afternoon, ladies," the plump British woman said with a welcoming smile. "Do you know what you'll be having?"

"Every carb you offer," Gabby said, then sighed. "Or the high tea lunch. Coronation chicken sandwiches, please."

Nicole hesitated a second. She generally ordered the salad, but something told her that sugar and gluten were going to be required today. "The same for me."

They passed over their menus. Their server promised to bring the tea right away, then left. Nicole leaned toward Gabby.

"Tell me."

"I honestly don't know if I can talk about it," she admitted. "What's beyond stunned, because that's where I am."

Nicole waited patiently. She'd known Gabby just over a year. The other woman was smart, capable and caring. She wasn't overly dramatic. Instead, she saw the problem and came up with solutions. If she was this rattled, it was bad.

"We talked about Makayla being pregnant," Gabby began.

Nicole nodded. "When we had lunch at Gary's."

"Andrew and I have been talking about what's to come. Makayla and Boyd swear they're in love. They want to stay together and raise the baby as a family."

Nicole rolled her eyes. "Seriously? Will she even be sixteen when the baby's born?"

"No."

"Then how are they going to be together? Will one of them move in with the other? Are they going to quit school and get jobs?" She pressed her lips together. "Sorry. I interrupted."

"You're saying everything I've been thinking. Plus Andrew and I doubt that Boyd is really in this for the long haul. It's not just that he's a sixteen-year-old boy who isn't going to want to have a baby cramping his lifestyle. His mother is very angry and upset. We're pretty sure she's going to be pushing for them to break up."

Their server returned with a pot of tea and a tiered tray filled with mini scones and little pastries.

Gabby waited until she'd left to pour for both of them.

"We've been talking regularly," Gabby continued. "That's what has me so confused. Because I thought we were on the same page and we're not."

"How are you and Andrew on different pages?"

Gabby put down the teapot. "I thought Makayla would give up her baby for adoption and Andrew thought she would be keeping the baby."

"What? How? She's in high school. I'm assuming he expects his daughter to graduate. How would that happen?"

Gabby sipped her tea.

Nicole stared at her. "No," she breathed, unable to believe it. "He does not expect you to stay home with the baby."

"He does. He told me that he really appreciates all I have to give up to make that happen."

But Andrew was so nice, Nicole thought, shocked by the suggestion. So supportive and loving. Anyone spending any time with them could see they were a great couple. He'd always been so forward-thinking. So in tune with the women in his life. "How could he ask you to give up your life like that? It's not your baby."

"Thank you." Gabby reached for a scone. "That's what I said. Why does Makayla get to go on with her life as if nothing happened and I'm expected to give up everything to raise her child? It's not fair."

"You must be furious."

"I am, and confused. We've been talking nearly every day about this. How could I not have understood him?"

"Plus your job." Nicole sighed. "You've been looking forward to it for months. Hasn't he noticed?"

"He has. But somewhere along the way he thought I was on board with this idea."

"What are you going to do?"

"I have no idea," Gabby admitted. "He's out of town for a few days. We'll talk when he gets back." She reached for a pastry. "I know exactly how it will be," she said bitterly. "He says that Makayla will have to take care of the baby when she's home, but she won't. He never refuses her anything. There will be after-school stuff. Football games and dances. I'll be the full-time mother to a newborn that isn't even mine."

Tears filled her eyes. "I love him, but I do not want to

take this on. I want to go to work. I want to be more than a mom. Does that sound awful?"

Nicole reached across the table and touched her arm. "Of course not. You love your girls and you love Makayla. This isn't about caring, it's about what's right. You didn't sign up for this at all. Have you discussed adoption at all?"

"I thought we had but apparently not. Makayla is still convinced it's all going to be butterflies and roses. Until that changes and I get her on my side, I don't know what I'm going to do with Andrew."

"At least you have time."

Gabby nodded. "According to the doctor, she's due around the first of February. So yes, there's time."

But not much. Gabby didn't say that out loud, but Nicole knew she was thinking it. They all had to be.

"Is she nervous about school starting?"

"I think so. She hasn't said anything, but she must be. She's barely showing, but that's going to change. It will be hard for her to keep going to class while she gets bigger and bigger."

Nicole remembered her own pregnancy. She'd been thrilled, but after a while, her hugeness had gotten to her. How much worse to be an unmarried fifteen-year-old girl?

"I've tried to take her clothes shopping a couple of times," Gabby added. "She keeps putting me off. I think she's scared, which makes me feel badly for her." She shook her head. "I'm so out of my league here. I don't know what to do."

"Have you talked to your mom?" Nicole knew that Gabby was close with both her parents.

"No. I'm dreading that conversation."

"Why? She's raised what, five kids? She may have some advice."

Gabby took another scone. "Nothing like this ever happened with us. She's going to judge me big-time. I can feel it. I'm not sure I can handle whatever it is she wants to say. I know that's making it about me and not Makayla, but jeez."

"How can I help?"

Gabby sighed. "You are, just by listening. Right now I don't think there's much for anyone to do. I have to wait for Andrew to come home so he and I can straighten this out. Then we can talk to Makayla together. United."

"That sounds like a plan," Nicole said. But the truth was, she had her doubts. Gabby and Andrew weren't even close on the issue. How were they supposed to find common ground? And if Makayla and her dad were the ones who stood against Gabby, there was going to be all kinds of trouble.

"Enough about the soap opera that is my life," Gabby told her. "What's going on with you? Are you still seeing Jairus?"

Nicole told herself not to blush. "Sort of. We had a second date."

Gabby raised her eyebrows. "And?"

"It was nice. I like him. I'm terrified, though. My marriage was a mess and I couldn't figure out why until after it was over. Plus, he's a writer. I've been married to a writer."

"Oh, please. That's like saying you dated a contractor once and it went badly, so no more contractors for you. The problem with Eric wasn't the writing. That was a symptom. He was the problem. Look at how he is now."

"What do you mean?"

Gabby softened her tone. "He doesn't see Tyler. He's the dad and it's one afternoon, every other week, and he still doesn't show up. That's not about you, that's him. For whatever reason, he's not interested in anyone but himself."

Nicole hadn't thought about Eric in those terms. "You think there's something wrong with him?"

"I think he's not like the rest of us. Most people want to be part of a social collective. A family, a group of friends. Eric was never like that. He's into the industry stuff and he likes being famous, but he's not connected. Does that make sense?"

Their server arrived with a tray of finger sandwiches, along with a plate piled high with crisps—aka potato chips. Gabby took one of the small triangles.

"It's been over a year since he moved out," she continued, waving her sandwich. "There's no other woman, right?"

"Not that I know of."

"Trust me, he would have wanted you to know. He loves being photographed by the press and he's never with anyone. I'm not saying he's gay, I'm saying he's not into intimacy of any kind. I'm sure you had fault in the failure of your marriage. Everyone gets some of the blame. But you're not responsible for more than like thirty percent. It's not because he was a writer."

A lot of information, Nicole thought. "Jairus still scares me."

"Sure. He's a great guy who's successful and you like him. He's also the first guy you've gone out with since your divorce. Why wouldn't you be scared?"

"You make it sound so rational."

"I'm sure you can make my situation sound rational, too. Distance is perspective." Gabby looked toward the kitchen. "You think there are going to be cookies later?"

Chapter Seventeen

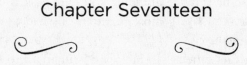

"I can't believe he did this to me."

Hayley heard the words, but they came from so very far away. Not underwater, exactly, but from somewhere else. She supposed the actual problem was she couldn't bring herself to care. Not about her sister's problems, not about anything.

She'd been home for a couple of days now. In her head, she felt her body start the healing process. She no longer got as tired. She was able to eat. But in her heart—there was nothing. An empty space. Whatever promise there had been, whatever child had waited, he or she was gone. Replaced with an absence that would never be any different.

Morgan sat next to the bed. She covered her face with her hands, then dropped her arms to her lap. "What was he thinking? He didn't ever talk to me about it. He just did it!"

"Maybe because you didn't talk to him about getting pregnant," Hayley said bluntly. She supposed she should be more gentle or diplomatic, but to be honest, she didn't give a shit.

"This is not the same thing at all," Morgan informed her. "He had a vasectomy. You can't take that back. It's permanent."

"No, it's not. They can be reversed. But a child is forever."

A child was connection and a piece of you that lived on. A child was everything.

"What are you talking about?" Morgan demanded. "A child is something we have together."

"Yes, you have three of them. You didn't ask Brent any of the three times. You got pregnant and he had to deal with the consequences."

"It's not the same at all. How am I supposed to keep him if I can't have another baby?"

Because the only reason Brent would stay was because there was a child? Hayley wanted to say that wasn't true, only she wondered if it was. The only reason Rob had moved back was because she'd been in the hospital.

According to Dr. Pearce, Rob hadn't left her side for a second. When she got out of surgery, he'd been there. He'd slept in her room. He'd brought her home and had moved back. But only to the guest room, she thought sadly. Only to take care of her. He hadn't been willing to talk about Switzerland with her before. Now that she couldn't have children, he had returned.

She'd always assumed they would be one of those still-in-love old couples, shuffling around in their nineties. But what if they weren't? What if what they had was broken? He'd put limits on their relationship. He'd walked out on her. Now he was back, but it was for the wrong reason.

She told herself not to think about it. That she couldn't possibly handle anything but getting better. That it would all work out in the end. But she wasn't sure about anything anymore.

"You're not listening," her sister complained.

"No, I'm not." Hayley looked at her.

Even with no makeup and dressed in shorts and a T-shirt,

Morgan looked good. Vibrant and sexy. She was a bitch on wheels, but for some reason, Brent adored her.

"Your husband is a really good guy," she said flatly. "He loves you and the kids. He comes home on time, he does more than his share around the house, he is involved with the after-school stuff."

Morgan sniffed. "You make all that sound like he's gone above and beyond. We're married. He's supposed to do those things."

"Yeah, and you're supposed to treat him like the treasure he is, but you don't. You treat him like crap and you know it."

Her sister glared at her. "Are you on drugs? Why are you talking to me like this? What's wrong with you?"

A question that would have been funny if it weren't so sad, Hayley thought. When had her life become the stuff of tragedies?

"I'm tired," she admitted. "And yes, still on drugs, which I guess means it's okay to tell the truth. You're a bitch. You've always been a bitch. You've been one your entire life, which is okay, but there are consequences for that. Brent deserves better than you, and you know it. So start acting like it. He's supportive and giving and you're never grateful. It's never enough. Honest to God, I can't figure out why he didn't leave you years ago."

Morgan stood and glared at her. "I'm going to forgive you, because you're not yourself. But let me be clear. I will not forget."

"We all know that, honey. You never do."

"Hayley!"

The word came out as a screech. Hayley winced at the sound, then figured it had been worth it. While she was being honest, she was going to admit that telling Morgan exactly what she thought felt pretty good. She should have done it years ago.

"I knew you had this dark side," her sister told her. "I knew it. You've hidden it behind your poor-me routine, but this is the real you. Selfish and mean. Do you know how much extra work I'm having to do because of you? All the prep work. All of it. You couldn't leave well enough alone. You had to obsess about having a kid."

Hayley looked at her sister. "I'm sorry my emergency surgery and nearly dying is causing a schedule upset in your day."

"You are such a bitch!"

"That's enough."

They both turned and saw Rob standing in the doorway of the bedroom.

"Morgan, I told you Hayley was still recovering. If you can't control your temper and visit like a normal person, then you need to leave."

"What? It wasn't me. You should hear what she said. She started it."

"Do I look like I care?" He pushed up his glasses. "I didn't think you coming over was a good idea and I was right. Get your things and leave. Don't come back without checking with me first. Is that clear?"

Hayley had the strongest urge to stick out her tongue at her sister, but she didn't. Morgan grabbed her purse and flounced out.

"I won't be back for a long time," she called over her shoulder. "You're going to have to figure out how to survive without me."

Hayley relaxed back against the pillows. If only that were true, she thought. But Morgan would be back, mostly because she didn't have any other friends.

She glanced at the clock. It was nearly three in the afternoon. Time for her to get up and walk around the house. She had to keep moving on a regular basis so she wouldn't develop a blood clot. She was also supposed to be eating right, drinking plenty of water and getting lots of rest. One out of three, she thought. That was something.

Rob returned to the bedroom. When he saw her getting out of bed, he hurried to her side to help her to her feet. Once she was balanced and nodded that she was okay, he stepped back.

"Better?" he asked.

She wasn't sure what he meant. Was she feeling better physically? She was—that couldn't be helped. But as to the rest of it, she was less sure about anything.

She walked out into the hallway, then turned toward the living room. At least their house was one story—she didn't have to worry about navigating stairs. She made it to the slider, then stepped outside onto the patio.

It was warm and sunny—a contrast to how she was feeling on the inside. The fight with Morgan had been the first thing she'd even somewhat enjoyed since coming home from the hospital. She didn't want to be in her own skin anymore, let alone live her life. Yet here she was, moving one foot in front of the other.

She looked at the backyard. It had been recently mowed and several of the dead bushes had been replaced with new ones.

"You've been busy," she said.

"I can only check on you so many times in an hour. I had to do something with my time."

"You should go back to work."

"I will. On Monday."

She had another couple of weeks until she was cleared to do the same. And then what? Keep going at her job until she was old enough to retire? Look forward to vacations every couple of years? Repaint the living room?

She felt the desperate sadness that haunted her, filling her, pressing down on her until breathing was impossible. She sat in one of the battered wicker chairs and fought against the tears.

Rob moved next to her. "I'm sorry."

"You're not."

"I'm sorry you're going through this. I'm sorry you had to deal with surgery. I'm sorry you almost died."

Okay, that she could believe. But the rest of it? "You're not sorry I have to give up."

"No, I'm not. I'm glad I don't have to worry that you're going to die trying to have a baby. You're going to get stronger and heal and then we'll figure out what's next."

"We?"

"I never stopped loving you, Hayley."

Maybe not, but he'd left her. Abandoned their marriage. "How am I supposed to trust you?" she asked. "Believe in you?"

"I'm here."

"Until I do something else you don't approve of."

"It wasn't like that and you know it. You were going to die."

"But I didn't die. You left because I wouldn't do what you wanted. I don't know what to do about that."

"Talk to me."

She looked out at the new plants. "What is there to say?"

"So after all this, I've lost you anyway?"

"I don't know."

"You were being unreasonable. No one could get through to you."

"You're saying, no matter what, you'll never leave again? I can depend on you?"

"You're asking for blind faith."

She looked at him. "So are you. I'm supposed to get over what happened and at the same time, welcome you back, all the while knowing you could walk out at any time. I had a hysterectomy, Rob. I can't have children, ever. My dream is over and dead and here we are. So you get what you want, but what do I get? What's different for me? Nothing."

"Is that what you think? That I didn't want children?"

"Not as much as I did."

He studied her for a long time. "You're right. I didn't want them as much as you. I wasn't willing to let you die. If that makes me the bad guy, I can live with that."

One of the hallmarks of a successful marriage was the ability to fight fairly. Every article and relationship book said that. Gabby knew it was true, and important. That both parties stay respectful. That people were able to speak and that they were listened to. That both sides were assumed to be coming from a good place. Voices were calm, facts and opinions shared, consensus reached. It was the right thing to do.

Only Gabby didn't want to do the right thing. She still wanted to scream and stomp her foot. She wanted to poke Andrew in the chest with a stick of some kind. Not enough to hurt him badly—she would settle for a slight, disfiguring wound.

As that wasn't going to happen, she'd prepared her points in advance. She'd written them down and practiced her Zen breathing. Or however close she could get for someone who didn't actually do the Zen thing.

Andrew had arrived home from his business trip the previous evening. They'd agreed to postpone their conversation until the morning, when they were both rested and the kids were in camp. Because no matter the crisis, life went on.

While Andrew had slept, she'd tossed and turned, working on her argument. Now the kids were safely out of the house and she sat in Andrew's home office, was facing the man she knew she loved.

She told herself they would get through this, but she honest to God wasn't sure anymore.

"Andrew, I believe you understand that going back to work is important to me," she began, careful to keep her voice neutral. "You've always been extremely supportive."

"I'm glad you think so. I know that you love the twins and wanted to be home with them, but you also enjoyed working. Being home alone with little kids all day hasn't been easy. You're a very good mother."

She briefly wondered if she'd made a tactical error in location. His office was too much like his power center. Not that she had a power center of her own. What? They would talk in the kitchen?

At least she had the pets on her side. Boomer lay stretched out next to her, his head on her lap, while Jasmine was on the arm of the sofa. Small comfort, but she was going to take all she could get.

"Thank you." She smiled, then glanced at her notes. "Andrew, I need to work. I love our girls, but I can't stay home forever. I need to use my brain. I need challenges that aren't about keeping the twins busy and teaching colors. I want more than this."

His dark eyes were warm as he nodded slowly. "I know, Gabby. I've thought about this a lot. You're giving up everything. I wish it were different. I mean that. If I could stay home with Makayla's baby, I would. It's my turn, right? But you don't make anywhere near enough to support our family."

He sounded so rational, she thought bitterly. So "I'm just like you."

"Of course I don't make enough. I was working for a non-profit when we met and I've been out of the job market for five years." Even if she got a job at a big law firm, she would be starting at the bottom. Andrew was a senior executive at a successful firm. He was well compensated for his expertise.

"I'm simply saying that having me stay home isn't an option."

"I get that," she said bitterly. "You get to be the hero, while I'm the bitch who won't listen to reason."

"Gabby! I never said that."

"No. You don't have to. It's like offering your kidney to someone when you know you're not a match. It sounds amazing and you're at absolutely no risk."

"Is that really what you think of me? That I'm more interested in semantics than intent?"

"I think you want to be able to tell everyone you did the right thing." She leaned toward him. "Why am I the only one expected to suffer in all this? I didn't get pregnant, but only my life is going to change."

"I think all of our lives are going to change."

"You know what I mean. Yes, there will be a baby in the house. That will impact all of us. But if I'm to understand what you're saying has to happen, Makayla will go on with her life unfettered by her child."

"That's not what will happen."

"Really? So she'll be the primary caretaker of the baby? Except when she's in school, she'll feed it and get up at night with it. She'll change the diapers and dress it while you or I supervise?"

He frowned. "I haven't thought it through to that level of detail. Is it really necessary all that gets defined today?"

"Yes, it is. I want to know what you think is going to happen. I want to know what you think *I'm* going to be responsible for with the baby. How much is me and how much is her." Because they all knew it wasn't going to be him. Not that she could say that.

"Will she be expected to come home directly after school to care for the baby? Will she have to give up after-school activities or time with her friends?"

The frown deepened. "You're angry."

"You're just now getting that?" She sucked in a breath. "Please answer the question."

"I don't know why you're insisting on making this baby a punishment for her."

Gabby stood and crossed to the bookshelves, then turned back to face him. Tears burned but she refused to let them fall.

"I'm not," she said quietly. "I'm really not trying to punish her, Andrew. But I'm also trying not to punish myself. Makayla made choices. There need to be consequences for her. From what you're suggesting, the only consequences are mine. That hardly seems fair."

"The baby will be a part of our family. We'll all pitch in. I'll help when I'm home. Makayla will help when she—"

There it was. The truth unfettered by anything pretty. Bold and ugly and real.

Gabby turned on her heel and walked out of the room. She couldn't do it. Couldn't have the rational fight. Not right now. Not about this.

Andrew stepped into the hallway. "Gabby? What's wrong?"

"You said it. You finally said it. I knew, of course. How could I not?"

"I honest to God have no idea what you're talking about."

She stopped and turned back toward him. As she gazed into the eyes of the man she would have sworn she loved more than anyone in the world, she wondered if their marriage would survive this.

While the chasm wasn't as obvious as an affair or a gambling problem, it was still building a wall between them. Not what he wanted her to do as much as his inability to truly grasp his part in the problem.

"You said Makayla would help," she said softly. "It's not Makayla's baby and I'm helping her. It's the other way around. As far as you're concerned, she'll give birth, then go back to living her life. Nothing will change for her but everything will change for me. That's wrong, Andrew. Worse, you can't see it. That's what I can't get over. You not being able to see it at all."

Chapter Eighteen

Nicole was as ready as she could be. The house was clean, the grill prepped, the food in the refrigerator. She'd gone with steaks because they were easy, along with her tarragon green bean salad that everyone seemed to like. She'd asked her friend Shannon to recommend a nice but not too insanely priced red wine and in case Jairus preferred beer, she had a six-pack of that. She'd stayed up late making brownies the night before.

Maybe she had been punishing herself for the failure of her marriage or maybe she was just emotionally stunted for not having dated before this, but she had to say living with those flaws was a whole lot easier than dealing with the painful writhing of her stomach and the steady hum of nerves through the rest of her body.

How did people do this? Date? Not worry and appear calm? Were they all faking it or was she a freak?

Questions that weren't going to get an answer, she reminded herself, before heading back to Tyler's room. Her own issues were one thing, but she also needed to make sure he was okay.

She found him sitting cross-legged on his bed, his Brad the Dragon books spread out around him. He looked up at her and smiled.

"I'm so excited!"

"Me, too," she admitted as she settled next to him. "Jairus is really nice."

"Uh-huh."

"You know he's busy with his book tour."

In fact he'd been gone for a couple of weeks and was just now back in LA. She knew because he'd phoned her a couple of times from different cities. The conversations had been relatively short and casual, but still. He'd called her. That had to mean something.

The problem was she didn't know what that could be, nor did she know what she wanted it to mean. None of which was what she wanted to talk to her son about.

"Jairus is a friend," she said carefully. "A guy friend, like Adam or Rob."

"I know." Tyler's brown gaze never left her face.

She wanted to say more, like *we're not dating*, only didn't saying that sort of hint at the possibility? Sometimes parenting was hard.

"I'm glad he's coming over," Tyler added. "Maybe he'll tell us about his next Brad the Dragon book."

"That would be amazing."

She kissed the top of his head and left him to his books, then spent the next ten minutes pacing her living room and telling herself she didn't actually care how the afternoon went. She wasn't really interested in Jairus. He was just a guy who wrote books her kid liked. Nothing more. But the lie sounded feeble, even to her.

Jairus arrived right on time. Nicole answered his knock and found the handsome man standing on her front porch. He had flowers in one hand, a small plastic blue briefcase in the other.

She'd said casual and he'd taken her at her word. His well-worn jeans hugged his narrow hips and long legs and his polo shirt emphasized his broad shoulders. It was a very nice combination.

"Hi," he said with a smile. "Thanks for having me over."

"Thanks for coming."

He handed her the flowers—a large bouquet of mixed blooms—then kissed her cheek. "This," he said, holding up the plastic case, "is for Tyler."

"Should I be nervous about what's inside?"

"Not even a little."

Tyler came running out of his bedroom.

"Jairus! You're here." The boy flung himself at him and wrapped both arms around his waist. "I've been waiting and waiting."

Nicole held in a sigh. So much for convincing her son the visit wasn't anything special. Jairus was his hero—or at least the author of his favorite character—which was probably the same thing.

"I've been waiting, too," Jairus said as he hugged the boy. "I brought you something."

Tyler stepped back and smiled shyly. "What is it?"

"Come see." Jairus pointed to the kitchen table. "May I?"

She nodded, not sure what to expect. Jairus helped Tyler into his seat, then moved another chair close and took it for himself. He set the case on the table and opened it.

Inside the lid were slots filled with pencils, crayons and markers in an array of colors. The rest of the case was filled with pads of paper. Jairus took one out and put it in front of Tyler.

"How would you like to learn how to draw Brad?"

Tyler stared at him, his eyes huge, his lips parted. "For real?" he breathed.

"For real. It's not hard. You start with a basic shape."

Jairus pulled out two pencils. They were both black. He

handed one to Tyler. It was only then that Nicole noticed they were chubbier than normal—just right for Tyler's small hand.

Jairus took a pad of paper for himself and showed the boy how to make the basic shape of the dragon. "I like to start with four circles," he explained. "One that will be his head and three for his body. Like this."

He demonstrated. Tyler drew similar circles on his paper.

"Great. We'll add his tail later. Let's start with his head. You'll want to add eyes and ears, like this."

Fifteen minutes later, Tyler had a pretty decent Brad the Dragon. He bounced to his feet and ran over to her. "Mommy, Mommy, look! Did you see what I drew?"

"It's fantastic. Can we put it on the refrigerator?"

Other drawings covered the white surface. Usually there was a discussion about what should be moved where and what would be sacrificed to make room. This time, Tyler raced to the refrigerator and began pulling down all his drawings. He placed the one of Brad right in the center, then turned to Jairus.

"Can we do it again?"

"We sure can. While you practice, I'm going to show you how to do the steps again. I'll draw Brad in stages. That way you won't forget."

Nicole felt the carefully constructed wall around her heart crumble to dust. How was she supposed to resist a guy who was so good to her son? Who was inherently patient and kind with children?

They sat back at the table. Tyler's brow furrowed as he concentrated on getting the circles exactly right.

"Is this how you learned to draw Brad?" he asked, his gaze glued to his paper.

"Uh-huh. I got a book on how to draw cartoons at the library and practiced a lot. I wanted to draw for my sister."

Tyler turned to him. "You have a sister?"

"I did. She's gone now."

Tyler nodded knowingly. "Like my dad."

Nicole stood by the counter. Now she took a step toward Tyler, then stopped herself. She knew that Jairus meant his sister had died, while Tyler meant… She paused, not sure what her son thought about his father. Eric was never here.

She told herself this wasn't the time for that conversation, but she would be sure to have it later. When she and Tyler were alone. While she didn't want her son missing his father, she hated that Tyler had no relationship with him. Eric had started out as a good father, but since he'd decided to write his damned screenplay, all that had changed.

Jairus and Tyler continued drawing for about half an hour. She retreated to the living room to read and give them space to just hang out.

"I'm going to talk to your mom," Jairus said gently. "But I'll be just in the other room if you have any questions."

"Okay."

Jairus got up and approached her. "I hope that was okay," he said in a low voice.

"Are you kidding? In his world, this is the best day ever."

Jairus flashed her a slow, sexy smile. The kind movie stars made famous. In person, it did funny things to her insides. She suddenly remembered how long it had been since a man had held her. Really held her. She and Eric hadn't been intimate the last year of their marriage. Which meant she was practically a reborn virgin.

Sex was not happening, she told herself firmly. At least not for a very long time. She had a child to worry about. Not to mention her own still-confused feelings. Besides which, Jairus wasn't asking.

But maybe he would, a voice in her head whispered. And if he did, maybe, just maybe a girl could say yes.

Two hours later, Tyler was still drawing. He'd moved on to the fat markers and had figured out the best shades of red to create his beloved dragon. Jairus stood by the barbecue, steaks ready to go on the grill. He had a beer while she'd poured herself a glass of wine.

"I could do a mural," he said as he eyed the cooking meat. "In his bedroom."

Nicole glanced toward the house. "For real? Like a Brad the Dragon mural?"

He laughed. "I'm more comfortable with him than say one of the Peanuts characters, so yeah. It would be Brad. If you don't like the idea, just tell me."

"Are you kidding? Tyler would love it."

"It'd be drawing on the walls. Some people might have a problem with that."

"I can live with it. When he's too old for Brad, we can paint over it."

Jairus placed a hand to his chest. "The cold practical streak of a nonbeliever."

She grinned. "You don't want your kids getting too old for Brad?"

"Never."

"You could continue the series through high school."

"I thought about it, but Brad dating? That would be too weird even for me." His humor faded. "I missed you while I was on tour."

The unexpected words caused her to flush. "Um, I'm sure you were too busy to even think about me."

He studied her. "Is it that you don't believe what I'm saying, or you do believe but it makes you uncomfortable?"

"Both."

"Because?"

She sipped her wine. "Eric's not dead."

"Excuse me?"

"Eric. Tyler's dad. You mentioned your sister was gone and Tyler said that was like his dad. Eric doesn't see him. It's frustrating. I can't figure out what's wrong. It's not like he's running around with a bunch of women. I'm not even sure he dates. But he's always busy with his industry stuff. Meetings. Writing. Whatever. It's as if Tyler doesn't matter to him anymore."

"Maybe he fell in love with Hollywood," Jairus offered, then put the steaks on the grill. "People do. It can be consuming."

"You ever tempted?"

"No. I write a cartoon character for kids. Not exactly fast-lane material. I've had books optioned, but there's never been a serious move to make a movie. Which is fine. It's not my thing. I like what I do, but I enjoy hanging out with my fans more. The kids are great."

She thought about the special event she and Tyler had been invited to. "You do a lot for disadvantaged children."

He raised one shoulder. "It's not that big a deal. I'm not uncomfortable around kids who are different. It's not like they can will themselves to be like everyone else. So we have to adjust."

It was the "have to" part of the sentence that spoke to her the most. Jairus didn't have to. He could write his books, go to signings, then spend his buckets of money, all without getting involved. He chose to make his work be about more.

"Back to me missing you," he said.

She winced. "I thought I'd distracted you enough that you'd forget what we were talking about."

"That might have worked if the subject had been less interesting. How many guys have you dated since the divorce?"

Not a happy question. "Um, counting you?"

"Sure."

She looked at him.

He raised his eyebrows. "So I'm your first. Okay, then. I'm going to have to be gentle and go slow."

"Very funny."

"I'm not joking, Nicole. Divorce isn't easy. I want to tell you that my ex is a hundred percent responsible for what went wrong in our marriage, but she's not. She gets maybe sixty percent. I still have skin in the game. The same with you and Eric. He walked out, but how much of that is you?"

He held up the spatula. "I'm asking rhetorically, by the way. I don't expect an answer to that."

"Good, because I don't always have one. I know I was wrong about a lot of things." She glanced at her house, then back at him. "When he left, he only took a few boxes. It's not that he was leaving me everything else, it's that I owned the house before he and I met and I think, after we were married, I never really thought of the house as ours. That's wrong. So when he left, there was almost nothing of his. He didn't leave a mark on anything."

She still remembered what it had been like when he'd packed up to go. She'd asked when he was returning to get the rest of his things. He'd looked at her and told her he had it all. That the house had never been his.

"Eric left the marriage a long time before it was over," she continued. "I blame him for a lot of what went wrong, but I'm guilty, too. I was willing to let him walk away. I didn't fight. I want to tell you that I didn't think there was anything worth saving, but now, looking back, I wonder if it was because I didn't care anymore. I'd never let him in so it wasn't a shock when he was gone."

Jairus studied her. "Good," he said, surprising her.

"What's good about it?"

"You didn't take the easy explanation. You dug deep for the truth. That's admirable."

"I'm not the hero here."

"No, but you're not the villain, either." His gaze locked with hers. "I missed you while I was gone," he repeated.

She held on to her glass of wine and told herself it was okay. She could take a single step into the abyss that was dating. She could be brave. If she fell, well, she'd survived tough times before. She would survive this.

"I missed you, too."

He smiled. "Was that so hard?"

"It was, but I'll survive."

Late Sunday afternoon, Gabby sat across from her husband in their backyard and wondered why it had to be like this. Why couldn't one of them be sick, or there be a financial crisis? That would be easier. They would have an external enemy to fight together. But this separation of expectations was impossible. She didn't know how to make him understand.

Part of her thought he was being obtuse on purpose. Because for him to see her side, he would have to acknowledge the complete unfairness of what he asked and expected. His position was indefensible, at least from where she stood. But Andrew was nothing if not fair. To survive the argument, he would have to say that purple was green and then defend that statement to the death. Or at least until they'd figured out what they were going to do about Makayla and her baby.

The afternoon was warm and sunny. The twins played on their swings in the shade of the trees on the edge of the backyard. Boomer sniffed his way through the plants by the fence, while Jasmine groomed in the sun and glared at the birds overhead. Makayla was with her mom. For the moment, there was peace. But there was also what felt like a thousand-mile-wide chasm between herself and her husband.

"Have you heard from Lisa or Thomas?" he asked.

She almost asked "who?" before remembering they were Boyd's hostile parents. "No. I'll call Lisa tomorrow. I suspect silence isn't good, but I have no proof at all. For all I know, they're decorating a room for their grandchild-to-be."

"Makayla hasn't said anything about Boyd?" he asked.

"Not to me."

Gabby leaned back against the cushion of the lawn chair. The weekend had been tense, at least from her point of view. She and Andrew were polite, but not especially friendly. They hadn't made love in days—unusual for them.

"I don't trust Boyd," he said. "Why isn't he hanging out here? If he cares about Makayla as much as he claims, why don't we see him?"

"I know. I want to assume all is well. That they're planning their lives together in the bliss that is young love, but I have my doubts."

"You sound bitter."

"No, I sound tired." She sighed. "I don't want to fight with you, Andrew, but you're making this hard."

"We're a team," he reminded her.

"I'm less sure of that than I used to be. Lately it feels like it's mostly me doing everything around here while you work." She held up her hand when he started to speak. "I'm not saying you're not supportive. You are always thinking of ways to be a good dad and a good husband. You work long hours to take care of us. I really appreciate that. But when it comes to the day-to-day life, it's all me. You're asking too much."

His dark gaze was steady. "What if there isn't another choice? Someone has to raise Makayla's child."

"It should be her, or she should give it up for adoption."

His expression hardened. "That's not an option. We've been over this. She isn't ready to be a mother."

"Then she shouldn't be having a baby."

"But she is. We have to accept what is happening. There will be another member of our family to deal with, Gabby. The baby is as much our responsibility as it is Makayla's."

She shook her head. "I don't accept that. We had no part in her decision to have sex. This is her doing. I'm not saying we don't help her. Of course we do. But Andrew, think about what you're saying. Everyone gets to continue with his or her life, except me. You want me to give up everything."

She felt tightness in her throat and burning in her eyes. "I can't," she whispered. "I can't do it. And I won't. I'm not giving up my life to stay home for the next five years and take care of your daughter's baby."

In the silence that followed, she felt her heartbeat pounding in her chest. Boomer must have sensed the tension because he raised his head to look at Gabby. Andrew's mouth twisted.

"I see."

Then she knew. What she'd said—what she'd done. She'd drawn a line in the sand. She'd defined Makayla as *his*. Not theirs, not almost hers, but his. With that handful of words, she'd given up the moral high ground.

Andrew had never treated the twins any differently than he treated Makayla. He'd never seemed anything but delighted about adding to his family. While she'd had to deal with a stepdaughter and, on occasion, his ex-wife, she'd never felt second-best.

"I see," he said again, his tone curt.

She wanted to say that he had to know what she meant,

but there was no point. She was instantly furious with herself, but also at him for what was going to happen. Because Andrew would be a jerk about this. She just knew it.

He cleared his throat, then glanced at his watch. "I'm sorry to have to excuse myself, but I need to call Candace and find out if I'm picking up my daughter or if she's bringing her here."

Gabby nodded. She told herself that the slight emphasis on the word *my* was her imagination, even though she knew it wasn't.

He went inside. Jasmine abandoned her bird-watching to jump onto the cushion beside Gabby. She stroked the cat, letting the cool, smooth fur soothe her. It was like that scene from the old *Terminator* movie. A storm was coming.

Kenzie and Kennedy jumped off the swings and ran over. They flopped on the grass and spread out their arms. Boomer moved close to his favorite girls and licked them both.

"Mommy, when is Makayla coming home?" Kennedy asked.

"Soon," Andrew said from the doorway. "I'm going to get her now."

"Can I come?" Kennedy asked.

"Me, too. I want to go with you."

Andrew looked at Gabby. "If it's not too much trouble," he said. "I'll take the SUV."

She nodded without speaking. It might be sunny and eighty in the rest of Mischief Bay, but at the Schaefer household, the temperature had just dropped very close to freezing.

Chapter Nineteen

Gabby stayed downstairs long after Andrew said he was going to bed. Things hadn't warmed up during dinner, although he'd been careful to be friendly in front of the kids. Now Gabby finished her grocery list for the following morning. Not spending the evening with her husband had given her some extra time to get things done. Just as soon as she was sure he was asleep, she would head upstairs.

She put the grocery list by her purse, along with several fabric shopping bags. She only had three more weeks before school started—and her new job. She needed to get things organized. There was clothes shopping to do and—

She heard a sound and turned. Makayla stood at the foot of the stairs. She was in her pj's, with her hair pulled back in a braid. She looked painfully young and small.

"Hey," Gabby said. "You okay?"

The teen shrugged. "I couldn't sleep."

Gabby pointed to the stools by the island. "Want some hot chocolate?"

"Thanks."

While Gabby collected milk and cocoa, Makayla took a seat.

"How was your weekend with your mom?" Gabby asked. Makayla had been home for dinner, but hadn't spoken much.

One thin shoulder rose. "She's mad at me."

"About the baby?"

Nod.

"She'll get used to the idea. It will take time." Not that Candace was the most affectionate mother ever, but Gabby had to believe she loved her child.

"She's mad at you, too," Makayla admitted in a small voice.

Gabby laughed. "Of course she is. I'm sure she said it was all my fault. That if I'd done a better job with you, none of this would have happened."

Blue eyes widened. "How'd you know?"

"A lucky guess."

Candace had never been a fan. Anything that went wrong in Makayla's life was Gabby's fault. A circumstance she found interesting. If Candace was so damned concerned about her kid, why was she seeing her less and less?

"She wants me to give up the baby for adoption."

Gabby continued to stir the milk in the pot. "Uh-huh," she murmured, doing her best not to dance with joy. Was it possible that after eight years, she and the bitch queen were finally going to agree on something?

"I told her I wouldn't. Boyd and I want to raise our baby together. We're in love."

Gabby held in a sigh. "I'm going to go out on a limb and say that didn't go well."

"No. It didn't. She yelled and said I was stupid and irresponsible. She said—"

The silence stretched on. Gabby turned and saw Makayla wiping away tears.

Gabby turned off the stove and sat down next to the teen. While the two of them were civil to each other, they weren't exactly best friends. So she wasn't sure what to say or do. She put her hand on Makayla's shoulder.

Makayla raised her head as tears filled her eyes. "She said Boyd was going to dump me. That I was fooling myself if I thought he'd last even a month after the baby was born. That we weren't in love at all. He'd just been out for what he could get."

True or not, there was no need to be harsh, Gabby thought, as she pulled Makayla close. The teen relaxed against her and cried.

"Boyd's still with you," Gabby pointed out. "He's not going anywhere, is he?"

"No. But his mom hates me."

"I suspect Lisa hates most people. You don't get to use her opinion of you to feel special, I'm sorry to say."

Makayla gave a choked laugh-sob, then sniffed and raised her head. "Do you think Boyd used me?"

"No." Gabby could speak the truth there. "Look how he's stayed by you. He stood up to his mom. That can't have been easy."

"You're right. He's a good guy."

Gabby didn't think he was going to stay "good" for long, but there was no point in going there. If they were wrong, then they would have to deal with Boyd and the baby. If they were right...well, time enough for that later.

The real takeaway was that Makayla wasn't interested in adoption. Which left Gabby firmly in the screwed column. She didn't want to have to deal with the baby and Andrew couldn't imagine anything else.

"Thanks," the teen told her. "That makes me feel better. I've been worried."

"I wouldn't be unless something happens. Sometimes, in a relationship, it's better to let the other person mess up, before you get mad at them. Getting mad in advance isn't really helpful."

Makayla smiled. "You always give the best advice, Gabby. Thank you." The smile faded. "I'm sorry about the baby. I didn't want this."

"I know."

The mature response, when what she really wanted to say was *You? You're not the one getting stuck, kid. Once you pop it out, your life will return to normal.*

Instead she patted Makayla's hand. "Want to try sleeping now? You have a big day of camp in the morning."

"Yeah. I feel a lot better." The teen gave her a quick hug, then headed upstairs.

Gabby poured the milk down the drain and washed the pot before slowly going to the master bedroom. Andrew was already asleep, as was Boomer. The combination of light snoring and steady breathing made her wish she and Andrew weren't fighting. That they could be the team he always talked about. Only what he asked for wasn't possible.

Not a restful topic, she told herself as she got into bed. She had to let it go or she wouldn't sleep at all. And the morning was going to come really early.

Which it did, she thought six hours later when the alarm went off. She was pretty sure she'd gotten maybe three hours of sleep. The day was going to be tough.

She got out of bed without saying anything to Andrew and headed for the bathroom. After pulling on her robe, she walked to the door so she could go to the kitchen and feed the animals. Andrew stopped her.

For a second, she hoped he was going to say something kind. Something that offered an olive branch, or at least a hint they were on the same side. Instead, he asked, "Do you mind picking up Makayla from camp today? I have a meeting and can't get there in time."

The unfairness of the question cut through her. He got

to demand she give up her life and that was fine, but she referred to Makayla as his daughter once and he now he was going to act like this?

"Don't be a jerk," she snapped. "It's not necessary."

His brows rose, as if he were confused.

"Oh, please. I don't have time for this," she told him. "It's been eight years, Andrew. When have I not picked up Makayla? When have I not fed her, clothed her, taken her to the doctor, to sporting events, to school and to friends, bought her birthday and Christmas presents? When have I not taken care of her? I've always been there for her and you know it."

She tightened the belt of her robe. "All I've asked in return is that she have chores. That she be required to contribute to the household, but you said no, she does nothing around here. I'm the one who said no boys in her bedroom and you explained to me that I was wrong. You knew your little girl *so* much better. So while you get to claim the biological connection, while you get to make all the rules because she's *your* daughter, I'm supposed to just go along with things. And because I *once*, and you know it was once, said your daughter, as in not mine, I'm the bad guy?"

She sucked in a breath. "No. I don't accept that. You're wrong on this. Wrong in so many ways, I can't count them. I want a life. That's not wrong or mean or evil. It's real. I want a job. I want to be able to make choices about my life. I don't want to stay home and raise her baby. I don't. I notice you're not expecting your ex-wife to participate in this at all. Just me. I have no idea how this is going to play out, but you know what? I'm sick of it. You're not going to dictate this one. If we are, as you claim, a team, then we get an equal vote and I vote no. I won't do it and I won't let you make me the bad guy."

With that, she walked out, Boomer and Jasmine close on her heels.

She made it to the kitchen before the shaking started. Until that very second, she'd never walked out in the middle of an argument. She'd never once not let him have the last word. She was sure she'd violated thirty-eight ways to fight fairly and she was confident a professional marriage counselor would tell her she was going about it all wrong, but she didn't care. Not one bit.

Hayley wandered through the house. The windows were all open, as was the back door. It was close to six in the evening and the breeze would pick up any second. Cool air would blow in from across the ocean, bringing the temperature inside down to a pleasant seventy-five degrees.

The days were getting longer—not in terms of daylight. That was actually getting less. No, what she noticed was how slowly time passed.

Physically she was feeling better. There was no escaping the body's ability to heal. As much as she wanted her outsides to reflect what was in the heart—things didn't work that way. She was trapped with cells that regenerated and a system that kept her moving forward. Which meant she had more energy, was more restless and just sitting and staring was no longer enough. She had to be doing something.

She glanced at her phone to see if Nicole or Gabby had texted recently. Her friends were in touch with her several times a day. But there was no new message. Because they had lives, she told herself. Something she was going to have to find for herself, and soon.

So far that wasn't happening. Last weekend Rob had primed their bedroom. Over the past few days she'd painted the trim. Only about twenty or thirty minutes at a time. She rested when she got tired. But as much as she hated to admit it, her energy was coming back and doing something productive felt good.

She would be returning to work next week. She'd wanted to go back sooner, but Steven had insisted she take extra time. Despite the emptiness inside her every second of every day, she could appreciate that he'd been traumatized by what had happened to her. She'd nearly bled out in front of him. Worse, the bleeding had been from her vagina, so it wasn't as if he'd been comfortable applying pressure.

The thought of her tall, strong boss wringing his hands as he waited for paramedics was almost funny, she thought with a smile. Then the smile faded because the results had left her half a woman.

Better to be dead.

She waited for that truth to settle in her. It had, at first. When she'd opened her eyes in the hospital, she'd felt that down to her bones. Now she was less sure. Because as much as she wanted to stay where she was—lost in her grief—her mind was moving on, too. Betrayal came in so many forms.

She heard Rob's keys in the front door and walked out to meet him. He smiled as he stepped into the house.

"Hi," he said as he loosened his tie. "How are you feeling?"

He always asked the same question, every night. The worry had faded over the past week or so, but he still asked. She wondered how long he would feel compelled to voice the question and if he would ever be able to completely relax about her body. Because while he hadn't seen her lying on the floor bleeding, he'd been the one who'd been told she might not make it. That the first night was going to let them know how it was all going to end.

"I'm good," she said. "I finished the trim."

His smile faded. "Hayley, I said I'd do that this weekend."

"I know, but I have to do something. I can't watch daytime TV and I'm already reading nearly a book a day. Besides, Dr. Pearce said for me to start moving around."

"I don't think she meant you should be painting."

"I'm careful."

He followed her into the kitchen. She'd been marinating chicken all day. Now she pulled it out of the refrigerator, along with the salad she'd made and a bottle of white wine. Rob opened the wine while she got glasses.

In the past few nights, they'd started having a glass of wine before dinner. She wasn't on any meds—she'd gone off all her hormones a long time ago. As for her postsurgery pain meds—she was done with those, as well. Over-the-counter ibuprofen handled any pain she still had.

They carried their glasses outside and to their small patio. The sun was still above the horizon, but trees and the neighbor's two-story house provided shade.

She sat on the old, stained plastic chair she'd bought at the Goodwill. The yard wasn't huge, but it could be pretty. Now that they weren't having a baby, they had savings. They could do everything Rob had suggested to fix up the house.

As she thought the words, she waited for the pain to slash through her, to cut her into tiny pieces and leave the chunks to blow away in the wind. Only that didn't happen. There was pain—plenty of it. Loss. Anger, even. She was moving too quickly through the stages of mourning. Sadly, she'd never had the chance to linger in denial. Having her uterus ripped out of her body had a way of doing that to a person. As for having a child, she was beginning to think she'd been on a fool's errand. Maybe that had never been her destiny.

She turned to her husband. Rob was such a handsome guy, she thought, smiling when he pushed up his glasses with that automatic gesture she'd always liked. He'd taken a week off work to stay home with her and had only been back at the company a few days. He called every couple of hours, made sure she had plenty of food in the refrigerator. He took care of her.

Now he rolled up the sleeves of his shirt. She studied his profile, the strength in his jaw.

They still weren't sleeping in the same room, let alone the same bed. Most nights she tossed and turned—her restless sleep broken by dreams of children she would never know. But sometimes she longed for the comfort of his warmth next to her. His arm around her, as he pulled her close.

She missed him, she thought sadly. Missed what they had been to each other. The road back seemed rocky and hard to navigate. She was angry that he'd left her. He was angry that she'd been willing to sacrifice her life and their marriage for a baby. An impasse—one she wasn't sure they could breach.

"How was your day?" she asked.

"Good. Busy." He picked up his wine, then glanced at her. "The usual."

There was just enough hesitation for her to know something was wrong, but that he didn't want to mention it, didn't want to stress her. He was careful these days. Careful to ask about her health, to lightly touch her forehead to see if she had a fever. Cautious about holding her, in case he might hurt her still healing body.

"There's something," she said lightly. "Tell me."

He leaned back in the crappy chair. "This client, Mrs. Turner. She's older. Rich. When I first worked with her, everything was fine, but lately she's always calling and complaining about her car."

"Is there something wrong with it?"

"No, that's the thing. It's working perfectly. We've checked it out a dozen times. She's hearing noises or says it hesitates when she presses on the accelerator. No matter what I do, it's not enough."

"Do you know why things have changed with her?"

"Her husband died," he admitted. "He'd been sick for a while, so I'd been dealing with her since taking the job." He shook his head. "I know what you're going to say. That this is because he's gone, but she knew it was going to happen. Besides, she barely knows me. Why isn't she torturing her kids?"

"She probably is. Or maybe she can't. You're a safe target. She's scared, Rob."

"Of what? She's loaded. Trust me, she'll be well taken care of for the rest of her life."

Hayley thought about her empty days. How she would stand in the middle of what was supposed to be the nursery and wait for the tears. Only there weren't any. She could cry in any number of places, but not in the baby's room. Maybe the space was too sacred for her foolish tears—she wasn't sure.

"Just because you know something's going to happen doesn't make it any easier to deal with," she murmured. "Before, she was his wife and now she's not. She's a widow. If he was sick, her days were probably filled with taking care of him. Even if they had help. Now she has nothing. No one's depending on her. It's hard to feel useless."

He turned to her. "You're not useless."

"I feel that way."

"Because you can't have a baby?"

A blunt question, she thought, surprised he would risk going there. "Sometimes. I wasted all that time and money and we have nothing to show for it."

Tears burned, but she blinked them away.

He moved quickly, putting his glass on the small table between them, then kneeling in front of her on the grass.

"Hayley, no." He rested his forearms on either side of her

thighs and stared up into her eyes. "There's no waste. We tried. We did everything we could and it didn't work out for us. We'll figure out another way. Don't give up."

"We're not going to have a baby, Rob. We are never going to hold our child in our arms. Do you know what that means to me? How much it hurts every second of every day?"

"No. I have no idea." He took her hands in his. "Did I want kids? Sure. But they were always an idea. You're here and real and I'm sorry about what happened, but I'm grateful every second of every day that you're alive and we're together."

He squeezed her fingers. "I'd rather have you than a baby, Hayley. I love you. I want us to get through this."

"I don't know if we can. You left me."

"I know."

She pulled her hands free of his. "That's it? You're not going to apologize."

She thought he might get up and walk away, but he stayed where he was.

"No, I'm not. Maybe I was wrong to leave, but you were wrong, too. You were making decisions without talking to me. You lied about wanting to fix up the house."

She started to protest, but he held up his hand. "Not that you wanted to, but why you did. You knew what I was thinking and you let me. You tricked me, Hayley." One corner of his mouth turned up. "I'm not so blinded by love that I can't see your flaws."

"Too bad."

"We'll both survive." He bumped her thigh with his elbow until she met his gaze again. "I'm sorry I left. I had no idea how to deal with what you were doing. I didn't want you to die and I felt you were beyond reason."

"I was." The confession came out as a whisper.

"But you weren't wrong?"

His voice was so gentle. She knew what he wanted—her to admit she'd gone too far. This wasn't about blame—it was about taking responsibility. He wanted to know that he could trust her in the future.

"Don't worry," she said bluntly. "I can't do anything crazy anymore. I can't have kids. That's over."

"Giving birth to a baby is over," he corrected. "The having kids thing is still a possibility."

"I don't want to adopt."

"I know. But there are other options."

She wished that were true. It wasn't, but Rob had always been an optimist. It was one of the things she liked most about him.

He rested his head on her lap. "I love you, Hayley."

The words hung out there. Not accusing, exactly, but expecting. She settled her hand on his head. Her fingers brushed his cheek. She felt the warmth of his skin and the prickliness of his stubble. Somewhere deep inside, the wall around her heart cracked just a little. Pain bled out, then faded.

There was so much more to deal with. Aches enough for five lifetimes. But maybe she was supposed to see the rainbow in the rain, she thought as she closed her eyes and whispered, "I love you, too."

Chapter Twenty

Gabby stirred the chili. She'd made a double batch so she could freeze the other half for a future dinner. Once she started work, she had a feeling she was going to be scrambling. While she was only going to be working part-time, getting back into the groove was going to take some time.

She had the salad made and rather than bake corn bread, she'd bought it at the grocery store. It was still August—no way she was turning on the oven, except in case of a cookie or brownie emergency.

She glanced at the clock on the stove and wondered when Andrew would be home. When he was in town, he usually called or texted her a few times a day. Since their big fight over the weekend, that hadn't been happening. She wanted to tell him to stop being so immature, but she wasn't exactly reaching out, either. At some point one of them was going to have to call for a truce. She figured it would probably be her, but not just yet. While her head told her that their marriage was more important than the fight, her heart told her not to surrender her hard-won ground.

A sharp scream cut through the quiet of the house. Gabby froze for a heartbeat, then turned off the burner and ran to the stairs. The twins were up in their room, playing dress-up and Makayla was in hers doing whatever it was she did before dinner. Probably texting with friends. No one should be in a position to—

The scream came again. Gabby's heart raced as much from fear as her speed. She hurried down the hallway and found the twins standing together, looking anxious. Kenzie pointed to Makayla's door. Gabby shoved it open and stepped into the teen's room.

Makayla stood by her bed holding her phone in her hand. Tears flowed down her cheeks. When she saw Gabby, the tears turned to sobs and she ran to her.

Gabby instinctively held out her arms. "What happened? Are you hurt? Are you bleeding?"

Makayla shook her head and burrowed into Gabby's embrace. Her thin body shook as she cried as if broken in two. The twins came in and hurried over to hug Gabby. She knew it was only a matter of seconds until they, too, were in tears.

Gabby pulled free of the teen and led her to the bed. She had her sit, then settled beside her. She motioned for the twins to come next to her, where she put her arm around them.

"Tell me what's wrong."

Makayla sucked in air, then started to cry again. "B-Boyd," she stuttered. "He's gone."

"What? Gone where?"

"Away. He's gone."

She held out her phone. Gabby took it and read the bluntly worded texts. Boyd had relocated to a prep school back East. He didn't know when he would be returning to California, so they should probably break up. He ended the text with a casual *hope you have a good summer.*

Asshole, Gabby thought grimly as she handed back the phone.

"You didn't know?" she asked before she could stop herself, then used her free arm to hug the teen. "Sorry. Of course you didn't. Do you know when he left?"

"N-no." Makayla wiped away tears even as new ones appeared. "He said he and his parents were visiting his grandmother, but he was only supposed to be gone four days. The last time I saw him, he didn't say *anything.* He said he l-loved me and would be back soon."

So he was a weasel and a coward. Gabby wished the kid was right there, so she could slap what she assumed was his smug face. She got that the decision to move hadn't been his, but he could have told Makayla to her face.

"I probably have an email from his mother," Gabby said.

Makayla turned to her. "Could you check?"

Because she was desperate for information. Boyd had been the girl's first love. She'd assumed they would be together always. Now she was pregnant and alone. Talk about a nightmare.

Gabby nodded and rose. The twins came with her as she returned to the kitchen. Her laptop was on the small built-in desk she used. There were only a handful of emails waiting and one of them was from Lisa.

It was short and to the point. Boyd's parents had decided it was best for him to be in a different environment, so they'd sent him to school out of state. They requested that Makayla not try to get in touch with him, that Boyd didn't want anything to do with her or the baby. Paperwork would follow, releasing him of all rights to the child. In return, no support would be requested or expected. Blah, blah, blah. Have a nice day.

Gabby stared at the last sentence. "Have a nice day? What a complete and total—"

Aware of the twins standing right next to her, she pressed her lips together, but thought plenty of words. None of them were bad enough to describe Boyd's mother, but it was the best she could do.

Makayla walked into the kitchen. "Is it true? Is he gone?"

"He is. I'm sorry, Makayla. He wants to give up his rights to the baby."

The teen started to cry again. Gabby rose and held out her arms as the girl walked to her. Gabby hugged her tight, then felt the twins holding on, as well.

While the news wasn't a surprise, it still sucked. Having Boyd out of the picture made things both better and worse. They didn't have to include him or his family in any decisions they made, but Makayla was hurt. With things bad with Andrew right now, Gabby felt stressed and hopeless.

"We'll figure it out," she promised, not sure what that meant.

"He said he loved me," Makayla repeated. "He said we'd be together always. How can he walk away from me and our baby?"

Gabby heard the garage door open. The twins released her and ran toward the door.

"Daddy! Daddy!"

She expected Makayla to follow in their footsteps, but Makayla stayed where she was. Gabby heard the door open and the girls greeting their father.

"Daddy! Makayla's crying and Mommy's mad and she screamed and we were scared."

Gabby winced. She knew it wasn't on purpose, but they'd made it sound like she'd been the one screaming, not the teen. Given how things were between her and Andrew, she could only guess how bad this was all going to go.

She braced herself for the accusations and waited for him to walk into the kitchen.

Kenzie came first, followed by her sister, then Andrew.

He looked at her holding his daughter, but his expression was unreadable.

"What happened?"

Gabby hesitated, thinking Makayla would want to tell him herself, but she only hung on, her head buried in Gabby's shoulder.

"It's Boyd," Gabby told him. "His parents sent him to a prep school back East. He's not coming back anytime soon."

"Is there going to be a baby?" Kennedy asked.

Gabby held in a groan. Because the twins didn't know their sister was pregnant. She and Andrew had been putting off telling them. But Makayla had said that Boyd didn't want her or the baby, which meant— Talk about a hell of a day.

The teen looked at her dad. "I don't understand! He said he loved me."

Andrew held out his arms. Makayla stepped into his embrace and began to cry again. Gabby took the twins into the family room and sat them on the sofa. They were both wide-eyed.

"Your sister's boyfriend moved away. She was in love with him, so she's very, very sad."

"Is he coming back?" Kenzie asked.

"Not for a long time."

"Will she have a new boyfriend?" Kennedy wanted to know.

"Not for a while. Her heart has to heal."

"Like when I skin my knee?"

"A little like that." Gabby thought about mentioning the baby, but figured she would wait. If the twins brought it up again they would have to talk, but with a little luck they would forget. At least for a while. One crisis at a time was so much easier.

Three hours later, calm had been somewhat restored. The

twins and Makayla were in bed, the dinner dishes done and a bottle of wine consumed. Gabby appreciated the fuzziness the alcohol facilitated because right now she didn't want to have to think about anything. Certainly not what was going to happen over the next few months.

She sat alone in the family room, her feet tucked under her on the sofa. Andrew had retreated to his office to answer a few work emails. She half expected him to simply go up to bed. It wasn't as if they were actually talking. But he walked in exactly when he'd promised and sat in one of the chairs.

"I hate that little shit," he grumbled. "How could he have done this?"

"You know it was his parents' decision."

"Maybe, but I doubt he put up much of a fight. He could have told her he was leaving. She's devastated."

"She is. Most first loves end badly, but no one deserves this."

"Thanks for being there for her." Andrew held up a hand. "I mean that, Gabby. She was in terrible shape and you were totally there for her. I'm not saying you wouldn't have been, I'm just—" He cleared his throat. "I'm grateful you supported her. That's what I really mean. Whatever you think of me, I trust you to take care of her."

An olive branch, she thought in surprise. "Thank you for that."

He gave her a brief smile. "We've got to stick together through this. We're going to have to be there for her. It might even be easier without Boyd."

"That's what I thought. We don't have to listen to him or his parents. God knows what kind of advice Lisa would have given."

He leaned toward her. "I know. But now Makayla feels abandoned and scared."

Gabby wasn't sure that was a bad thing. Maybe now she would consider adoption. But she would have to tread carefully when broaching the subject.

"I need to ask you something," he said.

She waited expectantly.

"Are you leaving me?"

The question left her openmouthed. "What? Leaving, as in leaving our marriage?"

"Yes."

"Of course not. Why would you even ask?"

"You've never been this angry with me before."

"You've never been this much of a jerk. Are you leaving?"

"No. I'm totally committed to you and the girls. Gabby, you're my wife and I love you. We have to find a way to make this work for everyone."

"I agree. And I think I get to be included in the 'making it work for everyone' statement." She used her fingers to make air quotes. "You can't make me do something I really don't want to do, Andrew. It's wrong. I need you to see that. I need you to understand that putting Makayla's needs ahead of mine makes me feel devalued. I don't want to punish her for getting pregnant, but I don't believe everything goes on as normal for her, either. We still have time to work this out, but I really hope we can find a solution that we can all agree on."

She waited for him to nod and explain how it was all so clear to him now. Instead he sighed.

"So it's still all about you," he said quietly. "I'd been hoping for more."

"What?"

"I'm disappointed, Gabby. Disappointed and a little surprised."

With that he rose and walked out of the room. She threw a pillow after him, but that wasn't nearly satisfying enough.

★ ★ ★

Sunday morning Eric texted right on time. Nicole almost didn't bother reading it. She knew what he was going to say. He was too busy, too important, too whatever to bother seeing his son. She didn't know why he was always blowing off his kid, but there they were—locked in a pattern that didn't seem to be changing.

Still, courtesy required that she answer, so she picked up her phone and glanced at the screen. Then nearly dropped it as she read the text twice.

I'll be there at noon to pick up Tyler.

Who would have thought? She texted back her agreement to the plan, then went to tell Tyler he was spending the afternoon with his father.

Her son was sitting at the low table in his room, working on his drawings. He'd pretty much mastered a basic Brad and was now experimenting with different colors. Traditionally Brad was a red dragon, but Tyler liked him green and purple and brown.

Nicole looked from the boy to the wall. Jairus had sketched out several large Brads. One version had Brad swinging a bat. Another showed Brad surfing. The third was of Brad lying under a palm tree, reading.

Jairus had promised he would finish the sketches on his next visit and then they could start painting the mural. Tyler talked about the project every night and had made Nicole promise to document the process with lots of pictures.

"I heard from your dad," she said, returning her attention to her son. "He's going to take you to lunch today."

Tyler didn't bother looking up. "Okay."

She wanted to say something like, "Hey, won't that be

fun?" or "Aren't you excited?" But she couldn't fake her way through the false enthusiasm. Eric saw Tyler so rarely, she had a feeling the visits were awkward for them both. They were caught in a cycle. The less Eric saw Tyler, the harder it was, the less he wanted to see him. Still, Eric was his father.

She sat on the floor. Her son smiled at her. "What, Mommy?"

"Do you ever think about your dad?" she asked gently. "About seeing him more?"

"No."

"Are you sad about the divorce?"

Tyler frowned. "No. You and me are a team." His expression brightened. "Maybe Jairus could be on our team. You know, when he comes to visit."

"Like an honorary member?"

"Uh-huh. That would be great!"

"It would." She hesitated, not sure what else to say. She wanted to be sure Tyler knew he could talk about anything with her. That she would always listen. But the kid was six. She didn't think he was hiding deep resentment.

"I'll let you know when it's time," she promised.

Tyler nodded.

"When you get back, we'll go to the POP and walk around."

He looked up and smiled. "I'd like that, Mommy."

"Me, too."

She retreated to the kitchen. Restlessness and unease gave her too much energy so she channeled it the way she always did—into cleaning. She took the burners off the stove and soaked them while she scrubbed the cooktop. By the time Eric arrived, she'd scrubbed the floor and cleaned out the pantry. She was tired, but feeling pretty darned righteous.

Her ex-husband pulled up in his BMW convertible, the top

down. Eric wore dark-wash jeans that probably cost as much as all her utility bills combined and a T-shirt that could have been made of silk. His sunglasses were designer and his smile seemed to be even whiter than the last time she'd seen him.

Don't judge, she told herself. There was no win in that. Eric and she were really different people. At one time she'd wanted to spend the rest of her life with him. If she thought he was a dick now, what did that say about her taste?

"Hi," she said as he walked into the house. "How's it going?"

"Good, and you?"

"Great."

They looked at each other. Silence stretched between them. There was genuinely nothing to say, she thought with some regret. They'd been married, had made a child together. Even so, it was as if Eric was someone she'd only known a little bit, a long time ago.

"I'll go get Tyler," she finally said. "I'll be running errands while you're gone, but I'll have my cell with me if you need anything."

"Thanks."

She'd barely made it through Whole Foods when her phone rang. She put the last recyclable tote in the back of her car, as she answered.

"Hello?"

"Hey, we're done with lunch and he wants to go home. You around?"

Nicole wanted to stomp her foot. It had been what? An hour? This was Mischief Bay. In summer! There were dozens of things to do. The Long Beach aquarium wasn't that far away. There was a kid's art exhibit at the POP and a farmer's market in Santa Monica. And that was what she could remember off the top of her head. Imagine if she really tried.

But this wasn't about her, and Eric obviously hadn't thought about what he would do with his son so he was ready to avoid his responsibility once again.

"I'll be home in less than ten minutes," she said. "I'll meet you there."

"Thanks."

She'd barely pulled into the driveway when Eric drove up next to her. Tyler jumped out of the front seat and hurried over to her.

"Hi, Mom. We went to McDonald's. I had a hamburger."

"Good for you." She smiled and held out her keys. "Want to open the front door by yourself?"

"Uh-huh."

He took the keys and let himself in. She'd thought he might come back out to say goodbye to his dad, but no such luck. Eric got out of his car and walked over to her.

"He's growing," he said.

"He is."

Eric shoved his hands into his front jeans pocket and drew in a breath. "I want to talk to you about something."

Relief poured through her. "I'm so glad you said that. This situation is impossible. Eric, Tyler needs you. You're his dad. But he hardly ever sees you and I worry you'll become less and less important to him. You can't get back this time in his life. He's still young enough to want to hang out with his parents. I don't know when that's going to change, but I know it will and then what? You'll want to be friends and he won't be interested."

She paused to draw in a breath. "I want you to have a good relationship with your son and I'm willing to make changes to the parenting plan if that will help. But if you want to keep things the way they are, I guess that's okay, too. Just know you can't keep disappointing him. You have to show up when you say."

Eric's gaze was steady. "I didn't mean Tyler. I had something else to discuss."

What could possibly matter more than their kid, she thought, both irritated and disappointed. "Okay. What?"

He reached into the backseat of his car and pulled out a large shiny blue envelope. "Two tickets to the premiere of my movie *Disaster Road*. I'd like you to come."

She couldn't have been more surprised if he'd held out a snake. "Why would you want me there?" she blurted.

"You were a big part of what happened to me." He smiled. "I know I wasn't the best husband, especially once I started working on the screenplay. But even though you didn't approve, you supported me and I'm grateful." He shook the envelope. "Please come. The movie's going to be rated R, so you shouldn't bring Tyler, but maybe a friend."

She took the tickets. "Thank you, and um, congratulations. You must be excited."

"I am. So I'll see you there?"

"Uh-huh."

Tickets to Eric's premiere. Who would have thought? And while she was happy for him, she couldn't help thinking he should be more worried about his son than his upcoming movie. But if he had been, there never would have been a problem, would there?

Chapter Twenty-One

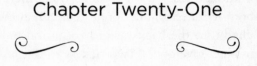

While Andrew always helped the mornings he was home, he also had a way of adding to the chaos. Or maybe that was just her temper talking, Gabby thought as she got the twins seated for breakfast. Either way, she found herself oddly grateful her husband was out of town.

"Guess what we're going to do after camp," she said as she portioned out eggs and bacon.

The twins both looked at her, wide-eyed and hopeful. "What, Mommy?" Kennedy asked.

Kenzie's brows rose as her mouth opened in a perfect O. "I know," she breathed happily. "I know. I know, Mommy. I know." She clapped her hands together. "We're going to get new school clothes."

Makayla, sitting across from them, shot Gabby a fearful glance. "Are we?"

"I thought we'd make our first pass at it. School starts in two weeks. I have no idea how that happened, but it did, so we're going to have to get ready." She felt her eyes begin to water. "My little girls, growing up so fast."

"We want dresses," Kenzie, the fashion princess, said firmly. "And new T-shirts and sweaters."

Kennedy turned her attention to her breakfast, obviously

uninterested in her upcoming makeover. "Mommy, did you tell the teacher we know all our letters?"

"I did and that you're starting to read. She was very impressed."

"Hair ribbons," Kenzie added. "With sparkles."

Gabby smiled at Makayla. "You have to respect that she knows what she wants."

"Sparkles for sure."

"Would you rather do your shopping another day?" Gabby asked Makayla, thinking with the pregnancy progressing, buying clothes could be complicated.

Relief relaxed her expression. "Yes, please."

"Then that's what we'll do. You and I will go out when your dad's back in town. We'll take care of the twins this afternoon. I'm picking them up right at one, which means you at one-fifteen. Is that okay?"

The teen nodded. "I can leave camp early. We're wrapping things up anyway."

"Great. Then we'll all go to the mall and when we're done shopping, we'll have dinner at Red Robin."

The twins both cheered.

Gabby knew that with the incentive of a favorite place, the twins would make their choices more quickly. Or rather Kenzie would. Kennedy tended to go along with whatever her twin suggested on the fashion front.

By the time they got home, everyone would be exhausted. She could sit the girls down in front of a movie while she figured out what had to be washed before it could be worn. She'd already sorted through their clothes to figure out what was school-worthy and what would only be for play. There was also the pile to donate that the girls had outgrown.

For a second she felt a flash of guilt about wanting to give it away. Makayla's baby...

She shook her head. While she didn't agree with Andrew's plan, that didn't mean it wasn't going to happen. The man had a way of being persuasive. She was determined not to stay home with Makayla's baby, but how long could she hold out? She was starting to miss him. Miss *them*. For the greater good…

But what about her? What about what she wanted? Plus, what kind of a message was she sending to her own daughters if she caved? All of which was a lot to think of before she'd finished her first cup of coffee.

"All right, everyone," she told the kids. "Enough chitchat. Eat. You have to get to camp."

The twins finished their breakfasts, then raced upstairs to brush their teeth. Makayla went with them to supervise while Gabby packed lunches. The teen came back down a few minutes later.

"They're putting on their shoes," she said as she leaned against the counter. "About the shopping…"

Gabby finished loading the dishwasher and waited.

"Thanks for taking me on my own. I don't really want to get anything new, but I do need a few things."

Which was not anything like the teen who worried about every item in her wardrobe.

Gabby turned to her. "What's your biggest concern?"

Makayla flushed. "That everyone is going to know I'm pregnant. I'm showing." She pulled her T-shirt tight across her belly. There was a small bump. "They're going to say stuff."

Kids could be brutal, Gabby thought, especially teenage girls. "Have you told anyone?"

"Not yet." Makayla dropped her arms to her side and looked away. "I don't want to."

"Your friends don't know?"

"No."

"Oh, honey, you have to tell them. At least a couple you can trust. You need the support. Friends can make all the difference."

Makayla looked back, tears in her eyes. "What am I going to say? I'm fifteen and pregnant and my boyfriend dumped me?" She started to cry.

Gabby crossed to her and held her tight. "I know this sucks," she murmured, "but it will get better."

"How?"

"I have no idea, but what I do know is nothing stays the same. This is a low, so there's going to be a high. I promise."

As she spoke, she hoped she wasn't lying. That things *would* get better. For all of them, but most especially for Makayla.

Hayley poured iced tea for her friend. "Thanks for coming by. I'm going crazy staying home like this. Steven made me take off until Labor Day."

"Nice boss."

"I think he's more traumatized than nice, to be honest."

Gabby raised her hands, palm up. "Can you seriously blame him? Don't take this wrong, but you almost died. That would traumatize anyone."

They were sitting at the small table in Hayley's kitchen. The day was warm and sunny, so she had the slider open. Later the breeze would pick up but right now it felt like summer. Exactly what Hayley needed.

There were times when she was so cold, she was afraid she would never be warm again. Telling herself that her condition had nothing to do with body temperature and everything to do with what had happened to her didn't help. She'd taken to wearing socks to bed and adding an extra blanket, but she was chilled to the bone. She wondered how much of that had to do with the fact that she was still sleeping alone.

"Just to be clear," Gabby said with a smile. "You're complaining about being given too much time off. Huh. I wonder who else would be sympathetic about that?"

Hayley laughed. "Point taken. I'll stop whining."

"You're not whining at all. We've all worried about you. Maybe you could look at Steven's actions through that filter."

"I'll try. It's just—I'm ready to be back at work. I need things to do."

"You've been doing a lot here. The new paint looks great. And the yard is coming along."

"Thanks." Hayley had signed up for a half-day class at the local nursery. Based on that, she'd come up with some simple ways to perk up the front yard. Rob had done the heavy digging over the weekend and she'd spent the past couple of days planting.

"I'm feeling better," she admitted. "Physically stronger." Not so much in her heart, but no one wanted to hear about that. "So what's new with you?"

Gabby made a face. "Nothing. Andrew and I are still fighting. Well, not fighting exactly, but not talking very much."

Hayley rested her elbows on the table and leaned forward. "He's still insisting you stay home with Makayla's baby?"

"Yup."

Hayley couldn't believe it. That was too much to ask. It was one thing if Gabby's great goal in life was to be a stay-at-home mom, but she'd been dying to get back to work for a couple of years now.

"You can't get him to listen?"

"Apparently not. I've tried to reason with him and we're not making any progress. The last time we discussed all this, he said he was disappointed in me." Gabby turned away. "Those were his exact words. I don't get it. Why don't I matter?"

"You do matter, Gabby. You have to see that. He loves you. He's trapped between you and his daughter. I know which side he should come down on, but he has to figure that out for himself."

"He's so damned stubborn." Gabby sipped her tea. "Did I tell you Boyd's gone?"

"What? No. Poor Makayla."

Gabby told her how the boy had simply disappeared. Hayley listened intently, wincing when she heard about the text message.

"That's crappy. Who does that?"

"A sixteen-year-old boy," Gabby said. "I feel horrible for her. It's just one more pile of shit on this road. Next up, we talk to Candace. Like that will go well." She leaned back in the chair. "I'm a horrible person because I keep hoping that she'll give up the baby for adoption."

"That doesn't make you horrible," Hayley said automatically, even as she emotionally distanced herself from the conversation. She could talk about this, she told herself, as long as she didn't think about it too much.

"It would solve a lot of problems. There are hundreds of wonderful couples who desperately want a—" She slapped her hand over her mouth. "Oh, God. I'm sorry."

"It's okay."

"No, I'm sorry. Talk about insensitive. For a second, I forgot."

Hayley allowed herself a slight smile. "Amazingly enough, I don't expect you to spend every second of every day thinking about me."

"But I'm your friend. I *should* be thinking about you."

"And you do. Gabby, it's fine. I know the prevailing wisdom on adoption."

"But you don't want to go that route."

"I can't."

"I thought your parents were good people."

"They were," Hayley said slowly. "It's not about good-ness. It's about…"

"Morgan?" Gabby asked. "You know she's having a cow with you gone, right? When I was there last week, she was completely insane. There's not enough help and the place wasn't set up at all. We had to open bags of cut-up vegetables ourselves and go find the spices."

Hayley thought about the three messages her sister had left on her phone. "We're not speaking. She got a little dif-ficult the last time she was here and Rob threw her out." Hayley wasn't sure how she felt about how he'd reacted. She must approve because she hadn't tried to get in touch with her sister since. She had to admit, a Morgan-free world was very peaceful.

"Tell me you're not going back," Gabby pleaded.

Not go back to Supper's in the Bag? She'd never considered otherwise. She had to help—Morgan was her only family.

Yet as the question sat unanswered, raw truth formed. They no longer needed the money. Even more important, she'd never much liked the job and working for Morgan was a nightmare. Her sister was bossy and demanding and…

"Oh my God," Hayley breathed. "I don't want to go back."

"Victory!" Gabby toasted her with her iced tea glass. "Good for you."

Was it good? Hayley turned the undefined sensation in her chest over a couple of times. Relief, she thought carefully. Maybe a little freedom with a giddiness chaser? She could sleep in on the weekends, like a regular person. Use her free time to discover a hobby or two she liked. There were pos-sibilities.

But as soon as she thought about how joyful that all would be, the sadness returned, nearly crushing her with its weight. She felt the heaviness against her shoulders and thighs and it was suddenly hard to breathe.

Gabby grabbed her hand. "I saw that," she whispered. "Oh, Hayley, how can I help?"

"You can't. I have to work through this on my own."

"No, you don't. Your friends love you. Rob loves you. You're not alone."

Hayley knew that was true and also that it didn't make a difference. "You don't understand."

"Then help me get it. Why do you have to have your own biological child? Is it the DNA thing? You want to pass on who you are? Is it having a true biological connection? Someone who comes from you because you don't know who you are and if you have a baby, you'll have that link?"

"You've thought about this a lot," she said, surprised at Gabby's insights.

"Of course I have. You're my friend. I want you to be happy."

Happy. That sounded nice. Not possible, but nice.

"My adoption was completely closed," Hayley said slowly. "I've left my information with several registries, but it's obvious my biological parents don't want to get in touch with me. I'm sure there are ways to hunt them down, but why? So that's some of it."

"Is Morgan part of it, too?"

"Yes. She's so—"

"Bitchy? Mean? Selfish?" Gabby drew in a breath. "Sorry, I interrupted."

Hayley managed a slight smile. "Yes, but it was a good one.

She's difficult. It's all about her, all the time. I'm starting to wonder if it's always been that way."

"Of course it has. She was born bitchy. If you're still thinking about your parents acting differently with her, it's because they had to. All that attitude and selfishness in a seven-year-old?" Gabby shuddered. "Talk about a nightmare. You were the good kid. Trust me on that. They didn't love her more. They loved her differently."

Hayley knew Gabby was exaggerating, but there was also truth in what she was saying. If she accepted the premise that her parents loved her just as much, then needing a child of her own was…foolish. And she wanted to believe, wanted to know that she could love an adopted child just as much.

Of course if she couldn't have children of her own, did it matter? Whatever love she could give would stand on its own—uncompared to… To what? Real love? But that was stupid. She loved Rob completely, even though he wasn't a biological part of her.

"I'm so confused," she admitted. "About everything." She smiled. "You're a good friend. That, I know for sure."

"No, I'm an average friend. A good friend wouldn't whine so much."

"You don't whine. You have a lot going on. Makayla, her pregnancy, Andrew being annoying."

Gabby laughed. "There is that." Her smile faded. "About Makayla's baby," she began.

"No," Hayley told her. "I couldn't. Even if I were to adopt, it's too close. Does that make sense? Makayla would be right there, as would you and Andrew."

"I get it," Gabby told her. "It's taking open adoption a step too far. For what it's worth, you'd be my first choice."

Another healing block filled in a bit of the hole in her heart. Hayley reached out and squeezed Gabby hand. "It's worth a lot."

Gabby had only been at Candace's town house once before. The three-story home was as coolly elegant as the woman herself. White walls, pale hardwood floors, white and ivory furnishings with the odd splash of deep orange as an accent color. There was a view of the ocean and plenty of open space. No toys, no pet hair, nothing to say that a real person actually lived here.

She and Andrew had left the twins home with Cecelia so the conversation would be more private. Makayla had begged to be left behind as well, but as they were discussing her pregnancy and the ramifications of Boyd's abandonment, her presence had seemed pretty necessary.

Andrew and Gabby still weren't overly friendly, so Gabby had some concerns about the meeting. She suspected that while Candace didn't want Andrew back for herself, she wasn't above the pleasure of knowing there was trouble in paradise. So Gabby smiled in all the right places and sat right next to the man she'd married. Surprisingly Makayla had sat on her other side, pressed against her, as if the three of them were there to offer a united front.

Candace didn't bother offering refreshments. Instead she glanced pointedly at her platinum-and-diamond watch, then said, "I'm not sure there's a point to all this. Boyd is gone. No one's surprised he ran off. Makayla is fifteen and pregnant. If it's too late for an abortion, she's giving up the baby."

Gabby couldn't believe she and Candace were on the same page. Even if Gabby's way of explaining their position would have been slightly less blunt.

"That's not what Makayla wants," Andrew told his ex.

Candace swung her cool gaze to her daughter and sighed heavily. "Really? You're going to be stupid and say you *want* to have the baby?"

Makayla flushed.

"Candace," Andrew snapped. "Don't be a bitch."

The other woman stiffened. "It's my house, I'll be how I want to be. It's also my daughter." She glared at Makayla. "The damage is done. Let's make the best of a bad situation. Are you seriously going to tell me you're throwing your life away by keeping that baby? Then what? Will you get a job at some fast-food place? Go on food stamps? Won't we all be so proud."

Gabby found herself standing up. "Stop it. Stop it right now. We're all dealing with the situation. Nobody is delighted by where we find ourselves but belittling your daughter won't help anything."

Candace studied her for several seconds. "Well," she said slowly. "The mouse roars. Who would have thought." She rose, as well. "I'm done with this. Makayla, you think about what you're doing with your life. Bad enough to have a baby. Worse to keep it."

With that she waved toward the door. "Now it's time for all of you to be going."

Makayla stood. Tears filled her eyes, but didn't fall. She started to say something, then turned and started for the door. Gabby hurried after her.

Andrew spoke to his ex-wife, but Gabby couldn't hear what he was saying. Nor did she care. Once they were outside, Makayla burst into tears. Gabby held her close and wondered how the hell they were going to get out of this alive.

Gabby made the decision to drive down to South Coast Plaza. Yes, it was ridiculously far when they had Del Amo not fifteen minutes from the house, but she figured Makayla would be more comfortable shopping in Orange County. The odds of running into any of her friends were remote, which meant the teen could relax. Plus, she hoped it would help the teen forget about the horrible encounter with Candace.

To that end, Gabby pulled Makayla out of camp so they could go early Thursday morning. They'd showed up right when the mall opened with the idea they could have plenty of time to shop and still get back to pick up the twins.

Unfortunately what had started out as a hopeful plan had turned into something closer to a disaster. Makayla brushed away tears as she walked out of the trendy store.

"Nothing fits," she complained. "The pants won't button and the shirts are all stupid. I hate this."

Gabby walked beside her, not sure what to say or do. Makayla had reached that awkward stage of her pregnancy where her regular things were starting to be too small but maternity clothes were weeks or months away. Not to mention weird for a fifteen-year-old.

They'd been to three stores and nothing had worked. Drawstring pants weren't in style and regular jeans that fit around her growing belly were ridiculously huge in the legs. They had found a couple of cute leggings that would work, along with a few tunic tops, but she would need more than that for school.

"What about dresses?" Gabby asked. "Come on. Let's go look at Nordstrom. They always have pretty things. It's going to be warm for a few more months. A nice A-line style will work. Maybe a couple of jumpers with a sweater underneath. You could wear tights and cute ankle boots."

Makayla sniffed. "I never wear dresses."

"So. You could try something new. You'd look adorable."

Makayla was a size two or four. It was hard for her to look bad. Even pregnant, she was adorable.

"I didn't think of dresses," the teen admitted. "Can we try some on?"

"I think we should."

They headed for the large department store. As they got on the escalator, Makayla looked at her. "Are you mad at me?"

"No. Why would I be?"

"Because of all this. It's hard. My mom…"

"Oh, honey, we so don't have to talk about her. Yes, it's been challenging."

Makayla smiled. "Because I'm pregnant."

"Really? I hadn't heard."

That earned her a second smile. The teen sighed. "I know Dad's mad at me."

Gabby told herself that defending Andrew made her the bigger person. "He's not mad, sweetie. He's unhappy about the situation. It's not what anyone wanted. I know you didn't."

"Tell me about it." She touched her belly. "If I could take those two times back, I would. Especially with Boyd gone."

"You still haven't heard from him?"

"No. Nothing. Just that one text. A couple of my friends heard he moved and I told them we broke up a few weeks ago."

Gabby supposed she should chide her for lying, but didn't have it in her. "I'm sorry he was a jerk."

"Me, too. I'm never having another boyfriend."

"Yeah, that will last fifteen minutes."

"It's going to last nine months. Or longer." They stepped off the escalator. "No one's going to want to go out with a single mother who's still in high school. My life is over."

The tears returned. Gabby pulled her to the side of the entrance and put her hands on the girl's upper arms.

"Stop," she said firmly. "Yes, there's a lot to deal with, but there's no point in worrying about it all, right this second. Boyd is gone. He turned out to be a very bad boyfriend and I'm sorry he hurt you. That's something reasonable to be thinking about right now. We're going to go try on dresses for you, because school starts soon. After you pick out some dresses, we are going to go spend a ridiculous amount of money on new shoes because I think it will help. Am I wrong?"

Makayla surprised her by hugging her. "Thank you," she whispered. "You're the only one I can count on, Gabby. You're being so nice."

The words surprised her. "I love you, Makayla. Sometimes you're really annoying, but even then, I love you. You know that, right?" The words were automatic. It took Gabby a second to figure out she meant them. She wasn't sure when that had happened, but it had. Somehow the disaster of the pregnancy had brought them together.

Makayla was crying again, but Gabby figured it didn't matter because she was fighting a few tears of her own.

"We're a mess," she whispered. "Both of us."

"Yeah, but soon we'll be messes with new shoes."

Chapter Twenty-Two

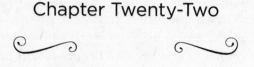

Nicole resisted the need to ask, yet again "How are you feeling?" Hayley had said she was doing better and Nicole needed to take her at her word.

They were sitting out in Nicole's backyard, enjoying the warm afternoon. Tyler was at a friend's birthday party. Rob was helping a friend with a car and Jairus was still on book tour. Not that Nicole would have expected to spend the day with him, had he been home.

They were in touch every day. Texting, mostly, with the occasional phone call. There had been a few pictures of his fans waiting to meet him and one very funny video of his empty hotel room, with the title *No hookers here.*

She hated to admit it, but she kind of missed him.

"Did you go Thursday?" Hayley asked.

Nicole raised her eyebrows. "To Supper's in the Bag? Yes. I depend on those meals. Shannon joined us. Morgan is not a happy camper."

The corner of Hayley's mouth twitched. "Gee, that's too bad."

Nicole laughed. "She is so missing you. I don't think she had any idea how much work you did for her. Are you really not going back?"

"I sent my resignation last week. I haven't heard from her since. Or before. We had a fight after I got home from the hospital."

"Let me guess. She said you were being selfish with your surgery and she needed you to get back to work right away."

"You were spying."

"I'm a good guesser."

Nicole studied her friend, taking in the faint bloom of color on her cheeks and sparkle of health in her eyes. Although she was still recovering from her emergency hysterectomy, Hayley looked better than she had in months. Maybe years. Nicole would guess it was a combination of rest, not being on hormones and not bleeding anymore. Hayley might not like the outcome, but at least the question had been answered.

"How's work?" Nicole asked.

Hayley rolled her eyes. "Ridiculous and nonexistent. My leave has been extended."

"Accept the coddling in the spirit in which it is meant."

"I'm trying, but everyone is treating me like I'm some delicate flower."

"You kind of are."

"Not really. How are things at the studio?"

"Great. I have lots of clients and have added two more classes, so yay." Nicole thought about the envelope tucked in her dresser drawer. "I saw Eric last weekend."

"You mean he showed up to see Tyler? Isn't that a surprise?"

"It was. He took him to lunch. Tyler said it wasn't very fun. They don't know each other anymore. It's sad." She shifted in her chair. "He, um, gave me two tickets to the screening or opening or whatever for his movie."

Hayley's eyes widened. "Seriously? Okay, is it just me or is that strange?"

"I thought it was. He says it's because I was a big part of him writing the screenplay."

Hayley snorted. "You mean you supported his ass while he typed and surfed."

"Look who has attitude."

"I can be tough. Not often, but every now and then. Do you want to go to the screening?"

"I can't decide. I'm embarrassed to say, I still don't know what the movie's about. I've read a bit about it online, but I never read the screenplay. Eric kept saying it wasn't ready. Then we were divorced and it seemed weird to ask. So I know as much as the rest of the world. Apparently the story's about a regular guy who saves the world. It's a thriller with heart and humor."

"Are you still seeing Jairus?"

The change in subject had her squirming. "He's on his book tour, so he's been gone."

"But you're still together."

"We're not *together*. We're, um…"

Hayley waited patiently.

"Yes, I'm still seeing him," Nicole admitted quietly. "We're texting every day."

"So take him with you. I've seen the photos. Jairus is a good-looking guy. It's not like events like this are part of your everyday life. Go have the experience with a handsome man at your side and call it a win. You'll look like the gracious ex-wife and you get your curiosity satisfied in one easy night. What's the movie called?"

"*Disaster Road.*"

"That's appropriate. You need to do this. It will give you closure."

When Hayley put it like that, going made sense. "I'm a

little nervous," she admitted. "I have no idea what to expect from an event like that."

"Ask Shannon. I'm sure she's been to premieres or knows someone who has. Jairus might have been, too. He's a celebrity."

Only to kids under the age of ten, she thought. Funny how Eric and Jairus were both writers, but they seemed so different. Eric was aloof, keeping to himself. He was mostly interested in the workings of Hollywood and how he could be in the inner circle. Jairus seemed to really care about his readers.

"Okay, I'll ask him," she said. "He might still be out of town on that day."

"I suspect he'll make it back if he can. So you like the guy?"

Nicole resisted the need to squirm again. "He's nice."

"And?"

"He's great with Tyler. Funny and patient. I'm surprised he doesn't have kids of his own. He'd be a great dad." She thought about how he'd been busy taking care of his sister as his marriage fell apart. She would guess that was one of the reasons. Maybe *the* reason.

Not that she would ask. Every marriage had its secrets. She had plenty from her time with Eric.

"I wish I could say the same about my ex." She raised her hand. "I know, I know. Old news. But I still can't reconcile what he's doing with how I feel about Tyler. He's everything to me." She sighed. "It's like with the house. I feel like he was never here. Not really. He moved in and when it was time to leave, he moved out. But nothing had changed. He didn't leave his mark on anything. Is that him or me?"

"It's both." Her friend raised her shoulders. "I think Eric is one of those people who simply doesn't connect deeply. It's not bad—it just is."

"That's what Gabby said, too." She thought about how

he'd been after selling his screenplay. "He's not into his success for the sex. There were pretty young women hanging all over him and I genuinely think he didn't care."

"You and I can't imagine not being involved. With our family, our friends. No matter how Morgan annoys me, I'm still going to call her in a few days because she's my sister. We're not islands, but I think Eric really is. He's getting enough. He not only doesn't need a close relationship with Tyler, he can't see what he's missing. It's like asking us to imagine what it would be like to live on planet Zenon."

"Planet Zenon? Is this a *Star Wars* thing?"

Hayley laughed. "You know it's not. You're as much a *Star Wars* geek as me. My point is, maybe it's not you. Maybe it's him."

"That's tidy. So I don't have to take any responsibility?"

"You know you do. You did plenty wrong in your marriage."

"Gee, thanks for the vote of confidence."

"Sorry, but you did. We all mess up. It's the nature of being human. The difference is you're looking at what happened and are searching for an answer. I suspect Eric has simply moved on to the next chapter of his life."

"You've become very wise, Obi Wan."

"If only that were true." Hayley sipped her lemonade. "I've had a lot of time to think. It hasn't been fun, but it's been good for me. To dwell on the fact that I'll never have a baby of my own."

"How much does it hurt?"

"A lot. Less than it did. Now I have to figure out what to do next. Rob and I need to repair the cracks in our marriage." Hayley sighed. "You can't go through what we did without leaving scars."

Nicole couldn't begin to imagine the stress all the fertility treatments had put on their marriage. "Rob's a good guy and he adores you."

"I know. I'm lucky." She smiled. "Maybe you'll get lucky, too. And when that happens, I want details. New man sex is so foreign to me. I'm going to have live vicariously."

Nicole laughed. "Get me drunk and I'll tell you everything."

"It's a deal."

"Hey, Mom," Gabby called out as she walked into her parents' kitchen. She was going to see the whole family in an hour, at her friend Pam's for a Labor Day party. But what she was here to discuss wasn't exactly party conversation.

She'd put it off as long as she could. Makayla could still conceal her pregnancy with flowy shirts, but eventually the truth was going to come out and the longer she waited to tell her mother, the worse it was going to be.

Gabby supposed she'd resisted for so long thinking that if she didn't tell her mother, it couldn't be real. Ridiculous, she thought. Wishful thinking. But there it was. She was an ostrich—burying her head in the sand and exposing her butt to the world.

On the bright side, despite everything that had been happening, she'd managed to stick with the classes at Nicole's studio and sort of stay on her diet. She was down ten pounds. A win she was going to hang on to with both hands. That would make it harder to reach for cookies.

"Gabby!"

Marie walked into the kitchen and smiled. She was dressed in white crop pants and a lacy shirt over a tank top. Gold earrings glittered, as did an armful of bracelets. When it came to jewelry, Marie was a big believer in go big or go home.

Her mother hugged her, then motioned to the bar stools

by the island. Because Gabby had told her she needed to talk, and all important conversations happened in the kitchen.

"You've had me worried," her mother admitted, watching her carefully. "You said no one was sick and all is well with you and Andrew, so what is it?" Her expression brightened. "You've decided to have another baby."

"Not exactly."

Gabby thought about everything going on. Her ongoing fight with Andrew, the way Makayla was so sad and confused, the twins starting kindergarten. Unexpected tears filled her eyes.

"Oh, Mom, it's a mess. All of it. My life is a disaster and I don't know how to fix it."

Marie took one hand in hers and squeezed her fingers. "Tell me what's going on. Then we'll come up with a plan together. We can fix whatever it is. You'll see."

Gabby's relationship with her mother might be uneasy. Marie could be opinionated and bossy, but in the end she was warm and loving. If Gabby was willing to admit she was in over her head, all the preaching would stop and the love would start. She just had to be willing to show her belly.

She sucked in a breath. "Makayla's pregnant."

Marie's mouth dropped open. "No. She's just a child."

"Fifteen. Believe me, we were just as shocked. We didn't even know she liked Boyd that way."

"The father's name is Boyd? Who names their child that?"

"Mom, that's not really the point."

Gabby explained how they'd found out and that Boyd and Makayla had wanted to stay together. She recounted the conversation with Boyd's parents and how he was gone now and Makayla was worried about what would happen at school.

"She won't even talk about adoption," Gabby continued.

"It makes me crazy. Andrew is totally on board with her having the baby."

"Of course he is." Her mother smiled sadly. "Sweetie, he's a man. This is his first grandchild. Not only does he get to see his dynasty continuing, but he has no idea what it means to stay home and take care of an infant. He expects you to do it, I assume?"

Now it was Gabby's turn to be stunned. "How did you know?"

"He's traditional. You both made such a big deal about you staying home with the twins. You made the right decision, of course, but it's such a generational thing. In my day, a woman stayed home to raise the family. Now everyone wants a career and what happens to the children?"

She pressed her lips together. "Which doesn't help you. I take it you're not happy about what he wants."

"No. I want to work. I know it's different from what you did, Mom, but I'm so ready to get out of the house."

"Of course you are." Marie released her hand. "Do you think I don't long for something other than being everyone's mother? That I didn't dream about a job where I was respected for who I was instead of always being Gabby's mother or your father's wife?"

No, Gabby thought in confusion. She hadn't known that. "But you were always so happy."

"My family is a blessing. I'm grateful every day for the life I have, but sometimes, I've wondered how it would have been different. So Andrew wants you to give up your job to stay home with Makayla's baby."

Gabby nodded. "He's promised that he and Makayla will *help*." She made air quotes as she said the word.

Her mother tsked. "Help? It's her baby. She should do more than help."

"That's what I said, but Andrew wants her to be a teen-ager. She needs to go to school and I don't want the baby to be a punishment, but what about taking responsibility? What about consequences?"

"So the two of you are fighting."

Gabby hung her head. "Some."

Her mother leaned close and held her by her upper arms. "Gabby, listen to me. I know what I'm talking about. The children come and go but your marriage should be forever. Andrew can be difficult, but he's a good man. Talk to him. When he doesn't get it, try again. Don't give up. You love him. I know you do."

"We haven't been talking very much," Gabby admitted, thinking about how she'd mostly been avoiding him lately. With school starting tomorrow, she'd been crazy busy, so keeping her distance had been easy.

"Talk to him," her mother repeated. "Work this out. Your marriage is worth saving."

"I know."

"I'm not going to tell your father until after the party. You know him. He'll say something and no one wants that."

Marie rose and pulled Gabby to her feet, then hugged her tight. "My baby girl. Let me know what I can do to help."

"I will, Mom. I promise."

"That's my girl."

"Pam never invites me to her parties," Morgan whined. "Why is that?"

"Because she doesn't know you." Hayley smiled at her sister. "I work for her son and I used to work for her husband. You have nothing to do with her."

"But you always say she throws really great parties."

"She does."

"Then I should get to go."

Morgan had simply shown up fifteen minutes ago, with no explanation, no anything. Just a knock on the front door. Rob was at the grocery store, picking up the wine they would take to the party. Hayley had thought briefly about not letting her sister inside, but then had decided she wasn't going to be afraid or back down. Not anymore.

They were standing in the kitchen. Hayley had to fight against customary politeness to keep from inviting her sister to sit down. She and Rob were leaving as soon as he got back—this was going to be a short visit.

"You're not coming back to Supper's in the Bag, are you?" Morgan asked.

"No. That's why I sent you a letter resigning."

"But I need you. The business sucks. I hate it. You did all the crap work. Now I have to. Or hire someone to do it. It's not fair."

Hayley realized that with great sorrow had come freedom. She no longer needed the job, so she didn't have to put up with anything she didn't want to. The word *victim* played in her head, but she'd never been her sister's victim. She'd been a willing participant.

There were nights when she woke up crying—not from any physical pain, but from loss. Deep, bone-chilling loss. But more and more there were times when she felt powerful. Because the choices were all hers now.

"You could sell the company," she suggested calmly. "Get a job working for someone else."

"Why on earth would I do that?"

Morgan's dark hair hung in thick curls. She was beautiful, as always, if one ignored her petulant expression. The permanent sulk was starting to give her lines around her mouth. Wasn't that just so very sad?

Hayley knew she was being bitchy, but was willing to go with it. She remembered their mother saying that it was okay to be a little mean now and then, as long as you felt bad afterward and didn't make a habit of the behavior.

"I miss Mom," Hayley said, thinking their mother would have had a lot of sage advice to give about so many things. "Do you still have the scrapbooks she made for us?"

"What? No. I have three kids and a husband. I barely have room for a pair of socks in my house. And who has time to look at stuff like that?" She used both hands to fluff her thick curls, then let them fall back onto her shoulders. "I can't do this anymore. There's too much stress. I need to get away. Can you take the kids for a long weekend?"

"Sure."

"Just like that?"

"I enjoy my niece and nephews and I haven't spent enough time with them lately. Of course they can stay with Rob and me while you get away."

"Good."

"Are you taking Brent?"

"God, no. He's part of what I need to get away from. Jeez."

Hayley found escape in humor. "You're not the nicest person on the planet, are you?"

"I don't have time to be. My best employee just quit. I'll text you the details."

"I look forward to hearing from you."

Morgan stared at her. "What's gotten into you? You're different. I thought you'd be all mopey and sad, but you're not. Don't you care that you can't have kids anymore? Was that all just a game?"

Hayley felt the path in front of her split in two. She could react from pain or from power. The choice was hers. Morgan was never going to be more or less than she already was.

This was as good as it was going to be for her. But Hayley could still pick her path.

She walked to the front door and held it open. "I'm happy to take care of your kids for a weekend because I love them and they're family. But you do not get to speak to me like that in my own home."

"What's with you? I didn't mean anything." Morgan grabbed her bag and huffed. "Fine. I'm sorry. Satisfied?"

"Not yet, but I'm getting closer."

Chapter Twenty-Three

Gabby inched her car forward in the long line of parents dropping off their kids at school. Makayla sat next to her, her hands clenched tightly in her lap. She radiated tension.

"You okay?" Gabby asked quietly.

Makayla nodded.

"It'll get easier after today. Once you're in a routine."

"I'm going to get bigger. People are going to find out."

As far as Gabby knew, Makayla still hadn't told any of her friends she was pregnant. She hadn't wanted Gabby and Andrew to tell the school, either. Gabby had insisted on having a conversation with her counselor so there would be a record of her condition, in case something happened. Makayla also had a three-week reprieve on gym class, so she wouldn't have to get changed in front of the other girls and then wear an outfit that would make her pregnancy obvious.

Gabby honestly didn't know what to say. The end result was inevitable. As Makayla had said—she was going to get bigger. There was no hiding where this was going. She probably had about two months until there was nothing anyone could do to conceal her condition.

Gabby reached out and placed her hand over her step-daughter's fists. Funny how in the past few weeks Gabby's emotions had shifted. She was no longer angry. Somehow she had moved to a form of acceptance, with a little sadness thrown in. She still wasn't ready to raise the child herself, but she was able to separate her feelings from what Makayla was going through.

"You have your cell," she said. "I'll be around. Call me if you need me."

Makayla nodded.

They reached the drop-off point. Makayla started to get out of the car, then, at the last minute, turned and hugged Gabby.

"Thank you," she whispered, tears glistening in her eyes. Then she was gone.

Gabby drew in a breath, before forcing herself to turn and smile at the twins. "Ready?"

They both grinned back.

"We're ready, Mommy. We're going to have fun." Kennedy spoke with confidence, as if there were no alternative to a good time in kindergarten.

"Yes, you are," Gabby told her.

She drove out of the high school parking lot and onto the street. The elementary school was only a few blocks away and the start time was such that she made it with minutes to spare. After finding a parking space, she helped the twins out of the car and walked with them to the classroom.

There were kids everywhere, from ages five to eleven. The differences in sizes and how they talked was amazing. Some of the sixth graders looked closer to twenty than ten with their trendy clothes. A few even had on makeup.

Kenzie had chosen the outfits for the day—summer dresses in matching fabric but in different colors. Gabby had already taken about a thousand pictures, but she used her phone to snap a few more as the girls paused by their classroom.

Kennedy hugged her. "Mommy, we're going to be fine."

"I know you are. You're both going to do great." Gabby crouched down and put her arms around them both. "You're both so smart and you get along so well with other children. I love you and I'm proud of you."

She stood and watched the girls walk into the classroom. They greeted their teacher and went to their seats.

Kindergarten orientation had been the previous week. There'd been a "practice" day with everyone arriving and having a chance to meet. Now the girls talked to other students as they waited for class to begin.

Gabby stood outside with a group of other parents. They all looked shell-shocked, as if unable to believe this had happened.

Andrew hurried up to join her. He'd been stuck home on a conference call.

"Did I miss it?"

Gabby wiped away tears and pointed through the glass in the door. "They're doing fine. It's going to be okay."

He put his arm around her and drew her against him. "Our little girls," he said quietly. "You did a hell of a job with them."

"It was both of us." The words were automatic but she found she actually meant them. Until recently, she and Andrew had always been a team. Now she leaned against him and wondered when they would be again.

Her mother's advice weighed on her. To make things work, she was going to have to be mature and didn't that suck.

"Want to get a cup of coffee before you go to work?" she asked.

"I'd like that."

He followed her to Latte-Da where they got their drinks, then settled at a table outside on the sidewalk. There was still a hint of morning coolness in the air and not many people walking around. It was as if they had Mischief Bay to themselves.

Gabby studied her husband. She loved him. Even when he made her crazy. Which meant she needed to establish communication between them.

"I'm sorry."

Words she'd been planning to say, only he'd been the one to say them first.

She stared at him. "Excuse me?"

"I'm sorry, Gabby. I never meant to hurt you. I was so focused on Makayla and how we were going to handle the baby that I couldn't see that by insisting, no, assuming, you would take care of him or her, that I was making you feel less important. I didn't see that I wasn't respecting you as a person. As a partner and the woman I love." His mouth twisted. "We have to agree on where we're going together. As a couple and a family. It's not a solution if one of us feels betrayed."

She wondered if she looked as shocked as she felt. Part of her wanted to reach out and touch Andrew's forehead. Did he have a fever? How on earth…

"My mother," she said slowly.

"Marie cornered me at Pam's barbecue yesterday. She lulled me into thinking she was on my side, then pounced." His smile was rueful. "Except what she said got me to thinking." He reached across the table and took her hand in his. "Gabby, I don't want you unhappy or mad at me. I don't want you to sacrifice everything for Makayla's baby. There has to be a way to make it work where the compromise isn't all about you."

Tears burned. "I'd like that," she whispered. "I don't want to be mad, either. And I don't want Makayla punished. I just need to not be the push point."

"I agree. Somehow we'll figure this out."

"As long as we keep talking," she said. "And we don't assume anything." She hesitated. "I'm worried about Makayla."

"In what way?"

She told him about their shopping expedition. "She hasn't mentioned the pregnancy to her friends. They're going to figure it out at some point and I don't think it's going to go well."

"Do you think she'll be bullied?"

"I don't know. I worry that she's withdrawn too much. She's a social kid. But since she found out she was pregnant, she hasn't had anyone over. With Boyd gone, she's on her own. That's not good. She needs her friends." She picked up her coffee. "None of this is easy."

"I couldn't get through it without you. Candace is less than no help. I swear she deliberately makes things more difficult."

"Maybe you should talk to her. Makayla needs support right now. More than she ever has. I'm not saying we need to coddle her, but this isn't the time for her mother to go off on one of her rants."

"I'll get with her." Andrew grimaced. "I can only imagine how that's going to go."

Gabby risked a subject she'd been thinking about for a while. "There are teen parenting classes. I think Makayla should take one. I don't want to have to teach her everything. I think it would go better if she were in a structured environment. Plus she would learn how to balance school and a baby."

She finished and held her breath. Would Andrew agree or would accepting the idea of the class be too much like saying Makayla had to do it all?

"That's a great idea," he told her. "You're right. She has a lot to learn. I remember how scared I was when she was born and I was a lot more prepared than her. Let's get her signed up."

Wow—that was unexpectedly easy. "I've found a couple of places that are local. We can talk about it tonight."

"Good." He smiled. "Okay—now for a more cheerful topic. Are you excited about starting work tomorrow?"

"I am. I'm nervous, too."

"You'll do great."

"I hope so." Makayla's pregnancy had sort of consumed much of Gabby's mental time so she hadn't obsessed as much as she had thought she would. Probably a good thing.

"I'm proud of you, Gabby, and lucky to have you in my life."

"Thank you. I feel the same way."

This was what she wanted, she thought. A good relationship with her husband. Her mother had been right about taking the moral high ground and about Gabby talking to Andrew.

"What does your morning look like?" she asked. "Do you have to get to the office right away?"

One eyebrow rose. "What did you have in mind?"

She grinned. "A little makeup sex. It's been a while."

"It has." He rose and tossed away his to-go cup, then reached for her hand. "I'm all in."

She smiled. "Good. Me, too."

Hayley put the sheets in the washer. Her first full day at work since the surgery had left her tired and a little achy, but she still felt good. At least she'd accomplished something other than sitting around and feeling sorry for herself.

She turned on the machine, then went to the kitchen to start dinner. Now that she wasn't working at Supper's in the Bag, she was fully responsible for the meals, but that was okay. She and Rob enjoyed barbecuing and she would figure out the rest. She had a Crock-Pot she'd never made friends with. That could be a start.

She pulled chicken pieces she'd been marinating out of the refrigerator and put them on a plate. Her cell chimed with an incoming text.

I booked my hotel reservation for the weekend. I'll drop the kids off at three on Friday.

Hayley stared at the words, then swore silently. In her smugness from standing up to her sister, she'd completely forgotten about her agreement to take her kids. She hadn't discussed it with Rob at all.

Before she could decide what to text back, she heard Rob's car in the driveway. He walked in a minute later.

"Hi," he greeted her with a smile, then froze. "What's wrong? Are you bleeding?" The color drained from his face as he crossed to her. "Hayley?"

In that moment she saw all that she'd put him through. How he'd suffered. It wasn't that wanting kids was wrong, she thought sadly. Of course it wasn't. But the price everyone had paid didn't seem fair.

"I'm fine," she said quickly. "Really, I'm good. Don't worry."

He relaxed. "Okay, then what's wrong?"

"I did something stupid. Morgan wants to get away for a weekend and I said we'd take the kids. I'm sorry—I totally forgot to ask you about it. Now she's made plans to drop them off on Friday. Is that all right or do you want me to tell her to reschedule?"

Rob pushed up his glasses, then cupped her face in his hands and kissed her mouth. "I love the kids. Of course they can stay. We'll have fun."

She smiled. "Thank you."

"You're welcome. Is it this weekend?"

"Uh-huh. We'll have to get out the blow-up beds for the boys. And, um, Amy's going to need the bed in the spare room."

The room where Rob was still sleeping.

He lowered his arms to his side. "You okay with that?"

She nodded. "I miss you."

"I miss you, too."

She wanted to say more. She wanted to ask if they were okay. Because since the surgery, Rob hadn't touched her. Not that they could have intercourse. She needed a few more weeks of healing, but still, there were other things they could do. Only there were issues standing between them. Things that hadn't been talked about. She'd gone behind his back with selling the house and he'd left her. They both had things to answer for.

He smiled. "Let me go change my clothes, then I'll start the barbecue. While it's heating up, I want to hear about your day."

Because that was normal, she thought wistfully. What they did now. But was it enough? She didn't know how much had been lost. Worse, she didn't know what the first move would look like, let alone who would make it. And without that, how could they possibly move on?

The world of immigration law, like much of the legal world, revolved around details. Facts, precedent, rulings, exceptions, exemptions, extensions.

Gabby found herself thrown in the deep end with her new job. She'd been given several ongoing cases and had spent her first few days trying to get up to speed. She'd done this sort of work before so had expected to jump right in. What she hadn't realized was that her brain had changed. She wasn't used to slogging through literally hundreds of printed or digital pages and retaining all the salient points. Eight paragraphs in, she found her attention wandering, so she had to go back and read them again and again.

While she'd been home with the girls, she'd tried to stay current with the changes in the law. She'd subscribed to a few online journals and had read them...or so she'd thought. What she'd actually done had been to skim them. Lightly skim them. And she'd apparently retained nothing.

Now it was Friday and she was exhausted. Not just by the change of having to be at a job—albeit only four hours a day—while juggling her family, but by her late nights. After the family was fed and everyone was in bed, Gabby had gone downstairs to read her cases, along with the applicable laws. Short nights, long days and plenty of legalese did not for perkiness make.

She glanced at the clock and saw it was a little after eleven. She had only been in the office two hours and she was on her third cup of coffee. That couldn't be good. Plus next week she had meetings three of her five days, which meant she would need to do the rest of her work at home.

She reminded herself that working at a full-time job in a big law firm would mean eighty-to-ninety-hour weeks. The concept daunted her. How did people do that? She missed her kids. Funny how when she got home, she was fine. She knew the twins were happy with their teacher and their new friends, but here in the office, she worried. She also found herself wondering about Makayla. The teen hadn't said much about school the whole week. She'd been sleeping a lot. Gabby worried she was depressed.

But the most startling part of working was more personal, and kind of sad. Peeing alone was not the thrill she'd thought it was going to be. Honestly, she missed Jasmine's little paw poking under the door and Boomer whining his displeasure if the door was closed.

Gabby got up to get another cup of coffee. As she walked down the hallway, she smiled at her new coworkers and told herself things would get better. That she'd argued about how she *needed* to get back to work. That she couldn't possibly continue to stay home.

Only, she'd thought it would be more fun. Or at least more interesting. Had working as a lawyer always been so dry?

"A first-world problem," she murmured to herself as she made her way back to her desk in her tiny office. She was making a difference. Helping people. Her brain would remember how to focus for more than thirty seconds at a time and she would make new friends. This was everything she wanted and by God, she was going to figure out how to enjoy it.

Chapter Twenty-Four

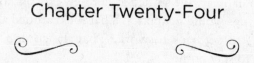

Jairus's place was not that far from Nicole's house. She was careful to take a more complicated route than necessary so that Tyler didn't figure out his hero was a short three-quarters of a mile away. Tyler's love of all things Brad had only increased since meeting the author and Nicole didn't want him stalking Jairus for the next few years.

Jairus was back from his book tour and had invited Nicole and Tyler to lunch at his house. Nicole told herself he was just being, you know, nice. After all, she'd had him over. But all the logic in the world didn't stop her palms from sweating as she made two more turns before going up to Pacific Coast Highway before going north for three blocks and then headed back toward the water.

"Do you think Jairus sold a lot of books?" Tyler asked.

"I'm sure he did."

"I'd go to a signing every day."

"I don't know. When you do something every day, it's not special anymore."

Tyler grinned. "Presents every day would be very special."

"Your room isn't that big. Where would you sleep? On the roof? In the car?"

"On the roof!"

She turned onto Jairus's street and found the address, then pulled into the driveway.

The house wasn't all that different from hers, she thought with some surprise. It was an old-fashioned Spanish-style bungalow. Many of the older, smaller homes in the neighborhood had been torn down and replaced with big houses that filled the entire lot, with only minimal clearance on each side. But Jairus's place didn't stand out at all. She thought maybe the windows were newer and the yard looked well kept. Still, there was nothing about it to distinguish it from others on the street. No flashing neon signing proclaiming *A number one* New York Times *bestselling author lives here.*

Tyler was already unbuckling his seat belt. Her son opened his door and took off for the front of the house. Nicole reached for her purse and the cake she'd made as her contribution for their lunch and followed him.

Jairus opened the front door before Tyler got there. He knelt and hugged the boy.

"Hey, sport. How are you?"

"Good. Did you have fun on tour? Did you sign lots of books? Did everyone want to talk about Brad?"

Jairus laughed. "Everyone did. Come on in." He rose and smiled at Nicole before taking the cake she offered. "You can come in, too."

"Thanks."

She walked into the house. The living room was big and open, with arched windows and large, comfortable furniture done in earth tones. The tables were wood, as was the floor. There was a fireplace at the far end of the room. Seeing as this was Southern California, she knew it rarely got used, but it was still pretty to look at. She guessed the house was a few hundred square feet bigger than hers, but built at the same time.

"I thought we'd hang out in the backyard," he said, motioning for her to lead the way.

They went through the kitchen where he put the cake on the counter. The space was large and open, obviously remodeled. She took a second to envy the stainless steel appliances and the smooth granite countertops.

"Where does Brad sleep?" Tyler asked.

Nicole turned to him and smiled. "Honey, you know Brad's not real."

"I know, but Jairus thought up Brad. He has to live here."

Jairus ruffled Tyler's hair. "You're a smart kid. You know that, don't you?"

Tyler grinned. "I'm smart sometimes."

"Brad does have a room. Would you like to see?"

Tyler nodded so hard and fast, Nicole worried he would hurt his neck. Then she followed the two of them back down a short hallway, past an open door that led to a good-sized bathroom.

Jairus opened the first door on the left. The room was small and painted white with floor-to-ceiling bookshelves on two walls, and storage cubbies on the third. The fourth was dominated by a big window surrounded by a huge mural of Brad's world.

She didn't know where to look first. Tyler began to laugh as he raced inside and sank to the floor. He started pulling out different copies of Brad books from the bookshelf.

"Tyler," Nicole began, but Jairus put his arm on her shoulder.

"It's okay," he said quietly. "He can't hurt anything."

The room was a testament to all things Brad. There were hundreds of books, mostly in English but also in several foreign languages. There were Brad stuffed animals and T-shirts and pens and flashlights, party favors, packages of balloons. In one corner was a stack of Brad towels by a Brad trash can. Possibly from the bathroom collection she hadn't known existed.

"Admit it," he murmured in her ear. "You're scared."

"No. I'm terrified. How do you sleep at night?"

"Brad's a great companion."

She had her doubts about that, but had to admit to being impressed by what Jairus had accomplished. He'd started drawing for his sister and now he had a Brad-driven empire.

After a few minutes, Tyler was enticed away from the Brad room with the promise of seeing Jairus's office. Nicole was equally curious about his writing process.

Jairus crossed to one of the other bedrooms and opened the door. Only they weren't in a bedroom at all.

The room was huge—obviously an addition. The style matched the rest of the house, but the ceiling was higher—maybe twelve feet. There were windows everywhere. Ceiling fans circled lazily overhead.

Beige paint offered a neutral backdrop for sketches pinned up everywhere. There was some kind of molding going around the room. Nicole stepped closer and examined the two-inch border of corkboard installed just above eye level. There were pins every couple of inches and they allowed Jairus to put his drawings up, in order. She saw the beginnings of a picture book—sketches of a tropical Brad in a Hawaiian shirt and holding a surfboard.

Jairus pointed to the drafting table at the far end of the room. "That's where I do most of my work." He showed them the big pads of paper he used, along with all the pencils and colored pens.

"It's not computerized?" she asked.

"Nope. This is how I learned to do it. I can't change now." He turned and pointed to the computer at the other end of the room. "I write the text there. For my manuscripts, I scan in the drawing so everyone can see how it will look."

Tyler walked along, staring at the story in progress. "Brad's going to learn how to surf?"

"He is."

Nicole had read enough of Brad's books to know that the adventure would probably not go smoothly and that the young dragon would learn a lesson along the way.

"When did you do the remodel?" she asked.

"Shortly after I bought the house. I thought my sister, Alice, would like the big windows and the backyard."

Nicole could see the east windows faced the big yard. There were trees and a sturdy swing set, along with a built-in barbecue and a seating area.

"You didn't want to be along the water?" she asked.

"It wouldn't have been safe."

For his sister, she thought. Because Jairus had known she would come to live with him. He'd been thinking of her when he'd bought this house and remodeled it. Because this was Southern California and the best light would be south, not east. But if all the windows were in the south part of the room, he wouldn't be able to keep watch over his sister in the yard.

She wasn't sure exactly what was going on in their relationship. There'd been that one, brief kiss, a lot of texting and some hanging out, mostly with Tyler along. So while she thought they *might* be seeing each other, the relationship was fairly undefined. Still, she couldn't help reaching for him, lacing her fingers through his.

Jairus squeezed her hand and drew her closer.

"It's beautiful," she said. "All of it."

"I'm glad you like it."

They went outside through the French doors in his office.

Tyler raced to the swing and jumped on. Nicole bit back the automatic "Be careful," and instead seated herself where she could see him.

"Tell me about your tour," she said. "You told me about the logistics and how you do a lot of media and stuff. You were gone a long time. Do you like doing it?"

"Mostly. I enjoy meeting my readers. The kids are great."

She knew he had events in most cities and there were private parties for children with developmental problems.

"I could do without the TV and the interviews," he said with a shrug. "They get old. New city, same questions. I have to keep reminding myself that even though it's the tenth time I'm telling the story, that for them it's new."

"Does Brad have groupies?"

"More than me."

She smiled. "I doubt that. I suspect there are more than a few single moms being very friendly."

His expression turned serious. "I didn't hang out with anyone, Nicole. And I sure didn't sleep with anyone."

She felt her mouth drop open. She closed it, then glanced to make sure Tyler couldn't hear them. "I wasn't asking that."

"Whether or not you were, I'm telling you."

There was an intensity to his voice—as if he had to be sure she understood. He wasn't teasing now.

"I appreciate that," she murmured.

Everything about the moment felt awkward. She wasn't used to talking about this sort of thing with a man. Jairus seemed to go out of his way to let her know he was interested and she didn't get that. It was as if he wanted to let her know she was special. She'd never been special. When she'd been younger, she'd never been good enough. Not to get into the American Ballet School, not to make it on Broadway. She'd come home a failure.

Eric had dated her and proposed, but she'd never felt he was swept away. And then he'd left.

"I didn't sleep with anyone, either," she said, her voice light.

His dark gaze stayed on her face. "You always do that. It's interesting. Whenever we start to talk about something intimate, you try to shift the focus."

She started to protest that she didn't, but she knew he was right. "I get scared," she admitted, then wished she hadn't. Why did they have to talk about this?

"Do you know why?"

She shook her head.

"Maybe I can help with that." He glanced toward Tyler, then back at her. "I like you, Nicole. I'm hoping you like me, too, and that we can get to know each other better. If there's a little naked in all that, then hey. I'm in."

She wanted to run. To bolt for safety. Because there was something about Jairus that terrified her. Or maybe it wasn't him at all. Maybe it was how she felt when she was around him.

Because she'd never been scared about Eric. Not until her marriage was falling apart. But that fear had been about the unknown, not the man.

"This is hard for me," she admitted. "Being with a man. Trusting a man."

He looked at her. "Is it any man or is it me?"

An interesting question. "Both. Dating anyone would be difficult, but you add a special element that confuses me." She swallowed, then forced herself to say the words. "Because I, um, like you."

"I like you, too." He sighed. "But let's just admit it. Mostly, it's the celebrity thing, right? Me and Brad. Fame sucks."

She burst out laughing. He touched the tip of her nose.

"Have a little faith. I'm a good guy."

"That part, I know." She glanced at Tyler, then back at him. "Listen, I have a strange invitation."

"Are there costumes? Because I love a good costume party."

"Where you always go as Brad, I'm sure. No, it's a screening for a movie. My ex's movie."

"Eric invited you?"

"Uh-huh. I think I want to go. I don't know much about the story, so it will be a surprise to us both. If you're interested in being my date."

"I am."

She casually rested her hand on his arm. "Me, too," she said. "In all of it."

The sound of happy children filled the backyard. Hayley smiled as she watched the elaborate game of tag that had everyone laughing. The sun was high in the sky, the temperature warm. In an hour or so Rob would set up the Slip 'N Slide on the lawn. Lunch was going to be hot dogs grilled on the barbecue.

In addition to her sister's kids, Hayley had offered to take Tyler, Kenzie and Kennedy for the day, figuring six wasn't that different than three. After lunch, when everyone was tired of playing outside, they were going to take on a craft project. She'd found a couple online and had bought the supplies. Then they would play outside again and finish the afternoon with a movie.

The visit was going well. Morgan had dropped everyone off after school yesterday. Hayley had gotten the three of them settled in their temporary room, then they'd gone to the POP for a couple of hours until Rob got off work. They'd had dinner out at The Slice Is Right.

Hayley had to admit that while her sister might be a bitch,

she knew how to teach her children manners. All three of them were incredibly well behaved. They'd ended the evening playing simple board games. No matter how old she got, a rousing couple of rounds of Candyland were always fun.

Now she watched her husband walk out of the house. Rob was so handsome, she thought, enjoying the sight of his broad shoulders and easy smile. He winked when he saw her.

"Have they found any of them?" he asked.

He'd hidden a couple dozen old Easter eggs all around the yard early that morning. They held silly things, like plastic rings, stickers and marbles. Just fun prizes the kids would like.

"Not yet. I'm going to say something soon."

The children continued to race around the yard.

He moved closer and put his arm around her. "I forgot to thank you."

"For what?"

"I took your advice with my customer. The one who lost her husband. You said she might be looking for attention, rather than trying to make my life miserable. So I started calling her after her appointment, to make sure everything was okay. Then I followed up the next day." He flashed her a smile. "Ever since that, she's been sweet as pie and not coming back with made-up problems."

"I'm glad the advice worked for you."

She spoke automatically, which was good, because her mind was elsewhere. If she were to count the number of times her husband had put his arm around her, it would probably be in the thousands. But this time was different. This time she was hyperaware of his body close to hers, of the heat of him and how he'd slept next to her last night.

Nothing had happened, but she'd enjoyed listening to him breathe while he slept.

She was, she acknowledged, healing.

Rob released her. "Okay. Time to let the wild things know there are prizes."

He clapped to get everyone's attention, then told the kids about the Easter eggs. Immediately the game stopped and the search began.

She watched Rob help the twins find eggs. He was so good with all the children, she thought. So patient and loving. A great husband. She'd been lucky to fall in love with him and have him love her back. More than lucky. Blessed.

Kennedy ran up to her with several stickers in her hand. "Look what I found."

"Those are very cool," Hayley told her.

"I know." The five-year-old hugged her. "You're the best, Auntie Hayley. I love you."

Hayley hugged her back. "I love you, too."

She'd meant the words. She did love the twins, and Morgan's kids and her friends and Rob most of all. Which meant that however damaged her heart might be, it wasn't, in fact, broken beyond repair. There was hope. And if she was very lucky, there was a happy future with her husband.

Gabby waited patiently in the parking lot. Right on time, a half-dozen or so teenage girls walked out of the building. Two more followed, a teenage boy in tow. Two minutes later, she spotted Makayla.

She walked directly to the car, her head slightly bent, her shoulders slumped. Gabby drew in a breath as she wondered what on earth she could say to make an impossible situation better.

"How was your parenting class?" she asked as the teen settled next to her in the car and put on her seat belt.

"Okay. We learned about how to tell if our baby's sick."

"That must have been a little scary."

"It was." Makayla shrugged. "Heather's boyfriend dumped her. He's going into the army or something." Her mouth twisted. "They were like engaged. He asked for the ring back. He told her he might want to give it to someone better." Tears filled her eyes. "He got her pregnant and he's acting like it's all her fault, you know? It's not fair."

Gabby squeezed the teen's arm. "I'm sorry. Boys can be idiots."

"Yeah, they can." She wiped away the tears. "I'm not crying over Boyd, you know. He's not worth it. He's a total shit head and I hate him. I'll hate him forever."

Gabby wondered if she should tell Makayla that kind of thinking wouldn't get her anywhere. But a part of her wondered if hating Boyd was kind of a good thing. At least it gave her something to focus on for the moment. Over time, the teen would have to figure out a strategy but for now, maybe having an enemy wasn't so bad.

"I hate him, too," Gabby admitted. "Because of how he hurt you."

Makayla surprised her by smiling. "Then he's in trouble, because you're really strong."

An unexpected compliment, Gabby thought, as she signaled and then pulled out of the parking lot.

They didn't talk as they drove home. Gabby kept listening for the familiar notes that indicated her stepdaughter had a text. Lately, her phone had been far too silent. Gabby wasn't sure about the balance between supportive and interfering, so she didn't ask too many question, but from what she could tell, most of Makayla's friends had drifted away. She wasn't hanging out with them after school or making plans on the weekend. There weren't any phone calls, no giggling conversations.

Cecelia and the twins were at the table coloring when they

got home. Boomer raced over to greet them, circling and moaning as if they'd been gone five years instead of a couple of hours. Gabby had a feeling his enthusiasm had a lot more to do with dinner than with missing them.

"How's it going?" she asked as she placed her handbag on the kitchen desk, then bent down to kiss and tickle her daughters.

"Mommy! Look what I did." Kennedy held up her picture. The princess was an interesting shade of green, with a purple dress and red trees in the background.

"Beautiful."

Kenzie smiled at her. "Hi, Mommy."

"Hey, sweetie."

Kenzie's picture was done in traditional colors and there was some kind of pattern drawn on the skirt. That girl was going to have a career in fashion or the arts, Gabby thought.

"Everything went great," Cecelia said as she rose. "You have the best-behaved twins I know."

Gabby grinned, knowing that hers were the only twins Cecelia sat for. "Thanks. We're working on it."

Makayla gave a halfhearted wave. The twins were having none of that. They rushed to her and hugged her tight.

"We missed you," Kennedy told her. "Every minute."

"I missed you munchkins, too."

As they embraced, Gabby saw the fabric momentarily pulled tight across the teen's belly. She was getting bigger by the day, she thought. There was a child growing inside her. A child that would one day be a baby.

That fact was no longer as startling as it had been. No longer as upsetting. She and Andrew still had their fragile truce. They were getting along, talking, making love, but they hadn't figured out what to do when the baby was born.

Gabby paid Cecelia, then glanced at the clock. It was nearly five. The casserole she'd prepped for dinner still needed a few ingredients added, then twenty minutes in the oven. But she also had to make cookies for the classroom tomorrow. Not just any cookies, but healthy, nut-free, low sugar, yet delicious cookies for twenty five-year-olds and their teacher. There was laundry and about four hours of work. She'd gotten up at five to start her day and figured she would be lucky if she got to bed before midnight. Sleep? Yeah, that was for someone else.

"Okay," she began. "We need a plan. I'm going to start the laundry, make sure we have what we need to make the cookies, then get dinner cooking." As she spoke, she turned on the oven. "How does that sound?"

"I can sort the laundry." Makayla's mouth twisted as she spoke. "I did all my homework at lunch and I don't have any tests to study for."

There was a lot of information in those two sentences. First, that Makayla was not hanging out with her friends at lunch anymore. Gabby had suspected as much, but her heart ached when the information was confirmed. Second, her offer to help was a bit of a surprise. She wanted to ask if the teen knew how to sort laundry, then decided it didn't matter.

"That would be so great," she said. "Thank you."

"We'll help, too," Kennedy added.

Kenzie nodded.

Which meant chaos, but beggars couldn't be choosers. Gabby pointed them in the direction of the laundry room. She collected pet dishes and opened cans. Jasmine materialized and wound her way around Gabby's legs.

Once the pets were fed, Gabby returned to the cookie prep. She had flour and—

A sharp cry cut through the relative quiet. *Makayla.* Horrifying thoughts of a miscarriage had Gabby running through the kitchen to the laundry room. Kennedy met her halfway.

"Mommy, Mommy, it's Makayla!"

Gabby had enough time to brace herself for blood. She rounded the corner and saw the teen curled up on the floor. Her phone was next to her and Kenzie was crouched close, stroking her hair.

"What happened?" Gabby demanded. "Are you bleeding? Cramping?"

Makayla turned a tear-soaked face toward her. She slowly shook her head and pointed to her phone.

Gabby picked it up. There was a text message. Her relief that Makayla was hearing from at least a few of her friends disappeared when she read the message. It was from Candace.

I've given this a lot of thought and I've come to the conclusion I can't deal with you right now. You're a chronic disappointment and I simply don't have time for all the drama you've created. I will not be picking you up this weekend.

The cold words cut like a knife. Gabby couldn't begin to imagine what Candace's text had done to the teen. No Boyd, no friends and now no mother. Words were useless. Not that it mattered. Honest to God, what was there to say? "Your mother is a bitch" wouldn't be helpful, despite the obvious truth.

Not sure what else to do, she sank onto the floor and pulled the teen against her. Makayla went willingly, then wrapped her arms around her, as if she would never let go. The twins joined in, the two little girls holding on to their sister. Makayla shook with her sobs. Gabby rocked her gently, but didn't bother saying everything was going to be fine. What was the point in that? They both knew it wasn't.

Chapter Twenty-Five

Andrew paced the length of his study. "I can't describe how much I loathe and despise that woman. Makayla is her daughter. No one wants her to be pregnant, but she is. We have to take care of her. To bail on her like that..."

He moved with controlled fury. With another man, Gabby might worry that he would throw something, but that wasn't Andrew's way.

"I know what you're thinking and you can't have her arrested," Gabby said flatly.

"I know that."

"I'm serious, Andrew. This makes her a shitty person, but it's not illegal."

"She's violating the parenting plan. I could take her to court for that."

"Yes, and then what? She'd be ordered to spend more time with Makayla. How does that help? The problem isn't the time, it's that she doesn't want to deal with this. She's abdicated any responsibility. Worse, she's hurt her daughter. You think I don't want to bitch-slap her? I do."

Gabby thought about all the teen had been through. "I'll admit Makayla and I haven't always had the greatest relationship, but this is different. She's scared. Boyd is gone, her friends have abandoned her. She only has us and we have to be there for her. But does Candace care about that? Of course not. She only cares about herself. I'm sorry, Andrew, but you made a sucky choice when you picked her."

Her husband stared at her for several seconds before crossing the office, grabbing her and pulling her close.

"I did," he said as he kissed the top of her head. "But I made up for it when I found you. Just so we're clear, I'm never letting you go. You're amazing."

Gabby let his love wash over her and give her strength. They would figure this out, she told herself. Get through all of it.

"I feel so bad for her," she admitted. "The hits keep on coming. Candace's timing really sucks."

"Because it's all about her," he said. "Damn that woman."

She stayed where she was for about a minute, then drew back. "I'm sorry, but I have work to do."

Andrew frowned. "You've brought home work every night this week."

"I know. It's just the load is incredible and with me working only twenty hours a week, I can't possibly get it done."

"Gabby, they hired you part-time but you're putting in full-time hours."

Something she was very aware of. "I know and I'm concerned, too. What I haven't figured out is how much of my struggle is them piling it on and how much of it is me being slow because I was out of the workforce for so long. Until I find that line, I'm not going to complain."

"They're taking advantage of you."

"Maybe."

Right now that was the least of her problems. More important to her was how much she didn't like her job. Had she lost her work ethic or was the job really not what she wanted to do? Hard questions considering how long she'd been imagining herself back at the office. She'd wanted this and now that she had it, she hated everything about it.

But to complain about it seemed wrong. She was so lucky, not to have to work if she didn't want to. She could do anything and sadly, she had no idea what she wanted.

"Don't wait up," she told her husband. "I'll be a few hours. And I'll check on Makayla before I go to bed. In case she can't sleep."

He kissed her again, this time on the mouth. She drew back reluctantly and headed for the makeshift office she'd set up in a corner of the family room. Her back hurt and she was exhausted, but those files weren't going to read themselves.

It was for the greater good, she told herself, although at this moment, she had no idea what the greater good might be.

Nicole told herself that she looked fine, that she had a handsome date and everything would be perfectly okay. Except for the handsome date part, she wasn't sure how much of it she believed. Going to your ex-husband's movie premiere was an event designed to get nerves quivering and stomachs roiling. She'd made herself eat because she'd known that no food wasn't a good thing. But the protein drink she'd forced down an hour ago now sat like an unhappy rock, low in her belly.

"I'm scared," she admitted, as they pulled up to the valet. A young man opened her door and she stepped out. Mostly because staying in the car didn't seem like a reasonable option.

Jairus, all sexy in a dark gray suit, complete with a tonal shirt and deep blue tie, walked around the car to stand next to her.

"Let's work this through," he said lightly. "We have tickets, we each have a date, although mine is much better-looking than yours. Did I mention you look totally hot in that dress?"

"You did and I appreciate it."

The dress was the most expensive article of clothing she owned. The Alexander McQueen pleated leaf crepe design had a squared-off sweetheart neckline that was cut low enough to be supersexy without showing too much. The dress itself was fitted to her hips, then flared out before ending well above her knee.

She'd nearly decided to wear something else. After all, this was a dress she'd bought for an event while she'd still been married to Eric. The need for something new had passed quickly. Her life hardly lent itself to fancy events, so why spend the money when she could recycle?

Jairus smiled at her. "We're going to have a good time. We'll watch the movie and then later we'll talk about it. Hell, we can spend a couple of hours trashing Eric. I'm game. Or we can go back to my place where I'll try desperately to seduce you. Desperate being the operative word."

Despite the nerves, his words made her relax. She smiled at him. "There's something wrong with you."

"I've been told that before. I wonder if it's true."

She stared into his dark eyes. He was very sweet. Not just with her but with Tyler. He was funny and kind and dependable. He got her. Talk about an unexpected bonus, she thought.

He held out his hand. "Ready to beard the lion in his den?" He frowned. "Is it lion or dragon? Do either of them have beards? Who thinks this stuff up?"

She laced her fingers with his and turned to the entrance to the theater. A few photographers stood waiting. There were small crowds of fans, there for the movie stars. Nicole wondered how many people were already inside and if she would see Eric at all. Not that she wanted to. It was just being at a movie premiere was so surreal, she wanted to be prepared.

"I'm ready," she said firmly, hoping that by saying it, the words would be true.

"Then I am, too."

They joined the short line of people being let into the theater. The photographers glanced at them, then away. They weren't anyone, she thought humorously.

The lobby walls were covered with huge posters from the movie *Disaster Road*. There were sofas and comfortable chairs set up in seating areas. Servers circulated with trays of appetizers and glasses of champagne. A hundred or so people stood talking.

Nicole wondered how many were with the production and how many were guests.

"Did you read anything about the movie?" Jairus asked.

"No. I thought about it, but then figured we were going to see it. Did you?"

"No. I wanted to be surprised."

"Let's hope it's a good one."

She laughed. "I alternate fear and apprehension."

"That it will be good?"

The question surprised her. "I expect it's going to be great. I don't mind if Eric does well. I don't wish him ill."

"A lot of ex-wives wouldn't be so generous."

She thought about the article his ex had written and the horrible things she'd said about him. "I'm not vindictive. I have flaws, but that's not one of them."

A voice over the loudspeakers directed everyone to their seats. She and Jairus went upstairs and sat in the balcony. The theater quickly filled up and Nicole spotted the stars, the director and Eric down in front. The executive producer appeared onstage and introduced himself and the main players, then promised to answer questions after the showing. Then the lights dimmed and the movie began.

Nicole hadn't known what to expect. Knowing Eric as she did, she wondered if she would hear his voice in the dialogue or see parts of him in the story. She'd been curious whether parts of their life would be woven into the action. What she hadn't expected was to find the hero's wife to be a caricature of herself.

The wife was blonde, shrewish and obsessed with her body. A former dancer, all she worried about was exercise and what she ate. She was a nag and so over-the-top annoying that she became the comic relief in a fast-moving action plot.

Nicole felt herself flushing. Heat burned on her face as she saw just enough of herself to know there was no mistaking what Eric had done. He'd taken the very worst parts of her and had blown them out of proportion to add humor to the story.

No wonder he hadn't wanted her to read the screenplay. She'd been his muse, but in the worst way possible.

Three-quarters of the way through the movie, the bad guys kidnapped the wife and the audience actually cheered. When the hero kissed the new love interest, Nicole heard sighs. And at the end of the movie, the wife was cast aside as the action star took up with his new lady love.

She didn't know what to say or do. Of course that wasn't her. She wasn't obsessed with her body. Yes, she cared about being healthy, but part of that was because she owned an exercise studio. It wasn't wrong to want to be fit.

She told herself that Eric's view of her was like a fun-house mirror—the truth was distorted. Yet a part of her wondered if that was how he really saw her. How much was poetic license and how much was his version of the truth?

The lights came on. She forced herself to relax, to smile, to turn to Jairus and say, "What did you think?"

"It was better than I thought it would be," he admitted. "I didn't like the hero as much as I could have, but it was good."

That was it?

"The wife was based on me," she said quietly.

"What? No way. Nicole, you're nothing like her."

He was wrong. Maybe he hadn't seen it, but she had. What she didn't know was what Eric had been thinking. Had she ever meant anything to him? Had she been little more than a means to an end? She'd always thought they'd married because they were in love. Now she wasn't sure. Maybe getting her to support him while he wrote his screenplay had been his plan all along.

Jairus stood and drew her to her feet, then escorted her out of the theater as the Q and A session began. When they were in the lobby, Jairus guided her to a corner and touched her cheek.

"It wasn't you," he said flatly.

"It *was*. She was so horrible. Maybe that's how he saw me. Maybe it's what he needed to do to leave the marriage. I've never understood him and now I'm more confused than ever." She thought about all she'd been through, all the blame she'd assumed. She pressed a hand to her stomach. "I'm not feeling very well. Could you please take me home?"

For a second she thought he was going to refuse, but instead he nodded. "Of course. Let's go get the car."

There were times, Hayley told herself, when wounds could only be healed by a burger, fries and a milk shake. And this was definitely one of those days.

She slid into the booth at Gary's Café. Nicole sat at her side while Gabby settled in across from them. Their impromptu lunch had come about through a series of quick text messages. The casual "Hi, how's it going" had spiraled to "I need some girlfriend time." So here they were.

Hayley realized she hadn't been out with her friends since her surgery. They'd been really good about coming to visit her, but there hadn't been a lot of her getting out. Now she looked around and admitted she'd missed the world a lot.

"How is everyone?" she asked.

"Good," Gabby said, her smile not quite reaching her eyes.

Nicole shrugged. "Same old, same old."

Hayley looked at them more closely. She saw tension in Gabby's posture and something that looked a lot like hurt in Nicole's eyes.

"Okay," she said, putting down her menu. "What's really going on? What aren't you telling me?"

The other two women exchanged a look. Hayley leaned forward.

"I'm not dying or breakable. I'm doing fine. Don't keep things from me. What is it?"

Nicole groaned. "I went to Eric's premiere a couple of nights ago."

"What?" Hayley wanted to slap herself. "I thought it was next week. I'm sorry. I would have called and asked about it."

"I'm glad you didn't. I needed time to process what I saw."

"How was the movie?" Gabby asked.

"I honestly don't know. The audience seemed to like it. Of course they were all friends and family, so what were they going to say?" She bit her lower lip. "No, that's not fair. The reviews have been good. Trust me, I've read them all."

Hayley knew there was a problem, but she wasn't sure what it was.

"You don't care that Eric's successful, do you?" Gabby asked, sounding doubtful.

"No. Not really. I just…" Nicole sighed. "I don't know him. I did, only I didn't realize it. I can't figure out how we got together, let alone married. And that movie."

Their waitress appeared. "Afternoon, ladies. Our milk shake of the day is peanut butter cookie, which is as good as it sounds. The guacamole burger is our deal of the day."

Hayley felt her stomach grumble in anticipation. She hadn't been very hungry lately, but now she felt as if she could eat two burgers and all the fries.

"I need a minute," Gabby said.

"I'll be back in a few," the waitress promised with a smile and left.

Gabby stared at her menu. "I'm going to have something decadent and I honestly don't care about the calories. I accept the wrongness of that."

"It's not wrong," Hayley told her.

"I hope you're right." Gabby looked back at Nicole. "What about the movie?"

"It was…" She glanced away, then back at them. "I'm the villain. Not the real one. He's trying to blow up the city. But the wife is based on me and she's awful. Whiny and self-absorbed. I recognized a few things and it was really hard. I'm so embarrassed."

Hayley turned toward her friend. "You're none of those things so I don't know how you could be in the movie."

"I just am. Trust me. Now I get why Eric didn't want me reading the screenplay. I think he took out all the frustrations he had in our marriage in that character. There's a rawness to their relationship that rings true. At the end, she gets kidnapped and is totally humiliated by the bad guys. Everyone cheered."

"You're an awesome person," Gabby told her. "We love

you. You're a great mom, your classes are popular. It's not you."

Nicole didn't look convinced. "It's more than I'm afraid people will guess it's me and think that's what I'm really like. It's that… Eric's view of me is so different than my view of myself. It's scary, in a way. Plus, I thought…" She sighed. "I know we're divorced, but I didn't think we were enemies."

"Maybe he got carried away," Hayley said. "Listening to the voices in his head. We all tell stories. Like me with Morgan. Saying my parents loved her more. Lately I've been wondering if that's true. She said something a while ago. About me being chosen. All this time I've thought she was the special one because she was theirs. What if it wasn't that way at all? What if all this time, she's been jealous of me?"

"Why wouldn't she be?" Gabby asked. "You're the one everyone likes."

Hayley thought about the last few months and how Morgan had acted. "My sister is kind of a bitch."

Nicole laughed. "You're just now getting that?"

"Seriously," Gabby added. "We all have T-shirts for the 'I hate Morgan' club. You want one?"

"Maybe." Hayley shook her head. "No. I take that back. I don't hate her. I think she's difficult and selfish and she takes advantage of people. All my life I saw her getting attention. I believed our parents loved her more because she always got her way. But lately I've been thinking. Maybe it's different than that. Maybe they acted the way they did out of self-defense."

"To keep her from burning down the house?" Gabby asked.

"Something like that."

"I always thought it was so interesting," Nicole said. "How you two are different. I know you're adopted, but it's more than that. Talk about different personalities. You're kind and gentle. A real giving spirit. Morgan sucks all the air out of a room. Everything has to be about her."

Hayley nodded. "She certainly screamed louder than me. Than anyone, really. So they listened because they had to. Morgan swears I was the favorite. I wonder if I simply looked at the situation from my perspective for so long that I forgot there was a bigger picture. Maybe it's like that with Eric. You're caught up in your point of view."

"What would be a different one?" Nicole asked.

Their server returned. Hayley opened her menu, then surrendered to the inevitable. "A cookies and cream milk shake," she said. "And the guacamole burger."

"Wow," Gabby breathed. "I am so impressed. I'll have a vanilla milk shake and the bacon burger."

"Chocolate mint for me," Nicole told their waitress. "The guacamole burger with sweet potato fries."

"Wild woman," Gabby teased.

"You know it."

Hayley waited until their server left before continuing. "Eric abandoned his wife and child. I can accept your marriage ending. It happens. But he has no excuse for what he did to Tyler. I think deep down he knows he was a jerk, but most people can't live with that, so they tell themselves another story. Whatever you saw on the screen isn't you, Nicole. It's what he tells himself to justify what he did. We all have our own personal truth, but I don't think it has much relationship with reality."

They both looked startled.

"Wow," Nicole said slowly. "That sounds really wise. I never thought of Eric having to make things right with himself. But he does, doesn't he?"

"He's the one who quit his job without discussing it with you," Gabby reminded her. "He's the one who withdrew from the marriage. You tried to make things work and he wanted out. Now he basically ignores his son. Everyone gets part of the blame in the failure of a marriage. You did things wrong, I'm sure. But most of it falls on him. He has to reconcile that. Maybe the character in the movie is part of that."

Nicole relaxed a little. "I hadn't thought of it that way. I just felt so humiliated. Like everyone was pointing and staring."

"What did Jairus say?" Gabby asked.

"He didn't think it was me."

"Then no one else will. People are amazingly self-centered and dense."

Nicole looked at her. "Speaking about anyone in particular?"

"Candace."

It took Hayley a second to place the name. "Andrew's ex?"

"That's the one. While we're on the subject of parents who deserve to be bitch-slapped, Candace has decided she doesn't want to see Makayla anymore." Gabby brought them up to date on what was happening with her family.

Hayley thought about all she'd been through to have a baby. She genuinely couldn't understand people who were blessed with a child and then ignored them. It made no sense. She would have given anything to have that relationship. She'd nearly died because of it.

"Makayla must be crushed," she said.

"She is." Gabby sighed. "I don't know what to say to her. I know I can't make it better, but boy, do I want to try. I hate feeling so useless."

Their waitress arrived with the milk shakes. Hayley let the cool, thick, sweet treat melt on her tongue. She felt the beginnings of a sugar rush as her world righted itself.

"There's no bad in this," she whispered.

"You know it, sister." Gabby grinned.

Nicole laughed.

"It's kind of funny," Hayley said. "You and Makayla seem so much closer than you used to be. I never would have guessed things would work out that way."

"Me, either. Andrew and I still carefully avoid the topic of what to do when the baby's born." Gabby sipped at her milk shake. "Okay, this is going to sound completely crazy, but I've actually thought he might be right. About me staying home with her kid."

Hayley felt her eyes widen. Nicole's mouth dropped open. "Are you serious?"

"Maybe. I don't know." Gabby looked down at the table, then back at them. "I'm not loving my job. It's so boring and I'm working way more hours than they're paying me for. For the first week, I figured it was because I was rusty, but now I think they're shoving things at me to see how much they can get out of me. I know it's a nonprofit, but I'm only supposed to be working twenty hours a week. I'm working more like forty."

Hayley winced. "When? You have three kids, a house, a husband."

"Tell me about it. I stay up late, get up early. It's hard. Especially when I think about how little I'm getting paid. I don't know. Then I think about all the women who are struggling just to put food on the table and I feel guilty for complaining."

"You get to complain," Nicole told her. "We all do. Someone else's circumstances have nothing to do with you."

"That sounds completely rational," Gabby agreed. "If only I could believe it."

Hayley got that. Guilt was powerful. It was like fear—it sucked up all the air until a person couldn't breathe.

"What does Andrew say about your potential change of heart?" Nicole asked.

"I haven't told him. I'm still working it through. I want to be sure I'm not running from work, if that makes sense. I want to make the decision from a position of strength, not to escape a job I don't like. Committing to raising Makayla's baby is huge. But I can't help thinking what I'm doing now isn't enough."

"Is the baby the only option?" Hayley asked.

"No. I've been thinking about going back to college. I don't think I want to practice law anymore. But I've never considered what else there could be."

"That's a big step," Nicole said.

Hayley nodded. She'd never gone to college. Just a couple of semesters, and then she'd met Rob. What would she be doing if she'd finished her education? She'd never thought much beyond being a wife and a mother. If she could do anything, she would...

"I'd study nursing," she said, surprising herself. "If I went back to school."

Nicole smiled. "No surprise there. It's the sweet spirit we were talking about before. You're good at taking care of people."

"I wish that were true." Hayley sighed. "Lately I've only been thinking of myself. With wanting to have a baby and all. Poor Rob. We're finding our way back together, but I could have lost him. I'm glad I didn't."

"We are, too," Gabby told her. "What about you, Nicole. What would you do differently?"

"I don't know. I love my business. And I can't say I wouldn't have married Eric because I needed him to get Tyler. I'm going to accept where I am and be happy."

"Can you let the movie thing go?" Hayley asked.

"I'm going to do my damnedest to try."

Nicole raised her glass. The other two clinked theirs against it.

"To doing our damnedest," Hayley said.

"Every day," Gabby added. "Even if that means getting up at four in the morning."

Chapter Twenty-Six

Nicole shifted her weight from foot to foot. "I really appreciate this," she said, both worried and late. "Kristie is usually so dependable and I'm not comfortable canceling a class at the last minute."

Jairus put his arm around her and led her toward the front door. "Go," he said. "We'll be fine. Right, Tyler?"

Her son beamed at her. "Mommy, we're going to *paint*!" He spoke with a charming combination of awe and anticipation.

"I look forward to seeing what you've done when I get home." She hesitated, not sure what other instructions she should give him.

When Kristie had called to say she'd unexpectedly come down with food poisoning, Nicole hadn't been worried. She could easily take over the early-evening classes. What she hadn't counted on was that none of her usual sitters were available. Cecelia was helping out another family. Pam was traveling. Neither Gabby, Hayley or Shannon were picking up their phones. Not knowing what else to do, she'd put in an emergency call to Jairus who'd instantly agreed to watch Tyler.

Jairus opened the front door. "Go," he said with a smile. "We'll be fine. Call every fifteen minutes, if it makes you more comfortable. We'll be right here. I promise."

She couldn't remember the last time a man had promised her anything, she thought suddenly, then shook her head. She didn't have time for this.

"Thanks," she said as she ran down the walkway toward her car. "Tyler, be good."

"I will, Mommy."

Three classes and a quick drive home later, she was back. Despite his offer to field her calls every fifteen minutes, she'd forced herself not to check in with Jairus. Tyler knew her work phone number. He would have called if there was a problem.

As she stepped into the living room, she saw there were a couple of lamps on, along with the TV. Several things occurred to her at once. First, that Tyler was still up. Well, not *up*, exactly, but curled up next to Jairus, asleep, rather than in his bed. Second, her pajama-clad son looked amazingly comfortable with the man, as if he trusted him completely. Which Nicole supposed he probably did. Third, Jairus and Tyler looked good together. Connected. As if they had a close relationship that made them both happy.

Last, and maybe not least, the second her gaze locked with Jairus's, she felt something sexy and liquid and hot deep down inside her. The sensation had been absent so long, it took her a bit to recognize it.

Desire.

The information shocked her. Sure, they'd kissed and it had been nice, but she'd been careful to keep things light. While he always joked about wanting her, she figured that was just a reflex rather than actual information. But what if she'd been wrong? What if he felt this way, too?

She lost herself in a nanosecond-long image of tangled arms and legs, of his body easing into hers. Her breath caught and she looked away to get a bit of control. Only to notice what was paused on the television.

Wanting fled as humiliation flooded her. She groaned. "He didn't."

Jairus smiled. "He did. Tyler told me about how you were a beautiful dancer and then offered to show me proof."

The DVD they'd been watching was a familiar one—a compilation of her various dance auditions and performances. They were years old and mostly silly. But at the time she'd thought maybe she could have a career as a dancer. Just one more thing she'd been wrong about.

"You could have stopped when he fell asleep," she whispered.

"I was enjoying myself. How were your classes?"

"Good."

Jairus shifted so Tyler stretched out on the sofa. He turned and picked up the boy, then carried him toward the bedrooms.

"He brushed his teeth already. We'd agreed on just one more minute when he fell asleep."

"Once he's out, he's out," she murmured, following them to Tyler's room, then scooting ahead to fold back the covers on his Brad the Dragon bed.

Jairus lowered him to the mattress, before stepping back to give her room to kiss Tyler good-night. When she turned to leave, she saw that progress had been made on the mural.

Most of the scene was outlined in black paint. Parts of Brad were painted in red and judging by the uneven brush strokes, she could guess who'd been doing that painting.

"You let him help," she said as she closed the door.

"He did a great job."

They returned to the living room. Jairus switched off the TV.

"The dancing was cool," he told her, his dark gaze settling on her face. "You're talented."

"Not really, but thanks for saying it anyway."

"Why do you have so much trouble accepting a compliment?"

"I don't."

He moved closer. "Yeah, you do. You deflect them."

Maybe, but if that was true, there was no way she wanted to talk about it. "I tried to make it as a dancer, but couldn't. I nearly starved to death in New York one winter. What I do now is better."

"But you're still a dancer at heart, I think." He smiled. "Tango Girl. That's how I thought of you after our first meeting."

"The costume makes an impression."

"Tell me about it." He reached up and stroked the side of her face. "Still scared?"

She knew he wasn't talking about her dance career. They'd switched to a more intimate topic. "I'm not scared."

"Sure you are. It's okay. I'm nervous, too. It's been a while, so hey, what if I've forgotten how? Plus, there's the whole 'it's you' part."

Sex, she thought frantically. They were talking about sex. Because they were going to do it? Was she ready? Would it be okay? What underwear had she put on that morning?

"Me?"

He moved closer and rested his hands on her shoulders. "Yes, you. You knock me out. You're sexy, funny, a great mom and those legs. You keep me awake at night, thinking about possibilities."

What on earth was she supposed to say to that? "Jairus, I..." She swallowed, knowing she could say no. He wouldn't push. He was that kind of man. The kind who listened and respected and painted murals in her son's room.

She *was* scared. Scared and nervous and apprehensive. Pick a word—any word. But she also liked Jairus and maybe, just maybe, she trusted him.

"Are you going to make your move?" she asked.

"Not until you're done thinking this through. I want it to be right. I want both of us to be sure."

She stared at his face, taking in the too-long hair, the wide eyes, the full mouth. She thought about his hands, always gentle and sure. She thought about how she looked forward to being with him and how she missed him when they weren't together. Then she raised herself on tiptoe and pressed her mouth to his.

They'd kissed before. Many times. There had even been a little passion in some of them. But this was different. This time there was anticipation.

She leaned into him. His arms lowered and his hands moved down her sides to settle at her waist. His mouth was warm against hers. He moved back and forth before brushing his tongue against her bottom lip.

She parted for him and felt need flower inside of her. Hunger grew, consuming her until the wanting was a tangible beast that had to be satisfied.

There were so many hours before dawn, she thought as she kissed him in return, meeting him stroke for stroke, letting the heat burn through her. So many possibilities.

She drew back and took his hand, then led him to her bedroom. She released his hand to turn on a bedside lamp, then shut the door. When she faced him again, she realized there was no fear, no uncertainty. She knew that everything about this was right.

Jairus's eyes burned bright with passion. "Before we get started," he said, his voice husky. "Do you have condoms?"

She thought of the box her friend Pam had given her several months before with the instruction to find someone to wear them, and smiled. "I do."

"That's my girl."

It was the last time either of them spoke for a long time. Jairus undressed her carefully, touching and kissing, exploring every inch of her. He took off his clothes and joined her on the bed. His body was long and lean, with just enough muscle to be interesting.

Nicole lost herself in the sensations of his hands on her body, his mouth on her nipples and then between her legs. It took seconds for her to come. The sensations were almost unfamiliar—her release nearly rusty from disuse. But when he entered her, she came again and this time was better. New and pleasurable. Right.

Later, when the condom was in the trash and they'd cleaned up and were lying in her bed, the tangle of arms and legs just like she'd imagined, he kissed the top of her head.

"Go to sleep, Tango Girl."

"You're staying?"

"I'd like to."

She relaxed against him, her eyelids heavy. "I'd like that, too."

"I'll be gone before Tyler wakes up."

She nodded, knowing she could trust him. Jairus shifted, holding her tightly against him.

"I'm going to say something," he told her. "Your job is to listen. Don't say anything back to me. Promise?"

She'd been feeling a little sleepy, but was suddenly completely awake. She nodded, feeling apprehensive. What was he going to tell her? Something awful? Did he not want to see her anymore? Was his divorce not final? Had she just made love with a married man?

"I love you."

She turned so she could look at him. Before she could speak, he pressed his index finger to her lips.

"Not a word. You promised. I don't want anything in return, Nicole. I just wanted you to know."

Hayley knew she was dreaming, but that didn't make the experience any less real. She was alone in the house. The rooms were familiar. She knew the shapes and the placement of the windows and which floorboards creaked. But that was where the similarity ended. The furnishings were all gone and the house was empty. She was in it completely alone.

"Rob?"

She kept calling for him, but he wasn't there. No matter how many times she circled through the unfurnished rooms, he was gone. Fear kept her moving. She knew that if she stopped, she would remember and the remembering would be too much.

"Rob?"

Her voice got louder and louder until she was screaming. Only there wasn't any sound. Just her frantic search. He had to be here! He had to be! Without him—

"Hayley?"

She came awake with a start. Rob leaned over her where she lay on the couch.

"Honey, what's wrong?"

She sprang to her feet and looked around. Everything was where it was supposed to be, including her husband. She flung herself at him and hung on tight.

"I had a bad dream," she whispered, breathing in the familiar scent of him. "You were gone." Because *gone* was so much easier to say than what she'd actually thought in the dream. That he was dead.

The babies she'd been unable to carry had been faceless. Real in her heart, but imagining them had been difficult. All their promise had been in the future. But Rob was different. He was now. To lose him was to lose everything.

He stroked her back. "I'm right here, honey. I'm sorry my meeting ran late."

She held back tears, knowing he wouldn't understand them. "I was reading and I guess I fell asleep," she whispered.

Her heartbeat slowed and the taste of fear receded. He drew back and looked at her.

"Better?"

She nodded. "You must be hungry."

"Starved."

They went into the kitchen where she heated some pot roast and the vegetables from their dinner the previous night. Rob loosened his tie as she worked and put his suit jacket over a chair.

"The service reports are good," he said, sounding pleased. "Customer satisfaction is up twenty-three percent from this time last year."

She clapped her hands together. "That's fantastic and all you, right?"

"Yeah. They're happy with me." He grinned. "We're getting a raise. A big one. Plus a bonus. Want to go to Fiji?"

She ran over and hugged him. "I'm so proud of you. Not surprised at all, but very proud."

"Thanks, Hayley."

He kissed her. "I'm serious about the trip. Want to go somewhere?"

She thought about how long it had been since they'd taken

a vacation. They couldn't because all their money went toward fertility treatments.

"Maybe not Fiji," she told him. "But yes, let's take a few days off together." She tilted her head. "Then maybe we can talk to a contractor about the kitchen. I still want to fix up the house, if you do."

"Sure. Kitchen, then bathrooms."

The microwave beeped. She checked his dinner, then put it back in for a couple of minutes more. When she turned back to him, she saw he wasn't smiling anymore.

"What?" she asked.

"I was thinking. About kids."

Her bubble of happiness burst. She tucked her arms behind herself and grabbed hold of the counter. "What about them?"

"Are you still against adopting?"

There it was. The inevitable question she'd been dreading. "I don't know. It scares me, because of what happened in my family." She held up a hand before he could speak. "I know my parents loved me. I know Morgan is a bitch and that's why she got all the attention."

His brows rose. "Are you sure?"

"I've been thinking about it a lot. About her and how things were. I think some of what I felt was real, but some of it was a story I told myself."

The microwave beeped again but they both ignored it.

"I need more time," she admitted. "Before I can put all the past behind me, but I'm trying, Rob. I know you want children and you don't care that much if they're yours or not."

He nodded slowly.

"I'm trying to get there. I want to get there."

He relaxed. "That's good to hear. We're not in a rush, Hayley. It'll happen. In the meantime, I want to look into ways to work with children. Maybe as a coach or scouting or something."

"You'd be great at that. Kids like you."

"I enjoy spending time with them."

She pulled his dinner from the microwave and set the plate on the table. "There are a lot of organizations that need volunteers," she said. "Maybe we can look together."

"I'd like that."

It wasn't having a baby. She would never have that. But it was time with Rob and if she kept busy enough, the pain wasn't so loud. She also liked children. Being with Morgan's had been fun. If she avoided babies and reminded herself that healing, like life, was a journey, not a destination, then she would keep moving forward. And one day, she would realize the hole in her heart had filled in just enough to be survivable.

Gabby told herself she was fine. That the weird shaking feeling was just because she was tired, nothing more. She was still in her first month of work—there was no way she could call in sick.

"No work tonight," she promised herself as she parked and walked toward the office building. She wouldn't take anything home. Instead she would make an easy and early evening of it. With Andrew out of town, it would be girls only. Maybe a Disney movie-fest and pizza.

While she was sure the girls would love the idea, she had to admit that the thought of pizza made her stomach flip over a couple of times. She shook off the sensation and went up to the third floor.

She managed to get through a short meeting on upcoming state immigration legislation without groaning out loud. The churning in her stomach didn't seem to be going away. She circled by the vending machine and got a Sprite, hoping that would settle things down. She had a headache as well, and a general feeling of exhaustion.

"I'm tired, nothing more," she whispered as she settled into her chair. She couldn't be sick. With Andrew in Chicago, she was on her own. Everything would be fine. She just needed to focus.

Thirty minutes and a Sprite later, she was starting to feel a bit more perky. She'd finished the last brief she needed for tomorrow, which meant she was officially not behind. A first since taking the job. That evening off was looking more possible by the minute. She was still smiling when her cell phone rang.

"Hello?"

"Mrs. Schaefer?"

"Yes."

"It's Matilda Dennison from the school. Kenzie's thrown up twice in the last hour. I'm afraid she's caught a bug. I need you to come get her."

"I'll be right there."

Gabby threw work in her bag, then checked in with her boss before heading out. Luck was on her side along with all green lights and she made it to the school in less than fifteen minutes.

A very pale Kenzie was curled up on a cot in the nurse's office.

"How are you feeling?" Gabby asked, touching her daughter's forehead.

"Yucky. I threw up."

"I heard. Let me get you home."

Kenzie sat up and Gabby put her arm around the girl. At times like this, her babies seemed so small.

"I'll need to get Kennedy, as well," she told the nurse. "If one of them has it, so does the other. It's just a matter of time."

Matilda, a kind-looking woman in her late fifties, nodded. "That's a good plan. We've had a few children out sick this week. Stomach flu. I suspect it's going to get worse before it gets better." Her gaze narrowed. "How are you feeling?"

Gabby thought about her own woozy stomach. Not that it mattered. She was the mom. Getting the flu wasn't an option.

"I'm fine," she said brightly, willing it to be true.

She signed out both girls. The nurse went and collected Kennedy. One look at her other daughter's pale face told her there was going to be trouble.

"Mommy." Kennedy started to cry when she saw her. "My head hurts."

"Okay, sweetie. We're going home."

She ushered both girls to her SUV. They climbed in without being prodded. She buckled them into their booster seats and closed the door. Not two seconds later, Kennedy vomited all over herself and the car.

Gabby opened the back door and felt her stomach churn.

"It's okay," she told the sobbing girl. "It's okay."

Kenzie gagged, then she threw up, as well. The smell filled the car. Gabby thought about the package of wipes in the front seat and the mess that went way beyond that. She swallowed against the bile rising in her own throat.

"It's five minutes," she told her daughters after she cleaned them up as best she could. "Hang on and we'll take care of the rest of this at home."

Kennedy started screaming. "Mommy, no! Mommy, please. Help me."

Kenzie joined in. Gabby felt tears fill her eyes. She honestly didn't know what to do.

"Five minutes," she repeated and closed the door.

The trip seemed to take forever. Both girls were screaming. Kennedy threw up again, then continued retching. By the time they reached the house, Gabby thought she was going to pass out from the smell.

She parked in the driveway and got out, then opened the door for the girls.

"Straight up to your bathroom, right away," she said firmly.

She got them inside. Boomer wanted to investigate, but she shooed him away and got the girls stripped down and into the shower. They were both shivering and crying. Boomer was howling at the closed bathroom door and somewhere in the hallway, her cell phone went off.

Gabby started to ignore it, then wondered if it was the high school. Was Makayla sick, too? She glanced at the screen, saw it was Nicole, sent off a prayer asking for forgiveness and hit the Ignore button.

By the time the girls were dried off, they'd stopped crying. Gabby hustled them into one of the beds, figuring it was better to share. She was pretty sure the vomiting wasn't done and there were only so many sets of sheets. Then she got them Sprite and ice chips and told them she would be right outside in the hall.

She rinsed off clothes and started a load of laundry, then checked the sheets. There were two sets for each twin bed.

"Mommy!"

She got back into the bedroom in time to watch both her daughters throw up. Only Kenzie made it into the trash can Gabby had placed by the bed.

Sometime around noon, Gabby was able to get outside to work on her car. The stench was incredible. She did the best she could to clean everything up. By the time she was done, she was shaking and weak and her own stomach was threatening. She told herself it was the stink, then headed back inside. The first load was done, so she put in the second and added bleach.

The house phone rang.

"Hello?"

"Mrs. Schaefer? This is the nurse from the high school. I'm afraid your daughter is sick."

Gabby sank onto the floor. "Okay," she said weakly. "I'll be there. It's just, my other daughters have the flu and..." Her stomach heaved. "Oh, God." She panicked. She couldn't get sick. Not yet. Not with everyone down for the count. Andrew. She needed Andrew. Who was a couple of thousand miles away in Chicago. That wouldn't work. Her mother.

Gabby told the nurse a family member would be there shortly, then dialed the familiar number and prayed for her mom to pick up.

"I was just thinking about you," Marie said cheerfully. "How are you, Gabby?"

"Not good." The tears flowed freely. "Mom, I need help."

"What's wrong?"

"Everything. The twins have stomach flu. They threw up all over the car and I don't feel good myself. Now the high school called and Makayla needs to come home. Andrew's in Chicago and I simply can't do it myself."

"I'll get Makayla, then I'll be right there. Call Andrew and tell him to get his ass home. I mean it, Gabby. You call him or I will."

Even as her nausea grew, her tension eased. "Thanks, Mom. I'll call him right now."

Chapter Twenty-Seven

"How are you feeling?" Nicole asked as she held her phone with one hand and pulled the pork chops out of the refrigerator with the other. "It sounds awful."

"I'm not dead," Gabby said, her voice still weak. "It was a pretty hideous three days. We were all sick. My mom stayed until Andrew got home, then he took over. I'm so grateful to have help. We wouldn't have gotten through it otherwise."

"You sound like you're not a hundred percent yet."

"I need another day or so, but at least I can keep food down."

"Want me to bring something over?"

"We're good, but I'll let you know if I need anything from the grocery store."

"Absolutely. Hang in there."

"I will."

They said goodbye and hung up. Nicole shuddered at the thought of everyone in the house being sick. Talk about a nightmare.

"I'm going to get the mail," she called to Tyler.

He looked up from his coloring book and nodded. "Okay, Mommy."

It was a Thursday afternoon. Warm, sunny and perfect in every way. She supposed part of her good mood was the residual quivering she felt inside. Even after several days, she was still having delicious flashbacks to her night with Jairus.

He'd been very sweet after the fact. Getting up in plenty of time to be gone before Tyler was awake. But he'd called later. And texted. And sent flowers. Then he'd gone out of his way to say it wasn't all about the sex. That he really did love her.

Love, she thought as she opened her mailbox and pulled out a couple of bills. She wasn't sure how she felt about that. Of course she *liked* Jairus. How could she not? He was a great guy. Funny and sweet and totally great with Tyler. But love terrified her. She'd loved before and look what had happened. She didn't want to make another mistake.

She walked back to the house, then flipped through the bills. The last business-sized envelope wasn't from a utility. Instead it was from Eric. That was odd. He'd never mailed her anything before. The child support payments were automatically deposited into her account from his bank. What on earth?

She stepped into the kitchen and started reading the letter. It was only a few paragraphs long. She read to the end, then started over because she couldn't believe what she was seeing.

I've thought a lot about what you said. About me being a part of Tyler's life. You're right. He needs stability. He needs to know what's going to happen. What that means is I need to take a step back. To get out of the way. I don't want him wondering if I'm going to show up. We both know I'm not.

There was more. About how it would be best for Eric to simply relinquish responsibility. How he wanted to pay her a lump sum rather than keep paying monthly child support.

That of course she could take him to court and force him to see Tyler, but how that wouldn't be right for either of them.

Nicole sank into a kitchen chair. Her heart pounded and every part of her hurt. How could he do this?

She read the words again, searching for some meaning, some hidden message to make it all make sense. She could do as he said—go to court and force him to be a father. Why should she have to? Tyler was his son. Didn't that matter at all?

Aware of the boy in the next room, she struggled to contain her tears. She couldn't let him know what was going on. If he saw she was upset, he would get upset, too, and what was the point of that?

She grabbed her bag from the small desk by the pantry and reached inside for her cell phone. After pushing a couple of buttons, she prayed for Cecelia to answer.

"Hey, Nicole, what's up?"

"Could you come over to look after Tyler for an hour or so? I know it's short notice, but I—" She paused. What on earth was she supposed to say?

"I'll be right there," Cecelia told her. "Give me fifteen minutes."

"Th-thank you."

By the time the teen arrived, Nicole had managed to get control. She washed her face a couple of times and smiled at her reflection. She was still a wreck but hopefully she could get out of the house without breaking down in front of Tyler.

When Cecelia arrived, Tyler yelled with excitement. He showed her the Brad the Dragon coloring book he was working on and how he'd put stickers around the pictures.

Cecelia looked at her. "Take as much time as you need."

"Thanks." Nicole knelt down to hug her son. "I won't be long. You be good, okay? Oh, and show Cece your mural. It's looking really cool."

"I will, Mommy." He hugged her, then grabbed Cecelia's hand and tugged her toward the hallway. "You have to see this!"

Nicole got into her car. Once there she wasn't sure who to call. Gabby was still recovering from being sick. Shannon would make herself available, as would Hayley. Pam was out of town. She hesitated only a second before scrolling through her contact list.

Jairus picked up on the first ring. "Hey, this is unexpected," he said.

At the sound of his low, steady voice, her tears returned. She clutched the phone tightly as she asked, "Can I come talk to you?"

"Of course. What's up and how can I help?"

"I honestly don't know."

Nicole held the mug of herbal tea. She'd tried sipping the hot liquid, but her throat was too tight. She wasn't sure she was ever going to stop crying.

"I don't understand," she whispered. "I don't care about him hurting me. He can do that forever. I don't care that he made me a fool in his movie. But this is his *son*. His child. My God, how can he walk away?"

She sat on the sofa in Jairus's living room. He was in front of her, on the coffee table, facing her. He stroked her free hand.

"I'm sorry," he murmured. "I don't understand, either. Tyler's a great kid. He's fun to be around. Easy. Eric's an idiot."

Probably true, she thought, but not an explanation. "You don't know, either, then."

"I don't. I'm sorry. I wish I could say it's a guy thing, but it isn't. It makes me angry, but I can almost understand my ex not wanting to deal with my sister. But this is different. This is his blood."

"Do you think I should take him to court? Force him to have visitation with Tyler?"

"How does that help?"

An excellent question and the entire point of the matter. Only Tyler mattered. Would his life be better if he saw his father because Eric was forced by the court? Or was it best to simply let the man walk away?

"A boy needs his father," she said. "That's what everyone says."

"Does Tyler miss Eric?"

"No. He rarely talks about him. You know that. Remember when he said his dad was gone? Like he was dead or something? I've talked to him about his father. It's clear that Tyler stopped missing him long before we were separated. They never had anything to do with each other."

Jairus nodded without speaking. Nicole knew he wasn't going to give his opinion. Not on something like this. She had to decide. She was Tyler's mother.

"I should probably talk to someone," she said at last. "A child psychologist or something like that. To make sure I'm not hurting him or doing something wrong."

"You love him. You're always going to make the right decision."

That made her almost smile. "I wish that were true, but it's not. I can easily screw him up."

"You won't."

"I appreciate your faith in me."

He leaned in and kissed her. The touch was light. Reassuring. He was offering comfort, not making a move. Funny how she hadn't known him all that long, but she was sure of so many things.

"I love you," she said unexpectedly. The words had come from nowhere, but having spoken them, she found she didn't want to call them back.

The corners of his mouth turned up. "I love you, too."

"I mean it."

"I know."

She smiled. "Now that you've won me, whatever will you do with me?"

His humor faded as he took both her hands in his. "Whatever you want."

Oh, to be young again, Gabby thought as she walked into the kitchen to make lunch. The twins were back in school. They'd been sick for two days, then had recovered seemingly overnight. She'd kept them home an extra day, just to be sure, but this morning, they'd begged to return to class.

In contrast, Makayla had asked for another day and Gabby had agreed. Tomorrow they would both return to their regularly scheduled lives. Gabby wondered if the teen was dreading it as much as she was.

Physically she was close to 100 percent. Her appetite had returned and she hadn't thrown up in nearly forty-eight hours. There was no reason not to go back to work. Except that she didn't want to.

There it was—the ugly truth. She hated her job. Nothing about it was what she'd imagined. She missed being home, she didn't like the long hours or minimal pay and the work itself was tedious.

She wrestled with what to do with that information. She knew what Andrew would say—he would tell her to quit and find something else that fulfilled her. Which she would like to do, if only she could figure out what that was.

She logged on to the laptop in the kitchen and checked her

email, then found herself revisiting a site on homeschooling. The crazy idea had come to her between bouts of throwing up. There were online programs that provided all the material. It would only be until Makayla had the baby, she told herself. At most through June. The teen would return to high school the following fall.

Could she do it? Did she want to? Did Makayla? She had a feeling she knew the answer to the latter. Being pregnant wasn't the thrill ride she'd anticipated and losing Boyd had only made things worse.

She logged off the site and found Makayla in the family room. The TV was off and the girl wasn't reading anything. She was just looking out the window.

"You okay?" Gabby asked.

Makayla shook her head. "I'm not."

Gabby moved toward her. "What's wrong? Are you feeling nauseous again? Do you have a fever?"

She sat down on the sofa and touched the teen's forehead. It was cool. Makayla was a little pale, but didn't look sick.

"I'm okay," she said, looking at Gabby. "I feel fine." Tears filled her eyes. "I can't do it. I can't have the baby."

"You mean keep the baby? You want to give it up for adoption?"

"No. I want to get rid of it. I want to have an abortion."

The words were a slap. Gabby drew back. She had no idea what to say.

"I can't do it," Makayla said again, her voice rising. "I can't be like you. I saw what happened, when we were all sick and you had to do everything, even though you were sick yourself. You take care of everybody. You're always running around and doing stuff. I don't want to be like that. I want to go have fun with my friends. I want my friends to like me again."

Gabby told herself to take a breath and think before speaking.

"You're getting over being sick," she said slowly. "You're upset."

Makayla stood and glared at her. "I know what I'm saying. I want an abortion. Today. I want to get rid of the baby. I hate it. I hate being pregnant. This is awful. Get it out of me. Get it out!"

Gabby rose. "Stop screaming. You're acting like a toddler having a tantrum. Sit down so we can discuss this like adults. If you're old enough to have sex, you're old enough to have a reasonable conversation."

She wasn't sure if her firm tone would work, but Makayla surprised her by wiping her face and sinking back onto the sofa. Gabby retreated to one of the chairs so they could face each other.

Dear God—what to say?

"An abortion isn't an option," she said, trying to sound as calm as possible. "You're too far along."

"I still can. In some places."

So she'd been doing research? "It's not an option for you."

"Why not? You believe in a woman's right to choose." The words were defiant.

"You're not choosing. You're reacting to a series of circumstances. To being sick and hating school and losing Boyd. I do believe a woman should have control over her body, but an abortion isn't a decision to be made lightly. Not like this. And not for the reasons you have. We're in a position for you to carry this baby to term and you will. If you want to discuss adoption, that's fine, but there won't be an abortion."

Makayla sprang to her feet again. "You can't make me. I'll talk to my dad. He'll agree. You'll see."

"Maybe he will, but if he does, he's wrong."

"I'm going to tell him you said that."

"Me, too."

★ ★ ★

The longest afternoon in history turned into the longest evening when Andrew called to say he had to attend a dinner meeting. Gabby picked up the twins and kept them and herself busy playing games and making cookies. Makayla shut herself in her room. After weeks of a relatively easy relationship with her stepdaughter, Gabby was stung to realize how quickly the goodwill could evaporate.

Shortly after eight, Andrew walked in.

"I'm home," he called.

The twins went running to their father in their pajamas. Makayla appeared at the top of the stairs.

"Let me get the girls into bed before you bring this up, please," Gabby said to her. "They don't need to hear the conversation."

She wondered if the teen would protest, but Makayla surprised her by nodding her agreement and returning to her room.

Bath time passed quickly. Gabby and Andrew tucked the twins in and read them several stories before they fell asleep. As soon as they stepped into the hallway, her husband turned to her.

"What's up?" He touched her cheek. "You're on edge. I could tell you wanted the girls in bed before we talked. Are you okay?"

"I'm exhausted and you need to talk to your oldest daughter."

Andrew took her hand in his. "Only if we do it together."

"That's not going to go well."

"Makayla's going to have to get over that."

They walked to her room. She met them at the door, then stepped back to let them in. Once the door was closed behind them, the teen put her hands on her hips.

"Dad, I want an abortion. I'm not carrying this baby anymore and you can't make me."

Andrew stared at her. "What happened to keeping the baby? You wanted to raise it yourself."

"What? No. I don't. I'm a kid. I don't want to be a mom. Have you seen what Gabby does in a day? It's ridiculous. You should get her some help. I don't want to have a baby. I don't. I'm fifteen. I want an abortion. You have to let me. Gabby said no, you have to say yes."

Andrew glanced between the two of them. "You've been talking about this?"

Gabby thought about the shouting earlier. "Makayla told me this afternoon. She's too far along. Plus, it's not a decision to be made lightly. These are the wrong reasons to have an abortion. I told her she should carry the baby to term and then give it up, if that's what she wants."

Makayla stomped her foot. "No. I won't. I want it out of me now. Dad, tell her!"

Gabby braced herself for the inevitable. The rational discussion that would result in Makayla getting exactly what she wanted. Because that was always what happened.

"No," Andrew said calmly.

They both stared at him.

"Excuse me?" Gabby felt her mouth drop open and consciously closed it.

Makayla looked equally stunned. "Daddy, you never tell me no."

"That's not true."

"It is," Gabby said before she could stop herself. "Makayla always gets her way."

How comical they must look to an outsider, Gabby thought as Andrew's eyes widened. Everyone slack-jawed in amazement. She supposed that made this one of those life-changing moments people were always talking about. She should try to remember every detail. The problem was, she was exhausted and so ready to move on.

"I want an abortion!" Makayla shouted.

"And I want a daughter who isn't pregnant," Andrew roared back. "Now we're both disappointed."

Makayla burst into tears. Andrew's expression turned stricken. Gabby groaned. She went to the teen and hugged her.

"It's going to be okay," she murmured.

"It's not. I hate my life and I hate this baby. I don't have any friends, school is awful and now I can't have an abortion."

Gabby pointed to the door. "Go on downstairs," she told her husband. "I'll deal with this."

He hesitated.

She shook her head. "It's fine. Trust me. There are powerful hormones at work. Let us work this through."

He escaped before she could say anything else.

Makayla turned to her and began to cry.

"If only we could harness all our tears," Gabby murmured. "California wouldn't have a water shortage."

"You think this is funny?" the teen demanded.

"I think it's not tragic. It's hard, it's uncomfortable and what you're going through is going to change who you are, but it's not the end of the world."

"It is to me."

"No, it's not. You're going to have the baby. We'll find a nice couple to take it. This time next year, you'll be back in school." She almost said *just like nothing ever happened*. Only she had a feeling there would be scars—at least on the inside.

Her stepdaughter sighed. "You're really not going to let me get rid of it?"

"I'm really not."

Makayla surprised her by wiping her face. "Is there any ice cream?"

"I don't know. Let's go find out."

Chapter Twenty-Eight

Hayley sat in the meeting room of the local church and listened as the women talked. Her friend Shannon had told her about the support group for women trying to adopt a baby. This was her second meeting and it was just as depressing as the first one.

So far she'd listened to stories of failed adoption attempts in multiple counties. Of surrogates who couldn't get pregnant or made legal trouble. Of IVF and fostering first.

She'd spent the last couple of weeks doing as much research as she could online before attending the group. She knew that everyone wanted an infant and that going through public channels could take years. That private adoption was a matter of knowing the right people, and she wasn't sure she and Rob did.

The meeting ended and Hayley left without speaking to anyone. It was Thursday and for reasons she couldn't begin to explain, she drove to Supper's in the Bag. Maybe she needed a good dose of Morgan to set her world to rights.

The store wouldn't open for another hour, but Morgan's SUV was parked in front. Hayley parked next to it, then walked to the glass door and knocked. Morgan appeared a few seconds later and let her inside.

"What are you doing here?" her sister said by way of greeting.

"I thought I'd come by and say hi."

"Can you talk while chopping because I'm running late."

"Sure."

"I don't suppose you want your old job back?" Morgan asked.

"Not really."

"I figured. My luck isn't that good."

Morgan locked the door behind her, then went back to the prep tables where she was distributing bags of vegetables into bowls. Hayley washed her hands, pulled on gloves, then joined her sister.

"How are things with Brent?"

Morgan wrinkled her nose. "Fine. He annoys me. He's a man and I tell myself he can't help it. The kids exhaust me. I need to get away."

"You were just gone."

"For three days."

"How much time do you want to take off?"

"I don't know. A year."

Hayley glanced at her sister. "You're an idiot."

Morgan stared at her. "Don't get on me. You're the one who came here. I didn't ask for this."

She continued to rant, but Hayley wasn't listening. She recognized the psychological trick. Deflect and attack. Possibly not in that order. But that was what her sister was doing. Switching the focus, ignoring the question. It was clever, if not very helpful. Because while they might end up not talking about Morgan, at the end of the day, her sister was still unhappy. Or at least complaining.

"Is the bitching a habit or are you really disgusted with your life?" she asked, interrupting the tirade.

"Excuse me?"

"I know you heard the question. There's nothing wrong with your hearing."

Morgan's eyes widened. "What has gotten into you?"

"I'm tired of playing these games. You're my family and I want us to be close, but I'm not putting up with your crap anymore. Be nice or we're done."

"You don't get to say."

"Yeah, I do. At least for my part of it." Hayley breathed in a very calming sense of power. "Brent couldn't be sweeter to you. Why don't you appreciate him more?"

"I appreciate him," Morgan muttered, turning her attention back to the vegetables. "Why do you have to make such a big deal out of all of this? You always do. It's exhausting. Is this because of the surgery? Are you still on drugs?"

"And there you go again—sidestepping the question. You've always done that, haven't you? Deflected the difficult conversations. Is that why you never fully grew up?"

Morgan pointed to the door. "Get out."

Hayley shook her head. "No. You're not the boss of me. We are going to have a conversation without you yelling or acting like a shrew. Just answer the question."

"Which one?" Morgan's voice was a scream. "Which goddamned question?"

"Are you happy with your husband and your kids?"

"Yes!"

The single word was sharp and loud, but Hayley heard the truth behind it. She smiled. "I'm glad. You're lucky. You kind of have it all."

Morgan's mouth opened, then closed. "I hate you."

"No, you don't. You love me. In your own twisted way."

"You're annoying."

"So are you."

Morgan picked up a bag of cut broccoli. "I don't feel lucky. I feel like I'm constantly scrambling. I don't have a second to myself. Do you know how much laundry I do in a week?"

"You should appreciate what you have."

Her sister surprised her by nodding. "I know. I'm sorry. You're still upset about the hysterectomy, aren't you?"

Upset didn't exactly describe what she was feeling, Hayley thought. But it was close enough for this conversation.

"Yes. Every day. I try not to think about it, but it's always there."

"Are you and Rob going to adopt?"

"I'm thinking about it. Adoption isn't easy. Not if we want a baby. There are waiting lists."

"What about Gabby's stepdaughter? She's pregnant. Is she giving her kid up for adoption?" Morgan paused. "Never mind. That would be too hard. They're in the same neighborhood. You'd never feel like the baby was yours, would you? There would be too much connection."

"That's very insightful."

"I'm not insightful."

"No, you're just selfish and bitchy."

Morgan raised her eyebrows. "It beats being sanctimonious and smug."

"I'm not smug."

"You are. Constantly. In your perfect marriage with your perfect husband and friends. But I love you anyway."

Something she couldn't remember ever hearing from her sister before. "I love you, too."

Morgan glared at her. "I'm not interested in being part of one of those ridiculous families that says they love each other all the time. Just so we're clear."

Hayley grinned. "No problem. As long as we both remember you said it first."

"You are so annoying."

"Back at you. Now give me the celery and I'll chop it."

Nicole handed over the frosted cupcake. Jairus dusted it with sprinkles and put it next to the others. Tyler was having friends over tomorrow and she wanted to get the baking out of the way. Jairus had offered to help.

He studied their completed cupcakes. "Nice. We're a good team."

"If only you did windows," she teased. "Then this would be perfect."

"I have the name of a company that does windows. Does that count?"

"Not in the least."

She carried the empty frosting bowl over to the sink and filled it with water. There were a dozen cupcakes. Eight for tomorrow and four for them. Well, three and one spare that she was planning on sending home with Jairus.

Because, despite the fact that they had been lovers for a few weeks now, he wasn't spending the night. She was careful about that. Their time together consisted of stolen moments. No matter how much she enjoyed having Jairus around, she didn't want Tyler getting too attached. In case things didn't work out.

When she found herself thinking there was a chance…that this was special, she remembered what had happened with Eric. How he was so disinterested in his only son that he was willing to sign away his rights.

She'd been to a lawyer, had talked to her friends and still didn't have an answer. Next week she would speak to a child psychologist to get her take on the right path. Forcing Eric to be a father when he didn't want to be wasn't right, but letting him simply disappear—was that so much better?

She wanted to believe he would change his mind. That one day he would regret what he was giving up. But she wasn't sure that would ever happen.

"What are you thinking?" Jairus asked gently.

"The Eric thing. I don't know what to do. No one has the answer."

"You're looking for someone to tell you what to say that will change him. You think there are words that will turn him into someone who wants to spend as much time with his son as possible." He put his arm around her. "A great sentiment, but it's not going to happen. Eric is what he is."

"A selfish jerk?"

"Pretty much."

She knew Jairus was right. There wasn't a magical solution. There was only what was best for Tyler.

"Speaking of my son, he's been quiet for a while." She started for his bedroom.

Jairus kept pace with her. "He said he wanted to work on a few drawings."

"Thanks to you, he's getting good at doing Brad."

"Maybe he has a future as a cartoonist."

"I'm not sure I'm ready for my son to become your apprentice in the Brad department," she said with a laugh. "I already feel that dragon overwhelms me."

"He's a good guy and you can handle it."

They walked into Tyler's room. He sat at his small table. There were crayons spread all around. On the far wall, the nearly finished mural glowed with light and color. It was an impressive piece of art, she thought. A thoughtful gift from a man who genuinely liked kids. Jairus would never walk away from his child. He would give 100 percent.

"What are you working on?" she asked.

Tyler grinned at her. "I did a drawing of all of us," he said proudly and showed it to them.

The picture was clear. Tyler and Nicole and Jairus stood together, along with Brad. They were all holding hands.

"Cool," she said, kneeling next to him. "I really like the colors."

Brad was his usual red, while the rest of them wore clothes.

"You're getting better all the time," Jairus told him. "Great trees there in the backyard."

"Thanks." He pointed to the paper. "Did you see we're a family, Mommy? You and me and Jairus and Brad. Brad's like my brother."

Nicole nodded and kept smiling. It was easy because she couldn't actually move and she'd been smiling before he spoke. Cold numbed her and dread made her so heavy, she was a statue. Only her mind kept moving.

The thoughts tumbled through her. Regret. Fear. The knowledge that she should have seen this disaster coming.

She'd been so careful to keep things light. To not let Tyler know she and Jairus had fallen for each other. But her son hadn't needed to know any of that to assume. To care. All he'd needed was time with a good man. Because while Tyler might not miss his father, he had a hardwired need to have a father figure in his life.

Nicole tried to tell herself that no harm had been done. That Jairus wouldn't hurt the boy. Only, what happened if the relationship ended? Tyler would be devastated. She'd wanted to spare him that and she hadn't. She'd put her child in harm's way. All because she thought Jairus was sexy.

Jairus pulled her to her feet. "We have cupcakes," he said, his expression tight but his voice friendly. "Want me to bring you one?"

Tyler nodded. "Yes, please."

Jairus drew her out into the hallway and then down to the kitchen.

"Don't," he whispered urgently. "Nothing's different. Nothing's changed. Don't read more into it than there is. I love you, Nicole. I'm not going anywhere." He grabbed her upper arms and stared into her eyes. "Don't do anything. I love you."

She nodded. "I know. I love you, too."

"Then let that be enough."

She didn't say anything. This wasn't the time or place for the conversation. But she knew what she knew. Loving someone wasn't enough. Not by a long shot.

Friday afternoon Gabby worked late. The twins had a playdate until five, which meant she could put in an extra few hours at the office. She'd stayed caught up all of fifteen seconds before the flu attack had seriously derailed her schedule. She figured if she continued to bring work home, she would have everything done in about two weeks.

She was exhausted from only getting four or five hours of sleep a night. Her boss had given her plenty of praise for what she was accomplishing and had hinted she would like to hire Gabby full-time. The thought of having more responsibility had nearly made her weep.

If she had to work forty hours to get paid for twenty, what would it mean to be responsible for forty hours of output? An eighty-hour week? At half pay? Not that she would mind so much if she liked what she was doing, but she didn't. She wanted to be excited about what she was doing. She wanted to look forward to showing up at the office and hey, she wanted to be paid for the time she put in.

She pulled into the driveway and parked with the car windows down. Despite the detailing, the smell of vomit lingered.

She had a bad feeling it was never going away. She got her tote and her handbag, then walked into the house.

For maybe five seconds, there was blessed silence. Just the empty living room and her own quiet breathing. Then Boomer bayed from somewhere in the back of the house and the twins came running out to greet her. She hugged them automatically.

"When did you two get home?" she asked. "I thought I was picking you up at five."

"Daddy sent Cece to get us," Kennedy informed her. "She's staying with us tonight."

What? Cecelia? But that would mean that she and Andrew were going out. Was there an event she'd forgotten about? Some work function or fund-raiser she would have to rally for?

The thought of it made her want to sink to the carpet and sob. She was bone-weary. She hadn't totally recovered from the flu before jumping back into everything. She felt as if she hadn't seen her kids in forever. She wanted to sit and read to them, to bake cookies with the twins and Makayla. Speaking of the teen, nothing had been settled, so that still loomed. Going out? It couldn't be lower on her list of priorities.

"Where's your dad?" she asked.

"In his study."

Gabby dropped her bag and tote onto the sofa, then walked down the hallway. Everyone trailed after her, including Jasmine who trotted to the front of the parade and meowed to be picked up.

Gabby obliged. Stroking the soft fur always made her feel better. Hearing the rumble of the purr eased her tension. She walked into Andrew's office.

Her husband looked up at her. "You're home. How was your day?"

"Fine. Why is Cecelia coming over?"

He smiled and rose. "I'm taking you to dinner. I know how hard you've been working. I thought you could use a night out." He winked at the twins. "It was a surprise. Thanks, girls, for not telling Mommy."

"Yes, thanks, girls," she said. "Could you please check on Makayla? We were going to bake tomorrow. Does she still want to help with that?"

The twins grinned at the prospect of one of their favorite activities. They went careening down the hallway, Boomer following on their heels. Gabby kept hold of Jasmine as she carefully closed the study door and faced her husband.

"Hi," she said tightly. "I don't want any more surprises. I don't mean that in a bad way, Andrew. I just can't take on one more thing." She thought about the full-time job offer and knew this wasn't the time to discuss it.

"Don't you want to go out to dinner?" he asked. "I'm sorry. I thought I was helping."

"I know." The road to hell and all that, she thought. "Look, you're very sweet and I appreciate the effort, but I have a question. Why do we hire Cecelia?"

"Because the twins are too young to be left on their own." He frowned. "I don't..." His expression cleared. "You're not asking that, are you? You want to know why Makayla doesn't babysit sometimes."

"Yes. She's fifteen. She's their sister. She needs to be a part of the family. She needs to be helping out. Things are better. I'm not complaining. I'm simply pointing out that she could do more."

Gabby set down the cat and faced him. "Andrew, I'm not doing well. Between the twins and the baby and my work and your travel, I'm being pulled in forty-seven directions at once. I need a break. I need help. I can't do it all."

"So I should cancel Cecelia."

Gabby started to say yes, then shook her head. "No. Keep her. Order in a pizza for everyone."

"I don't understand. Are we going out?"

"No. I'm going to bed. I'm going to sleep. You and Cecelia can keep the twins busy. I'll deal with all this in the morning." She started to leave, then turned back. "Do you know how to feed the pets?"

"Um…"

It wasn't his fault, she told herself. It was hers. For not asking for more. For not making him take responsibility. Just like the situation with Makayla. She'd been so careful to let Andrew take the lead. After all, the teen was his daughter.

But not only his, she thought. Not anymore. Things had changed and they were going to change more. There was a lot to consider, but again, all that could wait until morning.

"Makayla knows. Ask her."

"Gabby, are you okay?"

"I will be. Just let me have tonight," she told him. "Please. In twelve hours, I'll be healed."

She left before he could say anything else. After putting on her pajamas, she closed the shades in the bedroom, turned on the overhead fan and climbed into bed. In the distance she heard conversation. She thought Kennedy was asking why Mommy couldn't be with them. The need to sleep battled with comforting her daughter. She would get up and talk to her. In a second.

When Gabby next opened her eyes, it was two in the morning and she desperately had to pee. She returned to the bed and settled back down. What seemed like seconds later, it was seven-thirty and light peeked from behind the shades.

She rolled onto her back and stretched. She felt better, she admitted. Not healed, but definitely on the way to recovery. Things didn't hurt so much. Her head was more clear.

Andrew's side of the bed was empty. Jasmine lay curled up on his pillow. Gabby knew he'd joined her in the night, so she wasn't worried he'd slept on the sofa. Still, it was unusual for him to be up first.

She collected her robe, brushed her teeth, then made her way downstairs. She heard the twins laughing at something and the low hum of the television. She walked into the kitchen and saw that the girls were already up and dressed. Andrew was as well, although he hadn't showered. There was an open box of doughnuts on the table, along with several to-go containers of coffee and hot chocolate.

"Good morning," he said when he saw her. "How do you feel?"

"Mommy!"

The twins ran over and wrapped their arms around her. She hugged them back, savoring the feel of their little bodies so close to hers. Her babies, she thought happily. They were what mattered. Her children and her husband.

She walked over to Andrew and kissed him on the mouth. "Much better. Thank you for letting me sleep. I needed it."

"I could tell. You barely stirred the whole night. I kept checking to make sure you were breathing."

"Afraid you'd be left alone with all this?" she asked, her voice teasing.

Andrew didn't return her smile. "No. I was worried about you. I love you."

The intense statement surprised her. She shifted so she

could free an arm and held it open to him. Andrew joined the group hug.

After breakfast Andrew showered, then took the twins to the park. Makayla made her way downstairs about nine. Gabby was sitting at the kitchen table, planning menus for the week. She looked up when the teen walked in.

"Hey," she said. "How are you feeling?"

Makayla crossed to her and sat down next to her.

"I'm sorry," the girl said. "About not helping more. Dad talked to me last night." She looked away, then back. "I didn't mean not to help. I love Kenzie and Kennedy, you know. They're sweet and fun. But even if they weren't, I want to help." Her chin raised. "I'm part of this family, too."

A thousand thoughts descended. Gabby realized that there was a part of Makayla that wasn't sure where she belonged. The rejection of her mother had been devastating and with the baby and no friends and no Boyd, she was truly alone.

Gabby took her hands in her own and squeezed her fingers. "I'm the one who's sorry. I love you. I hope you know that and I'm sorry I haven't said it enough." Or at all, Gabby thought, suddenly feeling awful. "Makayla, you and I have been through a lot together. I learned how to be a mom with you. I know I made a lot of mistakes." She smiled. "You're right. We're a family and sometimes that's messy and sometimes it's annoying but it's forever. Your dad and I will always be here for you."

Makayla's eyes filled with tears. "I know. It's just everything is so awful. Gabby, please don't make me have this baby."

Gabby drew her close and hugged her. "I'm sorry. You have to. You won't be alone, but you're carrying the baby to term."

Makayla began to cry harder. "I don't want to."

"I know. We'll figure it out. Together."

Makayla straightened and wiped her tears. "This is really hard."

"I know." She hesitated. "Are you serious about not keeping the baby?"

Makayla nodded. "I want to give it up for adoption."

"You have to be sure. You can't go through the process, allow another couple to hope, then keep the baby at the last minute."

"I'm fifteen. I want to be normal again. I want to go to classes and hang out with my friends and do my homework. I can't do that with a baby. I can't do that now."

"Have you told your dad?"

Makayla ducked her head. "I thought maybe you could talk to him."

"I will. About all of this. Then we'll go meet with a lawyer. You can pick the family, if you want. The baby's parents."

"I don't want to know anything. I just want this never to have happened."

"Okay. I'll talk to your dad when he gets home."

Makayla nodded, grabbed a doughnut and went back upstairs. Gabby watched her go. She understood that the teen was hoping that after the birth, it would be like it was before. Only life wasn't that simple. There would be complications. She would talk to Andrew about that, too. How they were going to have to trade parenting classes for emotional counseling. Maybe for all of them.

Later, when Makayla was outside playing with the twins, Gabby walked into Andrew's study.

He got up and joined her on the sofa.

"How are you feeling?" he asked.

"I'm fine. I was tired. I'm better now."

He didn't look convinced. "I'm scared, Gabby. Whatever happens, I don't want to lose you."

"Let that go. Please. I'm staying. We're going to work this through."

He ran his hand through his hair. "I've been such an asshole. I was trying to make up for Candace's rejection by giving in to Makayla. That didn't help anyone. I taught her the wrong lesson and frustrated you. I was totally unreasonable on the pregnancy thing. You can't give up your life."

"Funny how you're saying that now." Talk about irony.

"Because she wants to give up the baby?"

Gabby stared at him. "How did you figure that out? She asked me to talk to you, but there hasn't been time yet."

"She wants you to talk to me rather than talk to me herself?" He swore. "Okay. Sure. She's scared I'll be disappointed in her. As for the adoption, it hasn't been hard to guess where this is all going. She's miserable at school, she has no friends anymore. Do you think we should send her to one of those unwed mother places? At least there no one would judge."

"Boarding school is the last thing Makayla needs," Gabby said firmly. "She would only feel more rejected. I think we can make things work here."

"How?"

"Give me a few days to figure it all out." She looked at the man she loved and knew he wasn't the only one who had screwed up. "I was wrong, too. I should have stood up to you more. I should have talked to you more, pushed back harder instead of letting you win by default."

"Like with the booster seats. I thought I was being nice, but instead I undermined you. I'm sorry, Gabby. I never meant for it to be like this."

She moved closer and he wrapped his arms around her. The feel of his warm, familiar body comforted her. Andrew had his faults, but they were the kind she could live with. He was, at heart, a good man and a father who loved his girls.

"We'll talk more," he promised. "I'm going to work on not assuming I'm right all the time."

She laughed. "Now won't that be nice."

He kissed her, his mouth lingering.

"Tonight?" he asked.

She smiled. "Always."

Chapter Twenty-Nine

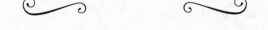

"That is amazing," Hayley said, her voice laced with awe. "I know you're not a fan, but wow."

Nicole wrinkled her nose. "I hate Brad less these days. Although Jairus confuses the heck out of me."

They stood together in Tyler's room. It was Saturday afternoon and her son was at a friend's birthday party. Nicole had invited Hayley over for some girl time and they'd ended up here—looking at the nearly finished mural.

"Tyler has got to love this." Hayley walked to the wall and lightly traced Brad's head. "It's huge and colorful and his favorite character ever. So why are you freaked?" Hayley studied the painting. "Hmm, let me guess. Eric lived here all those years and was able to walk away with little more than a few boxes. You've known Jairus only four or five months and look how he's left his mark on your house."

"Ouch," Nicole murmured. "Can we at least pretend my problem is subtle and deserving of an elegant metaphor?"

"Sorry. This one seems to be very on the nose. Am I wrong?"

Nicole led the way back to her living room. "No. I wish you were, but no."

"Are you dying to paint over it?"

"Every day. The cans are in the hall closet."

They sat on the sofa. Glasses of iced tea waited on the table, along with a plate of new pineapple Paleo muffins Nicole had made that morning.

Hayley took a sip of her drink, then pointed at the muffins. "Are they gross?"

"They're weird, but not gross."

"You don't need to lose weight."

"I know. I'm just trying to eat more healthy."

"Good for you. I'd rather have chocolate." Hayley put down her glass. "So what's the problem?"

Talk about the blunt question. "Jairus makes me uncomfortable."

"How and why?"

Nicole resisted the urge to squirm. "He's in love with me."

"That bastard!"

"Stop it. You know what I mean. He's nice. He's affectionate. He shows up when he says, he's good to Tyler. He painted a Brad the Dragon mural. He's good in bed."

Hayley raised her eyebrows. "I want more details on that last one, but not now. We're not getting distracted from the main point."

"I don't want to think about the main point."

"Which is kind of the problem." Hayley sighed. "So I'm just going to say it. Are you braced?"

Nicole crossed her arms over her chest and drew in a breath. Before she nodded, she reminded herself that she'd wanted to talk to her friend for a reason. To figure out what was wrong. To understand the gnawing sense of panic that filled her whenever she thought about Jairus and her relationship and the future.

"Go," she said firmly.

"You're scared." Hayley shrugged. "You picked Eric and

he was a dud, so now you're gun-shy. It's hard to risk yourself, to give your heart. You're older now, you have a son and a life. Jairus is too good to be true. He's nice and sweet and funny and successful. What if he breaks your heart? What if he breaks Tyler's heart?"

"I know. I worry."

"Which makes you want to run. But here's the thing, Nicole. The real problem isn't what might happen. The real problem is you. You don't think you deserve him. For whatever reason, you don't believe you're good enough."

Nicole scooted back on the sofa. Her face got hot and she didn't know where to look. "That's not true!"

"It is." Hayley's voice was soft. "I don't know if it's because of your mom or how you never made it as a dancer or what, but you don't believe in yourself. You have a successful business and a great kid and you own your own home. You're amazing. But you don't see that. It took you nearly six months to get the courage to buy a new car, even though you needed one and had the money. You're so scared of getting it wrong, you retreat rather than go forward. You don't try and therefore you lose out. It's like when you need clothes. You buy used rather than new. Which is fine, except in your case, it's a symptom."

Hayley leaned forward. "You don't have to start buying designer, but indulge yourself a little. You've earned it. Trust your judgment. I get playing it safe. I do, but men like Jairus don't come around very often. Wouldn't it be horrible to lose him just because you're scared?"

Nicole sank her teeth into her lower lip. Hayley was wrong. About all of it. Hayley didn't understand. Nicole wasn't like that. She couldn't be. She was…

"I'm a mess," she admitted. "Oh, God. What if you're right? I'm a total wreck."

"You're not. Stop it. You can't only hear the bad stuff. Conversations don't work that way. You have to hear the good stuff, too. Look at all you've done. Have a little faith in yourself, Nicole."

Was that possible? Faith? Admitting the good stuff. She wasn't sure why it terrified her, but it did.

"If Jairus up and left today," her friend said. "What would you do?"

"I don't know. Miss him. Help Tyler understand what had happened. Be hurt. Be mad."

"Would you sell your business?"

"What? Of course not. That has nothing to do with him."

"And the house? You'd keep it?"

Nicole saw where Hayley was going. "You're saying that I would survive. That I would keep on with my life. That Jairus is great but he's not the center of my universe."

"Something like that."

There was too much to think about. Too much to understand. It was all so confusing.

"He loves you," Hayley reminded her. "This I know for sure. Love doesn't come along every single day. You have to make your own decisions, but if it were me, I'd hang on with both hands."

Hanging on was scary, but losing him was worse. Nicole sighed, then looked at the coffee table. "I have M&M's in the pantry."

"A much better choice. See, you can do the right thing."

Nicole laughed. "I'm not sure picking M&M's over a Paleo muffin is exactly the same as committing to Jairus."

"Maybe not, but it's a start."

★ ★ ★

"Thank God you're here!" Morgan shouted and lunged forward. She clung to Hayley with amazing strength. "It was so horrible. He broke his leg and the bone was sticking out."

Hayley swallowed hard to keep her stomach from rebelling. Even without details, the image was plenty frightening.

"What happened?"

"Christopher was playing at school, hanging off the monkey bars and trying some stupid trick he saw on a video game." Morgan pushed Hayley to arm's length and glared at her. "A video game! They're not *people*. They're not even alive. But does he get that? Where's Brent? He said he'd be right here."

"Breathe. There's traffic. He'll get here. What did the doctor say?"

Morgan covered her face with her hands. "He needs surgery. They have to set his leg and he has to stay at least overnight. I can't think."

"Where are the other kids?"

"With Brent's mother. I'm sure she's using the time to turn them against me."

Hayley stifled a smile. Even in the middle of a disaster, Morgan maintained her sense of place in the world and knew what was important.

"You're a freak, you know that, right?" she asked.

"Maybe, but you're stuck with me."

Hayley nodded as she admitted, if only to herself, she could live with that. Her sister wasn't perfect, but they were still family. No matter what.

They sat down in the hospital waiting room. Morgan clutched her hand, squeezing occasionally. The frantic call had come just over an hour ago. Hayley had left work and come directly to the hospital. She thought about calling Rob, but he was busy with work. Brent would be here soon and he would take charge.

Sure enough, not ten minutes later, Brent ran into the waiting room. He hurried directly to Morgan. She raced toward him and they hung on to each other.

"Tell me everything," Brent instructed.

While Morgan explained what had happened to their oldest son, Hayley watched the couple. Gone was the tension and Morgan's restlessness. For all her complaining, she loved her family. Maybe the crisis would draw them closer. Hayley hoped so.

One emergency surgery, time in recovery and a bunch of drugs later, Christopher was finally in a room on one of the pediatric floors. Morgan and Brent had argued about who was going to stay with him. In the end, they decided they both would. Hayley had hugged them good-night and headed for the elevator.

There were a lot of children in the hospital. She hadn't realized the number. Of course it made sense. Kids got sick or injured. She passed rooms that were dimly lit, with parents hovering or asleep on cots. Some of the rooms were filled with balloons and stuffed animals. Others had drawings on the wall—as if the stay was a long one. Just past the elevator bank, she saw light spilling from a room.

Giving in to curiosity, she eased in that direction and saw a boy sitting up in a bed. He was maybe nine or ten, bald and wearing a hospital gown. His room was empty. Oh, there was plenty of medical equipment, but no balloons, no stuffed animals.

He was thin, with big brown eyes. As she stood in the doorway, he looked up from the book he was reading and smiled.

"You're working late."

"What?"

"You're from social services, right? I sometimes get late visits, but not this late." He raised the bed a little more. "I can save you some time. Yes, the treatment is going well. Yes, I understand what they're doing to me. The food is okay. Sometimes the nurses give me extra ice cream. When I can keep it down. I'm current with my schoolwork. Math is still my favorite subject, which is weird, so don't tell anyone."

Hayley stepped into the room. "I'm not a social worker."

The boy chuckled. "So now you know too much about me. Who are you?"

"Hayley. Who are you?"

"Noah. Why are you here?"

"My nephew fell and broke his leg. He had surgery. I was visiting and I saw the light on."

"Too bad for him. That's gonna hurt." Noah's mouth twisted. "But he'll be going home soon, right?"

She nodded. "Can I sit down for a minute?"

"Sure." He pointed to one of the plastic chairs. "I don't get many visitors."

"How come?"

"I don't have any family. I'm an orphan and I live in foster care."

His tone was casual, as if the information didn't matter anymore. Hayley felt the words cut her like a knife.

"I'm sorry."

One bony shoulder rose and fell. "Nothing I can do about it."

"How long have you been in the hospital?"

"Awhile. I have a few more weeks. It's cancer. Lymphoma. I don't mind talking about it. My foster parents always whisper when they say it. Like it's contagious. But it's not. It's the kind they can cure. Doing chemo sucks, but it beats the alternative."

"How old are you?"

"Eleven."

He sounded so much older. Wise, even. He'd been through so much.

"Do your foster parents come visit you?" she asked.

"Naw. They're busy. There are other kids and I can take care of myself."

Sadness swept through her, although she did her best not to show it.

"What do you like to read?" she asked.

"Everything. Adventure stories are my favorite. But I'm not picky. I'm a fast reader." He glanced around as if making sure they were alone. "Don't tell anyone, but I really like the Harry Potter books. Even though they're for kids."

"You're a kid."

Noah flashed her a smile. "Sometimes. Did you know at the new theme park, they have a replica of the train? And you catch it from Platform 9—"

"I didn't," she admitted. "I read the books, but I haven't been to the park."

"I'm going," Noah told her. "One day. You know, when I'm grown up."

Because there was no one to take him now. If his foster parents didn't bother to visit, she was sure there was no way they would take him on vacation.

She wanted to say she could help. That she and Rob would pay for the trip. But who would he go with? He didn't have anyone.

"What are you reading now?" she asked.

He held up the book. "*The Hunger Games*. I've read it before. It's good. Violent. I find it strange that there are so many books written about this country after a big disaster, but things are never better. Why is that? You'd think if there was a big war or something we'd learn our lesson and act right."

"That wouldn't be a very interesting story."

"I guess not."

Hayley studied the boy on the bed. "Okay, this is going to sound totally weird and you can for sure say no, but would you like me to read to you for a bit?"

Noah stared at her for a long time, then held out the book. "That would be nice."

Despite the talk she'd had with Hayley, despite her promise to be strong, Nicole had come to the conclusion that there was only one solution to the Jairus problem. And that was not to see him anymore.

She sat across from him at Latte-Da, their untouched lattes between them.

"I have a bad feeling about whatever you want to talk about," he told her. "Nicole, don't."

"You have no idea what I'm going to say."

"I don't have to. I can feel it. You're scared. I get that. I'm scared, too. I haven't been in love in a long time and I've never felt about anyone the way I feel about you. I love you and I love Tyler. Don't punish me for that."

If he wanted to hurt her, he'd found exactly the right words. "Jairus, there are a lot of things I have to consider."

"No. There aren't. I know Eric hurt you. I know you're worried about making another mistake. I know you have Tyler to consider. Don't give up on us. Don't walk away."

He stretched his arms toward her. "Nicole, I want to marry you. I want to have kids with you and grow old with you. I want to give you everything I have, be there for you."

His words hammered against her. They were wonderful

and painful and while a part of her wanted to say yes, a thousand times yes, the rest of her said to run. To escape while she could, while neither she nor Tyler would be damaged.

"I can't," she whispered.

He put his hands on his lap. "Do you love me?"

She hung her head. Was that what it came down to? "I don't know."

"You said you do. Before. I think that's what frightens you the most. Loving me. Knowing I'm not going anywhere. Because to make this work, you have to be all in and you're not comfortable with that. You want to hold a piece of yourself back."

He rose and walked around to stand next to her. "I won't accept that. I want everything you have, Nicole. No holding back. No excuses. Just your heart." He put his hand on her shoulder. "I'm not going anywhere. Take your time. I love you. That's not going to change."

And then he was gone.

She sat in front of her cooling drink and did her best not to cry. This was better, she told herself. This made sense. Being safe. Making the sensible decision. She and Tyler were fine on their own. If it was just the two of them, she could keep him safe. Yes, their world was smaller, but wasn't it worth it? To be sure?

She reached across the table. There was no one there to take her hand. No one to smile at her. To laugh. To say the right thing. She felt herself weakening. Jairus wasn't Eric.

But he also didn't come with any guarantees. Eric had promised to love her forever. She would accept the divorce, but not that he'd walked away from his own son. That he'd sent papers from his lawyer so he never had to see Tyler again. Because it was too much trouble.

She wanted assurances. She wanted to know and all Jairus could do was promise. In her world, a promise simply didn't count. Not anymore.

"You can interview the families, if you'd like," Amanda, an attractive fortysomething African-American woman, said. "We have several dozen in our files. You can pick your top two or three and we'll go from there."

Gabby sat close to Makayla, her hand on the teen's back. Her stepdaughter was tense and she had trouble meeting the adoption counselor's gaze.

"I don't want someone close," she said in a whisper. "I want a couple who lives on the other side of the country."

"Of course. That's not a problem. Any other criteria?"

Makayla shook her head. "Just that they'll be good to the baby." She sniffed. "Gabby and I went to the doctor yesterday. It's a boy. Does that matter?"

"No." Amanda's smile was kind. "Most of our prospective parents aren't concerned about gender. But it's nice that you know already."

Gabby hadn't been sure Makayla would want to know but when the technician had asked if she was interested in the sex of the baby, the teen had said yes.

"It doesn't change anything for me," Makayla said now. "I just wondered."

Amanda walked them through the process. They talked about how the parents would be chosen.

"What we find works best is one or two meetings as soon as you have your finalists, then you make the choice. You can stay in touch with them through the rest of your pregnancy, if you'd like."

"They'll be here when the baby is born?" Makayla asked.

"They can be."

"I want them right there. I want them to take him as soon as he's born."

Gabby moved her hand to Makayla's lap. The teen gripped her fingers tightly.

"I don't want to see him."

Amanda nodded. "I understand. Now about the biological father. You mentioned something about him signing away his rights?"

"I have the paperwork," Gabby told her. "He has no problem with Makayla giving up the baby for adoption." She'd phoned Boyd's mother, just to be sure. "If there are more forms, he'll take care of them."

"Then this should all go very smoothly. Let's talk a little about a few of the couples we have who meet your preliminary criteria."

Gabby stayed close while Makayla looked through the folders of prospective parents. While she tried not to offer an opinion, Makayla kept looking at her and asking, "What do you think?" After a couple of hours, they'd narrowed the list down to three couples. One was from North Carolina, one from Florida and the last couple was in Maine.

"I like them best," Makayla said as she and Gabby walked to the car. "They both work for the forest service, so he'll get to be outside a lot. I liked their letters, too."

Gabby nodded. "Hers especially." The wife had gone through surgery while still a teenager and it had left her unable to have children. "Plus, they're both from big families, so there will be lots of cousins to play with."

"It's an important decision." Makayla sounded tired. "I don't want to make a mistake."

Gabby put her arm around her daughter. "You won't. They've all been thoroughly vetted by the agency. Any one of the three would be a great choice. If you start with that premise, then it's just the matter of which couple speaks to you the most."

Gabby unlocked the SUV.

"Let's talk to your dad tonight and get his opinion. The choice is yours, but maybe the three of us talking it out will help you decide."

"I'd like that." Makayla sighed. "I guess you should take me to school. I can still get to all my afternoon classes."

The girl's obvious discomfort at the idea made Gabby want to protect her from the world. She couldn't imagine what it would be like to have to walk the halls of high school while pregnant. Talk about a nightmare.

"Why don't you take the afternoon off?" she offered. "You can get your assignments online and do them at home."

"Really?" Relief brightened her whole face. "That would be wonderful. Thank you."

"No problem."

Gabby got in the SUV and started the engine. As she drove out of the parking lot, she told herself this was it. She had to commit, one way or the other. Was she really willing to do it? Because once she committed, she couldn't back out.

She searched her heart and found only love for the teen next to her. As for her job, well, that had been a mistake. She'd been trying to recapture who she'd been when she'd quit. That woman was long gone. She needed to think about who she was now and what she wanted. Which was going to make for a very interesting conversation with Andrew later that day.

Chapter Thirty

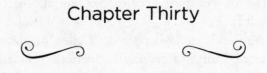

Hayley hesitated outside the hospital room. She felt nervous, which was silly. She was bringing lunch to a sick kid, nothing more. Well, that wasn't true. In addition to the burger, fries and a milk shake he'd requested, she'd brought a stack of books. Still, what if Noah didn't want to talk to her?

She drew in a breath, squared her shoulders and walked into his room.

"Hi, Noah."

The boy looked up and grinned when he saw her. "Hayley. I wasn't sure you'd come back."

"I said I would, didn't I? Plus, what was I going to do with this?" She held up the bag from Gary's Café. "As requested, a cheeseburger, fries and a chocolate shake."

Noah raised the bed. "That sounds great. Thank you. I don't know how much I can eat. I had a bad night."

Hayley pulled up a chair and sat next to his bed. "You don't have to eat any of it. I won't mind at all. I can throw it out so the smell doesn't bother you."

"No way. I want to try." He grinned. "It's been a long time since I had a burger."

She moved the rolling table closer and set the bag in front of him. As he pulled out the burger, she tried not to stare at his bald head. It was just...he looked so vulnerable, she thought.

Defenseless. To have to deal with cancer as a kid was awful, but to do it alone. She couldn't begin to imagine. If it had been her, her parents would have been camped out in the hospital. They would have dragged Morgan along. Her sister would have complained loudly about Hayley getting all the attention, but they would have been there for her.

Because they were her family, she thought. Flaws and all. She regretted taking the scenes of her childhood and twisting them into something bad. Something that had scared her. Especially when it hadn't been necessary.

Noah took a bite and chewed. His eyes widened with pleasure.

"Wow," he mumbled, then covered his full mouth.

"Yeah, I know all the best burger places," she joked. "Stick with me, kid."

He grinned and took another bite, then offered her his fries. She took one. It was still warm and salty.

"How's your nephew?" Noah asked.

"He's good. The surgery went well and he should be going home in the morning. He'll miss a couple of weeks of school, which he's very excited about."

Noah rolled his eyes. "A lot of kids don't like school, but I do. It's fun to learn new stuff. Better than being home sick."

She would guess that nearly anything was. "How long are you going to be in the hospital?"

"A couple more weeks. This is my second round of chemo and they think it's going to be my last." He put down the burger. "Sorry. I can't eat any more right now."

He'd taken two bites.

"It was really good, though."

Hayley shook her head. "So you're saying that whole burger-fries thing was cheap talk?"

He grinned. "Yeah. But I think I can drink the milk shake."

"Don't worry if you can't."

A nurse in cheerful scrubs walked in. "Hey, Noah."

"Hi, Minerva. This is Hayley."

Minerva looked surprised. "Nice to meet you. Are you Noah's foster mother?"

"She's a friend," Noah told the nurse. "Her nephew broke his leg and she's visiting."

"Oh, sorry about the accident." Minerva turned to Noah. "I need a blood draw."

Noah sighed. "Minerva's part vampire, but I like her anyway."

"I can't help it. Your blood is so appealing."

Hayley stood. "Let me get out of your way."

Minerva waved her back into the chair. "You're fine. I have a port I use."

"It's easier," Noah explained. "They can get blood when they need and give me drugs. It's kind of gross, but I'm used to it now. It doesn't hurt."

Hayley watched the nurse fold back his hospital gown to reveal an IV connection in his upper chest. Minerva pulled a sealed needle out of a protective sleeve. Hayley instinctively reached for Noah's hand. He squeezed her fingers.

"It's okay," he promised.

"I'm trying to reassure you. Not the other way around."

He grinned. "Okay. If you insist."

"I do."

When Minerva left, Hayley stayed a few more minutes, then glanced at her watch. "I have to get back to work. Want some company tonight?"

"Sure. If you want to stop by." He looked at her. "You don't have to, you know. Visit me. I'm used to taking care of myself."

"I'm sure you are, but I'd still like to stop by. Anything else you wouldn't like to eat?"

He laughed. "Chocolate chip cookies."

"You're on."

Gabby didn't bother closing the bathroom door. There was no point. It was close enough to dinner that the pets were following her everywhere. No matter how many times she pointed to the clock and explained they had another hour, they didn't bother learning to tell time.

So she peed with Boomer sitting patiently on the mat by the tub and Jasmine rubbing against her legs. When she returned to the chaos of the kitchen, Makayla was at the table with the twins coloring. The smell of rosemary and garlic from the rub she'd made filled the room. The brownies she'd made earlier were cooling on a rack. A salad was in the refrigerator. She'd marinated vegetables that would go on the grill along with the pork chops. Andrew had promised to be home right at five-thirty. If he made it, he would be in charge of the cooking—otherwise she would get it started.

She walked over to the table and put her hand on Makayla's shoulder. The teen smiled at her, then handed Kenzie another crayon.

This was what she wanted, Gabby thought. Time with her family. Not the crazy stress of her supposed part-time job. Not reading briefs and analyzing new laws. She wanted to be working with actual people. Kids and adults. She wanted to help in a way that made sense to her.

Several hours later, when the twins were in bed, Gabby, Andrew and Makayla sat around the kitchen table. They'd already discussed the three couples Makayla was considering. Andrew had asked several good questions about them, but then had agreed with Gabby.

"There's no wrong decision. You have to do what you think is right."

Makayla nodded. "I like the couple from Maine the best. I want it to be them."

"Why don't you take a couple of days," Andrew began.

Makayla cut him off. "Dad, I'm not going to change my mind. I know I've been immature about a lot of things. Especially when I first thought I might be pregnant. Thinking that Boyd and I would be together always. Well, that was stupid."

Gabby leaned toward her. "No, it wasn't. You trusted him and believed in him. That's not immature. That's not wrong. The person making the mistake was him, not you."

"I was unrealistic. I'm fifteen and he's only a year older. How were we supposed to like raise a child together? This is better. I'm not going to want to keep the baby. He needs to go to a good home where the parents are ready for him."

Gabby hugged her. "You're doing really well."

"Thanks."

Gabby straightened. "Okay, my turn." She looked at her husband. "I've been thinking about this a lot. Makayla isn't comfortable at her high school and I don't think she should keep going there."

His expression was cautious. "We talked about this. Where would she go?"

Gabby thought about the research she'd done. "It's just a suggestion, but I could homeschool her for the rest of the school year. I've looked online and there are some excellent programs."

She had more to say—that scholastically, it would be a challenge. Makayla wouldn't be skating through her studies. Instead, Gabby would choose a well-respected program that would be the equivalent of advanced placement in several subjects. That when Makayla returned to high school the following September, she would be ahead of her classmates.

But there wasn't a chance because Andrew was staring at her openmouthed and Makayla was out of her chair and jumping up and down.

"Yes!" the teen crowed. "I want that. I'll do everything you say. I'll do my homework and study and be the perfect student. Yes. Yes!"

Andrew pulled himself together enough to ask, "Gabby, are you sure?"

"I've been thinking about it for a while."

"You'd have to quit your job."

"I know. To be honest, I don't want to work there anymore. I hate it. I'm not a lawyer anymore. I don't know when that changed, but it did. I want to homeschool Makayla and then when she goes back to high school, I want to return to college and get my master's in educational administration."

Andrew laughed. "You want to be a principal?"

"Eventually, yes. I've learned a lot dealing with Makayla and her pregnancy. I think I could help."

"Damn, you constantly surprise me. Good for you." He looked at his daughter. "All right. So we're in agreement? Gabby's going to homeschool you through June."

Makayla hugged them both. "Yes. It's going to be great. You'll see."

"It's going to be interesting, at the very least." Gabby held on to her. "I have a lot of ideas about different things we can do."

"I can't wait to hear what they are," Makayla said. "Now I'm going to go upstairs and write a letter to the couple in Maine. Oh, once I tell Amanda they're the ones, do you think we'll get to know their names?"

"I'm sure we will."

392   SUSAN MALLERY

"Cool."

The teen left. Andrew stood and drew Gabby to her feet. He kissed her.

"How do I thank you?" he asked. "For all of this?"

"You don't have to. I want to help." She put her hands on his chest. "It's strange. When I first found out she was pregnant, I felt trapped and angry. But somehow her being pregnant has brought us closer. She's important to me, too. I want her to be happy. The next time she gets pregnant, it's going to be our grandchild, not just yours."

He kissed her again. "Thank you, Gabby."

"Thank *you*. If we hadn't fallen in love, I wouldn't have any of this." She leaned against him. "You're my handsome prince, Andrew. Even when you make me crazy."

"Then my work here is done." He bent down so he could whisper in her ear. "So, what are we going to do with the rest of our evening?"

"How about something naughty?"

Nicole wiped her hands on the sacrificial towel and stepped back to look at the mural. She'd been working on it nearly every day. The painting had gone slowly. She had neither Jairus's talent nor his patience. But it was important to Tyler and if her son couldn't have the friend he adored, at least he could have his work.

Nearly a week had passed since she'd last spoken to Jairus. A week of sleepless nights and long, sad days. A week of Tyler asking when Jairus was going to be home.

Because for the first time in her life, she'd lied to her son. Rather than tell him the truth, she'd said he was back on tour. She kept promising herself she would explain everything, just as soon as she figured out what she was going to say. Or rather how to phrase it. Because what had happened had been awful...and her fault. She was going to have to tell her son that they weren't going to be with Jairus because she was afraid.

Afraid to love, afraid to be hurt. Afraid to trust. She was a coward. And rather than face those fears, she would walk away from him. Had walked away, hurting not only herself, but Tyler, too.

She studied the mural, the bright colors, the careful lines that brought the ever cheerful Brad to life. A boy and his dragon, she thought sadly.

The doorbell rang. For a second she allowed herself to hope that it was Jairus. That he'd shown up to talk some sense into her, to insist that she give him another chance. But when she pulled open the door, there was only a uniformed delivery woman with a slim package.

"If you'd sign here, ma'am," she said, handing over her tablet.

Nicole scribbled her name, then took the envelope. She hadn't ordered anything. There was no return address.

She turned the package over in her hands before opening it. Inside was a book. No, not a book. Just loose pages bound together. The cover showed a familiar red dragon and the title: *Brad the Dragon and Tango Girl*.

Nicole sank to the floor. She was crying before she turned to the first page.

The story was simple. Brad met Tango Girl—a pretty blonde dragon who danced. Brad and Tango Girl went to dinner and out on the beach. Brad fell in love with Tango Girl and asked her to marry him. Only Tango Girl said no. The second to the last page showed Brad crying big, fat dragon tears. The last page was blank, except for a Post-it that said: *I'm hoping for a happy ending.*

There was nothing else.

Nicole closed her eyes and told herself she would be fine. That this wasn't a big deal. Yes, it was a lovely gesture, but it didn't have to mean anything unless she wanted it to. She'd made her decision. She wasn't going to be swayed by...

A book? The story wasn't the problem. Nor was the unwritten ending. The real problem was her. She'd always prided herself on being self-sufficient. On taking care of business. On being a good example for her son. So what was all this? Her teaching him it was better to lie and be afraid than tell the truth? What was she showing herself? That she would rather be alone and safe than take a chance on a wonderful man who loved her?

She got up and walked back into Tyler's room. The mural dominated the space. Everything about it was happy and positive. Jairus had only been in their lives a few short months, yet he'd already left his mark. Was she really going to lose him because of something he might never do?

Fear battled with hope and love. She knew what she wanted and she knew what was right. For once, they were the same thing.

She ran to the kitchen and collected her purse, along with her cell phone. She was still holding the book.

It only took ten minutes to drive to Jairus's house. She raced up to the front door, which opened before she got there.

He stood in the door and smiled at her. "I hoped Brad would get through to you when I couldn't."

She flung herself at him. Her purse and the book fell to the floor as she buried her head in his shoulder.

"I'm sorry," she whispered. "I was so scared. No. Terrified. I love you and I want to be with you. I love you, Jairus. I'm sorry for not being able to deal with that sooner."

He drew back enough to kiss her. "It's okay, Tango Girl. You were worth waiting for."

★ ★ ★

"I know there's someone else."

Hayley stared at her husband. He was pale as he stood in the kitchen, looking at her. His shoulders were slumped and his mouth a straight line, laced with pain.

"I've tried to ignore it," he continued. "But you've been taking long lunches every day and disappearing in the evening. You're not even trying to hide it."

"How did you know about the long lunches?" A ridiculous question, but the first one that came to mind.

"I stopped by to see you and Steven told me."

Betrayed by her boss, she thought, knowing that under any other circumstances, the situation would be funny.

"There's no one else, Rob. Not in the way you mean."

He didn't look convinced. "I love you, Hayley. I thought we'd gotten through everything. I know you still hurt and that the pain of what's been lost will never go away, but I had hoped we were making progress."

"We are." She moved closer to him. "Rob, I love you so much. You are the only man I've ever loved and that hasn't changed. I swear."

He didn't look convinced. "Then what have you been doing?"

"Going to the hospital."

He went white. "You're sick?"

"No. I'm fine. I'm sorry. I should have said that differently. There is nothing wrong with me."

He took a breath. "Tell me what's going on."

"There's a boy. His name is Noah. He's eleven. He never knew his dad and his mom died in a car accident three years ago. He didn't have other family, so he was put into foster care. What do you know about lymphoma?"

An hour later Rob was looking more relaxed. The color returned to his face as he continued to ask questions.

"What about a baby?"

"I talked to a couple of people," she admitted. "Went to some support group meetings. You've talked about older kids, but I could never understand why we'd want that." She sighed. "The truth is the waiting lists for an infant are really long. We'd be starting at the bottom. It can cost so much money and there's no guarantee. That frustrated me. I want us to have a family. I know you want to be a dad, and you'd be a good one. I want to be a mom. But until I met Noah, I couldn't figure out how that would happen."

Rob smiled at her. "Why him?"

"I don't know. I saw the light on in his room and walked in. We started talking. I like him. He's an old soul. He's been through a lot. He's sweet and strong and still a kid. He needs us, Rob. From what I've read online we'd have to get approved to be foster parents. Once we have that, we can bring him here and see how it goes. If we're all on board with it, then the next step is to adopt him."

She clasped her hands together. "I know I'm just about four hundred steps ahead of where we really are, but I can't help it. What do you think? Would you at least meet him?"

Rob looked at her for a long time, then smiled. "Can we go now?"

It was nearly seven when they arrived at the hospital. Families filled most of the rooms on the pediatric floor. Conversation and laughter spilled out into the hall. There were a few cries, but most of the conversations seemed happy.

Hayley led the way from the elevator. At the entrance to Noah's room, she paused. Nerves danced in her stomach. Not because she was worried. While so many things could go wrong, she knew in her heart they wouldn't. Instead, the flutters were more about anticipation. Because she could feel this was the very beginning of a wonderful journey they were all going to take together.

She took Rob's hand in hers and led him inside. Noah looked up from his book and smiled.

"Hi, Hayley."

"Hi, yourself. Noah, this is my husband, Rob. Rob, please meet Noah."

"Nice to meet you, Noah."

The two males shook hands. Hayley dragged over chairs.

"You're looking better," she said, noting the slight color in his cheeks. "Today was a good day?"

"It was. I didn't throw up once."

Rob looked startled. "You need to raise your standards."

Noah leaned back his bald head and laughed. "You're right. Not throwing up is a pretty sad benchmark."

"It could be worse," Rob pointed out. "Like not finding rat turds in your food."

Noah grinned. "Or cockroaches in your bed."

"Or—"

"So…" Hayley said, interrupting him. "Maybe we could talk about something else."

"Girls," Rob said, his voice affectionate. "They can be delicate."

"Tell me about it." Noah looked at Hayley. "Minerva said if I felt up to it, I could go down to the cafeteria for ice cream. Want to take me?"

"Absolutely."

"I'm in charge of the wheelchair," Rob announced. "And we're going fast."

Noah pushed the button to call the nurse. When she came with the wheelchair, Rob lifted the boy onto the seat while

Hayley made sure his IV line didn't tangle. They made their way to the elevators. While they waited, Rob smiled at her and gave her a thumbs-up.

Deep inside, she felt yet another piece of her heart heal. There would never be a baby of her own to hold. But there would be a family. Love and joy weren't dependent on DNA. They were a gift. One for which she would be grateful every day of her life.

EPILOGUE

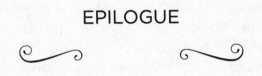

The Friday before Christmas was warm and sunny. It might be snowing across much of the country but on the Southern California coast, there was never going to be a white Christmas, and that was how the natives liked it.

Gabby looked at the green shiny bow Kenzie had tied around Boomer's neck and gave it about five seconds before the dog figured out a way to remove it. Jasmine, sensing trouble, and impending company, had hidden under the bed in the master.

"Hurry up," Andrew called. "I need pictures of my girls."

The twins were dressed in plaid dresses for the party. Makayla wore a plain black dress that did its best to conceal her condition. But she was far enough along to make that an impossible job. To celebrate the season, she had on a little crown of red-and-green glitter with ribbons that trailed down her back.

Gabby wore a festive lightweight sweater over black ankle pants. She'd managed to lose the rest of the weight she wanted. Helping Makayla eat right had been a big part of it, as were the twice-weekly killer classes she took with Nicole.

Andrew took several pictures, then released them as the doorbell rang. The Masons were the first to arrive. Jill and Carson hugged everyone. The young couple from Maine had been even better in person than they'd been in their paperwork. The first meeting, in October, had gone so well, there had been two more. They'd wanted to spend time with Makayla at the holidays and had flown out three days ago. They were heading home to Maine in the morning. Jill would return the week of Makayla's due date and stay until baby Michael was born.

Makayla hadn't wavered in her desire to give up her baby. In fact meeting the Masons had seemed to cement her decision. She was doing well with her studies and looking at different colleges. What could have been a disaster for all of them had turned out to be the oddest blessing ever.

Andrew got everyone drinks while Gabby took a very sad Boomer to the master. The dog was given a new rawhide bone to ease his loneliness. She returned downstairs to find that Hayley, Rob and Noah had arrived.

"You look great," she told the boy. He ran his hand over the inch of new hair that had grown in.

"I'm thinking I'll be getting a call from a modeling agency any day now. Because I'm so handsome."

Gabby laughed and hugged him. "I'm sure you will. But you'll have to tell them no. There's no way Hayley and Rob would let you out of their sight."

Noah looked at his foster parents. "Yeah. Isn't that the best?"

Gabby pointed Noah toward the far end of the room where Makayla sat with the twins, Jill and Carson. Noah picked up a soda on his way over. Hayley linked arms with Gabby.

"Doesn't he look good? His last checkup was perfect."

"He's doing great. You all look so happy."

"We are," Hayley told her. "The adoption is moving forward. It's going to take close to a year, but that's okay. He's with us until it's final." She beamed. "Then we're stuck with him forever."

"That is so wonderful."

"It's not what I expected, and that's okay. It's so much better."

Andrew let in more guests. Pam arrived, along with Shannon and Adam. Nicole, Jairus and Tyler were right behind them.

Gabby dragged Hayley over to greet them. "Did you do it?" she demanded.

Nicole held up her left hand. Nestled against the diamond solitaire was a slim, platinum band. Gabby shrieked.

"You did it! You eloped!"

"Last weekend," Nicole admitted. "We took Tyler and ran off to Lake Tahoe. It was wonderful."

Gabby wanted to hear all about it, but this wasn't the time. Still, she hugged her friend, then Jairus and finally Tyler.

She crouched down in front of the boy. "Does this mean Brad is your brother?"

He beamed. "Uh-huh. I'm lucky."

"Good news?" Andrew asked.

Nicole showed him the ring.

"Congratulations." He hugged her and shook Jairus's hand. "A little bird told me it was a possibility, so we have some champagne ready. Let me get it out and then you two can make the announcement."

When the glasses had been filled, everyone gathered around. Gabby looked at her friends and family and knew this was a year she would never forget. They'd all been through so much. Tragedy had turned to joy and what had once seemed broken had been made whole.

She raised her drink to the happy couple and let her gaze shift to her husband. Andrew tipped his glass toward her and winked. The twins gathered close, as did Makayla. Her family, she thought with gratitude. Three beautiful daughters, a circle of friends and a promising future. For all of them. Honestly, it didn't get any better than that.

★ ★ ★ ★ ★

THE
FRIENDS
WE
KEEP

SUSAN MALLERY

Reader's Guide

MIRA®

*Please note: these questions contain spoilers.
You should wait to read them until after
you've finished the book.*

*Visit www.MischiefBay.com for a printable PDF
you can hand out at your book club meeting.*

1. *The Friends We Keep* has three intertwining story lines—one each for Gabby, Nicole and Hayley. What are the common themes that tie together these three plots?

2. What does the title mean to you?

3. How did the events of the story change Gabby, Hayley and Nicole? What lessons did they learn? Do any of those lessons make you think differently about something that's happening in your own life?

4. Susan Mallery is noted for her keen insight into our inner lives, and her ability to elicit deep emotions from her readers. Which scenes were the most emotional for you? Which parts made you laugh?

5. Susan makes a promise to her readers that they can relax into the reading experience knowing that the characters will pull through, even after facing the hardest of

circumstances. Did you find the ending satisfying for each character?

6. Which of the three stories was your favorite, and why? Which of the three women is most like you? Did your opinion of any of the characters (including secondary characters) change as you read the book?

7. Did you feel that Gabby was being selfish by refusing to raise Makayla's baby as her own? What would you have done in her situation? Have you or has anyone close to you had a baby at such a young age?

8. Did Hayley's husband do the right thing when he left her? Why or why not? What else could he have done to get through to her?

9. Did you expect Hayley to adopt Makayla's baby? Do you think that ending would have been better or worse than what happened in the book? Explain.

10. What did you think of Jairus? Why do you think Nicole was so reluctant to meet him, and then to go out with him? Go around the room and state whether you read the start of Nicole's journey in *The Girls of Mischief Bay*. Does the perception of those who read that book differ from that of those who did not?

Join the mailing list at www.SusanMallery.com to be notified of upcoming new releases, contests and news!

BOOK CLUB
MENU SUGGESTION

Chicken Enchilada Casserole
from *Supper's in the Bag*

15-ounce can of tomato sauce	½ cup sour cream
10.5-ounce can of cream of chicken soup	½ cup frozen corn
2 teaspoons chili powder	2 cups shredded cheddar-jack cheese, divided
1 teaspoon garlic salt	12 corn tortillas, cut into 1-inch slices, divided
15-ounce can of black beans, partially mashed	2 cups baby spinach leaves
6 cups cooked chicken, shredded (1 rotisserie chicken works nicely)	Sour cream, green onions, and tomatoes for garnish (optional)

1. Mix tomato sauce, cream of chicken soup, chili powder and garlic salt. Set sauce aside.

2. Mix beans, chicken, sour cream, corn and 1 cup cheese. Set filling aside.

3. Preheat the oven to 400 degrees. Line a 13 x 9–inch pan with foil and spray with nonstick spray. Spread about ¾ cup of sauce into the prepared pan. Layer half of the corn tortilla strips on top of the sauce, partially overlapping. Put the filling on top of the tortillas, and the baby spinach on top of that. Spread another ¾ cup of sauce over the spinach leaves. Cover with the rest of the tortilla strips. Top with all of the remaining sauce.

4. Cover with foil and bake for half an hour. Top with re-maining cheese and bake for another 5-10 minutes, un-

covered, until cheese has melted and started to brown, and mixture is bubbly. Let sit for 10 minutes before serving. If desired, garnish with a dollop of sour cream, green onions and tomatoes.